YEAR OF THE RHINOCEROS

Year of the Rhinoceros

* * *

M. B. Neff

RED HEN PRESS | *Los Angeles, California*

Year of the Rhinoceros
Copyright © 2009 by M. B. Neff

All rights reserved

No part of this book may be used or reproduced in any manner whatsoever without the prior written permission of both the publisher and the copyright owner.

ISBN: 978-1-59709-137-4
Library of Congress Catalog Card Number: 2008942730

The California Arts Council and the National Endowment for the Arts partially support Red Hen Press.

Published by Red Hen Press
www.redhen.org

First Edition

TABLE OF CONTENTS

PROLOGUE xi
God Games — Idols and Ideals — The White Oz

CHAPTER 1 1
Morlocks and Star-Eyes — A Bad Boss Stereotype — Blue Balls at St. E's — A Memorable Whistleblower — The Golden Nadir — The Guy From Epanoma

CHAPTER 2 26
Reagan on Golf Tee Legs — Rochambeau's Note — Strong Chins, Blazing Eyes — Dreaming America Like a Bayou Moon — The Evolution of Eden

CHAPTER 3 34
Pretend You Are Manny — The Hitchcock Effect — Go Gators! — A Science Fiction Princess — Manny Near Paralysis — Do Not Think and Be

CHAPTER 4 44
The Sublime Perception State — In Search of JB — Manny Eden Meets the Staff — Tammy Pon and The Mental Douche — Like a Moral Volcano

CHAPTER 5 54
Nixon's Favorite Photo — The Eye Comet of Hunsecker — Manny's Training — Hart Crane in BLT — Mzz Dracos Scares Manny Into the Men's Room

CHAPTER 6 71
A God Without Conscience — Early Days of OWC — Coming of The Morlocks

CHAPTER 7 79
A Letter to Mommy K — Answer Their
Panic With A Pumpkin — Varsana's Tongue
Fries Mzz Dracos — Manny Meets Worm
and Union Head

CHAPTER 8 90
Potential Prosecutorial Merit — Manny Goes
With Flow — Becky Tests Manny — Big Fines
for Improbity — Ms. Linderhart Lacks the
Team Player Edge

CHAPTER 9 103
The Pissoir of Anomie — A Candidate For Wax
— Espresso on the Mozartplatz

CHAPTER 10 107
Joe Blow On Menu? — No Reasonable
Grounds — The Pickering Disruption Test —
Threshold Maneuvers in The Light — Laney
vs. The Hunsecker

CHAPTER 11 125
Like Warm Rubber Massacre — Washington,
Inc. — Nursing Gertrude — Laney vs.
Emperatriz — Laney vs. The Gipper — Laney
vs. The First Nancy

CHAPTER 12 158
Ladies Night At Scandals — A Mongo Moon
Goddess — Laney vs. Manny Eden — Sneaky
Shit Theories — Personalities Are Such Fragile
Creations

CHAPTER 13 172
Deputy From Luna Hell — Cosmic Epiphanies —
Death of a Thousand Bites

CHAPTER 14 178
Un Peu du Chose

CHAPTER 15 181
Un Coup d'Eclat

CHAPTER 16 187
Manny Advises Dictator — Manny As
President — The Origin of Morals and Idols

CHAPTER 17 195
On Revolution Time — Ceremony of The
Watch — Utopia By 2000 — Laney Becomes
A Sword Goddess — Manny As "Mr. God"

CHAPTER 18 205
Silence of The Wimp — The Rodent Snack —
Glyphs Pressed to Mutter — Luna Attacks —
The Impossibility of Morality

CHAPTER 19 217
Hunsecker Fears an Act of Congress —
Hunsecker Enlists Help of Manny

CHAPTER 20 220
Like a Morose General Patton — Magical
Thinkings Beyond Good and Evil — Ashley
Madison Befuddles The Democrats and
"Rolls With The Punches"

CHAPTER 21 231
The Powers of Rodin — Pecking Order —
Year of The Rhinoceros — The Glue of
Common Loathing — Something As Basic
As Heat

CHAPTER 22 246
The Needful One — "Carry Us to Blockula" —
The Stone in Laney's Head

CHAPTER 23 255
Ashley Gets Even — They Won't Survive
Dr. X — Laney Goes Rhino

CHAPTER 24 261
Manny Loses It — Dropping the "Utopia Stone" — Up From The Slime-House-of-Saud Office Park — Hebrews, Hittites, Greeks, and So Forth

CHAPTER 25 273
Throbbings of Worm — A Desperate Catfight — The Cops Bust Laney — A Note About "Self"

CHAPTER 26 282
Madison's Version of Events — Manny Goes Mannequin — A Moral Obligation — "They Just Wanted to Kill Her" — What Really Happened at Childe Harold

CHAPTER 27 289
The Sublime Perception State — Seven Screams — Death of a Counsel — As Far From God As Angels Can Fly — Deejah's Final Peace

CHAPTER 28 294
The CEO — Varsana Claims Grope — Keat Linderhart's Car Accident — The Dong Hobbit — Uncle Pharaoh's Flea Tent — A New Life

EPILOGUE 300
The Whistleblower's Lament

Tyranny is a habit; it grows upon us and, in the long run, turns into a disease . . . A society which can watch this happen with equanimity must itself be basically infected.
—Fyodor Dostoevsky

There are times I wish I hadn't done it . . . If you asked me would I do it again, do I think it's worth it? Yes. I think it's worth it.
—Whistleblower Jeffrey Wigand
Sixty Minutes 02/04/96

Get that son of a bitch.
—Richard Nixon

PROLOGUE

God Games — Idols and Ideals — The White Oz

SAY TO YOURSELF, *I AM GOD.*
That's right. Imagine it.
Now, do some tricks, try out Your powers.
Hide in a far *Nothing* at the edge of light. Drift near Far Tortuga in a leaky turtle boat. Melt an icecap, craft a crop circle, have sex with a virus—etc.
Now, go to the city of Washington and read a few minds. Pick up a copy of the *Post.* Hang out in a senatorial *hideaway* with an oil or weapons lobbyist. Try to reconcile the biases, irrationalities, and politics You encounter there into something that makes sense for the good of all.
In other words, try to un-Babel this city . . .
You cannot.
It is impossible, even for You. Being all-powerful, You have "created" a place even You will never sort out.
Short of flaming snakes from the sky (at least twice a week), two worlds will always prevail in Washington and trump all Godlike efforts: the *World of Idols* and the *World of Ideals.*
If contrast is necessary to resolve doubt, or if you are unable to decide which *World* is more important to Washington, nix the God imitation. Buy a ticket, and come autumn, fly to the city. Stay there for days, weeks, whatever it takes. Stroll around and compare the *Worlds.* Glide like the ghost of Thomas Paine or Clara Barton beneath the power-aired vaults of the Supreme Court. Cup your hands in the starry black Reflecting Pool. Stroke the faces of marble head in the Capitol and touch the shimmering surface of the White House. See your own soul in the architecture of hope. Then at dawn, call room service. Order Eggs Norwegian, kiwi fruit on the side, black

coffee, and a Bloody Mary with lime. Eat and drink slowly as you gaze from your balcony across the Potomac over the acres of dome, obelisk, and temple winnowed out dark by the morning sun. At such time you will feel dazed, and it will appear to you that this Grand Republic Babylon of *Idols* (and partisans), this White Oz of *Ideals* (and fools), is none other than the fabled Atlantis itself, a rumored utopia restored from the ocean strata and made to assume its rightful station as an omphalos of the cosmos awaiting extinction once more.

If you try to inhale it, or realize its synergy, you will find it impossible. The human mind cannot grasp *Infinity*, and neither can it contain Washington. Only by creating a God, or a president, do things begin to anchor. Each generation demands an idol, and sometimes more than one, worship always preferable to despair.

CHAPTER 1

Morlocks and Star Eyes — A Bad Boss Stereotype — Blue Balls at St. E's — A Memorable Whistleblower — Golden Nadir — The Guy From Epanoma

EVEN BEFORE THE AGE OF THIRTY, Manny Eden's liberal politics and smartass nature improved his years of incarceration at one of America's most renowned mental institutions, and as a result, he was denied many things, including the solace of hope, Hell, God, and comfort food. Early one Tuesday morning in 1992, while reclined upon a vomit-smelling couch in the St. Elizabeth's day room, he stared up at an old RCA television suspended from the ceiling, his neck beginning to ache as he watched Tom Wolfe on the comedy show, *Saturday Night Live.*

"*SHEEEOOOIMEEEEEAMUGGERRRRFUGGERRRAWWWTHURR!*" Wolfe yelled at the camera. He couldn't help but dapper about the set in his usual slappy white suit, his aging face puckered and supercilious, his body dodging water balloons hurled at him from off stage. Manny wondered if the face came naturally to Wolfe or if he wore it for theatrical show.

"*SHEEEOOOIMEEEEEAMUGGERRRRFUGGERRRAWWWTHURR!*" Wolfe spewed again. Someone must have told him to make fun of the opening of his latest novel. Why? Because it also contained a long and bizarre sound that made no sense. The sketch bored Manny, but Wolfe's face never changed, not even when a bucket of chocolate-like bilge poured onto his suit from above. "*SHEEEEOOO... yechk!*" The studio audience guffawed at the vision of a bilge-splattered Wolfe. The author spit at them, winked, and the TV cut to a commercial of a fat black poodle on two legs strip-dancing to the rock song *Losing My Religion* by REM. The fur fell away piece by piece as the dog transmogrified into Sammy "Pink Bone" Bartowski—a wealthy pet dealer from Chevy Chase with a mouth big enough to swallow a litter in one gulp.

Manny flipped Pink Bone off and lowered his head, rubbing his neck as he looked around. The day room was quiet, only Belinda Hearns, the ex-mayor of D.C., using hands to act out her latest Spanish Inquisition fantasy on an imaginary bureaucracy. Manny knew that St. E's nursing staff would soon treat her nail wounds with raw alcohol and tape her fingers to palm while she screeched as if tortured.

Feeling restless, and tired of reruns, Manny stood and walked to a window that overlooked the St. E's grounds in Washington, D.C. It was still early in the morning, around 7 AM. Outside, the lawn engineers from El Salvador chopped and hosed, tidying up shrubbery and flowers beneath the glare of Venus. Manny saw the planet in the eastern sky, like distant car headlights atop a blue mountain. For some reason, it reminded him of his status as a true prisoner of Earth, and he said quietly to himself:

Let the asteroid hit.

The thought wasn't original, placed in his mind long ago by the fated and righteous woman he loved. And he had no choice but to agree. The world of the nineties was stupid, cyclical, and fucked. NATO fought the Serb genocide squads, Africa bled itself to bone in civil war, South America burned in poverty, the Party elite of China tightened their death grip, and the author Tom Wolfe entertained America by dodging water balloons and taking on bilge.

What could be worse?

Before he could answer, a scuff of shoe on tile disturbed him. Manny turned to see the soft blond face of a man who had shot an American president. Fifteen minutes later, the two of them were playing chess in a large and dimly lit utility closet just off the day room. As usual, John Hinckley teased Manny about his past, made fun of his beliefs and enthusiasms, till Manny said,

"Shut the fuck up, Johnny."

Manny knew he must be playfully harsh with John, otherwise he would just keep jabbering and poking like he did every time they played chess. St. E's had pushed new meds on him, so he was much better than in the old days when he fixated on Jodie Foster.

"No medications will ever help you, Manny," said Hinckley.

"Shut the fuck up, Johnny."

"We're both diseased and your disease is *outlook*. You're no different than when you landed in D.C. ten years ago to kiss the Gipper's ass."

"That's crap, Johnny, and besides, the two of us are nothing alike."

"But we both love the women who imprisoned us. No?"

Manny's blood pressure whistled in his ears. He resisted an urge to tip the game board into Hinckley's lap—the fellow was pushing his hot button again. Why did he let him do it? The women referred to were Jodie Foster, the actress of course, and Manny's murdered love of years past, Laney Dracos—a woman whose spirit warmed and defended him at St. E's. He noted her presence in his St. E's journal, and only the day before she'd told Manny's most loved psychiatrist, Doc Blue Balls, where to stick his latest conclusion:

```
St. Elizabeth's Hospital, May 22, 1992

Laney Dracos moved my mouth yesterday, just
after lunch. She told Blue Balls to go fuck
himself following his monthly evaluation of me
as an incurable sociopath. No surprises there.
Course, Blue Balls didn't like it, smiled at
me real cold, but I'm not escaping this mental
health dungeon regardless. Even after all these
years Laney still makes me feel like the crazed
Heathcliff in Wuthering Heights, the scene where
he throws open the window to call to the ghost
of his Catherine. Only in my case, Laney is
fused to my nerves and thought, as if I were so
consumed that I have, at least in part, become
her—and unknown to the therapists at St. E's,
the best part of me is Laney. They can't name
it, but being followers of Sigmund they want
to expose it and remake it into something sick
and harmful. I'll hold out though because I
love her beyond their ability to comprehend.
In other words, she's dead and I refuse to move
on. Is that clinical? I don't think so, espe-
cially not in a place where the guy behind you
at the water fountain claims to be the reincar-
nation of Mary, Queen of Scots.
```

> In other news, last night I dreamt the mad poet
> Ezra Pound stalking the halls of St E's, curs-
> ing America. He woke me up around three, after
> I shouted at him to return to his cage.
>
> God of sorry bastards, protect me.

And so it went. But there were good times also. When not struggling with staff, Laney Dracos proclaimed her goodness and wisdom till Manny made demon love to her on the shore of his imagination—she appearing like his old vision of an American poster goddess from WW I, only a bit wilder: her hair free and dark as a Virginia night, her eyes brightening to moons above the Chesapeake, yet always a star-dimming blue by dawn, while her face in contrast to that purity looked sassy and Hollywood, and at times, more needful and sadly tragic than she would ever admit.

Regardless, Manny knew he must not give Hinckley an edge.

"Not true, Johnny, now shut the fuck up. Checkmate in three."

While Hinckley sweated his next move for minutes on end and made insect-like clickings with his mouth, a bored Manny hit rewind, to relive his strange days with Laney, and just as importantly, his love of The Gipper in the eighties—a time when a great many star-eyed youth like himself left their hometowns and herded to the White Oz of Washington. Fed with hope, lies, and videotape campaign pledges, the kids had come from all points, from as close as Georgetown University and from as far away as American Samoa. Like Manny, their ambitions and enthusiasm were channeled into thoughts of change, productive and peaceful revolution, their backgrounds of Key Club civics and valedictorian speech demanding nothing less. Like rabid baseball fans full of stats, they chatted the nuances and quirks of government and its many personalities, and unlike the average bureaucrat or American, quoted Jefferson and Chomsky with equal skill, bragged of points scored and votes received in playful college games of Congress, and became giddy at the prospect of accidentally meeting The Gipper on a White House tour. They took the form of high school grads and college kids, nerds and quarterbacks, honor rollers and cheerleaders, Evangelicals and Humanists, young Republicans and Democrats, chess clubbers and pro-wrestling fans—the most dedicated America could send. Driven and incredibly naive, they were willing to lick stamps or join in idol-worship at a moment's notice.

In other words, like Manny—obsessed.

Surprisingly though, upon settling down in the Grand Republic Babylon, they often found estrangement to be the norm. The *World of Ideals* was not their own. No sooner did they compare their notions of democracy to the motives of bureaucracy than panic would set in.

How could these poor "Star Eyes" have prepared?

First, to imagine oneself destined for things more useful and immortalizing, and then, days or weeks or months later, to be rudely confronted by those who contradicted and denied all belief, who classified themselves as the "realists," created for the young people a circumstance worse than demoralizing. Like Morlocks of *The Time Machine*, their dream killers belonged to an underworld of dark and petty carnivores, also known as federal managers.

If the rest of America could have been there, during the eighties, they would have seen how these Morlock types forced the thousands of Star Eyes to either flee the city, submit and join the Yes-Mammal Nation (also known locally as "Star Base Brown-Noser Alpha"), or else resist as whistleblowers, and fail.

If *only* America could have been there.

* * *

THE MOST MEMORABLE AND INFAMOUS Star Eye who *was* there, Manny Eden (middle name Achan, pronounced *â-ken*), considered himself no different than the others—his goal back then to secure a reason for being. And what did this mean? Helping his country in a selfless way while serving his boyhood idol, The Gipper. What else? Young Eden was a true democrat, and the son of a liberal activist mother, though a political hybrid not usually seen east of Sacramento. Nevertheless, in 1984, at some point between the discovery of AIDS and the film debut of *This Is Spinal Tap*, he fled his hometown of Kenosha,

Wisconsin, to find a career in Washington, and like the thousands before him who had landed in that city for the first time, he felt afraid and powerdazed.

Only months before, he'd been fired from his crappiest job ever at the Burger Chef in downtown Kenosha for whistleblowing to district manager Bob Shorts about his boss's failure to wipe the cheese blocks clean of bug larva. Just when things couldn't get worse, an article in *Newsweek* magazine levitated him to the status of hero.

The "Office of Whistleblower Counsel" (OWC) had come into being: a special agency created by a Democrat Congress (*Civil Service Reform Act of 1978; Public Law 95-454*) to enable brave whistleblowers to safely defend their nation against bad bosses and criminal acts of government. And even though a Republican, The Gipper applauded, giving a speech at the agency and shaking hands with the new agency head, Ashley W. Madison, the two of them smiling and backslapping—course, the agency had started a few years before under the presidency of Jimmy Carter, but after standing up and falling a few times, it was really ready to get going!

As Counsel Madison said at the ceremony (according to *Newsweek*):

> "I could not be more pleased that President Reagan has chosen me to lead such an important mission to protect the American people from the harmful practices of bad government. Our men and women of conscience must be free to speak out. The Constitution of the United States gives them that right, and if we deny this basic freedom we become nothing but a government of yes persons, and such a government can never benefit a freedom loving nation."

Finally, someone gave a damn! As *Newsweek* pointed out, it was all part of The Gipper's plan to reform Washington. He promised America, and he wouldn't let the people down. In response, Counsel Madison publicly called for workers from around the country and all across the political spectrum to help him succeed in his "brave, new mission."

How could a Gipper-dazed, jobless, honest liberal resist?

Manny called the OWC personnel office in Washington at least a dozen times, received contradictory information more than once, and after a resume polish (that included accomplishments at the University of Wisconsin rather than his loser Kenosha jobs), and a criminal background check that lasted nearly a month, he made peace with a saddened mother and booked his flight to Washington D.C. for the job interview.

Days later, at the O'Hare terminal in Chicago, a tearful Mommy K (his mother's nickname) smiled and kissed her son. *I love you, Manny Eden*, she said, and added, "If it doesn't work out, I can probably get you a job at Ed's Plant Emporium in Milwaukee. Just a plan b, cause you never know, hmm?"

A speechless son gave Mommy K a corpse-like grin and ran to catch his plane, the cactus of Ed's pricking him to extra effort.

He could hardly wait to get to Washington.

Upon arrival he herded through the White House, puffed to the peak of the Monument, breathed rotunda till it made him giddy, gawked at the Smithsonian's Tyrannosaurus, then quietly parked himself across the Potomac at the Rosslyn Marriott, ordered a Bloody Mary with lime, and soon enough, the opportunity to land his Washington dream job arrived.

Of course, he was determined not to blow it, but only ten minutes into the interview with an OWC federal executive at Cafe Artaud on 19th Street and Manny asked himself:

What kind of assholes do they forget to wipe around here?

* * *

IN HIS WHOLE TWENTY-TWO YEARS, Manny Eden had never met a man like this. First of all, Mr. Basil R. Hunsecker acted and looked the stereotypical bad boss: a middle-aged prick in three-piece gray and tacky pink tie who disturbingly resembled Al Pacino in *Dog Day Afternoon* (narrow head and brooding Italian look), only an older version, with a thinner face, pock-marked cheeks, and big, protruding, blue-bone eyes that sucked in everything and contrasted in an irritating way with his sallow brown skin—as if he were the victim of one too many spray tans. His odor, somewhat unique, like cooked shellfish marinated in mildew. What Manny didn't know was that Hunsecker remained the owner not only of a rare, painful, and mummifying disease that ate away the body fat between his skin and muscles, but also of more than one post-pubescent social trauma, his memory way to full of punky kids screeching at him:

Hey, pizzaaa face, you fucking shithead pizzaaa face!

Of course, it wasn't Manny's fault, but beyond Hunsecker's eyes of fuzzy blue, he mulled over a single best opportunity for revenge—the subject occupying this stereotype every day of his life, and whether he realized it or not.

"Who are you smirking at, Mr. Eden?"

"It's just my face. I was born that way."

"Are you a registered Republican?"

"Uh, no . . . I'm not registered yet, but I did vote for—"

"Are you Jewish?"

"My mother is Jewish . . . my father—"

"Died in a boating accident on Lake Michigan when you were only five. He drowned himself looking for you in the water, dived down so deep he couldn't make it back."

Manny's face shivered as if slapped. "How did you know?"

"I know what Uncle Sam knows. Remember, we did a background check on you."

"Yes, sir," Manny said and thought to himself, *This stereotype can't be the only one. There must be more of him . . . Is it because he's a boss? A Republican?*

"And have you resolved your guilt after all these years?"

"Over?"

"The death of your father."

"I don't . . ." Manny was confused. To his surprise and embarrassment, his hands began to shake ever so slightly. He couldn't answer.

"And your odd middle name, *Achan*—why did your parents name you after a Jewish criminal?"

"*What?*"

"Achan was a thief who angered God so much that he punished all the Israelites in retaliation. It's right in the Old Testament. I know my Bible."

Manny decided to rebel, just a bit. "My mother believes Achan was really a hero, sir."

Hunsecker raised a hand and flattened his hair, front to back, reminding Manny of a 1950s greaser. "Oh? How is that?" he asked.

"She ... uh, said that Achan confessed his theft to save the Israelites from God's wrath, and for his efforts he and his entire family were stoned to death."

"What of it?"

"She believes Achan was scapegoated for their problems, that God had nothing to do with it, and she thinks Joshua was really the bad guy, and that—"

"All right then ... So you love *whistleblowers*, Mr. Eden?"

"Sir, I—"

"And you've come to Washington to *save them*? I'm afraid I'm skeptical. Do you have some sort of savior complex?"

Manny smiled, though inwardly he squirmed. Under the glare of Hunsecker, he imagined the Washingtonians of Cafe Artaud watching him and squirming also in a state of sympathy and irritation—hundreds of minute vibrations worming up Manny's legs and into his face.

"Tell me, Mr. Eden, what are you trying to prove? What is your real goal?"

"To-to save America from herself?" Manny blurted out.

"What? Are you trying to be *flip*?"

All Hunsecker motion stopped. His scrutiny of Manny was frighteningly prognostic and bellowing without sound. Manny sat up straight in the chair, struggled for composure. Hunsecker looked like a cross between a dead bass and a pissed off gargoyle—a classic, bad boss face, another stereotypical reaction. Ed's Plant Emporium beckoned. Manny reminded himself to just *tell the truth*.

"I've come to be part of the Reagan Revolution, and—"

"And you think I haven't? Look, Mr. ... *Garden-of-Eden*, humor has its place," the Hunsecker said, leading the Manny fowl, squeezing the trigger, "but I think of this job interview as an obstacle you must hurdle."

"Yes, I—"

"And furthermore, *dolores capitis non fero. Eos do.*"
"Sir?"
"That's Latin. One of five languages I speak."
"What does it mean?"
"It translates to *do not taint these moments with frivolity.*"

Hunsecker smiled really big, catching Manny off guard, sighed as if disgusted, and returned to his plate of mussel appetizer. He considered the interview with Manny Eden to be routine business, unpleasant and boring, yes, certainly not an occasion to suspect anything unusual; and though suspicious in the extreme, even Hunsecker could not predict the future catastrophe Manny Eden would cause, and one that would not only threaten Hunsecker's own existence, but that of the Grand Republic Babylon as well.

* * *

BEFORE HE COULD THREATEN BABYLON, or anything else, Manny had learned to sustain himself on a cornball devotion to democracy and America. While studying in the poli-sci program at the University of Wisconsin he stupefied roommates and girlfriends alike with New Order predictions for a Pax Americana society going into the year 2000—complete with Martian colonies, gasless aqua-cars, low taxes, free health care, cities sans ghettos and security for all. Being a headstrong and pugnacious political personality in his hometown of Kenosha, he had worked hard to defeat the mayoral bully, "Mob Boss" Rosetti. He'd also blown the *Chicago Sun* whistle, loud as the evening freight, on the Drummond family who ran the local newspaper, the *Kenosha Morning Sentinel*. They supported the mayor's various binges and catastrophes, and he believed the cretins to be genuine threats to democracy.

Even decades later in St. Elizabeth's mental hospital while playing chess with Hinckley, Manny's mind reached out to embrace Washington, drifted like a wind-blown memo through the idol airs and sacred pillars. He was an incurable idealist given to fantasy, and he created within himself a martyr symphony of whistleblower souls who would one day rise phoenix-like from the power struggle ash to restore the city to democracy.

Though imprisoned at St. E's for pleading insanity after ridding Earth of the White House hyena who murdered the love of his life, Laney Dracos, Manny remained a loyal beast of burden to all. He couldn't help it. *The big lug!* It never left him, even during those occasional bouts of misanthropy provoked by hospital therapists—and why would they do such a thing? Because they didn't like the look of his face, and often as possible, unfairly used it as an excuse.

As for the rest of his body, Manny stood out lanky and dish-white wherever he went, a six-foot-one-inch high chiaroscuro without meaning: hair and eyes of darkest brown against that pale Wisconsin skin. If he walked naked into a bare, sunlit room, he morphed into a smear of shadow. His real physical handicap though was what Kenosha elders, cosmeticians and convenience store clerks termed, "a punch-it face." Even Mommy K said he sported a "smirky mug," the kind people liked to hit, and that's why Dr. Killany, chief therapist at St. E's, and Manny's biggest enemy, often imagined Manny to be dismissing him as a loathsome bureaucrat for deliberately falsifying Manny's condition in order to keep him a political prisoner of Washington.

Of course, this fact was true, and Killany abhorred that Manny judged him for it. Therefore, whenever he saw the chance, the doctor would smile really big and say to Manny with a gentle tone:

"Smirking like that *only* supports your diagnosis. Remember, you once murdered your own boss."

Manny, fully expecting the jab, and with a low and dry voice, would usually respond with something like:

"My apologies, Doctor *Human Kind*. I was simply imagining you performing on stage at the Kennedy Center."

"Oh, and what was I performing, Mr. Eden?"

"Swan Lake in a swastika tutu, while your White House buddies watched with opera glasses and clapped."

"So I'm a Nazi homosexual?"

"No, doc, a Nazi transvestite with blue balls."

And so it went.

No matter his face or therapist, if he failed to express remorse for his crime in St. E's, the staff termed him a "sociopath in denial." If he expressed remorse, the staff termed him a "sociopath with a manipulative agenda"—whatever it took to keep him locked away. St. E's was determined not to risk angering the White House or Congress. They all feared that upon release, Manny had the potential to go national, perhaps talk radio, or worse, *Sixty Minutes*.

* * *

MANNY NOW PACES WITHOUT LEGS and fumes. This interview with Hunsecker has devolved into cliché, the stuff of bad movies, so bad that no one would ever believe him.

Does The Gipper know about shitheads like this?

In the meantime, what can he do about it? Nothing. The fellow is obviously a grave-digging dictator. From the very first handshake, Hunsecker had squeezed his fingers (and if it's one thing Manny *hates* it's guys who squeeze fingers during a handshake). At any moment, Manny thinks he'll lose it. One or two more growls from this stereotype and his mind will imagine all sorts of dangerous fauna floating out of nothing and performing strange tricks, some of it even seeking victims—a coping habit learned since age six when he magically poofed into being the Marvel comic superhero DOCTOR STRANGE to scald out from beneath his bed a pack of foot-eating trolls.

But such displays of phantasmic violence might not be necessary.

"Enjoying your Monte Cristo and rob roy?" Hunsecker asks.

Manny can't answer. A knot of cheese and whiskey flatus has just lodged like putty in his throat. As he stares at the boss person, holding back his own eruption, he unexpectedly feels a reluctant pity, and wonders why he hadn't felt it earlier. After all, Hunsecker poses before him as a simulacra of a Hollywood Al Pacino—one broken and hastily restored on a face more obnoxious than noble, more pitiful than tragic.

"The food, Mr. Eden? The rob roy?"

Manny forces speech through the flatus knot. "Fine. This place makes the best roys, Mr. Hunsecker." Hunsecker grins. Manny decides it's time to lighten things up further and use his JFK voice. *"Ask not what your country can cook for you, ask rather why you should not fricassee your country."*

Imitating JFK had always been a party favorite in Kenosha.

But not here.

Manny watches the growing scowl on Hunsecker's face. He realizes what a huge mistake he's just made. So what's the big deal? JFK is still a popular president, and besides, Manny had been clevering out funny imitations ever since he was a kid. Between black eyes (so many that his friends nicknamed him Achin' Eden), his old Wisconsin prairie pals, Tommy Cox and Steve Field, nagged him to be a stand-up comic like their parents watched on late night television, and so, by the age of fourteen, much to their glee, he was able to produce fair imitations of both popular and relatively obscure personalities, including Jimmy Stewart, JFK, Stevie Wonder, Groucho Marx, Wo Fat from *Hawaii Five-O*, Johnny Rotten of the Sex Pistols, Lily doing "I'm Tired" from *Blazing Saddles*, as well as cartoon characters like the Tasmanian Devil, Rocket J. Squirrel, and Daffy Duck's most famous "despicable."

Friends and enemies alike were either impressed or infuriated by his antics—the difference, of course, being Achin' Eden's timing and application.

Now, even though he's beaming at Hunsecker like a comic-relief Disney dwarf, the man's bellicosity sucks in with a heave and blazes forth, narrowing and focusing long enough to scorch out a hole in Manny's future.

The Martian death ray pivots.

"Mr. Hunsecker, the *uhhhhh*—"

"The *what?*"

"Nothing . . . nothing."

Things are out of control. Hunsecker's jaw line and chin, as symptoms, whiten hard, flush bone to air with the tremendous effort of chewing his final mussel before the entree arrives. It's suddenly all or nada for Manny Eden. Even though the concept of pushing his nose to within even an inch of Hunsecker's ass is abhorrent, he MUST make it clear.

"I want this job, Mr. Hunsecker," Manny says, demanding and weary, pricked by the cactus of Ed's. "I've been sleeping on it for weeks, dreaming it, living it. I mean, it's a good thing, and not just like working in a corporate Skinner box, if you know what I'm saying? I want to do *my part* to help President Reagan clean up government. Isn't that worth it? Won't we as Americans benefit from that?"

Hunsecker appears dumbfounded.

"*Nulla mensa sine impensa.*"

"Sir?"

"Translated roughly, it means, *I don't get it* . . . And by the way, Mr. Garden-of-Eden, how did you learn of my office?"

"I read an article in *Newsweek* explaining how the Office of Whistleblower Counsel helped a whistleblower regain his job at the Justice Department. It was amazing. He'd reported certain district attorneys taking bribes from drug cartel bosses and his own boss—"

"Telling the truth is risky business in this city, my friend. You might get your head shot off."

Manny lifts his glass to drink, imagining a nearby explosion of head. He can't believe human beings in positions of trust really act so badly. Does it matter if they're Republicans or Democrats? Would he ever know the truth?

"The real problem is finding a memorable whistleblower to begin with," Hunsecker says.

At the edge of Manny's eye, Hunsecker's body subsides further. Manny may *still* have a chance. He MUST impress the stereotype *now*. "I know something of bureaucracies throughout history, sir. Once I knew I wanted to work in Washington, I studied—"

"Bureaucrats have been around since before Babylon, Mr. Eden," Hunsecker says dismissively. "We adjust the law when Congress turns its back. As a matter of fact, and most people don't know it, but the regulations we write have the *power of law*. Did you know that?"

"That's astonishing, sir. I had no idea."

"It's a good thing because Congress won't stop creating monsters they are unwilling to leash . . . Why if we didn't act, even my office would have become one." He sighs, deflates again, removes a roll from the bread basket at the center of the table and begins to butter it—a very good sign.

Perhaps Manny can relax?

While Hunsecker chews, the man-boy from Kenosha imagines CONGRESS and its lumbering Frankensteins of pork and compromise, impotent bullets fired into sluggish Executive waters, blind and stupid energies unleashed and forgotten like decaying nukeheads beneath Nevada. *Shine, Perishing Democracy*! Only now, the Office of Whistleblower Counsel exists, a "heartfelt brainchild" (according to *Newsweek*) that reflects by its charge the "American tradition for democracy, integrity and fair play." Congress drafted the magical incantations necessary to raise the Excalibur of Hunsecker's office from the lake floor of vague but good intention, and the implications for the redemption of America were rippling in effect, beginning with those very few women and men possessed of sufficient courage and moral conscience. Hunsecker's office tuned in to their frequency, injected an army, amplified their howl till it inevitably burst the friable walls of corruption. No bureaucrats or cabinet heads, no White House appointees or senators or Pentagon generalissimos were immune.

And Manny knows The Gipper wouldn't have it any other way.

Neither would he.

Politics and do-gooding were turkey and pecan pie to a guy like Manny Eden, and once the Jimmy Carter years of the American presidency passed, he settled into his philosophical niche—and not surprisingly, this "niche" hadn't won him any friends among the powers-that-be in Kenosha, namely, City Hall, and the town newspaper (the conservative *Kenosha Morning Sentinel*) owned by a man named Drummond who appointed his nineteen year old son, Syd Drummond (an obese and alien-looking bully known to Manny since grade school), to the position of senior political editor.

Like his father, and the rest of City Hall, Syd termed Manny an "unholy cross between Ralph Nader and Barry Goldwater," for as the young Eden grew and his rare-vision politics matured, he pushed both his *democratic* for-the-people and *conservative* less-government views with the uncompromising zeal of a televangelist.

Syd never could figure what made the kid tick. He knew little of Manny's family and background, and out of ignorance, nicknamed him "The Golden Nadir," changing the "e" to "i" because that got him laughs around the coffee pot. Besides, anything that diminished Manny made the Drummonds happy. Indeed, they had every reason to loathe him. The kid's "bicycle sermons" (Manny often barked at Syd from atop his old banana-seat stingray) beginning at age fifteen were the stuff of barroom jokes. He would needle the Drummonds for the *Sentinel* being too soft on corrupt city politicians. In the face of Syd's sausage-sized middle finger, The Golden Nadir would rant on and on about the *Sentinel* dumbing down the good citizens of Kenosha, turning them into "goldfish awaiting death by BB gun"—the final battle between the two of them taking place at the City Hall spring picnic at Paycock Park on Lake Michigan in 1983.

* * *

BACK AT CAFÉ ARTAUD, A DAZED-BY-THE-SEAT-OF-POWER Ms. Idaho appears. She is the waitress. She plucks away Hunsecker's plate and replaces it in one smooth motion with a small football of game hen. She then hollows him out with a river of blonde hair, two ponds of green eye, a sun of forehead (all the wait staff in Cafe Artaud are blondes), inquires if he is a congressman—having learned this much self-promotion tact as she fiddles with the plates.

Hunsecker looks up at her, grins like a snarling whale. Ms. Idaho bubbles out something about "fresh baked" and evaporates into a nearby palm. Hunsecker begins to munch his bird. Foreheads of golden wait staff smear the air. Manny glances around Cafe Artaud at the shutter-diced blocks of sunlight and the many faux-plants-in-glass decorating the salmon yellow walls.

Manny grows nervous.

He thinks of something to say, fearful of prolonged silence.

"Has OWC rescued any memorable whistleblowers lately?" His tone is subdued, anxious as he is to avoid a new dilemma. But surprise, the stereotype smiles, and in a way that appears genuine.

"*The Office of Whistleblower Counsel is a child of men no less wise than the Founding Fathers. She is a woman, pure and strong and beautiful, like America,*" he says, magniloquent as a Washington socialite high on status. "We are forever searching for memorable whistleblowers, Mr. Eden. And as soon as we find one, we'll all celebrate."

Manny glosses over. He has a vision of OWC as an American goddess, her sword protecting the brave and swinging in circles like sunlight above her head, the power of its force and purity holding the yipping Morlocks at bay. As Manny looks on, Hunsecker carefully wipes his mouth clean of hen sauce. He refolds and places his napkin on the table in a genteel *L'Ecole Des Jeunes* fashion—as if he'd attended that finishing school for wealthy women—while his face, uncompromised by trivial task, waxes pensive with visions of anguished and sorely outnumbered patriots. Within moments, Hunsecker is idol-jawed with solemnity, poised in eternal requiem before the Tomb of the Unknown Whistleblower.

"The duty of my office, Mr. Eden, is to defend responsible persons from reprisals against those who would destroy them for speaking out. It is vital that witnesses of courage and a sense of public duty be free to speak, for good government cannot be conducted on the basis of lies."

"Yes, sir."

"Conscientiousness must be valued, or we become nothing but a culture of yes-men, um . . . yes-persons."

Curtain call.

Once his meal is picked clean to bone and puddle, Hunsecker clears his throat, and portraying a block-hauling self-discipline, inhales a few cubic tons of Cafe Artaud air before crunching down. "Mr. Eden, there are things you *must learn* about our management culture," he announces, "on the slim chance you might be chosen for this job from among the many candidates available."

Now the real test. How enthralled can Manny look?

"Though I am the supervisor of the Whistleblower Counsel Investigation Division to which you've applied, I think of myself as a true leader, not simply a manager." He hesitates, takes a quick glance at

Manny to make certain he's fixated. "Leaders such as myself thoroughly understand the beneficial use of *power*, as well as *aggression*. This should tell you something." Manny's gas knot steams loose through his nose.

"I've done a thorough self-inventory, Mr. Eden, turned inward so deep, towards my own personal philosophy."

"Yes, sir."

"Essence, hardtack, the gristle of tough decision, this is *my* religion. Are you listening?"

"Yes, I am."

Manny's attention shifts as Ms. Idaho returns. The Hunsecker clears his throat again, irritated at Manny's momentary lack of attention. Regardless, he orders a cherry cheese cake from Ms. Idaho. She nods and leaves.

"Now, tell me, Mr. Eden . . . pop quiz. What have you learned about my management culture?"

"Huh?"

"What did I just tell you? Weren't you listening?"

"Yes, of course. Your personal philosophy, or, the culture . . . I don't—"

"Can't you be honest?"

"It's not that."

"Then you can't be *decisive*."

"Not that either—"

"I think it is. You're coming off as rather boneless."

Manny's expression is extragalactic and Hunsecker notices. He would now call a quick end to this job interview if not for the fact that his cherry cheesecake is missing.

Harrumph!

The boss plucks a sugar packet from a bowl, and after opening the contents into his iced tea, begins to stir.

"I'm waiting for an answer, Mr. Eden."

Manny sees the dead man's curve ahead, his voice a lonely whine in the rigging, "I've learned . . . that essence and hardtack, uh, that your management culture is powerful, like a religion in the sense that it, uh, promises hell if a thing, I mean, if the whole group teams up to, uh . . ."

Hunsecker goes from red to purple. His shirt collar, like a garrote, pinches his head to a mutated beet. With one hand he reaches up and runs a finger between his collar and skin in an attempt to relieve the sensation of choking. He thought he'd cornered Manny's attention, victory at hand, but somehow the fellow had wiggled loose.

Damn him!

Honor is at stake and a test must be given, immediately. Either Eden will ball a fist and bake Hunsecker's face to coffee-table size, or he will submit, sputter down to softness—and of course, Hunsecker knows how badly the small towner needs the job, so he's betting his teeth on the second reaction.

Unfortunately, he doesn't yet realize that despite Manny's idealism, or perhaps because of it, the small towner has a real problem with authority. Especially, *boss types*. Even the word "boss" makes Manny feel wormy.

Only a year before his journey to Washington Manny was fired from a job for which he'd shown great promise (manager trainee at the Furniture Heaven in Milwaukee) not only because he decked a psychotically irate store manager who had slapped his co-worker, Sherry Dobbins, in the parking lot, but also because he taunted the boss afterwards (according to the *Kenosha Morning Sentinel*) by terming him "a low life weenie bastard."

Then came other firings.

Manny was terminated from a Kelly Boy temp job at Kenosha City Hall for exchanging words with his boss, Mr. Kyle Stickle, the Director of Public Safety, over the fact that the Kenosha Police Department was overstaffed with "blackjack-dumb Barney Fifes" who had nothing better to do than "speedtrap honest citizens to justify their salaries." An outraged Mayor Rossetti only found out afterwards that Manny actually worked there.

Following that, he was fired from an apprentice bartender job at O'Shaughnessy's Lounge for refusing a direct order from O'Shaughnessy himself to charge "all black-hearted fucking immigrants" (bicycle assembly plant workers from Cuba and El Salvador) almost double for rail drinks.

Then things got worse.

* * *

AFTER HIS FIRING FROM O'SHAUGHNESSY'S, Manny returned home to find his mother weeping—not due to his untimely yet predictable termination, but all because of a distressing news story about The Gipper on CBS news.

Mommy K sprawled herself on the living room couch, her long dark hair undone and falling on one side to the carpet, her face pushed down in a pillow as she repeated to herself in a tone of unflinching despair:

"*My poor country. Oh, God, my poor country!*"

Alarmed, Manny asked her what had happened and she sat up in his arms. As he gently stroked her hair, she said between sobs, "It's that Reagan creature, Manny ... He's wrecking our nation ... bankrupting us and selling us out ... to special interest pirates."

Unknown to Manny, this was Mommy K's last ditch effort to reclaim him from the wiles of The Gipper. She'd been a liberal activist in Wisconsin for many years, even worked on presidential and congressional campaigns in the early sixties, but her ploy was doomed to failure. Manny was still fifty percent Hollywood, still lying on a couch at nine years old watching the chimps and footballs of the actor Ronald Reagan. He couldn't believe what he was hearing. He said to his mother, "It ain't the president, Mommy-K, just some political frogs who work for him. He'll pith the bastards, you'll see."

Rather than be calmed by her son, his utter denial caused Mommy K to lurch to her feet and screech at Manny:

"HOW DARE YOU SUGGEST THAT ASSHOLE, SIX-SHOOTING, CORPORATE PITCH-MAN IS NOT RESPONSIBLE!"

"Mommy-K—"

"Manny, you've been living in la-la land for *too long*. You've got to flush the Jeffersonian dream shit you learned in college. And no more superheroes or American sword goddesses. These are the products of fantasy. Our heroes are dead ... They've all been killed by The Combine!"

"The Combine?"

"Read Kesey. It's all there."

Manny stood to face his mother, trying to stay calm, though looking concerned. He held her, but she shrugged him off and glared at him. Manny used his JFK voice (because he fancied himself a comedian of sorts) in an attempt to soften Mommy-K: "*Whoa, Mommy-K, the Gipper is like old JFK, he'll—*"

"What?" His mother verged on ballistic. "You can't compare a Republican like Reagan to John Kennedy. That's blasphemy! *Blasphemy!* Can you be more hellishly ignorant? You're a Democrat, Manny!"

"But—"

"Your naivety makes me sick. You've learned nothing from me."

Manny sputtered. "Why don't you grow up, mom? We have to live in *the now*, don't we?"

Manny's final mistake. Mommy K became so irate and impossible that her son went into hiding. No dinner for days afterwards. She barely spoke to him for weeks. Meanwhile, Manny was forced to hunt for another job, only the task proved even more difficult. Word was spreading like rancid butter all over Kenosha that the hothead crusader, Manny Eden, was not employee material.

Some even believed he was Irish, despite the fact his mother was Jewish.

* * *

HUNSECKER BEGINS WITH A BLOAT. After that, change occurs rapidly. Swelling to a self-righteous enormity, the ominous dislodging continues until the hemisphere of his shadow falls across Manny's hand and chills his fingers. For further effect, the boss swivels his head like the Great Toad God of Mambia, as if searching for Ms. Idaho, and booms forth at Manny with:

"NO CHEESECAKE!"

Manny Eden gulps a big shot of Rob Roy. Hunsecker's left eyelid twitches. "Find out about my cheesecake, Eden. *Now!*"

Manny can't help ask himself: *Okay, so what? Will any of this bullshit matter if I get the job?* Regardless, he feels the old dreamy hate return in the light of Hunsecker's glare. Instinctively, Manny wants to scream, spit, gag, hurl scalding hot soup at Hunsecker, burn him from life with the power of DOCTOR STRANGE, the superhero wizard, but before any retribution can begin, the front door opens several feet away and washes him in sidewalk light. Ms. Idaho drops a glass on the floor, breaking it.

The sound expands like a tiny shriek.

A pause then. A nervous laugh.

In a simple and calm way, Manny replies: "I'll do it."

Hunsecker observes an on-the-brink Manny Eden glancing anxiously around for a member of the wait staff—the reality of his affliction propping the Hunsecker delusion.

The internal *schadenfreude* is obvious.

Once more, the boss face grows calm as a hurricane-eye. He intends to approach as a shrewd dick, recover his potency, reevaluate Eden's aptitude for loyalty (and that was important above all things, for the Office of Whistleblower Counsel needed protection from leaks and liberals). But even now, his plans are in doubt, for Cafe Artaud waxes vague and finicky, intolerant of all human presence. No one suspects that Manny Eden's imagination possesses the power to denature and transmogrify the quivering atoms of the Georgetown eatery.

Before the boss can utter another word, Manny lashes out. He starts with a simple frying pan. He imagines it hurtling out of the kitchen. It skims Hunsecker's head and whirls across the dining room like a loose helicopter blade to knock one of the Washingtonians unconscious, ricocheting off his forehead with a loud *kuh-whang* and skidding to rest in a plate of Caesar salad. At the same time, the faux-plants in glass begin to squirm and seep loose into the walls. Some of them imbed snugly in the gypsum and crisp to fossils. Others slide like melting plates of wax to the floor, congealing there to fly-trap mouths that squeak like tortured mice and scurry around in search of toe prey.

The entire dining room begins to scream.

Manny cannot locate Ms. Idaho. He figures she must be with the kitchen help, all of them huddled quivering behind the steel fryer, watching as the soup du jour thickens and rises ominously from the cook pot like a red fist looking for Hunsecker jaw. Before it can punch through to the dining room though, Manny rises up from his chair. Hunsecker raises his hands to protect his face. His jaw drops to the floor, pulled like gum, for Manny's true nature now gleams forth from beneath a facade of mundane flesh. He has become DOCTOR STRANGE, his entire head a roaring sun devoid of spots. While his tormentor howls and evaporates like water on a hot sidewalk, Manny proclaims:

"YES, OH WRETCHED ONE, I AM YOUR SUPERIOR!"

Unfortunately though, the real Hunsecker is still solid.

Hunsecker's eyes reveal to him the lachrymose face of Manny Eden blooming whiter, and groping: a face of dark brow and eye cast against a skin as pale as the tablecloth. The throat beneath swallows hard.

"Mr. Eden." Hunsecker struggles to portray sincere incredulity. "You seem to be a man less concerned with ambition, and more concerned with accomplishment?"

"Well, I . . . yes."

"Accomplishment for the sake of itself?"

"For the sake of an end, sir."

"Part of the Mother Theresa *help-whistleblowers-thing*?"

"Uh . . . maybe. Look—"

"Then if I ordered you, as your boss, to cease and desist all aid to a whistleblower, any whistleblower, what would you do?"

Manny watches Hunsecker's eyes. They flash like bulbs before thinning to crescents of neon moon. A door has opened within the subterranean pallor. A party of shadows drifts into the obscurity of Cafe Artaud.

Manny replies, "I would naturally defer to you, since you would never order such a thing if . . . it were not in the best interest of the government and, uh, the nation."

"Good answer, Mr. Eden. I believe you might be a true patriot."

Hunsecker smiles and clears his throat, taking full measure of the other's trembling hands resting flat on the table top. He sees in that quiver an eager motivation for success, as well as a potential for absolute pliancy. At first, Manny Eden squirmed in him as just another ball of barking nerves, only now, he resolves, slots in well at the Procrustean factory. At such time Hunsecker saw fit to fill the air with the implausible in the presence of the doubtful, Eden would bloom the true poseur, exorcise the demons of negativism whatever the source.

Manny, sensing the shift, once again attempts to engage Hunsecker in a way he believes the stereotype will accept without complaint. "At the office, sir, how do you find a memorable whistleblower? How do you tell good from bad?"

"It's a sense of *evil*. You develop a nose for it after a few years."

"But do real whistleblowers suffer retaliation?" Manny asks.

"Yes, Mr. Eden, and the sad thing is, most of the time, we cannot prove it, but at OWC we do as little bad as possible, and as much good as we can—that is, with the resources available."

"I only hope I can serve as one of those . . . sir."

"We receive complaints," Hunsecker says, "deep throat stuff of all kinds, and plenty of suffering, usually through the mail. The letters claim abuse, persecutions, criminal activities and such, but even ones which appear to have substance usually prove trivial or false upon close analysis. A lot of crazies, paranoids and malcontents out there."

"I bet."

"Some of the letters are hysterically funny at first, then just when you think you've seen everything, here comes a wallapoloozer to bowl you over."

"No doubt."

"You see, Mr. Eden, our government is not nearly one percent as corrupt as the media portrays us."

"Corruption sells Chevys, Mr. Hunsecker. "

"A few years ago, oh—and this one is a gem—a few years ago a Democrat editor of a small town newspaper in Illinois wrote OWC to claim the CIA had implanted a telepathic listening device in his brain, so that whenever he thought something foul about President Reagan, an electric shock would be triggered that jolted him so hard his dentures fell out. He even included receipts from his dentist."

"Unbelievable!"

"Here, let me give you an example of a truly *memorable* whistleblower. I carry this one with me for laughs. It was sent to us last month by an EPA emissions inspector in the Midwest—a real psycho."

The grinning Hunsecker reaches inside his jacket, pulls out a coffee-stained square of paper and hands it to Manny. He unfolds it and reads:

```
Dear Whistleblower Justice League,

Do you know pimp city EPA? Can you name the
whores? Do they look surprised when you show?
Why did they refuse to pass that mustard? Why
did they spit on our wives in Rawlin's All-
You-Can-Eat-For-Whores Buffet? Do you have a
feel for these atomic levels of whoring? Are
you appointed by a precedent of the United
States? Will turds rise to the top here just
like in a dictatorship? Will the EPA boss we
want to murder, Mr. Russo, deny he's a homi-
cidal sludge-for-blood toxic waste whore, the
guy from Epanoma? And what about Jan Darcy,
the state biologist? Do you know why he blew
about the hundreds on slabs? Or why the state
whores ran him out on a slander then smoothed
everything over with a thick cream of tumor?
Do you know what affected us when Russo, act-
ing like a cumsucking jackass from dickville,
said then if it's so bad why doesn't Washing-
ton do something about the goddamned problem?
Is it none of our business then?

Sincerely,

The Mudslinger Mob From Marengo County
```

Manny hands the letter back to Hunsecker who refolds it and slides it inside his jacket.

"Well, Mr. Eden, what do you think?" This was the final test. "Is that one *memorable* enough for you?"

Manny answers, "Real strange. Borderline schizo, sir."

"So true. You have no idea how nearly impossible it is to choose a letter not written by an eccentric malcontent or a mental patient." Hunsecker then sighs loud and deep, as if longing for days more Nixon-like and halcyon, and says, "I believe you are a *true* patriot, Mr. Eden."

He winks, and reaching across the table, places his hand atop Manny's, and leaves it there.

The Golden Nadir can only smile, and wonder whether or not Hunsecker will demand sex at some point in the future.

CHAPTER 2

Reagan on Golf Tee Legs — Rochambeau's Note — Strong Chins, Blazing Eyes — Dreaming America Like a Bayou Moon — The Evolution of Eden

THE NIGHT FOLLOWING THE INTERVIEW, Manny Eden awakes shivering in a bed of cold tub. A muffled pounding in the distance alerts him to the presence of some cheeky son-of-a-bitch who won't stop slamming a fist on his hotel room door. Manny staggers out of the tub, freezing and shriveled, and more than a bit dizzy. He figures the bottle of cheap Bordeaux he'd finished off earlier that evening must have numbed him too well.

To celebrate a successful end to his bullshit interview with Hunsecker, Manny had ordered the Bordeaux up to his room, along with a crab-stuffed trout filet and a slice of key lime pie. He ate, drank, and after watching several hours of late night television—including a rerun of *The Beverly Hillbillies* (the one where a band of hippies worship Jethro for smoking crawdads) and a bad psychotronic movie, *Plan 9 From Outer Space*—Manny finally dozed, writhing into a scary dream hours later. The oneiric flow, pitter-pattering through his brain on dream-water feet, resolved itself into a Daliesque image of Ronald Reagan. It hopped around on golf tee legs, the torso cracked open to a column of drawers filled with blue jockstraps, their groin cups inked with Virgin Mary heads—all of them screaming at Jesus to make more wine.

Then things got really strange.

Rarefied atmospheres of marble hall and white office tore free and clogged Manny's motor skills. A herd of yes-mammals assaulted him with slogans of culture preservation, slogans like GO WITH THE FLOW and NOT IN MY BACK YARD; and before consciousness gratefully interrupted, Manny's nose poked at the air, barely able to plug the rectum of a game hen from Cafe Artaud. The apparition bobbed before him like a black snowflake on a breeze. And the last thing he remembered? The hen turning around to glare at him, its head replaced by Hunsecker's beakless, skin-sucked face.

At the sight of that, Manny shrieked himself awake, his arms flying, awkwardly knocking his wine glass off the end table and onto the floor. He picked it up, tried to get back to sleep, but the horror inspired by recalling Hunsecker's face looking goofy and pissed atop the neck of a game hen made him nervous. So he drew a hot bath, hoping it would calm his nerves—and it did. Only now, it's one A.M., cold as Hunsecker's eyes, and some fucking maniac won't stop banging.

In a bathrobe, and still quaking, Manny goes to the door and opens it. But no one is there. He sees a white envelope at his feet and bends to pick it up (the whole circumstance reminding him of a scene in the old Vincent Price movie, *House on Haunted Hill*).

The envelope is addressed to: THE NEW EMPLOYEE.

Manny shuffles back to the bed, sits, and turns on the light to read:

Dear Mr. Eden,

    My name is Rochambeau. I used to be a whistleblower. They called me the human wave machine. If you have any real sense, you will soon see that our country is self-destructing. We prod our heroes to attention with high and mighty words, encourage their conscience, then let them rise to the occasion and we become angry, even indignant. Do we hate them because they remind us of our own guilt and hypocrisy? Regardless, I know where you are, Mr. Eden, and while at OWC you might have a chance to meet my friends, and it won't matter to them whether you are conservative or liberal in your political beliefs. They will contact you if you are true to your nation. We hope you will join our resistance as a brave member of THE AMERICAN WATCH. Our duty is to fight the hell of corporation that Washington has become. The future of America depends on it. Anyway, they call me Rochambeau because I live in Lafayette Park, wear a tri-cornered hat, and point accusingly at the White House. If

```
you go there looking for me, no one will help
you. I live in secret, but I'll be watching.

Sincerely,

Rochambeau
```

Manny tosses the letter onto his nightstand. He can't figure it. *The American Watch*? No. It's Hunsecker—must be. He's verging on psychotic break. He typed the letter after the interview, or else returned to his office to photocopy it from a file. All to test my reactions, no doubt, Manny says to himself. What else? A hazing of some kind by the staff? But at *one A.M.* in the morning? Maybe Hunsecker was out on a drunk all night and finally snapped. If I'd opened the door in time, the strange bastard might have exploded in here and demanded even more ass-kissing.

Only a bigger question remained. Manny can't avoid asking himself: *Would I have puckered?*

At this moment, he's burned out by his performance at Cafe Artaud. He compares the humiliating experience to drinking a bowl of voodoo brew, a mystical mare-sweat-bird-drop-iguana-tongue concoction necessary to relieve an alien blood fever, fatal if endured one more day; and besides, the cure only had to be experienced once, one gathering up of grit, one pinch of nose and the choking indignity of it slopping hot and fuming down the throat . . .

But *what the hell*, he'd won, the method justified.

Upon landing in the new job (Hunsecker told him to connect with personnel and arrange a start date ASAP) he'll have the letter and ask Hunsecker about it, watch his face. Somehow, Manny knows the phenomenon of the American Watch will make sense.

One final glass of '83 Bordeaux and he snuggles under the blankets to contemplate his future. He imagines himself a Teddy Roosevelt of the little people. Imagines himself so merciless and morally volcanic in the pursuit of justice, of course—and Rochambeau, or Hunsecker, whoever he is, will have to approve. Manny is sure he can be effective, and without having to *suck up*. Certainly qualifying him to be a partisan in The American Watch?

No matter. *The whole thing is probably a fraud anyway.*

He continues to sip wine, and his thoughts wander to the OWC. He imagines the nature of his future colleagues. Realizing broad strokes are necessary, Manny creates visages of fierce and sagacious vitality, the strong chins and blazing eyes he knows he will soon encounter within the vaulted chambers of the Office of Whistleblower Counsel. Would not an Olympus with a sense of sacred mission compel the creation of a divine posse? If The Gipper's friend, Counsel Madison, supervised the hiring, the outcome was inevitable. That ass Hunsecker had to be an anomaly, a legacy of some kind, or maybe just some poor bastard they all feel sorry for.

After finishing his wine, Manny verges on sleep, and before consciousness evaporates, he transforms himself. He becomes a teary lug of a man, moist with emotions—the kind that might seem naive and laughably melodramatic if expressed to any streetwise cynic—for now, mounting before his eyes arrives the source of his motivation: a land of meteor-born beliefs and dreams of freedom poised on the edge of the universe like a true Titaness. *Flaming eyes and flowing hair, broadsword in hand, body of an Amazon queen.* It is *his* America, protectoress of the weak, enemy of the Hun and bad bosses alike. He imagines her like a full moon, floating up enormous, resplendent, yet airbrushed free of blemish, her love-polished face sifting up like a balm through the wavy cure and heat of the trees, her pale hills and facial swellings of national rage now tender, softening to Manny, ghostly and soothing as a summer rainbow in Chesapeake twilight.

* * *

BY THE AGE OF EIGHT, Manny imagined America's sunny blade rising above his head like a whisper of good. In her arms she cradled a small child, and all around her, dark men of "The Hun" circled. And as the Hun hounds of Germany snarled, America swung her sword, and the child stared with fearful eyes. The child was Manny's make-believe sister. He called her Ava. She lost his hand as their family fled

Antwerp in 1914, the hot iron of Hun burning the world behind them to flames. Alone, and with a panicky mob surging in the streets, Ava became lost—finally knocked cold and left for dead.

Only America could save her.

Manny watched as She stepped forth from a gleaming hole in the clouds above the city, her sword held high, only a brief glimpse of the purple peaks fading behind her. The Hun charged and their iron horses broke like squall against the mighty headlands of her bosom. Their hound life was spilled by the sun of her blade. Ava, Manny's sister, raised her hand and America held it till Ava was safe, and Ava never let go. Why? Because she wasn't his sister, only an imaginary being.

Manny had always wanted a sister, but in fact, his family consisted of only two other people: his mother, Gloria Swanson Barrow (nicknamed by Manny "Mommy K"—Mommy plus Kennedy), a dedicated JFK liberal and former civil rights worker from Colorado; and his grandfather, Edward "Eddie" Eden, a Teddy-Roosevelt-type conservative and World War I vet who often mesmerized Manny with tales of the hero Sergeant York—Eddie having served with York in the Argonne Forest, capturing German machine gun nests and shooting flame throwers on German backs to make them blow up, and such wicked stuff as that.

Eddie also possessed a collection of WW I memorabilia that included recruitment posters of *America The Beautiful* battling "The Hun." Not an evening passed that Manny didn't see the following words shining down on him from the dining room wall:

> AMERICA AWAKE! CIVILIZATION CALLS
> EVERY MAN, WOMAN AND CHILD!

From a young age, Manny therefore not only saw his country as needful, but also as a strong, stately woman, sometimes blustery and violent, yes, and always for the right cause.

As counterpoint and complement while dreaming Ava and America, Mommy K taught Manny the value of democracy, justice, and responsibility to the community. She often coaxed her son into helping with local charity events by asking, *What can you do for your country, Manny*

Eden? She encouraged him to be active, smart and brave, and to involve himself in making his little part of America a much better place.

When Manny was ten, the two of them witnessed a mid-afternoon bank robbery by the Houlihan brothers in downtown Kenosha. They stood directly across the street, in Sanford Park as the alarm bell echoed off the buildings downtown. Manny would always remember the flashes of gunshot through the window, the suffocated sound of a scream, and the black-hooded men bursting out of the bank like germs in search of a host.

At the police station afterwards, Mommy K told Manny that if he let bad stuff go by without speaking up then he was every bit as responsible. Manny just looked up at his mother and said, "BANG! BANG!" But the lesson stayed with him all the same, and well into adulthood, even through all those many years of incarceration at St. Elizabeth's. Mommy K also taught respect and emulation of America's wise leaders, struggled hard to provide her young son with a paternal role model in John F. Kennedy. She read him the JFK lore, substituted JFK speeches for bedtime stories, and even made him watch JFK assassination footage. One of his earliest memories was that of Jackie O crawling over the car trunk to retrieve that shot-off piece of JFK's head (Mommy K saying the murder happened because JFK was such a good and conscientious person). But much to her horror and anguish, and following a Ronald Reagan movie marathon on Channel 44 in Kenosha, a headstrong Manny adopted his own political father: Ronald "The Gipper" Reagan.

Nine-year old Manny had been laid up with the flu. While Mommy K was at work, he and grandfather Eddie lazed around on the couch, drinking juice and rob roys and watching Ronny get the bad guys, run touchdowns, and frisk with monkeys. *Hell's Kitchen* was one of Manny's favorites, starring Ronny and The Dead End Kids. Though Ronny wasn't exciting, or much of anything, like in *Knute Rockne* or *Bedtime for Bonzo*, or *Brother Rat*, the fact that he was in a movie with The Kids was good enough.

In contrast, JFK hadn't made any real movies. Little Manny was surprised. Wasn't he famous enough? Ronny's flicks were way better than the footage Mommy K showed him. Ronny was more of a hero. It was easy to see—and of course, old Republican warhorse Eddie agreed, saying to Manny, "You know a real man when you see one, son!"

Per Mommy K's advice, Manny wasted no time involving himself.

As his quietly outraged mother edited and coached (and Eddie snickered), Manny wrote nearly two dozen letters to Governor Reagan of California, like this one:

```
Dear Governor Raygun,

    I hear that hippies are smoking on your front
lawn and throwing banana peels at you like
Bonzo chimps. Just get some fire hoses and
wash them off the grass. If that doesn't work
then pay them to leave because most of them are
poor anyway and could use a job as movie extras
or something. Will Bonzo be back? I miss him.
Why don't you make a movie where you switch
places with Bonzo? I mean, he gets your brain
and you get his, and you could call it Bonzo
Gets Elected. Then if things screw up in Cali-
fornia you can blame your Bonzo brain. But it
really won't matter about the brain switch
because we both know Bonzo is real smart, just
like you. Maybe he could become president of
the United States. Anyway, what a funny movie
that would be, huh? If you come to Kenosha,
I'll do my chimp imitation and groom you, and
Nancy too. Please say you'll come.

Cool Bananas!

Manny A. Eden
```

Stirred therefore by his childhood idol, the Hollywood Gipper, his mother's Kennedy lore, and Eddie's crusading posters and tales (together with a potent dose of Huck Finn and Holden Caulfield), Manny entered Stephen Douglas High wanting to do the right thing, be a hero of some kind. Even before high school, at age thirteen, he fantasized that he was a wise and benevolent U.S. president with super powers—a cross between JFK, Ronald Reagan, and the Marvel comic book hero, Captain America.

During the day, President Eden foiled the forces of corruption, and at night, fought Soviet spy thugs on the streets of Capitol Hill. Manny would pretend on weekend mornings, frisbee-tossing a trashcan lid and knocking down old Chlorox bottles he'd lined up on a sawhorse until the biggest bully in Kenosha, Syd Drummond (nicknamed "Fat Alien"), caught him at it. Jumping the fence, Fat Alien rushed in with a tree branch thick as a giant's wrist and smashed it against Manny's upraised trashcan lid while repeatedly shrieking:

"I AM THE GHOST OF ADOLF! NOW DIE!"

CHAPTER 3

Pretend You Are Manny — The Hitchcock Effect — Go Gators! — A Science Fiction Princess — Manny Near Paralysis — Do Not Think and Be

PRETEND YOU ARE THE DUCHESS OF ALBA posing for the famous Goya, or perhaps Ivan the Terrible ordering the death of his court, or maybe the author Ron Hubbard inventing a science fiction religion or Queen Zenobia defeating the legions of Rome, or perhaps a great magician, The Amazing Randi, exposing the top cons of psychic fraud. Or just imagine you are someone far less important—like Manny Eden ... Can you? Can you be him, if possible, just for *a short time*, a fly on the wall of his future?

Try it.

On the count of nine, you will be him.

1 ... 2 ... 3 (your throat is tight with tie)

4 ... 5 (you are young and incurably idealistic)

6 ... 7 (you are loveless, gaseous, sweaty)

8 ... 9.

It's two weeks since you received the mysterious note from Rochambeau. You've found a small room for rent in Arlington, Virginia, and you've taken the subway from Rosslyn to arrive at your new job at the Office of Whistleblower Counsel (OWC).

At 7:59 AM the elevator doors open onto the eleventh floor of 2915 K Street in Washington.

Now, step from the elevator. Look around. The floor is dark. Immerse yourself and realize an Alfred Hitchcock effect. Perhaps *Vertigo*. Observe how the scheme sunsets down to a twilight-on-black-hole. The walls, papered blunt and overcast-white, affect you with an odor of slashed budget. The carpet beneath you appears like a slab of frozen black cola. To either side, strips of luminous green plastic fuse wall with floor, and above, the ceiling is a long, black block, set with a pyramid tripwire (or so you imagine) and poised to collapse. At intervals, halos of feeble yellow light gasp forth from the walls. You note how gently they jaundice your hands.

As you absorb all this like a sponge sucking mud, your lungs struggle for air thinned to a cough. You wonder what unknown law of Murphy is at work here. You imagine also that the wrong move in this place of darkness will result in your death.

But no matter.

Shrug off this new fear.

The power of optimism compels you.

Walk through the darkness toward a single glass door at the end of the hall. Note the surface embossed with gold-flake letters that read:

OFFICE OF WHISTLEBLOWER COUNSEL

Open it. Pass through.

Move down a stubby hall and into a cramped reception office smaller than the men's bathroom in Cafe Artaud. Look around. See an exotically coiffed, young African American woman who pilots a desk that looks like a gray tank of metal.

Wave at her.

Smile with lots of teeth.

Watch her stare back as if you were a new species of cockroach. Note from her faux-brass nameplate that she is Ms. Yolanda Peel. Look at her hands. They are long, thin and candle-lit with stiletto nails hot as pink flamingo. See the creek-stone texture of her punk-shaved head, her earrings like ponds of pewter contoured soft as ears. Watch in a stupor as she motions her head ever so slightly, the overlapped plates bangling, hollow as wind chimes.

Recover and speak first. Try hard to be clever:

"My name is Manny Eden. I was hired by Mr. Hunsecker as an investigator for the Office of Whistleblower Counsel... And you look cool, like a Miles Davis number."

But Ms. Yolanda Peel, unwilling to acknowledge you in any meaningful way, snatches up a phone, punches and announces casually, "It's me, Deejah, can you *stand it?*" While her every eye and muscle droop with infinite boredom, she tells the Deejah person that "a new shammer has arrived." A whiny fly response on the other end of the line forces Ms. Yolanda Peel to scowl.

She replaces the phone, gazes up and informs you that Mr. Hunsecker's secretary, Deejah Thoris, knows nothing about a new hire, hasn't seen one piece of paperwork, and can't believe Mr. Hunsecker is even looking to fill a new position given current budget restraints; and furthermore, "You'll just have to stew here in this waiting room till his *old bad self* shows," or until Ms. Yolanda Peel hears differently.

At this point, you search for size ten ruby slippers. You fumble for explanation, but options are few. You thank her, tell her you're sure it will all work out, and you sit down, uncomfortable as possible, wondering what the hell is going on.

You are afraid to consider the worst.

While sitting, you distract yourself with the name *Deejah Thoris*. It sounds familiar, like a name from a sci-fi novel, only you can't place it. Regardless, you begin to feel out of place, and out of sorts, like a jellyfish caught and slapped on a blazing dock.

It's summer and you are drying out.

You opt to make conversation with Ms. Yolanda Peel in an attempt to distract yourself further. "Ms. Peel," you say, your face concerned, "please tell me, what is the whistleblower situation now?"

"*Huh?*" Ms. Yolanda Peel frowns.

"Any whistleblowers the office is protecting?"

"That's not my job," Ms. Yolanda Peel says and opens a drawer in her desk, her chimes bangling. She rummages around as if looking for something.

"You just started working here? With the American Watch?"

"Huh? Watch *what?*"

"You been here for awhile?"

"I've been ridin' this government rhino goin' on five years."

"Long enough to enjoy it?"

"*Huh?*"

"Do you like working here?"

"All I gotta say is, everyday I pray to Jesus."

Ms. Yolanda Peel finds what she's been looking for—nail polish—and begins the touch up. Ignored once more, you focus on your surroundings. You note how pasty the interior of this waiting cubicle is, how drab with a wallpaper skin of ochre ripples. You begin to wax sluggish. You wane to Ms. Yolanda Peel's head-in-a-vise attitude before moving on to more complex thoughts of termite state.

A fight to control panic comes next.

You wonder what might happen to you if it has all been a mistake: the long flight back to Kenosha followed by an application to Ed's Plant Emporium in Milwaukee. A land of dirty nails, bitchy customers and daily cactus stabbings. But an article about The Gipper "on the stump"—as reported by a *Time* magazine laying on an extra chair beside you—temporarily blunts the cactus.

After a minute or so, you imagine yourself as president. You travel briskly through the nation by train, like in old times, skimming the pale-boiling rows of Midwestern plain, leaping the Great Divide and the moon-towered ranges, trudging the yellow and red teeter-stone deserts You trickle along the grinding seam of plate fault towards the Central Americas that yet simmer hot and betrayed with the remains of Asiatic races, cheering mobs wombing you wherever you go:

Fry them sickos in Washington, President Eden! Make democracy work!

"FLAME ON!" is all you can reply.

Suddenly, the door beyond Ms. Yolanda Peel quivers with a muffled voice.

Is it the Hunsecker?

No. You are afraid to hope, but you hurriedly refresh your memory of schmooze skills and haul in the slack on your face as a tedious unbolting occurs.

The door moves.

A tiny crack appears. A twinkling fairy light gleams forth.

Poof!

The door opens wider. Only the movement is plodding, and at the sight of this painful yawn, a heavy exhaustion fills you just as the entire cubic volume of air in the room shifts.

At last, the pressure is off.

The door swings towards you. You stare inside. A narrow and low ceilinged corridor comes into view like a long and hollow needle that you intuitively guess must be used to inject all newcomers of compatible blood type into the magical body of agency.

A deep sigh is heard.

Ms. Yolanda Peel grins, winks at you, and announces:

"THE DEEJAH. She *comes!*"

You don't understand the import of this comment until a moon to mask the sun appears from behind the vanishing door. Her red hair, frazzled out thick to either side of her head, strikes out at you like a single hurled orange. Her body, hazardous as a knife, appears thin as the door crack. Her eyes, black as bowling balls, grip and gutter you. And as she looms closer, you note with a little alarm tingle that she flaunts a bulky gray sweatshirt with the words GO GATORS! emblazoned in orange impact letters on the front.

For a few long moments, no one in this tableau says a word. Then following a spew of *fuck-this-wimp-ass-bullshit* breath expelled from between the lips of the no-nonsense Ms. Yolanda Peel, the Deejah with the gator sweatshirt speaks to you. Her man-like voice is disturbingly reminiscent of Hunsecker himself:

"I am Deejah Thoris. Mr. Hunsecker's secretary."

What choice do you have? You stand and move towards her; but just as you raise your hand to shake hers, the sounds "I'm Man—" drumming out from your mouth, her entire body shudders, as if pumped with panic toners.

Go Gators!

The sight of this dysfunctional display paralyzes you. You are afraid to imagine the sleeping powers of utter repulsion, terrified to guess what this person might do if aroused to real passion or fury—and you can't deny or sugarcoat this impression. Perhaps her opposed hemispheres are partitioned off by a zipper in her scalp. At any moment she might pinch it and peel down to her waistline to reveal a ravenous alien mollusk, or a demon servant of Satan, or maybe just the *Horror of Party Beach*. But then she gives your whole attitude the once over. She verges on utter contempt until forced to focus suspiciously on your loitering hand still hanging in the air.

Finally, she shakes it, cold and quick as a slap.

Next, she pivots and is sucked—no—injected down the length of the hollow hall behind her, the air mass in the reception office restored like elastic to the memory of form.

Baffled by the surreal disappearance, you nevertheless recall your manners. You turn back to thank the pink-bangling Ms. Peel for her professionalism. She stares at you as if feeling pity, and perhaps, a desire to warn you or wish you luck.

You're not sure which.

No time to ponder though.

Only a *sang-froid* approach makes sense now.

You notice too that though the anorexic gator person has mysteriously vanished, you can hear the *swish swish* friction of her denim and the wheeze of her lungs filtering out pints of oxygen somewhere beyond.

Poised for a bubbling first impression, you start forward. You follow the *swish swish* and quickly arrive at an intersection of blank hallways. You pause, search for a scarecrow in need of a brain, toss an invisible coin and turn right. Before you have gone even a few paces though, a new apparition erupts from a door on your left.

The face of it sobs with rage.

It belongs to a severe man in his forties, his forehead the size of a baseball diamond, his hair white as a polar bear tummy. A double-breasted blue suit and a purple tie complement the rage. And the apparition doesn't stop or slow for a moment as it hurtles straight for you.

"Oh, ahoy there! Excuse me," you blurt out.

"You're *not excused*," the apparition replies savagely, jerking you around and barreling on.

As you turn to watch him vanish, your entire face winces to the right several inches. Then once more, as if to refocus you on your sacred mission of cure, the nurturing *swish swish* of denim goads you on, this time from an open doorway further down the hall.

You step quickly.

Upon entering another small room, you glimpse a smear of gator disappearing into a hole on your right, and you're certain she won't escape, not this time. Pressing forward, you glance around just long enough to note the ad hoc shabbiness: several metal folding chairs flush against the wall, a well-ringed coffee table and a chipped end table crowned with a percolating pot of coffee, its scuffed and cold trunk rearing beside towers of styrofoam cup. On the wall to your right, a black-on-white sign is taped on high, and it says:

THE COFFEE ROOM

Passing through, you arrive in a much larger space. Before you, the gator woman is seated behind a gray desk tank. She opens mail with machine-like slashes of letter opener, and you can only think of one throat after another being slit.

Cautiously, you move towards her.

Still lingering in her present human form, yet on the fringe of a transmogrification more violent, she slits the envelopes all the more abruptly as you draw closer, preparing to ask her a question. You've just recalled the source of her name, and you're extremely curious.

"Your name, uh, *Deejah*. It's the same as a character in an Edgar Rice Burroughs novel, right?"

"I've been told that," Deejah says, her face emotionless.

"Wasn't she a princess of Mars?"

"That is so."

"Well ... it's kinda cool to be named after a science fiction princess, huh?"

No answer.

"Did Mr. Hunsecker call, Deejah?" you ask.

"Not this time."

She refuses to meet your gaze.

"The situation must have changed, or I wouldn't be here ... I suppose."

No answer.

"He hired me as an investigator ... He'll be in later?"

"That is so," she replies.

"Do you know what time?"

"What I said."

"You said he didn't call."

"He left a note."

"Ah. Anything special? I mean ... any instructions for me?"

"To wait."

"*Pardon?*"

"Wait."

"Is this his office?" With a hitchhiker thumb you motion to a spacious and imposing room behind you with a window in it.

"That is so." She scoots her chair behind an IBM Selectric typewriter on her left and rolls in a blank envelope.

"Then do you know what time he'll be in?"

"He didn't call."

"I know that, but the note said nothing else?"

"What I said."

"You said it only told me to wait."

"He told me to tell you before he left."

"Tell me what?"

"What the note said."

On the verge of slapping yourself, you think fast. You don't want to come off like a hothead, especially on the first day. Then as if to prove divine intervention, a framed photo on Deejah's desk distracts you. You can't stop staring at the object in the photo: a plume of white rocket exhaust capped with a human head. "*Danilo Plato-Prophet,*" you remark with a tone of sarcasm in your voice, as if in whimsical contemplation of higher bunko artist forms.

Deejah abruptly stops slitting after you say that. She meets your gaze with eyes become slag pits from Hell. You wallow in them, screaming, dissected without mercy, your many cold parts discarded in abandoned mine shafts from Utah to Mingo County. Eager to please as you are though, you dumbly attempt to retrench and get on Deejah's good side.

"I've read a lot about Ms. Plato-Prophet. She, uh—stirs controversy, to say the least. Have you seen her? I hear it's expensive, $500.00 a pop."

"She is *The Hierophant*."

Deejah's eyes don't slacken. You imagine yourself diced and dribbled out at 5,000 feet like warning propaganda.

"Harmusal, right? That's the god she channels?"

"Yes," she answers, resuming her slitting before adding in a solemn, prayer-like voice, "*The God. The only God. My Harmusal.*"

"Isn't Harmusal from the ice age?" you ask.

"Yes."

"And doesn't Ms. Danilo Plato-Prophet live in a castle in Oregon, one she had imported from Belgium?"

"That is so," Deejah says.

You recalled this bit of information about Danilo from an article in the *Chicago Sun*, but what really scars your mind even now is the photo that accompanied the piece: Danilo Plato-Prophet, unearthly as usual in translucent white robes, and posed beside her, the "companion witchdoctor," an Incan dwarf by the name of Antipater who wore an orange wizard cap slashed with tinsel comets. According to the *Sun*, he functioned both as her "spirit guide and chief deputy."

Curiosity now forces you to examine Deejah's photo more closely. Billowing up like a demonic kite, the theatric she-god poses in an ankle-length robe white as borax. Her arms outspread, Christ-like, sci-fi platinum head lolling stuporous on her shoulders, mouth gaping as if caught at the peak of a ripping snore. You would recognize this image anywhere: Danilo's famous "channeling pose." A superimposed aura ignites the air above her head with a peacock nimbus of whore-madam velvets, faux-leopard yellows and cough lozenge greens—these "psychokinetic hues" spewing out to erase the background—and floating above this toxic halo, a big drip of cartoon flame, and above that, embossed in brassy, drop-shadowed letters, Danilo's timeless reprimand:

DO NOT THINK AND BE

You next dream a way to compliment Ms. Plato-Prophet's choice of supernal wisdom delivery; but the conjuring of Deejah's teeth snapping tight on your jugular prods you into blowing retreat with the whispered words:

"*Go Gators.*"

Back to lobby mode now.

No slouching though, no bolts or bangling ponds of warning. You must look poised, on edge, prepared at a moment's notice to blow off the mounting disappointments and hurl your patriotic body into the fire. But right now, all is quiet and no one is in the coffee room. You slip out to make yourself a cup, return and sit on a green vinyl chair pushed against the wall. On your right, Hunsecker's office echoes with the ghostly thunder of rolling heads, and on your left, the pre-homicidal votary of Harmusal begins to hum and meditate.

You reason that none of this makes any difference.

You choose to ignore the symptoms.

You tell yourself that only deeds and vision are important.

CHAPTER 4

The Sublime Perception State — In Search of JB — Manny Eden Meets The Staff — Tammy Pon and The Mental Douche — Like a Moral Volcano

DEEJAH'S CHAIR SQUEAKS. She hates it because it makes it difficult for her to focus, especially if she's trying to meditate. Only no time to gripe now—she has three memos to punch out before Hunsecker arrives.

After a short prayer to her god Harmusal, she rolls OWC letterhead into the IBM Selectric, trying not to glance at the new hire, but doing it anyway, noting how he averts his eyes as if afraid of her. She smells an OWC yes-mammal in the making, *almost* feels sorry for him. But hadn't he flipped her off with his smart tongue? And only a few minutes ago? Also, his new gray suit, perfectly combed black hair and smirky face are *really* annoying.

She feels a sudden urge to slap him, an urge she cannot understand.

In seconds, the urge to violence grows overwhelming.

Just as she's about to jump up and whack the Eden prick with a full palm of fury, she stops. Tries to calm. Says quietly to herself:

I must relax. This man is doomed. I will speak with the Hierophant instead.

And then, as she does so often, Deejah transcends her limitations.

She withdraws memories of her last visit to Danilo's land. She imagines herself wet and thin as fog, her bare feet molding into the dark mud of the Oregon coast. Raising her head, she sees her body in the distance, a tiny fire-ant upon the rim of a black cliff. In a moment, she is there. Stepping, and oh so delicate, she teeters upon disks and balls of damp stone, her mind alert as a shriek, immersing into what Hieorphant Danilo calls:

The Sublime Perception State.

Deejah seeks testimony to return to the Hierophant, one snatched by her alert perception from this land of fog-soaked earth and smoky black sequoia—and it wasn't as if the age-forgotten things had to jump up and tusk-prick her. Wisps and apparitions were acceptable to report. These chimera were, as she learned, *protophysicals.*

Projected reflections of what-had-been.

The Aborning Solids struggling to regain their essence.

Such phenomena hailed therefore as presagements of Harmusal's return, *Phase I* proof of His *Transepochal Resurrection* reclaiming the earth—for the god, as a supernatural rake, was dragging the entire Ice Age back with him as he fought to regain the human plane.

"WHAT HAS BEEN SHALL BE AGAIN!" Hierophant Danilo had triumphantly screeched from atop her cliff dais.

"THAT IS SO!" Deejah bellowed with thousands of others in ritual thunderclap response, all eyes rolled white to the scalp.

"WE SEE THEM NOW!"

From the slopes of the Coastal Ranges to the dark promontories of Harris Beach, *The Aborning Solids*, like psychic soap bubbles, appeared and popped every few hours while whole geologic epochs advanced in bole-snapping, tidal crust waves and receded, leaving behind each day the scars of glacial drudgery.

* * *

DEEJAH BEGINS TO TYPE, the letter—a standard we-hear-you response to a government employee claiming whistleblower status. After a moment though, she stops, and listens. She detects movement in the coffee room. A woman's laughter.

Who is it?

At least two people. Sounds of cup and pour.

The smirky prick, Eden, hears it too. Deejah notes his face on alert. He sips his coffee. His eyes are wide, motionless.

What does he expect now?

From within the coffee room, a feminine voice proclaims:

"Female whistleblowers have fewer death-threat fantasies than males. You think, Varsana?"

A second female voice, this one older and with a trace of Bahamian accent, responds:

"You know me, Babs. I'm old enough to tell the truth about things now. I don't have to be afraid anymore cause I'm fireproof."

Deejah listens carefully while staring at Eden.

"Ring around the rosy, a pocketful of matches," Babs says.

Eden can't figure that one. Look at him raise that eyebrow!

"Where's the—" Deejah hears Varsana suddenly lower her voice. Deejah can't make out the last two words of the sentence, but it sounded as if Varsana used the words, *Triumphant Beast*—and she's heard this before. It's a nick around OWC for Mr. Hunsecker. Even Counsel Madison uses it.

After a pause, Babs answers. "Schmoozing at the Pentagon."

"Hunsecker's endless career search?"

"That's it."

Both women chuckle.

Deejah smiles at the astonishment on Eden's face.

Is he stupid?

Silence for a few moments, then Deejah hears a coffee slurp, *ahhhhh*. Sugar tap and tinkle.

"So, Ms. Babs, what does the perfect lover want now?" asks Varsana.

"To slap the face of the nearest woman better off than me."

"I'm surprised. Maybe I should duck?"

"It's just that Sven's parents gave us a townhouse in Manassas."

"Well, yes, that's enough to make you violent."

"It's a wedding present, Varsana, but it's too big, God, like a cave! And I just collapsed Saturday morning. I wanted to beat my fists on the floor because we don't have enough furniture to harmonize with the spaaacccce."

Deejah wants to gag.

When will the end come?

Varsana says, "It's funny how the little things—"

"Can make you so miserable? Just talk to me about my case load," says Babs, "it has doubled in the past two weeks."

Coffee slurp, very *ooooh* on the lips.

"So what's new in the Lawrence debacle?" Varsana asks. "Any JB?"

"No, no JB. Now he says the whole Customs Department is after him." Both women chuckle again.

Eden's raising both brows. His forehead will ache soon, very soon.

"Next, he'll claim he sang backup for the Rolling Stones!" Varsana says. Deejah hears more footsteps. Someone else has arrived to get coffee. *Who?*

"MY BABSHEBA!" A man's voice impacts the air. Deep and booming like heavy logs over the Frostbite falls. "QUEEN OF BABYLON! How deep's the mud?"

"Boyden!" shouts Babs, exuberant as a child. "Mud's fine. Pour a cup."

"Will do," Boyden says, "but what's this about Customs?"

"The Lawrence case," says Varsana.

"A confirmed *pisaki!*" Boyden says with comic vehemence.

"I prefer *kritikany!*" says Babs with equal gusto.

The Eden prick doesn't know what they're talking about. Who would?

Glass and sugar tinkle-tankle. Creamer tap and tinkle.

"But what of Lawrence's speech?" Varsana persists with her query, in a cold voice now. Deejah knows she hates being muffled by Boyden.

"Tainted by ink," Babs says. "Mr. Hunsecker decrees—"

"His words must be fresh, his speech clean!" Boyden proclaims.

"Well, speech unclean. Lawrence whined to the Dallas media. Claims no other choice. Trainloads of Peruvian snow were allegedly poised on the border."

"The law according to Hunsecker," Varsana announces in magniloquent fashion. Small laughter, a hiccup. "Everyone has a choice, Babs."

"Exactly, and best of all, Lawrence says he returned to his apartment last week to find a chalk effigy of himself scratched on his wall, man-sized, and a hole punched through the heart with an ice pick."

"O.H. S.H.I.T.!" Boyden spell-shouts.

"*Please!*" implores Varsana.

"Customs must be taking lessons from the Mafia," Boyden says.

"Nope. Nothing more complex than insubordination," says Babs. "Lawrence was ordered to keep it classified. Customs has already fired him . . . Oh, yesssss, and speaking of nutty asses deserving termination, where is the biggest ass in Washington, our very own *Laney Dracos?*"

"I meant to tell you," Varsana says. "I was at Counsel Madison's cocktail party in Old Town last Saturday night when the monster decided to attack."

"I don't believe it!" Babs says.

Fucking bitches! They won't leave her alone.

"She howled like a wounded cat as soon as the butler let her in, and then hassled everyone at the party, acting like an imbecile and asking if JB had been invited. Is JB here? Are you JB? . . . And she wouldn't shut up."

"But why?"

You shut up! Shut the fuck up!

"To attract attention, why else?" Varsana says. "You know how she craves to be the center of things. You ever seen that big mouthed comedienne, Judy Bermuda, Tanaka, or something like that? She reminds me of her. And get this, *Mzz Dracos* wore a tin foil dress, very mini, and with hideous, zebra-stripe heels—strictly Star Whore."

"Why hasn't anyone fired her yet?"

Bitches! Bitches! Bitches!

"Then she began to recount her most recent punk-rock adventures."

"Adventures? Gaaaahhhdd!"

"She bragged about the uniquely tasteless stunts she performs on stage with a simple glass of water and a microphone stand."

"Washington City Paper!" Boyden interrupts. "She's on the cover of September WCP—Tammy Pon and the Mental Douche!"

"What?" Varsana asks.

Laney Dracos is *Tammy Pon.* That's her alias," Boyden says. "She won't admit it, of course, but get a copy of WCP. You'll see. It looks just like her."

"That whore," Babs says.

Who's the whore, Babs?

More coffee pouring, more slurping. Deejah does recall seeing Tammy Pon and her band at the 9:30 Club in D.C., and Tammy did look *a lot* like Laney Dracos—only it was hard to say for sure. Tammy's face that night was slashed with heavy rouge and purple eye shadow.

"Oh, by the way, don't we have a new hire coming in?" asks Varsana.

Deejah turns to stare at Eden. He looks up and sees her boring into him with big fanatic eyes as if he were a production of her god, a reflection of what-had-been. She raises her right hand, slowly, ominously, and points to the coffee room.

Manny sighs.

Did he dare disobey a science fiction princess?

* * *

EDGING OFF THE CHAIR, gripping his coffee, Manny stands and floats through the imaginary air of sacrificial knives hurled by Deejah. Effortless and unwounded though, he passes into the lobby. All heads swivel. He opens with a big smile and says:

"Hello, I'm Manny Eden. The new hire."

Things blur off to the sides. Manny realizes instinctively that the face nearest him belongs to Babs. Her eyes are swimming pools, huge and chlorine-aqua, her face brimming with a Kansas-like purity, cute and clean, her hair bronze, cropped short and stylish above her collar. She wears a frilly white blouse and an office-grey wool skirt and she smells like Old English aftershave.

"Hi, Manny. I'm Babs Easton. What's your category?" she asks him, extending her hand to shake.

"Category?" Manny asks.

"Are you an Accommodator, an Evader, a Sniper, a Super-Amiable, or a Manipulator?"

Manny hesitates, then says, "None of the above. Just a man scared of gator."

"What?"

"No, seriously, I don't get it."

"We have to know what category you fit into so we know how to defend against you. It's part of the agenda thing. Mr. Hunsecker has divided everyone up into an agenda."

"Well, then, I'm what you might call a superhero." Manny winks at Babs and sails his hand through the air with a whoosh. He considers a

JFK or a Bullwinkle imitation at this point, but holds off, figuring it's too early to act funny.

"Yes, you are most certainly the Garden-of-Eden," says Babs.

"Why?"

"Cause Mr. Hunsecker said you might talk like a lunatic."

"Yeah, uh, I'm a lunatic, but I'm not Garden-of-Eden, just *Eden*."

"Oh?" Babs chortles in an irritating way when corrected. She tries to smile, her face partly cloudy. Her left hand clenches nervously at her skirt while her other hand raises a cup of coffee to her lips. Manny notices for the first time a small gold cross shimmering below her adam's apple. Babs sees him staring at it and says to him matter-of-factly, "I'm a Catholic, Mr. Eden. What religion do you belong to?"

"Religion? I'm not—"

"SO YOU FOUND JB?" The brawny voice of Boyden. Manny pivots into a an onrushing torpedo of hand flesh. "I'm Boyden McCarthy. Good to have you on the investigator team, Manny."

Boyden strikes Manny as an adult version of Billy Mumy, the red-haired child actor from the old TV show *Lost in Space*—his eyes small, his mouth soft, his entire face verging on goofy. Nevertheless, he's wearing an impeccable, blue-pinstripe suit and a red tie with an American eagle tie-pin (gold plated); as a bonus, he's got that incredible Captain Ahab voice full of gravel and command—a voice that might belong to a general.

"Thanks, Boyden, but I gotta ask. Who is JB?"

Boyden laughs. "Joe Blow! The perfect whistleblower. We're hunting him down, but something always happens to rub out the trail."

"And *pisaki, kritikany*?"

"Russian terms for various species of malcontent in the Communist Party. Mr. Hunsecker borrowed 'em from some book about whistleblowing in the Soviet Union. "

"So the pinkos have whistleblowers too?" asks Manny.

"Sure, Manny, every country does." Following this explanation, Boyden's head motions once toward the open doorway to Deejah's area. His throat warbles with an eerie, sci-fi melody. His eyes roll one complete orbit. "You *uhh* met—" He leans closer to whisper, "*the Harmusal cult psycho?*"

Manny wearily nods *yes*, and as he does, Varsana pushes herself in front of Boyden. "Now introduce yourself to *me*," she says. Manny notes the inky blackness of her hair, the neck tails colored a bleeding rust. Her face is large-boned and teakwood tan, inset with a pair of cat-hazel eyes. She's wearing a flower-print dress and looks way too skinny for her height (nearly six feet). Another anorexic? "I'm Varsana Pardo, from Nassau, and I don't waltz."

"Manny Eden, from Kenosha, Wisconsin. And I don't waltz either."

"Eeeeden?" Her nails, long as Ms. Yolanda Peel's, shimmer a glossy magenta. They irritates Manny's wrists as he shakes with her.

"You're married?" she says.

"No."

"Good, I may have someone for you."

"I need someone . . . Meanwhile, I'll, uh, just have to settle for the rewards of muzzling corruption," Manny says, trying to be clever.

Babs blinks. She looks perplexed. "Pardon? What *corruption*? Who is corrupt, Mr. Eden?"

"Well, maybe these people the whistleblowers are complaining about?"

Babs forces a grin. "Oh, *of course*."

She locks eyes with Varsana for a moment, then refocuses on Manny, blinking rapidly. For some reason, Manny feels if he were suddenly back in high school. "Have I met the whole office now?" he asks.

"Everyone in the Investigation Division, except for Mr. Quigley, Rebecca Bergstein, and *Mzz Dracos*," says Varsana.

"*Backstabbing bitch*," Boyden whispers and glances around as if wary of hidden eavesdropping devices. The *Lost-in-Space* boy then smiles to himself—as if recalling something amusing—and says, "Manny, you *must* see this. Hold on!" He swivels around and bolts out of the room. Varsana and Babs gawk at each other, apparently surprised by his behavior.

Immediately after Boyden leaves, Deejah Thoris appears in the doorway, her body rigid, thin and orange-headed. Babs and Varsana stare at her, their faces blank. Deejah's man voice booms forth:

"MR. HUNSECKER CALLED. HE WILL ARRIVE IN MINUTES."

Having announced, Deejah turns and disappears. Before anyone can recover, Boyden returns, triumphant and brandishing above his head a folded newspaper. "Check it out!" he says, assuming a maestro-like stance while drum rolling with his mouth. Varsana appears vexed, but before she can complain he snaps the paper open, exposing the cover page at arm's length.

"Sorceress most foul!" Babs hoots, her face stumbling in mock horror, her trembling finger pointing at the cover.

"Is she, or *isn't she?*" Boyden asks with his deep and rustic Gregory Peck voice. He raises half his face over the top rim of the paper. His crossed and goofy eyes roll up and skirt the edge. At the same time, Varsana Pardo's left hand lifts ever so slightly, as if instinctively preparing to claw. "*Yessss,*" she says, enthralled to the outer limits. "*Mzzzz Laney Dracos* . . . It must be!"

Manny stares at the cover. He sees what appears to be a microphone stand thinning to a hair, dropping away like a long fire pole into the black, howling mouth of a George Washington face, and tightened as an erotic leg-scissor about the circumference of this dropping pole, a fleshy spider of female form, her head tipping back, and only the underside of her chin visible, her starry black hair erupting to an enormous and inverse question mark that sweeps up and over the top half of the page before jetting like a gush of black oil under the *Washington City Paper* title. Below her, near the bottom of the page, the words arrayed in impact type:

TAMMY PON AND THE MENTAL DOUCHE PURIFY DC!

"She's naked!" Varsana says, "Except for those hideous, zebra-stripe heels. And I really, *really* wonder if her good friend Senator Ormsby knows about this?"

Babs shakes her head slowly, appearing anguished at the sight of Tammy Pon's naked body. "You have to accept things for *what they are.* I mean, at some point, you just have to wake up and stop fighting city hall."

Boyden chuckles at Babs and refolds the paper. The *Tammy Pon* image vanishes. Varsana growls. Manny appears stupefied. The trio of Boyden, Varsana, and Babs are soon left hanging. To overcome the awkwardness, and at Boyden's suggestion, they agree to tour "superhero Eden" around the OWC offices. On the way, they point out Personnel, Legal Division, Counsel Madison's office (on the floor above), Budget (only two gnome-a-crats wearing green eyeshades), Congressional Relations, and then back to the brink of Investigation.

Manny, unable to suffocate his curiosity any longer, finally decides to ask:

"Oh, by the way, anyone here know *Rochambeau?*"

Sudden silence. Varsana looks blank, uncertain on how to respond. Babs' face shows genuine fear. Boyden smirks and shakes his head in the negative. Manny continues. "You see, I got this—"

"We're not at liberty to discuss the hero of the revolution," Boyden interrupts. "You best ask Mr. Hunsecker."

Following this advice, all of them stand awkward and numb, and as Manny ponders his fate, a distant roaring begins. It grows louder with each passing second, as if a thing of hurtling velocity and dreadnought-size mass were shoving a few cubic miles of air down a narrow throat of hallway.

The investigation trio hears it and immediately stiffen.

An unknown figure enters the room.

She stomps through like a furious majorette, her breath hissing out with a sound of heel-crushed cobra. Is it a warning? Black reading glasses bruise the flesh of her nose, her reddish brown hair snapped slick and tight behind her head, her face a portrait of old fear turned dour with repeated focus. Oblivious to the rising alarm of consciousness, she takes a sharp left and vanishes into a smoky world of partitions, her hiss fading with distance.

"*Becky!*" Varsana exclaims.

The roaring stops.

Pavlov rules.

No lips move, no muttering, except beneath skin. Hands and limbs quiver, and jerk, smooth themselves out, gliding quiet and deliberate in a routine way, as though an excuse must be found, as if all meretricious motion, all peculiar and visible intention must be made unquestionably defensible.

CHAPTER 5

Nixon's Favorite Photo — The Eye Comet of Hunsecker — Manny's Training — Hart Crane in BLT — Mzz Dracos Scares Manny Into The Men's Room

WITHOUT EXPLANATION TO MANNY, the staff of the Investigative Division blend like heat into the air, scurry off to their respective lairs—all except for Boyden. He slips out his wallet, fidgets with it in a panicky way while removing a single square of white paper, wallet-photo size. He snaps it to Manny Eden like an experienced card shark, winks boldly at him and backpedals away.

Manny, now alone and dumbfounded, stares at a small photo of a dark and waxy man. His nose looks like a comma of flesh. He wears a tuxedo jacket, black bow tie, white shirt, and on his legs, sailboat boxer shorts. He is smiling and holding a bowling ball. A caption in a rectangular box below his bald knees reads:

MY FAVORITE PHOTO, BY RICHARD NIXON

No time for gawking though. The lobby is bathed in total silence, still as air in anticipation of beast.

Manny can't help but tingle.

A snort of hot breath fans the dust from his back. He turns, and following his about face, Manny's vision staggers him backwards, his eyes filling with a man-sized ray of pink. He notes with astonishment how this sizzling pink span is sliced down its center by a black and plummeting smudge that looks like a comet—and inside the tip of this comet, a red eye inset with golden pupil.

The eye is fixed on Manny.

As he watches, it sprouts limbs, torso and a face that belongs to Hunsecker. Manny tries to speak to it. He cannot. It is absurd to even try.

After a few moments of awkwardly stuffing the bowling Nixon in his pocket and fumbling for a spot to rest his coffee cup, Manny uses his legs to follow the eye trail past the suspicious face of Deejah. Once arrived, he stands demonstrably thrilled and expectant on the threshold of Mr. Hunsecker's office, the flag of his face snapping smartly, his sclerotic ego courting the moments till recognition occurs; and as a plus, he's smiling, not smirking at all.

But the Hunsecker won't look up.

He thumbs through a Rolodex on his desk, his mouth dropped open, his comet-eye tie flapped like a big pink tongue on his belly. As soon as Manny tries to speak, Hunsecker says:

"You are indebted to me, Mr. Garden-of-Eden."

"Sir?"

"I've just donated you an hour of OWC's finest."

"I'm flattered, sir."

"Becky Bergstein, outside, through the lobby and down the hall, take a left," Hunsecker says, attempting to rid himself of Manny with a hitchhiker thumb.

"Mr. Hunsecker, I have a letter, from *Rochambeau?*" Manny reaches into his jacket and pulls the envelope out. Hunsecker stops what he is doing and stares intently at Manny, his face surprised.

"What? Already? Bring that here."

Manny delivers the envelope.

Hunsecker rips the note out and reads it, his face scowling the whole time.

"Where did you get this?" he asks. Manny tells him. Hunsecker listens and keeps still, then says, "Do not discuss this with anyone. Say nothing about Rochambeau or the American Watch. Understand, Mr. Eden?"

"No problem, sir, but who is Rochambeau?"

"Never mind. Go find Becky Bergstein now. And remember, say *nothing*. Your career is just beginning."

* * *

HOLLOW AS A GIFT-SHOP WHITE HOUSE, Manny goes in search of OWC's finest. He has zero time to consider the implications of Hunsecker's fear and denial, so he simply follows directions.

He finds Becky Bergstein three partition cells down and on the left. He stops and stands rigid in the open gateway to her partition courtyard, recognizing her as the impressive woman who had just blown through the lobby with a hiss. Though no longer hissing, she yet smolders, feverishly gulping cigarette smoke while cursing and slashing wildly through a heap of carbon and bond atop her desk.

"Excuse me, Becky? . . . *Becky?*"

She doesn't respond. Manny decides to try humor.

"Richard Nixon is with me."

"Eh?" She glances up frowning, her glasses on the tip of her nose.

"Richard Nixon?"

"Goddamn this shit."

"Mr. Hunsecker said you'd procedure me. You are Becky Bergstein?"

"Give me time to piss, *okay?*"

"I'm Manny Eden."

He extends his hand. She ignores him, drags on her VA Slim cigarette, blowing the smoke out the side of her mouth. Cautiously, Manny lowers his hand and seats himself in a chair facing her. She swipes at the mass of paper a few more times, blows more smoke, then locates the slice she'd been searching for. Ignoring Manny further, she begins scribbling on it long and hard, muttering to herself.

Meanwhile, Manny looks around. He first notices the white coffee mug on the corner of Becky's desk. On its surface, black type reads:

YOU DON'T HAVE TO BE CRAZY TO GET HIRED HERE,
BECAUSE THEY KNOW THAT AFTER BEING
SURROUNDED ON A DAILY BASIS BY
IGNORANT, WISHY-WASHY,
EGO-MANIACAL,
BACKSTABBBING FREAKS,

YOUR SCREWS WILL LOOSEN SOON ENOUGH.

Manny absorbs the message and tries hard to distract himself. He notes that atop Becky's desk, but pushed to one side, squats a Comtech XT-PC and keyboard, and beside that, an onyx ashtray brimming with butts, suspended in air by a quartet of bronze dragon-legs. Also, stacked to a dozen parts collapse, and surrounding her on all sides, a tornadic sprawl of disassembled files, index cards, memo slips, sticky notes, copies of congressional bills, phone messages and OMB circulars. And it doesn't stop there. The loess of OWC bureaucracy spills over the edge of the desk and onto the floor to infect the surroundings, the paper ejaculation spewed onto the partition walls. In juxtaposition to a litter of tacked-up pronouncements and CYA miscellany, Manny sees three calendar photos of other-reality gleaming forth: the Disney spires of Mad King Ludwig, a cluster of Arizona buttes looking like purple fingers at sunset, and a patch of tulips bursting red against a background of green lawn.

Becky stops scribbling after a minute, looks up and frowns at Manny examining her space. "So you've met Richard Nixon?" she asks derisively, her face sharpening.

"He's right here." Manny taps the top pocket of his jacket.

"Did Hunsecker interview you at Artaud's?" she asks.

"Why?"

"The investigators are interviewed there because its cheap. The attorneys are always interviewed somewhere more exclusive."

"That makes me feel good."

"It was supposed to. Oh, and there were only three applicants for your job. The other two couldn't spell."

"I can spell, also read, and write."

"Real funny, but I don't have time for this shit."

"But Becky, I'm a special *shit*."

"Being a comic around here won't carry you, Mr. Eden."

"My intent is to work."

"At *what?*... Never mind." Becky places her cigarette in the ashtray, folds her hands tightly in front of her and stares at Manny as if he'd become a thing obscene and annoying—the ex-bass player of Mental Douche perhaps, or maybe a serial pedophile out on work release. How loathsome can he make himself? Then a phone rings in the office distance.

Becky visibly exhales.

She appears to calm, her repugnance reconsidered, her face slacking off. Nausea-glazed eyes lift and divert from Manny's face onto angles which intersect the partition walls—as if she seeks inspiration, the kind of solace that only madness and Ludwig may bring.

"Your predecessor, Julie Field, left a disaster here," she states flatly, her eyes returning to Manny. "Plus the task of updating the OWC files."

"What happened to her?" Manny asks, instinctively curious.

Becky glances at her partition wall again, a shadow of purple butte drifting in her eyes. For the first time, Manny notices her nose pulse: a tiny throb of vengeful heart just below the left septum. Meanwhile, her cigarette smolders to a long finger of ash, one about to overbalance out of the ashtray and onto a desk smothered in combustibles. And Manny's certain he'll be held accountable if the event comes off on schedule.

"Hunsecker showed her K Street, months ago."

"What? She was *fired*?" The wrinkle of irrational fear in Manny's voice is obvious. "You're serious?" The floor curls from under his feet till he finds himself helplessly pedaling in black space.

"Yes, I'm serious. Hunsecker termed her a sniper, a phony super-amiable, plus a dash of extreme manipulator."

"Where is she now?"

"Spudfuck, Idaho."

"Is she alright?"

"The tips are lousy, but Julie gets strawberries and whip cream waffles twice a week. She even got her heart-shaped ass on a Snappy tool calendar. I received a letter from her just last week. She might marry the owner of the local pool and beer joint, or else return to Washington."

"And do what?"

"Immolate herself, Buddhist monk style."

Trying to be cute, Manny says, "Julie sounds like a real *pisaki*, huh?"

Big mistake.

The way Becky Bergstein's face flares in violent astonishment at the sound of the word *pisaki*, you would've thought Manny Eden had accused her father of eight counts of seagull sodomy. Her hands grip her desktop like a terrorized cat, while Manny, desperate and awkward as a Republican senator forced to vote for gun control, tries to grin, the muscles in his mouth going soft.

"You'll burn a path here," Becky states acidly.

"Look, I apologize. Boyden and Varsana—"

"I don't have time for this shit. Get out of here and go read the investigator training package your master has concocted. It's in a file lying somewhere in Laney Dracos' office down the hall—I mean, *Tammy Pon's* office. Isn't that what you and your new totenkopf buddies call her?"

"My toto cough . . . *what?*"

"Down the hall," she says, cutting Manny off as the cigarette butt, still burning, drops off the lip of the tray and skittles across a stack of memos.

Manny points and Becky yelps, swinging wildly and slapping the cigarette off the paper. It spits through space like burning shrapnel to strike the partition wall, a firework of sparks spraying out on impact.

* * *

BEFORE BECKY HERSELF CAN DETONATE, Manny Eden pops out of her space and goes in search of Tammy's lair. It soon reveals itself as the last cell on the left—her real name, ELAINE DRACOS, on the nameplate. But she is not in. Only her paper-scattered signature remains.

Manny knows he must find the training file, and fast, before Hunsecker can check on his progress. First though, he must sift through a clutter as chaotic and profuse as Becky's. He skims over the desk, lifting up handfuls of paper and glancing underneath. Among other things, he discovers buried and warming beneath the sheets a number of unusual items. These include a subscription blank to *Archaeology* magazine, a *Best of American Poetry 1982*, a water-ringed copy of an old *Internationale Situationniste* newspaper proclaiming "The Revolt

Against Boredom," a foldout of a hung and restless Playgirl bimbo named Keith, and a 1984 edition of *High Weirdness by Mail* published by the Church of the Sub-Genius.

The fusion of these juxtaposed items excites Manny Eden in an unexpected way. It makes him wonder what kind of bizarrely protean creature this Dracos person really is.

In methodical steps, he moves from the desk to her credenza and its separate askew piles, finding nothing that resembles a training file. He notes the gun-metal cabinet pushed against the wall—the place most logical to search—and last on his list because taped across the top drawer is a strip of white paper, its surface slashed with letters in magic-marker red:

TO THE BIMBO DOGS: STAY OUT!

Manny knows he's not a bimbo dog. He hesitates nevertheless.

While he ponders, Becky Bergstein, still sitting at her desk, begins a ritual act of calming, one of her own invention that combines *Jnana yoga* with poetry and "projection."

A necessary event.

As a new puppet of Hunsecker, Manny had quite easily forced her into a stew, pulled those rods which served to dampen her critical nerve mass. But it wasn't Eden's fault she ignited on him.

The poor brown-noser!

Becky closes her eyes and expands, trying to ignore a sharp and growing pain in her chest. She deep breathes for a few moments till she calms. She opens a drawer in the bottom of her desk and withdraws from the coffee-spotted nest therein a book entitled, *The Hart Crane Anthology.*

A single sheet of paper, folded, slips from the book as she opens it.

Becky picks the paper up from the floor, unfolds it and reads once again a poem written about the poet Hart Crane. Laney had given it to her as a gift two years before. It concerned the final distribution of Hart following his suicidal leap from a steamer in the Gulf of Mexico:

```
HART CRANE IN BLT

By Elaine Dracos

Whatever form of corporeal flash
and tic submersed to join
with Belalcazar's Conquistadors,
phalanxed with salt-digested halberd
against the Horseshoe Crab Empires

Before looming globular with bloat,
nibbled gray as soap and risen like
a gas-punctured astronaut to pip-pop
among the motes and undersea sun-bars -

His Hartness sprayed out of shape,
a cloud of minnow frightened by a
roving goose fish.

Till he, a timid instance sloughed
to a fan of bitter scallop
on the shores of
  Jumento Cays—

And well up the food chain,
resolved as toenail or BLT on toast

From Pensacola to Oshkosh, an odor of poet
between the fingers,
and deep as coil.
```

Becky refolds the paper, places it in the book, and closes the cover. With the book on her lap, she shuts her eyes again and resumes her ritual:

Subtle energy of the vital breath. Control of the Prana. Pranayama and Hart. My breath deepening to a calming rhythm, and not with the heart-like surges of Nin's Atlantide, but with the air-through-needle softness of pines, bowing like worshipful beings to the lips of Hart's moon wind—

Before she can finish, a noise jolts Becky into OWC reality.

Warning scuffs on the carpet outside her partition.

Hunsecker? No.

Laney?... Yes.

Next, a jarring noise—the sound screechy and metallic—violence of a different kind. And Laney is not going to stand for it. She rushes past Becky's office, her alarm and anger blurring quickly down the hall.

That poor bastard Eden!

Only a minute before, Manny had jiggled and tapped at the forbidden file cabinet. He'd also hammered with the bottom of his fist on the top drawer, one of three, finding it nearly impossible to slide out. Then to his surprise, a capitulating groan and the old jaw opened. A quick perusal of the off-white tab fins . . . nothing there. He realizes with a sense of futility that he must heave open even more drawers. His neck vertebrae crack and his breath deepens in anticipation of further ball-buster contests.

Now, just as he's shoving against the tank-like bin and losing to three decades of friction grime, he detects the pitter-patter of suspiciously delicate hooves behind him. But before he can react, before the first breath of apology can brush his lips gentle as a mollusk foot digging sand, a God-awful feline bellow explodes in the air and jolts his nervous system clear over the partition:

"DAMN YOU, SIRRAH!"

Releasing the file cabinet abruptly, trembling in an involuntary and embarrassing way, Manny Eden turns to encounter what half a second of intuition has told him must be Earth's ultimate nemesis.

"WHAT BRAND OF PISSANT ARE YOU?"

Manny is faced with a tall and voltage-frazzled avalanche of black hair, and set within this rage, a pair of blue eyes like shards of glacial dross ripping to sea, devouring him in a fit of indignation to a dim point of shriveling bureaucrat. At once this woman reminds him of a mythic giantess ripped from a womb of smoking earth, a blustery daughter of Zeus born of political forehead.

"Look, uh, Aphrodite—"

"And where did you get the impudence to handle my personal files, sir? From the BIMBO DOGS?"

"Becky Bergstein said the training file would be in here so—"

"Becky! Eh? . . . *Becky, sir?*"

"Uh, yeah, and—"

"Well, it's *reality check* time, no?"

Laney Dracos pivots and stomps full of war goddess rage back down the hall, Manny observing her sharper-executive image of pinstripe wool and black heel gloss. He also notes the inflated contrast between this image of fire-eating, office extraterrestrial and the even more radical phenomenon of Tammy Pon—the erotically screwed work of fantasy so recently displayed on the cover of WCP.

Nearly incoherent though, and fearing further repercussion on the first day, Manny has no choice. He walks past the entrance to Becky Bergstein's office and catches a quick glimpse of his fierce and dark antagonist leaning forward over the desk, Becky's face enthralled, and she and Becky rushing with exclamations, only in subdued, whispering tones.

Neither of them look up as he passes.

No apologies.

No matter.

Manny Eden knows he must plod on in search of greater kinetic energy sources. He imagines tying himself to the nearest catapult, cutting the rope and impacting head first. Once outside the walls, he will wander the howling wastes of Monument Valley, sift between the purple buttes at dusk till he discovers, protruding as a cold megalith from the OWC sands, the door to the men's room.

In seconds, he locates a suitable stall and enters, bolts the entrance and slams himself down on the toilet seat cover. He fights back another surge of panic, still pricked by the cactus of Ed's, as well as the many dead-end hells of Kenosha he can't stop imagining. He questions his own courage, predicts a surge of self-loathing and quietly defends himself in a most natural way by recalling a day of courage—the battle at Paycock Park with that bully journalist Syd Drummond of the *Kenosha Morning Sentinel*.

He wasn't afraid then.

In those days, before he needed a real job, he wasn't afraid of anything.

* * *

ROARING UP LIKE A MORAL VOLCANO in his mother's '68 Buick Electra, a twenty-year old Manny Eden was galvanized by a column he'd read that morning in the *Chicago Sun*. It concerned the Kenosha mayor's office, under investigation by the Wisconsin state's attorney general. Why? Because Seawall Brothers, Inc., a firm contracted to repave the parks and streets of Kenosha, was kicking back enough money to buy the mayor a beach house in Sicily. So why hadn't that been reported in the *Sentinel*? Stirred to nemesis, Manny couldn't help but go hunting for a few Drummond bears to run up a tree.

After slamming out of the car, he prowed through the picnic crowd at Paycock Park. At least a hundred people showed up that blue April day, many of the attendees soiling the moment by turning a dark and suspicious face at Manny as he passed by. Only he didn't care. He felt he had to do the right thing, even if no one else in the town saw it that way.

Within a minute or so he spotted the garrulous Syd Drummond, big as a Chevy flatbed and gulping down franks and fries with Mayor "Mob Boss" Rossetti. The whole place smelled of grease and sleaze. In the background, a five-piece band on the gazebo played a clunky version of *Battle Cry of Freedom* that made Manny nauseous. Regardless, he strolled right up to Drummond wearing a face that could heave a stomach, but before he could speak, the editor stopped him cold with a rumor:

"Hey, Eden! Heard you got flushed from a job at the Public Safety Office. You good for *shit*, college boy?"

Rather than explain his latest firing from a crap job, Manny bug-eyed Drummond with a cartoon face on the brink of dynamite. Mayor Rossetti, backing off to bystander status, belched root beer and grinned like a used car salesman after a big sucker score (the mayor not liking the looks of Manny whom he considered a smirk-faced troublemaker). Manny executed an Elvis lip sneer in response to the mayor then returned attention to Drummond:

"What's more important to ask, *Fat Alien*, is when will *you* blow the whistle on Rossetti here?"

The mayor belched again and Drummond replied, calling Manny a "juvenile liberal asshole" forever unable to "get on board with the program." But Manny Eden, brimming with adrenaline, his crusader shorthairs standing on end, shot back:

"You're a traitor to the people, Drummond. This ain't Chicago!"

A crowd began to gather. Noting the audience, Manny fired off a Mr.-Smith-Goes-To-Washington rant about zoning fraud and excess tax profits for "friends of the city." The mayor signaled to an aide who called the police. After being called "Fat Alien" for the third time, Drummond flew into a rage and launched himself at Manny's throat. The two of them crashed through the picnic, punching and grunting. The band played a whiny version of *Wooly Bully* and several couples who were twisting stopped to watch. The mayor tried to chokehold Manny and got an elbow in his weasel face. Amelia Rossetti, his obese wife and school board president, grabbed a handful of Manny's hair and stuffed pizza crust in his mouth. Manny choked. Another woman screamed and Drummond's shovel-sized fist knocked Manny stupid.

Later, in the back seat of a Kenosha squad car, a dazed Manny ruminated on life, the universe and everything. He'd wandered off the prairie into the faded back lots and cold depression of Kenosha only to find what? A few billion years of stellar gas resolved to this moment: twenty-eight percent unemployment, an ugly need for survival sans politics and an ongoing hopelessness only rock-and-roll could cure. Why worry about Mob Boss Rossetti when you could twist to the *Wooly Bully*? Family taught Manny that self-respect was more important than the respect of others, especially if something really mattered; but the mean reception he'd got at the City Hall picnic stung. He felt shame, an overwhelming pressure to conform. It was like a thumb pressing hard on that little spot of his mind that made tears.

Helpless for the moment, Manny Eden used his imagination to set things right. He pulled a small wooden matchbox from the top pocket of his torn shirt and slid it open. Inside were Drummond, Rossetti and the cops, small as baby dung beetles and screeching at him. He just shut the matchbox and shook it vigorously, all of them ricocheting around inside like dry garbanzo beans.

* * *

ONCE MANNY FINALLY SNUGGLES behind his very own Eracto desk tank, his mood improves. And how does he know it is his? The only empty one. No pens or staple removers or excess paper ejaculation, only a single piece in his black plastic inbox, and a thin green file placed squarely in the center of the desk.

He scans the surface of his partition walls, sees nothing—no trace of former occupancy. His predecessor, Julie Field, scalded into anonymity.

He examines the green file, and as he waits to exhale, he observes with pleasant surprise that here before him, shimmering like a stillborn angel fetus, lays the Hunsecker training material for which so much blood had recently been spilled.

But first things first.

Manny removes Richard Nixon and slides him into the top desk drawer. Following that, he snatches the single piece of paper from his inbox and reads it:

ATTITUDE CHECK

FOR SEPTEMBER

-1- Do you value your job? If not, you will never be successful at it.
-2- Are you unhappy? If so, take charge and adjust your attitude.
-3- If you have a bad attitude, you don't feel good about yourself.
-4- Employees get good positions due to positive attitudes, not vv.
-5- Winners with positive attitudes strive to make themselves happy.
-6- Whiners with negative attitudes strive to make others miserable.
-7- If you do not stand for something, you will fall for anything.

Manny had no problems with attitude and figures this lecture must be meant for people like Mzz Dracos and Becky Bergstein.

Unable to restrain himself any longer, he opens the investigator training file and peruses the contents therein. He fishes out the memo from Mr. B. Hunsecker addressed to "All New Employees"—nothing unusual in its contents. A simple statement of intent and a sincere hope that all will "endeavor to excel" in their new positions as OWC investigators. Also included is a standard OWC investigator form, OWC-2036, and stapled on the back, two letters.

Hunsecker had written in cursive across the top of the first letter, *A Typical Crackpot "Whistleblower" Charge*, and atop the second, *Agency Response to Aforementioned Charge*.

Manny reads the latter first:

```
March 18, 1984

The Honorable Ashley W. Madison
Counsel
Office of Whistleblower Counsel
2915 K Street
Washington, DC 20005

Dear Counsel Madison:

This letter is in response to your query as
regards, once again, the ever evolving and ex-
asperating matter of Ms. Jacobs and her conten-
tion that CWirth Inc. intentionally neglected
the renovation of housing units in Philadelphia
while engaging in an ongoing practice of em-
bezzlement and fraudulent billing. You have the
Housing and Urban Development (HUD) report on
the eight housing parks in question as well as
the itemized evaluations which prove that all
specs are being met, and have been met since
the units were first opened for occupation in
1978.

The latest reiterations by Ms. Jacobs have, in
my opinion, the mark of accusations made by an
individual whose mental state must be called
into question. It is my contention that the
duration and tenacity of her allegations alone
will prevent her from altering her opinion no
matter what contradicting evidence is produced.

Regardless, the aforementioned HUD reports con-
tain no false statements, and no effort has
been spared by my staff to ascertain whether
or not all relevant evidence is included. Ac-
cusations by Ms. Jacobs that HUD or DOJ over-
sight has been compromised, simply because
```

CWirth Inc. exercises its constitutional right to make campaign contributions, are utterly without merit.

Additionally, we have learned during our own investigation of HUD that Ms. Jacobs is known by her regional director, and her former director, as an eccentric as well as an incompetent. Her complaints regarding what she terms improper HUD inspections, false reportage of data, and undue bullying tactics on the part of CWirth employees are all either delusory or contrived. Witness the fact that no other HUD staff who work closely with Ms. Jacobs will publicly support her reckless contentions. Her continuing correspondence with the OWC must be seen only as a ploy to gain an imagined advantage by working OWC against DOJ and HUD.

As before, you have my word the HUD report is one hundred percent accurate. I've spared no effort to verify this matter myself. Hopefully, we can act in concert in the future to resolve similar problems before they have a chance to get out of hand, or into the press. Not only do disgruntled people like Ms. Jacobs besmirch the reputation of fine government agencies and their conscientious employees, but they actually do physical harm by preventing those who suffer real injustice from receiving the OWC corrective action they have waited so long and patiently for.

I am sure you will concur.

Warmest regards,

J. W. Callaghan
Attorney General of The United States
Department of Justice

Next, Manny reads the "crackpot whistleblower" letter:

March 28, 1984

The Honorable Ashley W. Madison
Counsel
Office of Whistleblower Counsel
2915 K Street
Washington, DC 20005

Dear Counsel Madison:

Hello again. This is my fourth letter to you, but I have something new to tell. It appears that if you contribute an enormous amount of soft money to a political party, preferably during a presidential campaign, you can demand the lynching of any fool do-gooder you wish. I know word has leaked to CWirth employees, courtesy of management, that I alone am threatening their jobs. Their resentment and anger have produced as an end product my tortured effigy tacked on a No. 2 pencil. The Latin quote affixed, however, denotes some kind of twisted intellect, and this I find disturbing.

The tiny crucifixes began arriving week before last. As I noted, they are made from No. 2 pencils, these joined by a tiny copper nail. Attached to the wood by thumbtacks are paper doll cut-outs of myself, arms outstretched and feet tacked together. My name is scribbled on the forehead, and etched in ink across the chest, tiny letters which spell, QUOS DEUS VULT PERDERE PRIUS DEMENTAT. Translated from Latin it means: 'Those whom a god wishes to destroy he first drives mad.'

The first crucifix I found in my mail box, and the second, a day later on the front seat of my car. As an employee in the inspection division at the HUD office in Philadelphia, I've been deceived and manipulated by contractors and even threatened by executives who claimed to have pull with senators or congressmen, but never have I been persecuted by anything as deviant as this.

You must stop taking at face value those doctored reports on the housing units in question which abound in blatantly false statements made by HUD officials and that by design omit dozens of instances of tenant testimony, independent evaluations, and photographs that support my contention that CWirth and other contractors are systematically defrauding the government.

I hold you at fault, sir, for not taking action in this matter, and for allowing a situation to continue that will force tens of thousands to live in squalor without heat and often without running water. The practices I've been describing to you are business as usual on a nationwide basis, and in other major cities like Washington, D.C., and Los Angeles. It's hard to accept, but it's the truth. If you doubt what I'm saying, I can take you on a personal tour of the units in Philadelphia. Just let me know.

Regardless, how strange it is to watch a normal and quiet community, together with local government officials, act like one destructive force, both tribes joining together to form one mutually supportive organism.

Perhaps we're not so different from bacteria after all.

Sincerely,

Jennifer W. Jacobs
HUD Housing Inspector

CHAPTER 6

A God Without Conscience — The Early Days — Coming of The Morlocks

FOLLOWING A TYPICAL DAY OF MARTYRDOM and panic-hissing at OWC, Becky Bergstein sought to relieve her tension in any number of ways. Depending on her mood, she might stop by Clydes on the way home and force herself into a state of *margarita philosophy*, or else she might jog across the Key Bridge up to Roosevelt Island and back, or maybe just go straight home and repeatedly kick the tacky purple recliner she'd bought when really high and stupid last summer in Adams Morgan (or some combination of the above). But on this particular day, following the advent of Manny Eden, and a really nasty bout of Hunsecker—Hart and *Prana* notwithstanding—Becky yearned for nothing less cathartic than the absolute destruction of human civilization.

That evening, within the womb of her Georgetown apartment, she reclined on her leather sofa, her head propped with pillow. In the air, between her kitchen and the front door, Stravinsky's *The Firebird* crackled, providing a soundtrack of classic wax while the television translated for her a videotape from her father's library: *Mauna Loa, Volcano, 1978*.

As she listened to Stravinsky, smoked her second joint of Shenandoah Gold, and intoxicated herself with the video-lava rivulets of Mauna Loa, she bestowed upon herself the powers of a god without conscience. She imagined the Hawaiian hyle of 1978 floating past her eyes and forming all the absurd objects of human device and creation, her wrath dissolving each in turn to heat and puddle. Boulders the size of houses morphed softly into rows of glowing port-a-johns, puffs of pumice erupted into Reagan inauguration confetti, smaller stones collapsed and burst into clusters of flaming imps with Hunsecker faces—the raw tonnage of *pahoehoe* demanding sacrifice from Becky as it whorled scintillate and scabrous with a colder wreckage of McFood franchises, only-a-buck stores, federal hives of bureaucrat, and other items on a civilization shitlist too abhorrent to forget or ignore: Dapple-Doe-Lane gas lamps and Kmart hunter mannequins, Soviet coming-of-age novels and Japanese game show hosts, Anatolian fertility toads and Matusi skin needles, Olmec god heads and Byzantine monk skulls, Ms. Sunmaid bosom pumps and Fido Love dog girdles, and so forth and so on from age to age, plus all manner of horrific nasties like feces dolls and anal pears, cones of silence, Guatemalan shin-crackers, Torquemada femur-crackers, Old Sparky electrocution chairs and cargo cult shrines and many more shapes impossible to count or name.

Finally, as the methodical creation and destruction abated, *The Firebird* died, and Becky began to deep breathe, slowly, thoughtfully (as she always did with Hart and *Prana*), till she calmed, relieved herself of the further need for divine violence.

The John Coltrane album, *Ballads*, came next, and having grieved enough, Becky returned to her couch and dreamed herself a wistful and insouciant Alcyone, a woman transformed to a great bird and gliding on wings upon the uprise of heat, far above the *pahoehoe*, in a space where her flight blended with the odor of ripe and fired souls.

The jazz of Coltrane filling her thoughts with sax, she stared down through the darkness at the sun-boiling rent of Mauna Loa. She watched closely as it gargled its way up to the night and drained north to a cloud. Bellows of Pele pounded the skin drum of air around her bird-like body while buttes of steam, tourbillious where the legs of lava delta waded into ocean, stacked to the moon, colored it a judgment day pallor before chaotically rumbling southeast, heavy as a saltless tear metropolis to rain on another unsuspecting island—Bora Bora, or Galapagos perhaps.

Meanwhile, Becky's father, Hal Bergstein, near suffocation in a tinfoilish space suit, had gone forth to wallow in the heat drafts. From on high, Alcyone Becky watched the videotape and smiled serenely, noting her father as a silver splinter in the black earth skin far below—his most fervent desire to ford the lava rapids of Mauna Loa in a dream-created super canoe of his own construction. Becky recalled a vibrant discussion of the incredible folly with his closest business associates in the lobby of the Mauna Loa Hilton, the day she and her governess, dour old Marika, left to fly back to New York.

By the age of eight, Hal's "little skittle baby" Becky had already snapped his suspenders and buffed his shoes in scores of luxurious hotel suites around the earth—only possible because he made enough commission to not only hire a fulltime traveling governess from Belgium who taught Becky geometry, physics, and the romance languages, but to treat them both to a lavish lifestyle courtesy of his career as a freelance investment scout whose network web branched along a trail from Manhattan to Bonn to Singapore.

The seasonal trip to New York in December was *always* played up as the triumphant return of the supreme capitalist, the Rand-infatuated Caesar: European art spoils and conquered-nymph photo albums handsomely displayed, plus at least one client party at his NYC penthouse featuring booze-spewing ice nudes, Kabuki samurai servants, no less than half a dozen blonde and leggy Ursula Andress look-alikes (Hal obsessed over the actress) serving cocktails, Dave Brubeck himself whenever possible, as well as a bout or two of seize-the-day braggadocio.

But it was all to end badly for Hal.

During the winter of '78, Becky's father toppled like a sun struck animal. On the coast of Greece, in a rare moment of semi-relaxation, he posed, weepy as a sad clownface beside a Greek Orthodox parade of icons that solemnly, and with an air of pack-horse suffering, wound its way from village to village along the hot-white coast of Karpathos. A sixteen year-old Becky held the Nikon. Hal Bergstein motioned. Becky snapped, just in time. A face of wordless breath in the dark room: eyes rolled white within the mask of Hal's convulsion, and only she and Mr. Shaw, the photo developer at the drugstore, had ever seen it.

Diagnosed at Johns Hopkins in Baltimore with a malignant, skull base tumor the size of Becky's fist, Hal clumsily tidied his will, made arrangements with his sister Rachel to care for Becky, kissed his distraught and confused daughter farewell, and after videotaping his own suicide by morphine overdose, legally submersed the scalped bubble of his head into a liquid nitrogen vat owned by a company in Vermont named Timeslip, Inc. For $50,000, Timeslip cryogenically suspended the "personality" of any willing head—their theory predicting that the next millennia would invent enough superscience miracles to not only exorcize Hal's tumor, but grow him a pile of flesh virile enough to tote around his newly-cured brain.

Becky recalled how her father suicided with his fingers crossed, and she had watched that tape over a dozen times. It was available still, in her apartment, just to the left of *Mauna Loa, 1978*, though she knew she would never watch it while listening to John Coltrane.

Never.

She saved her Black Sabbath album for such an occasion.

* * *

WANTING PASSIONATELY TO BE THE OPPOSITE of her father's ultra-capitalist, Ayn Rand persona, Becky Bergstein attended Columbia and graduated with an MPA, later successfully interviewing for a White House Fellow position during the final days of the Carter administration in 1979. Like the many other Star Eyes who joined the newly-formed and congressionally mandated OWC, she adopted the nation's capital with an overdose of grateful enthusiasm, honored to play a role in shielding the nation's millions from the excesses of bad government.

Her zeal the first year was legendary. She quickly became tagged in agency circles as "Joan of OWC" for the dogged and clever manner in which she ferreted out evidence that those who resisted the Washington mob were being garroted for their attacks of conscience. But no sooner had OWC become effective than forces loyal to the blue flag of The Gipper awoke from a state of doze, and by 1982, the agency, known in White House circles as "a magnet for loose cannons", began to equivocate, and out of pure career-death terror, soon ceased to speak at all.

The clamoring and wailing of White House hacks in the agencies under OWC investigation was heard echoing like an exploding dock fire down Pennsylvania Avenue. OWC had become genuinely dangerous. Every corporate lobbyist and political appointee knew it. The entire city of Washington quivered like a giant yes-mammal whenever the ripples were felt, for each time OWC successfully defended a whistleblower, press stories broke, political beheadings followed and big corporate contracts died. By 1983, hearings on Capitol Hill were threatened by Senate Democrats, and the Reagan White House reacted *conjunctis viribus*, dispatching a platoon of staff to "secure the cannons."

Within only weeks following the crack down, a tongue thick as a county courthouse suffocated the *J'Accuse* mouth of OWC. Theomachy and reckless martyrdom ensued. Terrific battles erupted in the halls on K Street. Fistfights, catfights, memo-bludgeon duels took place between dedicated OWC careerists and White House staff. Local infirmaries were overwhelmed by the surge of back injuries, both human and camel. Three and a half weeks into her third year as an investigator and Joan of OWC was suddenly without pay, cut loose for two months, the entire workforce suspended in the ensuing panic once a congressional budget ax had fallen on the agency's fund appropriation—a scheme enacted "for the health of America" by both Republicans and Democrats in the House (all members of an appropriations committee hostile to OWC).

To those naive fairy children of America who watched from a distance, the darkness boiling like war seemed only a buzzing glaucoma of their own vision, for the press bites disgorged weekly from the White House proclaimed OWC a champion, a barb in the side of wasteful and corrupt government. But to those sufficiently digested within the leviathan like Becky, and to those who sought it as a source of counsel and justice, it had become the most subtle of Trojan Horses.

Things from the Reagan campaign's *terra incognita* were anointed and placed in supervisory positions. Waves of darkness and echoes of yes-barking filled the halls. Investigators and attorneys from the Carter days either quit or were fired by means of rigged performance appraisals presented on kangaroo court day. Joan of OWC herself—interrogated with Positive Mental Attitude (PMA) brain screws and threatened with demotion, insubordination and Siberia—collapsed and wept bitterly at night, crying often for nothing more than a boss who might allow her to escape with a decent job reference.

The Honorable Counsels themselves, appointed by the White House to lead the OWC in "correcting the grave injustice being done to the party, the president and the American people," proved to be aloof and often mysterious beings, reminiscent of omnipotent wizards entombed in black castles, their backsides protected by walls of hackish acolytes and minor chit-demons, their activities shielded by White Oz spin-spells and sorceries of black box, as well as the more mundane techniques of mind-wilting obfuscation—thus defeating invasions by "the liberal press" and the occasional Democratic congressman who might be looking to "cheap shot" The Gipper.

Distance from the average OWC employee did not, however, prevent these Counsels from exerting an eroding influence on same, for tagging along in their train were their own personal Morlocks, those who consorted in the Counsel's stead with the lowlier grades of being. Typically, they fleshed out to various boss types, deputy assistant deputies and scurrying Schedule-C staff pistols who were, in effect, loose fragments of each Counsel's peculiar personality, all of them thriving in a state of sycophant symbiosis with their Counsel host, their own will, intentions and reality *du jour* always tuned to match the idiosyncratic frequency of the host himself.

A portion of the Counsel's Morlocks, as Becky couldn't help but recall, made a splash more notable than the rest, and simply for the sheer amount of confusion, capriciousness and misery they injected into the struggling OWC ranks. Ms. Louisa B. Arenas, for example—a token Hispanic, Christian Right Morlock with fund raising ties to the Reagan campaign in Florida—impressed her "dearest Counsel" by commanding her aides-de-camp to mingle with the attorneys and investigators at OWC, establish trust after a few drinks at local bars, and report back to her whatever dissension regarding the subject of OWC ineffectiveness and abuse they discovered so that she might include the names of these "Democrat disruptives"—whose loyalty to the president she seriously questioned—to an ever growing RED LIST—this list prioritized in order that those included might be methodically culled from the organization whose "God-anointed mission was observed by President Reagan," and this culling usually accomplished by means of performance appraisals deliberately eroded to incompetence by her swarm of male and female mini-Morlocks (sociopathic imps from West Palm Beach nicknamed The Napoleons, and no taller than Ms. Arenas—only five foot three) who quaked under her absolute domination. And not only were these sub-types blessed with backbones of mush, they actually competed with each other to present the exposed neck of an attorney or investigator she particularly loathed for an immediate beheading, often on a trumped-up charge of office insubordination or impropriety, such as an "unauthorized" long distance call.

Becky fumed whenever she recalled the mean-spirited firing of Scot Bumpers—a good friend, a hire from the Carter days and the most effective and respected manager in the Investigation Division—in large part because Ms. Arenas labeled him an "untrustworthy inside Democrat, but in truth because, as she put it, "he was too damn good at his job." Included in the letter demanding his immediate resignation were shocking allegations made by African-American and female co-workers on his staff asserting that he was not only a "vociferous bigot and a vicious, sexual harasser," but also "a gross incompetent" who allowed good cases to "suspiciously slip through soft fingers."

Another notable Morlock, and one who Becky especially loathed, was Elizabeth Whitfield, a young Ohio *white stocking* fresh out of the Republican National Committee—appointed by the White House as deputy to the Counsel—who arrived with a mandate to mortify, harass, and otherwise bully with absolute impunity any unlucky wretch whose opinion, facts, or grasp of reality even slightly contradicted her own.

Liz Whitfield, the indefensible moron who changed to black stockings, dyed her hair blonde and blowjobbed no less than two Counsels in a row in an effort to permanently secure her job.

Liz Whitfield, who in a matter-of-fact voice, and at a lunch table full of staff, told one of the older investigators, Mr. Plumley, that he was an absolute drain on the "dynamic synergy quotient of OWC," and that perhaps he might benefit everyone by contacting as soon as possible the Right to Death Society.

Liz Whitfield, who permitted only the most avid and dull witted of yes-mammals to attach to her like parasitical remora; who for petty reasons deepsixed employee vacations at the last possible minute despite plans and cost to the one so affected; who phoned staff at 6 A.M. on weekend mornings, demanding (without ever bothering to identify herself on the phone) they leap from bed and race promptly to the office to draft a memo for her immediate signature on Monday, and she never signing it, but instead pointlessly revising it till the following week; who at the close of her crisis-wracked tenure at OWC (after having spent all her blowjob capital), phoned employees to meet her at her office on a Sunday morning at 8:00 A.M., and there, as she dripped her puddle of tears—and much to the astonishment of the groggy OWC staff—blubbered on and on for over a half hour about having to take her leave from them under adverse political circumstances, and how much she would miss their loyalty, affection and diligence, and so forth while her screeching five-year old son, Marcus Whitfield, maliciously pinched neck hairs, skewered thighs with No. 2 hunting pencils and bounced Nerf-like off the walls and floor, never once calmed or admonished in any way by his mother.

During the dark ages of OWC, Becky had experienced nearly every form of dysfunctional petty tyrant known to the human species, both male and female, and she realized, to her wonder and chagrin, how violent she could become whenever exposed to the Counsels and their servants. And while the mere thought of *The Great Contaminator*, Ronald Reagan—accompanied by his self-succoring train of frauds (state campaign chairmen), traducers (campaign focus-group leaders) and temporizers (campaign bag handlers)—stirred her to fury in the same way English possession of French lands must have thrown the original Joan into paroxysms of rage, it was the existence of Hunsecker and Madison that made her blood burn for heads at the marble feet of Lincoln and Jefferson.

But would she keep her job at OWC long enough to see justice?

She was afraid not to. Already she had survived many years, and not by means of collaboration or sycophancy, often projecting herself to successive coup leaders as a strange, know-nothing *Evader*, a harmless liberal crank not to be bothered with, easily dismissible due to being non-descript, hidden by smoke and frequently ill.

In short, non-threatening.

Having shed the armor of Joan since 1982, she nurtured goals once thought to be the exclusive right of a partisan or a prisoner of war: to survive, resist in secret and openly renew the fight whenever possible—John Coltrane, Stravinsky, and end-of-the-world catharsis notwithstanding.

CHAPTER 7

A Letter to Mommy K — Answer Their Panic With A Pumpkin — Varsana's Tongue Fries Mzz Dracos — Manny Meets Worm and Union Head

IN A LONG LETTER TO MOMMY K, written in Lafayette Park at lunch time, Manny Eden talked about his work, and the group house in Arlington, Virginia, where he lived. Only a GS-7 grade employee, Manny couldn't afford to rent his own apartment. Fortunately though, there were plenty of people in Virginia around his age, and with similar low income issues.

The house itself, a three-story, red brick colonial owned by Herb "Pitbull" Barker, a retired CIA contractor, had two bedrooms on high, one in a converted basement, and only a single bath. Happy to distance himself from his odd roommates, Manny quartered in the basement beneath a porthole-sized window with a view of the driveway, his only company at nights being a raccoon family from a nearby park—three or more often lingering for hours, staring eerily at him through the tiny window as he lay in bed drinking Sam Adams beer and listening to his favorite wax (Pretenders, Patti Smith, Boomtown Rats, New York Dolls, The Motels, Lene Lovich, Siouxsie and The Banshees, Steely Dan, etc.—Mommy K having packed and shipped Manny's turntable and records) or reading his recently acquired sci-fi novels like *The Left Hand of Darkness* and *Martian Chronicles*.

As he noted further to Mommy K in the letter:

```
My roommates are Molly Wong and the Elephant
Man (whose real name is Antoine Saul). I know
you'll think I'm cruel for calling him Elephant
Man. That's what he calls himself. I'm not kid-
ding. It's like a joke with him, and he does
```

resemble John Merrick, really. His head is huge, misshapen, and his face is lumpy with boils that disappear and bubble up again. He scares you at first. I moved in because the basement room was only $95 per month. E-Man's smart though, and he even loaned me some science fiction books. I like sci-fi now, especially one short story about this guy who changes the world to match his imagination. All he has to do is think of something and it happens. He tries to fix the human race, make a utopia, only it doesn't work out so well. Anyway, the sci-fi prevents me from getting too bored when I'm not at work.

The only other distraction around here is the ongoing war between Molly and E-Man. Just this past week she accused him of eating her pastries, farting on her favorite sofa, and messing with her <u>Playboy</u> collection (yes, you heard right). Is he doing all that? He says no way. Hey, I know you're going to think this is gross. Last night Molly flashed the Miss March foldout at me and said, "Good eating!" I'm not kidding.

E-Man smokes big Hav-a-Tampa cigars to keep her out of the living room so she won't hang around while he's watching TV. It's not fair, and I told E-Man that last night after Molly got home from work. All I could do was duck and run after Molly went ballistic.

A couple of times, E-Man and I have gone out to dinner. His favorite place is a Greek restaurant called Mt. Gyro and run by a guy named Daddy Papadopolis. The waiters there are jerks and they scowl at E-man behind his back, as if they think he tries to look scary just to annoy them. Anyway, the food is greasy and it's in a strip mall, one of the many around here. Virginia is beautiful, but the strip malls, one after the other, ruin the landscape. You just wish they would dissolve or burn.

Work is going okay. I haven't been given a whistleblower case yet, but that's supposed to happen soon. I'm in training. The boss, Mr. Hunsecker, calls me Garden of Eden. He thinks it's funny. Right now I'm just loading case file data into a computer. They've got boxes of it. The person who worked there before me, who was fired, screwed it up. And you know, I'm happy I got this job. It beats the Syd Drummond out of jobs in Kenosha, but I've got to tell you, there's something funny in the air here, like a smell of road kill. That sounds bad, I know. I can't explain it any other way. I've never worked in a place quite like this. Most of the staff in my division are friendly, so maybe I'm just depressed because there are no real windows here (just a few slits)? No sunlight. I figure once I get my first real whistleblower case to defend, I'll be fine.

By the way, I received this strange letter weeks ago from someone who calls himself Rochambeau. He says he's part of a secret organization called The American Watch, and that OWC isn't on the up and up. I don't know what to make of it. I admit it has bothered me. All very strange. I don't know who Rochambeau really is. The boss is an actor, and he likes to test people for reactions, so it might be just that. I even suspect he made the whole thing up just to keep the office on edge. Who knows? I'll wait and see. All that won't matter if something worthwhile comes from this.

Also, I haven't met anyone SPECIAL yet. Well, I did meet this really hot woman named Elaine Dracos. She screamed at me the first time we met because she thought I was trying to steal her stuff. Everyone here acts paranoid. I'm eggshell walking almost every day.

That's it for now.

Love You Much,

Manny

* * *

THE BOY-MAN FROM KENOSHA WRAPS UP his lunch break in the park and returns to dutifully resume his data entry at OWC, only this time in Varsana's office. Her caseload files are the largest for some reason. Maybe because she is assigned more cases? Manny can't figure it.

While Varsana lingers a few feet away, whistling show tunes and piddling with paper, Manny wisely uses the opportunity to discuss the whistleblower investigation process.

"But you must consider the *nexus*, Mr. Eden," Varsana says in a somewhat reproachful manner. "You must strain out frivolous complainers with the Substantial Likelihood Test, the Pickering Disruption Test and other tests like that."

"But what about the issue itself, Ms. Pardo, the reason for the whistleblowing in the first place?" Manny asks.

Varsana stares at him with damp, cookie-warm eyes, as if she feels maternal towards him. "Haven't you been properly trained yet, Mr. Eden? Wasn't that Becky Bergstein's job?"

"Well, I have some training, but—"

"The *source*, first, Mr. Eden. Consider the source. If it isn't pure, the issue is invalidated by default. I mean, you have to be realistic. Whose word are you going to accept in this he-said-she-said world of ours? The whistleblower? Or the hundred or more other employees and agency managers who say the opposite?"

"Why can't OWC just go and investigate—"

"It's not our job, Mr. Eden," Varsana says, quickly cutting him off, "and besides, we don't have the budget or staff to cavort all over the country checking on every wild tale that comes in here. It's not realistic."

"Sure, I see the problem," says Manny. "But I guess it's just natural that I want to get to the bottom of things."

"You mean you would rather clean toilets?"

Unknown to Manny, her outlook had been honed at La Salle and Associates, one of the most prestigious lobbying firms in D.C. Varsana once sat on the Phillip Morris account throne, the biggest and most important at the firm. She retired years ago after a bad bout of stressful back problems, finding OWC far less demanding. As a bonus, it was impossible to get fired as long as you went with the flow.

Using his best JFK voice, Manny says to Varsana:

"*I will erect a statue to each whistleblower, make them into prime time movies, paragons and parables to serve as an example to our nation.*"

"What kind of voice is that?" she asks.

"JFK?"

"Who?" Varsana's face goes blank. After a pause, and in a cold, quiet voice, she says to a stupefied Manny, "My friend, I think you're a *Manipulator*."

"Why?"

"Because you're trying to be funny at the wrong time. And if you're serious, your behavior is unprofessional, did you *know*?"

"No, I—"

"Life is gray, Mr. Eden. You can't be biased. You must distance yourself when you deal with these cases, not get involved with them on a personal level. The way it sounds now, you're ready to have them all over for dinner. "

Manny tries his Jimmy Stewart imitation next, certain he can get Varsana to lighten up. "*But Ms. Pardo, I'll come to them like a fairy godmother, answer their panic with a pumpkin and a sparkle-wand, save them from old man Potter.*"

Varsana considers a flare of indignation, but thinks better of it, not wishing to be manipulated. "You're a real comedian," she says. "and a bit of George Bailey from *It's a Wonderful Life*?" Varsana smiles. Her teeth are perfect chips of translucent moon.

Manny feels relieved. "Sure. When I was a kid, I wanted to be a comic."

"Well, um, all this Jimmy-Stewart-pumpkin-stuff makes you sound like Mzz Dracos, not a *comic*."

"I don't get it."

"I haven't told you *yet*," Varsana says, her face growing dark and determined. This is her favorite topic of discussion at OWC and she isn't going to be derailed. Mr. Eden must be educated sooner or later and now is as good a time as any. "Mzz Dracos wants attention so bad she pens long letters to the whistle blowhards."

"What?"

"No. Ask anyone. If you want, you can sabotage your new career at OWC by joining her Whiner Relief Agency, a private nonprofit she set up on her own without permission—and included in the package is the old Whistleblower's Home, a half-way house for lowlife office psychos."

"That's kinda funny. So it's all a joke?" Manny tries to smile.

"No, not at all. Mzz Dracos fashions her own response letters to these people . . . she goes over the Counsel's head."

"How?"

"Boyden caught her at it one day when she was up on the Hill. He was looking for a file letter in her computer when he found them, the letters, dozens of them written to ersatz blowers, dripping with phony admiration, godspeeding them and making them all into saints, encouraging them to press on, as she put it, to *the press*! She wanted them to roast us alive at the *Washington Post* and in *Time* magazine. I nicknamed her Vendetta after that."

"Good nick."

"The whole thing was an insult to all of us because of the horrible lies she made up in those letters. She only wants revenge because she hasn't been promoted in years—and she told the whistle blowhards how to do it, how to strike back with provocations sent to the newspapers and Congress."

"It's easy to believe," Manny says. "she's so hostile."

"And she conspires with them, has lunch with them, goes to their homes at night and *sleeps with them*."

"Huh?"

"They're a turn on for her, you might say. She even flew down to New Mexico once to sleep with a lawyer who was fired from the Justice Department for lying about his fellow prosecutors working with a drug cartel."

"Varsana, you hate her guts, right?"

"I can't deny it, Manny . . . and she would have been fired long ago, except for the connections who protect her."

"What kind?"

"She's chumsy wumsy with a powerful Democrat senator. She uses him as a weapon and she's betrayed the Counsel himself, vowed to ruin him! It's all politics, horrible, dirty politics."

"What do you mean?"

"The Democrats and Mzz Dracos! They want to destroy the president!"

"Uh—"

Varsana becomes conscious of her loud voice. She lowers it again, and as her words came faster and faster, she leans into Manny, her lips furiously whispering the words only inches from his ear:

"Oh, Manny, I can tell you this because I have nothing to fear from no one. Basil doesn't deserve her vicious attacks, her sniping at him in front of the whole office. He may be somewhat rough, maybe even a little theatrical, but the poor man's had a difficult time of it. His mother died last year, and a lot of pressure from Counsel Madison has come down on him—not that there's anything wrong with Mr. Madison. He's a courageous man."

"The Gipper approves, so he must be okay," Manny says matter-of-factly.

"And Mzz Dracos is not a Wonder Woman, not what she wants you to believe."

"What does she want me to believe?"

"Just ask her about the Ziska case. I dare you. He was a paranoid over in Health and Human Services who yapped about the Secretary ignoring billions in corporate Medicare fraud. Course, it was all a lie. She carried on and on about Ziska, fought with Deputy Counsel Liz Whitfield tooth and nail, then suddenly pushed the poor dupe off the dock."

"She was wrong about Ziska?"

"Of course, as usual, but this time it was the Senator who reigned her in. He was up for reelection just when the Ziska issue flared. He didn't want to risk controversy, and so the punk sorceress backed off because she's really a hypocrite first class and a coward. She knew her father protector might not last to shield her . . . so much for that poor dupe Ziska, eh?"

Varsana blinks at Manny, huge and drab, then cocks her head in response to a light scuff of sound. As Manny watches her face for signs of invasion, a hard thing with sharp points, like an iron rake or a loose bear paw, mercilessly gouges its weight into the partition fabric just outside Varsana's office. The sound is head-splitting, as if the skin of a plane were being peeled off at mach one.

In no time though, the sound unravels to a retreating pitter-patter of human feet, leaving Varsana in a state of total paralysis. Manny jumps up and pokes his head out into the hall. In the distance, he sees Becky Bergstein's eyes, two pinpricks of red, as she turns to observe him staring at her. She points at him and disappears around a corner without a smile or a wave, taking her body with her.

Following a pause of recovery, Manny notices a black rupture in the dull partition fabric a few feet to his right. A death wound begins at eye-level and rips down to the carpet, looking as if a knife or a pair of scissors had torn it.

Varsana slides up behind him with eyes of metal, her body edging slow and easy into the hall, evolving to a posture of cat. At once it becomes obvious to her that some malcontent fiend had escaped its tour of solitude. She gasps and bumbles out with *"Hera's Bile!"*

Manny says nothing, deciding to keep quiet about Becky.

Varsana runs her index finger through the frazzled rent once, removes it, sniffs her finger, and lifting her arm on high, jams it like a hot poker in the direction of Mr. Quigley's office. "Go to Worm Quigley," she commands Manny with an imperious tone, her body rigid as a Lafayette Park idol. "His case data needs to be input." Her face is alarmed yet already beaming with possibility. "Go, *now.*"

She quickly turns from Manny in a rush to get to her phone, her statue posture dissolved, only the light and blur of her one hand recalled chasing him from her presence.

* * *

"YOU CAN CALL ME WORM," Mr. Quigley says.

Worm is a bald bureaucrat in his seventies. Thin, sharp nosed, one muddy glass eye, pits jaundiced, Kmart-gray tie.

"It's okay. That was my fraternity nick at ATO back in 1930," he says.

Worm sets down his coffee mug, extends his hand that looks like a cold, speckled trout. Manny shakes it, shivering to himself as he does so, and briefly describes to Worm the loading of case data, asking politely if Worm can fish around for his own files so Manny can complete his task and by next week get on with "the more serious work of investigation."

Worm mutters something about "matter having its own agenda," and nods, apparently agreeing to Manny's request to look for the files.

As Worm grunts, wheezes, and digs through his desk, Manny glances around Worm's partition and sees dozens of photos of Civil War soldiers, weapons, battlefields and even recruitment posters. One particular photo, though, snags his attention. It is the head of a living Union soldier without a jaw, his tongue slapped big and limp as a wet calf liver on his neck.

Worm looks up to see Manny fixated on it, and says, "Some canister shot from a Rebel twelve pounder tore that boy's jaw clean off. Happened at Fredericksburg."

Manny's eyes are big and bulging with tongue.

"I feel it on my neck," Manny says.

Worm asks Manny if he is interested in the War. It is then Manny notices Worm's swampy left eye staring at his own foot while the other fixes oddly on Manny's forehead.

Being polite, Manny says, "Yes," and Worm diverges onto such Civil War topics as *The Rock, The Stump, The Crater,* Custer-Mosby duels in the Shenandoah, etc., until an hour later, Worm finally asks:

"Have you been to Fredericksburg, Mr. Eden?"

"No, sir."

"The poet Walt Whitman saw it for himself, what it was like."

"Saw?"

"The limb heaps."

"Sir?"

"The limbs of soldiers sawed off in the surgeon's tent. I suppose he wanted to acquaint himself with reality . . . his brother was bleeding on the ground there."

"Nasty stuff."

"After the war, Whitman got a job at the Interior Department. The Secretary soon fired him because he didn't like Whitman's *Leaves of Grass*. It offended him . . . you know how the powerful can be."

"Like some bosses, right?"

"But Whitman should have felt proud, because he made an impact. You only get fired like that after making an impact."

"How long have you worked for Uncle Sam, Mr. Quigley?"

"I've been ridin' this rhino for twenty two years now. Been working for Sam even longer, since the fifties, in the army. I retired at the rank of major." The face of Worm, turned up to Manny, remains bland. "I'll tell you son, war is hell in any age."

"Sir?"

"In Korea, we found dead prisoners the Chinese left behind—Americans mostly, wrapped up with barbed wire, sitting back to back. They'd been bloating for days. We had to clip the wire and pick them all up, pile them on a truck bed. They were leaking. I hoisted one onto my shoulders and he burst over me like a gooey bag . . . I was a lieutenant . . . I got the glass eye cause of Korea, this one." He points at the eye fixed on his own foot.

Manny says nothing.

Worm turns. With his good eye, he stares bemusedly at the monstrosity of the Union head for a few moments. He then bends down, sputters like a weary old horse, and heaves at a drawer handle fixed near the bottom of his desk. Upon opening the drawer and fumbling in a file, he withdraws several sheets which he hands to Manny. They are crinkled at the corners, coffee-spotted.

"Is this all, sir?" asks Manny.

"That's it, son," Worm says. "I'm just a back up around here. No one takes me seriously."

Manny thanks Worm nevertheless and flips him a solid salute. In response, Worm says:

"People think I'll fade, Mr. Eden, but I won't. No sir."

* * *

LATER THAT DAY, MANNY RETURED HOME to find a second note from the American Watch tacked to his front door. It was folded and sealed in a white envelope and addressed to him. He stood outside in the cold to read it.

```
Dear Mr. Eden,

Under no circumstances will we allow yet an-
other Reagan ass kisser to infiltrate this
organization. We will stop you if necessary.
Did you know you are on probation? You can be
fired rather quickly, so don't force us to
arrange that. We are masters of theater, ru-
mor, and the careful seeding of evidence.

We promise the guilty will be punished.

Sincerely,

Rochambeau
```

After a sleepless night of Kenosha job market, Manny believed he had little choice. The following morning he gave the letter to Hunsecker and watched him bake so hot and red that he looked as if he'd tried to run the mile in less than four minutes. Manny backed slowly out of Hunsecker's office, his mouth shut, certain the boss was incapable of any form of theater so profound and frightening.

Manny knew from that moment on that the American Watch was real.

CHAPTER 8

Potential Prosecutorial Merit — Manny Goes With Flow — Becky Tests Manny — Big Fines for Improbity — Ms. Linderhart Lacks The Team Player Edge

VARSANA COMPLAINED TO HUNSECKER that the new hire wasn't being properly trained and Hunsecker reacted by charging into Becky's office and slamming her with his tongue so hard that Becky was forced into three margaritas, two doobies of Shenandoah hay, and a fresh bout of *Mauna Loa 1978* before the night was over. As a precaution, Hunsecker also assigned Boyden to help Becky, and he commanded the two of them to get Manny "up and leaping tall buildings at a single bound" within three working days.

Manny had no choice. He became excited. The momentum of things diluted his termination worries over the American Watch—at least temporarily.

The flow was simple enough: letters of complaint entered the office, with or without supporting evidence, and were logged by Deejah Thoris and tagged with a case number. They were distributed to the investigative staff in a manner determined by Hunsecker, and the staff screened the alleged whistleblowers using an initial set of chopping questions:

1) Does the alleged whistleblower appear ostensibly sane?

2) Does the complaint itself fall within OWC jurisdiction (as opposed to the National Labor Relations Board or EEO Commission)?

3) Are specific disclosures made—as opposed to imprecise griping?

4) Do the actions alleged to have been taken by management against the alleged whistleblower fall into the OWC defined parameters of "prohibited personnel actions," i.e., demotion, termination, transfer, poor appraisal, reassignment of duties, etc.?

If the alleged whistleblower made it through this initial screen, the investigator typed up an OWC form A3-86, noted on it his or her remarks on the pertinent nuances of the case and a step-by-step narrative summary (for Hunsecker's benefit) as well as a triage analysis of "potential prosecutorial merit." If Hunsecker decided the case appeared sufficiently complex, it proceeded to a secondary review conducted by Hunsecker himself. The case would then linger in his office, sometimes for weeks or even months, before resurfacing with supervisory scribbles regarding matters of emphasis and procedure.

Communications with the alleged offending agency comprised the next phase. Regardless the review level of the case in OWC, the investigator always phoned a designated contact within the agency in question—usually within two weeks of receiving the initial complaint—and informed this contact (always an agency attorney) of the relevant issues and charges in the case—the identity of the alleged whistleblower not revealed unless prior written consent given. The attorney then informed the management within the agency of the complaints against them—including all alleged retaliations as well as all whistleblower-alleged acts of criminality, abuse and misconduct—and awaited an official agency response to the charges (usually weeks, or even months), promptly forwarding aforesaid response to OWC upon reception—usually an informal phone call, followed later by a letter signed by the head of the agency.

Immediately upon receiving the informal agency response, the OWC investigator noted the attorney comments in the case file and proceeded to weigh the complaint against the agency response in order to make a determination of "potential prosecutorial merit."

At this point, the case usually underwent a final chop at the bi-monthly Investigatory Division staff meeting wherein it was summarized, salient points reviewed, and based on a final determination of merit, a thumbs up or down decreed by Hunsecker. If thumbs up, the case proceeded to the legal division for further action, and if legal concurred, the OWC, via the Counsel, unleashed the weight and edge of paper necessary to both relieve the whistleblower and deter the agency from further retaliation.

According to law and OWC regulations, the offending agency was also charged with formally responding to Counsel as to agency plans for remedying the misconduct, abuse, and/or criminality in question.

Regardless the disposition, the alleged whistleblower was promptly informed in writing of the final decision, usually by close-out form letter.

* * *

OCTOBER WAS A HECTIC MONTH at OWC, would-be whistleblowers feverishly active in the great foggy bowl of discontent that was Washington. And as scores of these pariahs shamelessly unburdened themselves to OWC, Manny's rapport with his office mates improved, and as a consequence, he began to feel comfortable. The early estrangement of the first few weeks was chalked up to bad luck, as well as his tendency to expect the worst—a habit he'd acquired in the anti-human universe of Kenosha. Regardless, his anxiety brought on by the American Watch was not easily forgotten.

One morning, as soon as he arrived at OWC, a tiny figure of tin foil not more than two inches high and shaped like a Revolutionary soldier with a tri-corner hat, stood in the center of his desk, the toothpick thin right arm raised and pointing at Manny's empty chair. Manny showed it to the first person he saw in the office, Babs Easton, and before he could say a word, she gasped out "Rochambeau!" and turned on her heel in quick retreat. Manny showed it next to Hunsecker who snatched the figure and crumpled it to a tiny ball while his mouth made a sound like a drill boring wood.

Despite these American Watch events, Manny did whatever he could to distract himself. Together with Boyden McCarthy and Richard Nixon, he began doing lunch *al fresco*, either in Lafayette or Farragut Park—their dialogues often diverging, though never tediously, onto such topics as OWC shop, Boyden's adventures with his wealthy socialite relatives, the Soors, and his membership in the conservative thinktank, the Heritage Foundation (he concurring with their opinion that far too many moderate Republicans nurtured "liberal social nannyisms").

Boyden often expressed grave concern at Washington's "lack of political courage," and he praised The Gipper endlessly and more than once revealed to Manny his preposterous ambition to be nothing less than Secretary of Defense.

To a Wisconsin boy like Manny Eden, this kind of talk was cherry on the milkshake. Of course, being a liberal, the "nannyism" thing annoyed him, but he let it go rather than confront Boyden, telling himself he needed to harmonize with his space in order to be effective at this job. What good would it do for him to get fired, as he had from the Public Safety Office in Kenosha? Though not much chance of that, for nearly everyone in the office, even Worm Quigley, contributed to Manny's growing sense of warmth and belonging.

Worm would corner Manny at the coffee pot, or in the bathroom, drill him with Civil War trivia questions such as, *How many miniballs did it take to whittle The Stump? How many of Mosby's men did Custer hang in the Shenandoah? How many soldiers died of pneumonia at Cold Harbor?* etc., while Babs Easton, frisky and beaming, would sneak up on Manny, sly as a White House staffer, and clamping her long and bony hands over his eyes, demand he recite by heart all the tests for prosecutorial merit.

Both Varsana and Babs referred to him jokingly as "Peter Sham" or "director-in-waiting of the Whiner Relief Agency" or something like that, and Varsana kept insisting that he give her the green light for fixing him up with an unforgettable date. Even the Princess of Mars blurted good morning to Manny on Fridays, and Ms. Yolanda Peel had stopped staring at him as if he were a cockroach.

Still, Manny avoided any brush with Elaine Dracos (alias *Mzz Dracos*, alias *Tammy Pon*, alias *Vendetta*). Why? Because she had already collapsed his sum of ego with a single meteoric punch. Her powerful gait and chopping gestures he observed only from subliminal angles. He strained every corner eye muscle in an attempt to determine whether or not the blur of her white face ever turned to glance at him. It never did. Mzz Dracos was intent on remaining dismissive. And nothing could have irritated Manny more, especially when he recalled her disruptive and arrogant parting of the office sea that first day, and the manner in which she pinned him with her Nemesis voice and knock-out eye against that rusty file cabinet.

What a stammering oaf he'd been!

He couldn't deny that her extreme *brunette-ness* and Venus-de-Milo verve intimidated him, squirmed into his fingers and notes and tamed the grand sweep of his 'y's and other tail letters. Only prolonged dialogues with E-Man at his house in Arlington had provided any form of temporary cure. In short, whenever he imagined Laney Dracos, he gulped an invisible pill that could not be swallowed, the cumulative effect as if an answer vital to his survival had been forgotten and could not be recalled no matter how much he strained.

* * *

IN THE DAYS WHICH FOLLOW, Becky Bergstein awakens and realizes a curious Manny is attempting in subtle manner to engage her. She knows instinctively that he wants to learn more about Elaine Dracos. But she quickly becomes elusive, even annoying.

On several occasions, a flash of flesh pricks Manny's eye and he looks up from his desk to see her standing before him, pensive in posed profile or else staring at him for a few seconds in a screw-loose fashion, as if the mere sight of him makes her paranoid. On a Thursday morning in mid October though, the day before Manny's first bi-monthly review meeting, Becky takes pains to invade his office.

She bombs him with three new case files.

He makes no effort to hide his glee.

Even as Becky slides them like snapping piranha into his inbox, Manny can't stop smiling—and this annoys Becky in the extreme. She pulls up the one extra chair in his office and plops herself down to face him head on. Her face is cold and adamant, mission-oriented, Manny's grin reflects in the black walls of her eyes. She lights a cigarette and begins to talk while blowing big smoke rings in his general direction.

Manny imagines himself a detective in a film noir.

He decides not to ask about the rip-in-the-partition incident.

She informs him that the case files are his first real whistleblower cases and that he must screen them and make recommendations based on their potential prosecutorial merit at the upcoming staff meeting. One of them, the USSC file, is straight from Hunsecker's office. He had ordered Becky to "hand it over to *Mr. Garden-of-Eden*" for examination. She adds that the files, as a whole, are relatively uncomplicated, and he will be digesting more complex cases in the near future, depending on his progress.

"It takes no more than three months for neophytes to learn all the excuses," she says. Manny asks her what she means by that remark, and she replies, "Nothing a bullet won't cure."

He chuckles nervously. "But do any of these have potential?" he asks.

"Potential for *what*?"

"To be Joe Blows."

"I wouldn't be surprised, but that's no different from past history."

"I won't touch that one," Manny says. "Soooo, where's Tammy?"

Becky's face squirms at the word *Tammy*. She looks ready to ignite. "You trying to aggravate my ulcer, Mr. Eden?"

"No."

"Then do not refer to Elaine as *Tammy*, or *Vendetta*, not around me, okay?"

"Sure. I didn't mean anything by it."

Becky drags off her cigarette and says, "She's up on the Hill. When there's a crunch she volunteers staff work for the Senate Governmental Affairs Committee."

"I'm surprised she has the temper for it."

"She was sorry for laying you out your first day. It was my fault."

"I don't get it. What's her problem?"

In response to Manny's question, Becky blows a big smoke ring at his face and slowly leans forward. She closes to within only a few inches of him, her entire attitude and appearance darkening. "*Look, Mr. Garden of Eden*" she whispers. "*Elaine will crack this fucking OWC planet. The whole regime of Madison, Hunsecker, Babs Easton, all of `em, poof! poof! poof!*" Her lips and hands burst in sync with tiny explosions. "*You get it?*"

"Why are you telling me this?" Manny asks.

"*Maybe because I'm tired of the shit. Or maybe because I know more than you think and I'm taking a chance on you. Or maybe because I want to know who my enemies are,*" she says icily.

"How do you know I won't tell anyone?"

"*Tattle if you want. I'll just deny it. Besides, Laney has said worse, right to their face. Did you know?*"

Manny doesn't answer. Instead, he reacts by placing a finger to his lips. With his other hand, he reaches across his desk to grab a small note pad and a pen. On the pad he writes in small letters:

        ARE YOU IN THE AMERICAN WATCH?

He slides it before Becky's eyes. She betrays no emotion, just reaches for the note pad. Manny hands her his pen. She writes something and lifts it up to show him:

        IF I WERE, I WOULDN'T TELL YOU.

After a pause, she places the pad back on the desk and writes:

        YOU WILL BE CONTACTED.
        DO NOT FEAR.
        BE TRUE TO YOUR NATION.

She shows him this last note for a count of five, rips it out of the pad and crumples it.

Manny sputters, not knowing what to say.

Becky behaves as if rejuvenated. She unleashes a big smile at Manny, slaps both hands on her knees, and jumps to her feet. Before departure, she encourages him to midnight-oil the case files. "Hunsecker will try to rough you up a bit," she says matter-of-fact as she glides out of his office, her attitude visibly lighter.

For a time, Manny hears her pacing, as if she were contemplating a return to add a comment, or an observation or two, but her footsteps soon fade, and Manny is left alone, wondering whether or not he should tell Hunsecker.

Truth be told, he believes Becky a fool for confiding in him.

Maybe it's a setup?

He imagines Elaine Dracos cornering him in the elevator lobby and shrieking, SO *YOU ARE A PISSANT AFTER ALL, EH MR. EDEN?*, and though he owes her nothing, he decides to hold off, keep Becky's words to himself. Besides, the thought of infiltrating the American Watch excites him, all danger aside, especially after Becky's note. Manny figures the Watch will either help or hinder the achievement of his goals. If the latter, it hurts the mission of OWC and he will work to defeat it despite all warnings and tin foil soldiers. Regardless, he has no choice but to examine the case files Becky left behind.

Two of them are easy, not even in OWC jurisdiction, referencing alleged violations of the Freedom of Information Act. Not his problem. He disposes of them with a few cursory remarks and proceeds to read the final complainant letter:

```
July 8, 1984

Mr. Ashley Madison
Counsel
Office of Whistleblower Counsel
2915 K Street
Washington, D.C. 20005

Dear Counsel Madison,

My name is Keat Linderhart, and until recently
I was employed as Director of Field Research
at the United States Sentencing Commission
(USSC), the agency assigned by Congress the
task of choosing suitable sentencing guide-
lines for Federal judges. Due to broad dis-
crepancies nationwide in sentencing for simi-
lar criminal offenses, our services are in
great demand by the courts. Nearly two years
ago our emphasis shifted onto developing a
scale of fines and alternatives for use in
punishing corporate crime. The scale topped off
at $364 million for a single fine. If that
seems high, we're talking about executives who
```

launder drug dollars, openly bribe government officials, collapse financial institutions through embezzlement and fraud, treat the deaths of consumers or employees as an allowable risk of doing business, and so forth. Unusual punishments were also conceived. For example, we imagined a judge sentencing a seven figure CEO to three years spooning baby food to daycare infants.

Please forgive my unprofessional passion as I discuss this, but no sooner did USSC publish its first draft of proposed guidelines than the corporate blitzkrieg exploded. Lobbyists and attorneys, congressmen and senators who hadn't even known the USSC existed, began arriving in a a steady flow of limousines. Even now, they attend closed Commission meetings and employ every intimidation tactic you can imagine to force the Commission to obey their demands. Some of the bolder lobbyists, from La Salle Associates, for example, even have the nerve to hurl open threats at employees. I have witnessed this. A few of the more influential attorneys, connected by soft money to both the Democrat and Republican parties, have approached Commissioner Lester personally, handing him their financial impact statements and suggestions for level-by-level reduced fine schedules.

I know the emasculation of the Commission will not taper off till the fines drop to a wrist slap. One of our highest for the most egregious offense has already sunk from $280 million to only $580,000. Anyway, the whole effort here has become farcical, everyone joking about it, and many pretending it's all part of the democratic process. Dozens of staffers have quit in disgust. It appears that corporate punishment is well on the way to becoming only an acceptable overhead cost.

On June 16 of this year I was summoned, along with fifteen or so others at the Commission, to testify before the Senate Committee on Governmental Affairs as to events at USSC. Apparently, a story had made NBC news and stirred a sufficient amount of controversy. In answer to a direct question from Senator Breggar as to whether I believed the task and effectiveness of the Commission to have been compromised by the undue influence of outside business interests, I answered yes. No other answer was possible. Of course there were more questions directed to me, but the theme was the same, and I answered affirmative to all of them.

As a consequence, Commissioner Lester, as well as the Commission members and their assistants, may now be lumped into one of the three following categories: frightened, foolish, or treacherous. The foremost are those who want me dead, the second in line who actually believe their arguments, and the final category who will gladly deliver me in pieces. I have noted and logged significant events in the methodical cleansing campaign that kicked off the week following the hearing.

They are as follows:

<u>June 26, 1:05 PM</u>: I receive a memo from Ms. Judith Mazur, Assistant Commissioner at USSC (copy attached), stating that due to a reorganization, I am no longer responsible for research matters. My staff of three will be allocated elsewhere. I am effectively stripped of nearly all my duties, and an unknown woman arrives that morning to relieve me of my files. She said she was on detail from the White House.

<u>July 1, 12:00 PM</u>: I meet a good friend for lunch, Myrna Kelly. She is a fellow Director at the Commission. After some uncomfortable small talk Myrna blames me for being stupid at the Hill hearing, for exaggerating the truth, as she puts it, then informs me that because of my stupidity she can't risk being seen with me anymore. I thank her for her honesty. She apologizes, cries a little, then hurries out with her sunglasses on.

<u>July 7, 3:10 PM</u>: I stop by to talk with my former staff. None of them will speak unless spoken to. Their responses are terse and they

avoid eye contact. We had always been on good terms, and I trusted them, only today is different, and I can't help feeling as though someone had punched me in the stomach.

July 11 through July 30: At least once a day—and as many as half a dozen times—one of the two following individuals passes by my office: Erma Masters, Commissioner Lester's secretary, or Vilma Marchant, Judith Mazur's secretary. As they pass I see them staring at me out the corner of my eye. Once, Erma lingered, observing me while I was on the phone talking to my son. But when I turned to look at her, she moved quickly on.

August 3, 8:30 AM: I arrive at my desk to find a memo addressed to me from Judith Mazur. It is an official reprimand for what is termed excessive telephone use, tardiness, leaving work early, and it has been observed that I routinely take more than an hour for lunch. I am informed that such behavior cannot be tolerated in a professional office and that I will face disciplinary action if it continues.

August 3, 8:39 AM: I have a talk with Ms. Mazur in her office in regards to the contents of the memo. A new side of her personality reveals itself to me. She explains nervously, as if on the verge of hysteria, that she no longer can afford the time to be concerned with "my petty problems." I tell her the charges are laughably absurd. She replies that witnesses can be found to corroborate the allegations, then hastens to add that she herself has noticed my usual vitality slipping to a sluggish level. We begin to argue. She orders me out of her office as soon as I attempt to pin her down, and I am shouting at her in anger, and don't stop, even when she flings the door to her office open so that everyone can bear witness.

August 3, 11:30 AM: Vilma Marchant drops off a memo on my desk. It is from Ms. Mazur and it charges me with gross insubordination as well as dereliction of duty. The final paragraph, in a conciliatory tone, suggests I seek counseling for the obvious problem I have with accepting authority.

<u>August 4, 9:03 AM</u>: After making several phone calls to the Senate Committee staff I feel more isolated than ever. I speak with an aide to Senator Breggar. I tell him that my time is short. He sounds outraged, sympathetic in the extreme. He says he will call back later that afternoon with an answer. I contact a few reporters at the Post and they sound mildly interested. They ask whether anyone else at the Commission will confirm my suspicions of retaliation. I have to answer no. By close of business the aide in Breggar's office has still not called back.

<u>August 6, 10:30 AM</u>: My alienation is complete. I now exist in a place I have heard rumors of, but never believed till the overwhelming presence of fear and loathing convinced me. I receive a call from Erma Masters, instructing me to come immediately to the Commissioner's office for a meeting. I ask what it concerns. She will not say.

Before I go to the meeting, I slip a little flash camera into my purse. After I arrive, Commissioner Lester calmly informs me he has learned of my recalcitrant nature and this knowledge has brought him to a state of anguish because he always believed that I showed great promise as a competent and dedicated USSC employee. He expresses sincere disappointment that I now appear to lack the team player edge.

As a matter of course, I inform him of the facts as I know them, apologize for leading him to such a state of anguish, and tactfully indicate that I believe the issue of team playing irrelevant to my circumstance. He becomes very huffy when I contradict him on this matter. Even though I am very low key, he orders me to stop getting defensive.

Next, our conversation centers around the motivation behind my testimony to the Senate committee. He accuses me of vindictiveness and avoids all substance of the testimony, i.e., all facts and conditions which prompted the Senate hearing in the first place. They are nothing but political matters, he tells me, and he behaves as though I am lying, fabricating the events discussed at the hearing. He demands I recant my charges and undo the tremendous embarrassment I have caused him. I tell him no. He demands more strongly, and I still say no, and then he gets up from his chair and comes towards me in a rage. I slip my small flash camera out of my purse and begin flashing him over and over again as he screams at me. He tries to grab the camera. I won't let him.

I turn and run out of his office.

August 7: The story goes that I attempted a "shake down," threatened the Commissioner with a charge of sexual harassment if he continued disciplinary proceedings against me.

Of course, I must have forgotten.

I hope you can relieve me of this problem, Counsel Madison. Please don't hesitate to call me at 202-633-1412. I'm willing to pursue any avenue you think is best, and I can provide documentation to support my claims of USSC's capitulation.

Regardless, the USSC deserves a chance to make things right. I hope you can help us, and by doing so, help the American people.

Sincerely,

Keat Linderhart

Attachments

CHAPTER 9

The Pissoir of Anomie — A Candidate For Wax — Espresso On The Mozartplatz

MY WOMAN OF NO, my Antigone, my ineffaceable Keat, Manny says to himself. She lodged in his lunch hour like a tower of King Ludwig, soothed him like a full moon of Democracy afloat above the Chesapeake—his remaining afternoon at OWC occupied with restoring her to dignity and subtracting all but her passionate face and that dark force animating her crime-and-punishment land. If not for her reckless morality, he would be unable even now to realize that subtle yet permeating condition, that formless *loathing* which demanded retaliation for truth, and thereby reduced Washington and all its cells to a pissoir of perpetual anomie.

Manny whimsically decided on a different course home that evening. Worm had told him of the Civil War park off 16th street, near the White House—"a place of heroes," Worm said, and since Manny was in the mood for heroes, he searched until he discovered, rising above all, a bronze likeness of General Sherman: the scourge of the South.

Staring up at him, Manny retrieved his memory of Keat Linderhart's fall. He wished a bronze for her also. If Sherman deserved it, she deserved it even more. And as he transfigured her to tragic-angel-cast-down, he immersed himself unavoidably in the *loathing*, feeling at once a displacement of mind that substituted his musings with premonitory images of a discarded idol, an American Ozymandias (perhaps a statue in The Gipper's likeness, his elephant-sized head buried nine centuries from now in Maryland topsoil) as metaphor for the end of America herself—and this scary prediction he soon realized was nothing less than a warning of predators lurking nearby, all of them eager to squash democracy.

Within moments, Manny found himself surrounded by the Morlock gang.

Just like the old days in Kenosha, his imagination stepped forward with a foot the size of Chicago. He unslung his red-white-and-blue shield and immediately became President Eden. He surged with the special powers of Gipper, JFK, and Captain America. He reminded himself that glory counted for nothing, and he threw his shield at General Sherman's jaw, knocking it clean off. The General's blackened bronze tongue fell to his neck with a loud clang. The Morlocks became frightened and slid back to shadow. They were cowards, after all! Satisfied, Manny retrieved his shield and made for the subway.

He felt no remorse for Sherman.

The General had spared no one, not even those who loved him.

* * *

POISED TO REDEEM GOD, Manny tenderly bore Keat Linderhart home to his room in Arlington. Hour by hour, he rejuvenated her, inflated her to Florence Nightingale-like atmospheres, her surfaces and forecast radioactively tragic yet immune to oblivion. Her glow of martyrdom filled his water glass, his hands and walls, the sweet-iced *don't-touch-doughnuts* of Molly Wong, and even the bubonic visage of E-Man that unnerved him as he heated a can of bean soup for dinner.

On this special night though, as you might expect, Murphy's Law strikes.

A blasphemous event occurs.

It interrupts Manny's mental shrine erection to Keat Linderhart. Between the afterwork garbage stream in his head and the surface of mirror above his bathroom sink, Keat's face (having grown brighter and brighter) rises up to blind him like a big glow-blob of flashlight. Her head lifts and tilts back, as if in recovery from prayer, and her eyes open, just a little till they gleam scintillate and blue as the oaf-stammering eyes of Mzz Dracos.

How can he resist?

Keat's face acquires *the look* of Dracos, and Manny finds this "dracosmorphosis" of her annoying, even unsettling, but he can't maintain the purity of her image without the *Vendetta* usurping it in some manner.

By bed time though, he accepts the inevitability. He allows this new version of Keat Linderhart to ascend as a savior no different than himself, and as a perfection he is not worthy of. On-screen at the *cinema interieur* of Manny Eden, she hatches into a pretzel of dove-white limbs atop a black lake of hair: just a flash of chiaroscuro, a shriek of consummation, then onto chest-grazing breasts of milky teardrop.

But wait, Manny says to himself, *this is all happening too fast.*

The evolution of worship into bold erotica requires stage-play realism. The images of word must be chosen carefully.

At 1:00 A.M. a tapping in the dark awakens him. Keat's face has appeared at his basement window, pushing away the raccoons. Through the moon-pierced glass, he locks eyes with his first office hero.

Once he has coaxed her to the front door, calmed her inside with a smile and a beckoning hand, he notes how strangely her back is covered with wounds like open eyes. He holds out arms and she drops herself into his cradle. He wants to warm away the awful cold of her humiliation, but only several degrees later, she cups her face with his hand. Her wet, Dracos-like eyes, irritated at being unable to see the world of her desire, choose a simple gratitude instead.

He consoles her with words of hope and justice, as well as a glass of fine brandy, but she soon breaks away from him and into a shower. Afterwards, emerging fresh and marbly and unscathed, she becomes a Venus in terrycloth, a gentle Zenobia of Palmyra, legs unsheathed and smelling of lemons.

Later, as peace enraptures the two of them, his eyes grow pensive and his flesh rigid. Her bowl of pliant tummy lures affection while her breasts and knolls of white fever relieve him of will. In Washington, by day, her morality singes him and leaves him groping for excuse. But in Salzburg, months from now (for Manny has quit OWC to romp impoverished and Tropic-of-Cancer-like with her in Europe), she sips espresso on the Mozartplatz.

Beneath the cold blue suck of an Austrian sky, she tableaus for him a unique local psychology pincered between Soviets in the east and

Americans in the west, plus a salting of Bavarian nobility to complicate things. She tangents effortlessly onto topics more worthy of a genius, perhaps an American woman like Vos Savant, or a Russian like Kosmodemyanskaya.

He would not have it any other way.

* * *

AS A BALL OF ST. ELMO'S created with face, Keat follows Manny into the subway Friday morning. A quick stroll next from Farragut West metro to the cold office squares of K Street. On the way they speak of vacations, sex, and plans of resistance, and though absolute martyrdom might be a preferable news story, he wants to save her anyway.

Manny will be true to his nation by being true to Keat Linderhart.

Once inside OWC, she supplants the average bureaucrat. She creates her own horizons to ascend from and set upon. She bloats to tremendous proportions, drowns out all space, whole rooms in less than a second—or else miniscule and unpretentious as Manny's fingernail, she collapses inward, whirring about his eyes like the ghost of a fly or a gleam of Potomac moonlet upon the sea of his carpet.

CHAPTER 10

Joe Blow On Menu? — No Reasonable Grounds — The Pickering Disruption Test — Threshold Maneuvers in the Light — Laney Dracos vs. The Hunsecker

AT THE APPOINTED TIME of nine A.M., the staff of the OWC Investigative Division meet in the tenth floor conference room for the bi-monthly case review meeting. The room itself is windowless, wood paneled and hung with presidents. A pair of ten-foot high American flags frame a grand portrait of The Gipper at the far end.

Upon entering, the staff members sit down and place their case files before them on a long mahogany table. All are present, except for the Hunsecker and Laney Dracos—the former routinely late for the review meetings, sometimes as long as half an hour. But his inevitability is always foretold in the variety of *no nonsense* personas adopted by the staff—the only exception today being Worm Quigley who slouches in his chair, his mouth sputtering with reproach at some imaginary hobgoblin perched lightly on the tip of his nose. While one hand remains slapped atop his head, the other extends into the air, high and winglike, fragile and flapping, as if waving a grandfatherly farewell—the arthritis painkillers he'd taken earlier that morning already unhinging him a bit.

To his left sits Varsana Pardo, her extremities magenta-glossed. Her large face looks almost Chinese and it beams in professional fashion at no one in particular. Across from her, Boyden unleashes a macho head nod. Manny notes the male bonding feeler and refuses to react. Instead, he demands a glaring fix from himself, his thoughts only of Keat's future, his eyes black as eggs fried to a char on bureaucracy.

Babs Easton, sitting next to Manny, notes his severity. She watches it screw in and tighten. Ignoring it though, she smiles and effervesces with:

"It's back to school time, Mr. Eden. This is your classroom."

Manny doesn't respond.

Babs tries again. "*Mr. Eeeeeden? Don't be an Evaderrrrr.*" Manny looks up, says nothing. Babs continues. "The first staff meeting for any new employee is a learning experience. Your teacher, Mr. Basil Hunsecker, will make *certain* of that."

Becky Bergstein, two seats down from Manny, glares at Babs, her eyes a few degrees below absolute zero.

"Anyway, I hope you've done your *homeworrrkkk,*" coos Babs, the last word pealing out on a high note.

"I hope so *tooooo,*" coos Manny, turning to face her, the imitation scowling the face of Babs ever so slightly.

Becky suppresses a chuckle. But no time to predict an outcome.

Before another word can be uttered, a disturbance grows in volume and violence in the hall outside the conference room. A raspy and lengthy scrape starts it off, followed by what sounds like a single claw of iron-tipped nails cutting slowly into six feet of marble. Could it be Varsana's suspect returning? Had the fiend escaped its tour of solitude once again? Varsana links up with the after effect of gouge on her partition wall only days ago. Friction sparked by the noise evaporates all her faux gaiety. Her brows pinch like scorched caterpillars. Her entire face darkens with a rare form of cartoon rage.

Other members of the staff react also.

Boyden twitches at the noise, as though popped by a rubber shin hammer. Babs attempts a sappy grin. Becky simply looks irritated and shakes her head ever so slightly, as if regretting a pointless tragedy, and as she does, a second announcement overwhelms the clawing, only this new sound the more earth-devouring and oceanic, as if a heavy and segmented bulk several miles long were being monotonously dragged against the walls outside.

"*My God! What is it?*" asks Manny Eden, somewhat alarmed.

No one answers. Their minds have already lapsed as one into fear of allegation and reprisal.

To distract himself, Worm begins a schizophrenic muttering on the "astral intelligence of matter." Manny cannot pay attention. His eyes cast wildly about in search of Keat Linderhart's body. Too long before he finds her glowing flesh laid in winter and subjected to debilitating cruelty and humiliation—the kind only human beings can inflict. Her precious thoughts gnaw at him, her words and hope cradled by his morality. Seeing him, she bravely shakes off the pain and ice and throws herself into his arms once more. She weeps between the pincers of ideology on the Mozartplatz and cries out to him:

Oh, Manny Eden! Does it really matter? In a million, the ocean will rise, and Washington will die.

Before Manny can reply, an entrance is made.

The Hunsecker arrives.

He's wearing a Picasso tie, chair-brown pants, and a blue polyester jacket. Under his arm he carries a four-inch-thick, black "case bible" binder stacked with whistleblower documentation. Everyone looks up as he enters, and Becky, her thumbs pricking, wonders how long it will take before the *moral-reality-of-OWC* lecture begins.

Oblivious to Becky though, and like an idol of grim reminder, Hunsecker rivets himself at attention at the head of the table. The American flags rise to flank him, while The Gipper, like a slice of blue cheese afloat between the flag bread, peeks over the top of Hunsecker's head, observing and approving.

In order to pass judgment on all present, Hunsecker slowly lowers his massive black binder down onto the table. His face constructs a monument to self-righteousness, eclipsed as he is by his own sanctified bubble of *Deus vault*. And for what seems like the longest fifteen seconds of anyone's life, he unnerves the staff by prolonging this statue-like posture; and Becky knows you cannot stare up at him gleaming like a monstrous Ra above the prostrate crust without feeling foolish, or running a risk of insulting him with a curious or amused stare, so you just have to sit still and avert your gaze as if you are afraid of him (which you really are) and hope the ritual mood setting soon comes to an end.

It does.

Hunsecker stiffens a bit further before hauling his chair out from under the table. Positioning himself, and grunting like an old senator, he coughs and sits down, releasing the air from his legs. His polyester-coated forearms topple like pylons on either side of his case bible.

A pause.

The boss reconnoiters the room, searches eyes for discontents, halts for a count of three on Becky, then looks down at his binder. Upon opening the black portal of it, he briskly leafs through to *the proper page*, his face waning at last to a tone of judgmental efficiency.

Meanwhile, around the conference table, the human attitude reveals itself in harsh tones of *gravitas* and chastened attentiveness. Hands are folded like crypts, heads poised to nod—pointless and nervous scribblings on paper perhaps, but nothing able to divert focus from the boss godhead. For the second time in his life, Manny is rendered infantile, buffeted nonstop by the prickly hot wavefront of Hunsecker presence.

"I'm just meditating, Mr. Garden-of-Eden," Hunsecker's voice catches Manny off guard. "I have a habit of meditating several times a day. It places things in perspective for me."

Manny is unable to reply.

Hunsecker glances up once more to examine all faces, his lips peeling back to impress them with a big white smile. His lips then flabber, horse-like, but he smiles again and inquires in convivial fashion of those assembled:

"Well, heart breakers and life takers, is Joe Blow on the menu *today?*"

Half the room chuckles at the question. Manny nods a sincere affirmative. Varsana reacts with a loud "*Ah-Hah!*" Becky manages a weak grin. Everyone appears affected, except for Worm who makes little airy explosions with his mouth, as if imagining the opening salvo at Gettysburg.

"MR. GARDEN-OF-EDEN!" Hunsecker shouts, prodded by the sight of Manny's head nodding. The boss cocks his body, gapes as if astonished. "So, you think *Joe* is on the menu?"

"I think so, sir."

"Well, you'd better *think again*, son."

"I've been thinking about it all night, Mr. Hunsecker," Manny says.

"Okay, Mr. Blow Detective, your time will come," Hunsecker says and laughs in an exhausted way, the lids of his eyes grinding down to half mast. He begins to gravel out with an old recipe, but instead sneezes and sputters, his voice spittle-choked and twangy as a short-order cook just down from Mesa Verde:

"*Yeahhhhh, aaahhockkk! Shizzummm!*"

Immediately, everyone stiffens. As they attempt to filter this malapropos emission, Becky bites down on her lip to prevent a loud guffaw. She knows how Hunsecker goes berserk if he thinks anyone is laughing at him. She also knows he was born and raised in a south Texas trailer park, that he flunked out of UT, and that he keeps both facts a secret. Laney Dracos used her connections to dig into Hunsecker's past after he arrived at OWC, and Becky knew everything that Laney knew. She had also learned about his love of ballroom dancing and raising exotic cats, and the fact that at UT he was a theater major strangely obsessed with Eugene O'Neil.

Soon enough though, Hunsecker recovers, as if nothing had happened, and moving forward, announces somberly to Manny:

"Before we get on with this meeting, Mr. Garden-of-Eden, you must be reminded of several facts which pertain to the conduct of business here. I should not have to tell you, since by now you are supposed to be *trained*, but I'll do it anyway if for some odd reason you do not yet know."

"Thank you, sir," Manny says, looking sincere.

"The priority for protecting whistleblowers was established early in the administration of President Reagan." Manny notes how serenely The Gipper hovers above Hunsecker's head, rather like an Irish guardian angel, or a saint, maybe St. Pattie himself. "This is a *morality* imposed on us by law. Do you understand, Mr. Garden-of-Eden?"

Manny nods, as do Varsana, Babs, and Boyden. Becky smirks, only for second, not long enough to get caught.

Hunsecker continues. "The benefits which accrue from their conscience can be immense in terms of saving our country from the damaging effect of fraudulent, wasteful, and abusive government. We must never overlook a case with potential merit. The Counsel emphasizes timeliness of response and no one should be left hanging. We jump *in*, we jump *out*."

"I understand, sir," Manny says.

"OWC obeys the letter of the law. We are sacred to it, and we've established our own morality here, Mr. Garden-of-Eden, a righteous one. I've never been more convinced of anything."

"Yes, sir."

"But you must understand, we do not *owe* these persons who seek us out. We represent the public interest, not *individuals*. This is also part of our morality. Do you get my meaning?"

"Yes."

Manny stops nodding. The others continue. Becky sits still, her eyes wandering. Worm looks dazed.

"OWC requires a preponderance of evidence, a *prima facie* case before it will pass judgment on a manager or his agency. And why? Because OWC will *not* be compromised or humiliated, and I will *not* allow any complaint to be forwarded to our legal division that is highlighted by obvious defects in prosecutorial merit."

Hunsecker clears his throat and pauses, looking away from Manny to sample the mood around the room. He casts a casual glance to the right at Varsana. Without hesitation, her face pacifies to a slight pout, as if begging Hunsecker for something more than managerial expertise.

Quickly dismissing Varsana, compromised by her effort to fawn, Hunsecker's eyes drift off a few lazy degrees to find the image of Babs Easton.

They lock eyes.

Hunsecker says nothing as the memory rushes back to fertilize him. Like erotic steam, she brims to the top of his dome, viscid and bubbly as hot love fat girdling the well-seared flanks of his brain. Shortly after her hire, she selfishly consumed his time by adorning porn-movie marquees and GQ magazine ads. But soon, she unfolded poignant and unrelenting enough to suck in his belly and color his hair. Right now, she's got him expanding like a spiked cake in an oven. From across the table she watches his lips, the thin gravel milk of his eyes, and realizing a brilliant future, stokes him to the edge with only a wink, love biting the tip of his frontal lobe till he feels a tingle on his shoulder. Before

Hunsecker can prevent it, her blue-veined, tangerine breasts strain forward till they unmercifully close his eyes, her nipples plugging his dilated pupils.

Such play, as Babs is well aware, makes the boss shudder with visions of slushy pink mai-tais beside the Best Western pool bar in Fairfax.

How can Hunsecker forget?

He smiles and says to Babs matter-of-factly and with unquavering voice, "By the way, Ms. Easton, I've reviewed your pending African genocide case from the State Department, and we can go ahead and close it out . . . no merit."

"Alright, Mr. Hunsecker," she replies, soft as nipples.

Meanwhile, during the lull, Manny Eden has found it difficult to concentrate. His own dream, his precious and defiant Keat Linderhart, has bubbled up unexpectedly, liberated from her Austrian cafe. With psychic fishing lines he sets her afloat, her face and body adrift and humming above the conference table, intoxicating him like a magic dirigible of purest light.

Though perplexed by the disrespectful calm and lack of compassion elsewhere on earth, Manny taps the table with a pencil. Keat remains ignorant, but Hunsecker forcibly goads himself into supervision. Without hesitation, his face pokes into Manny's, and when Manny doesn't stop the tapping, Hunsecker unlocks himself, releases *The Lean*.

Manny finally notices. The tapping trails off.

"Be patient. We'll get to you directly, Mr. Garden-of-Eden," says Hunsecker, a dull spike of harrumph in his tone. "But for reasons of time and expediency I'll forgo discussion of the simpler open and shut cases and proceed directly to—Mr. McCarthy? Can Mr. Garden-of-Eden learn something from you today?"

"Yes, sir!" Boyden grins and opens his only case file, withdrawing a few sheets of paper and placing them on the table before him "I've got a Pentagon pariah here who says she knows just why America is going bankrupt."

"Another G.I. Joe Blow?" Hunsecker asks, feigning surprise.

"Yo!" Boyden's fingers snap, crisp and loud above the case file. "Once a week, as usual, sir. Only this time it's a Jane Blow, civilian scientist."

"Oh, dear Counsel, *deliver me*," Varsana says as if exasperated, her eyes still fiddling with her boss.

Further down the table, Becky watches in silence like a stage hand. She notes how fortunate that nothing escapes Hunsecker's notice—each orbit of office personality, like each case file or memo, remaining bonded to a conspiracy of balance.

How can she hold out alone?

And where the hell is Laney?

Hunsecker returns his attention to the notes in front of him, Babs' nipples temporarily retracted and filed. He runs his finger down a few lines on a page then flips it, glancing at the back. In the interim, Becky, suffering from boredom, removes her glasses to clean them with a tissue. The movement attracts Hunsecker. He looks up and neglects his perusal of the file to scrutinize her actions. With a mixture of *schadenfreude*, apathy, and relief, everyone at the table plays out their own volatile scenario.

"I cannot live without the face of Elaine Dracos!" Hunsecker discharges in Becky's direction.

Becky looks up at Hunsecker and says, "You speaking to me?"

"I believe so, Ms. Bergstein, unless you're *really* not here and I've gone insane."

Becky replaces the glasses on her nose, and says in a nonchalant manner, "Laney should be arriving soon. She got a call from Senator Ormsby's office early this morning. They're doing a cost benefit study on federal advisory committees."

"Well, I appreciate the role you play as her confidante, Becky."

"She'll arrive, Basil, I'm certain . . . any second now."

"I want a consensus on her responsibilities," he grinds out to Becky, eyes lambent, head nodding twice. "I'll *have* a consensus on her responsibilities," he promises, boring down on her when she doesn't twitch.

Becky, not foolish enough to reply in kind, folds her arms and places them on the table. Her eyes rove in search of hiding places. And who can blame her? The rest of the staff can't help but react. Babs blinks in a vacuous way at Hunsecker. Manny looks edgy. Worm Quigley gapes into oblivion. Varsana appears ready to claw, her "rage" focusing inexplicably on a spot just above Boyden's forehead while Boyden's face imitates that of a spoiled child feeling cheated at Christmas.

As if satisfied by the responses, Hunsecker grins, then turns back to stare at his favorite male employee. "Boyden!" he exclaims. "Run down your case for Mr. Garden-of-Eden, son. Give the agency rebut, and focus on the concepts and road signs we employ at OWC to determine whether or not we should defend or assist a whistleblower. Include nexus, motive, protected activity, Pickering Disruption, Mt. Healthy, and the Threshold Question. We don't want him to miss a thing!"

Boyden nods at Hunsecker and starts right in, not looking at Manny, but reading confidently from his notes:

"This particular case involves an alleged whistleblower at the Pentagon. The complainant's name is Dr. Esther Brody, and she's a fifty-five year old physicist who works for the Army's SDI bureau. She's been employed there eight years. Her claims are both wild and narrow. She puts in a lot of malcontent time squawking about defense procurement and contractors in general—similar to stuff we've heard over and over—bribery of generals, congressional pork, rigging of bids, intentional cost overruns, bogus quality tests—"

"Then why so many years before our darling Esther's conscience turned sour?" Hunsecker asks Boyden, his brows raised.

"I don't know, sir . . . but the nitty gritty—"

"Read the paragraph in the letter," says Hunsecker like an impatient maestro, "the one just before she mentions the specific allegations. I want Mr. Garden-of-Eden to hear everything."

"Certainly . . . it goes, *Early on in my career I was told the Defense Department wanted contractors to maintain a sublime profit margin so that opportunities might be discovered for certain Pentagon officials in their twilight years. I suppressed my anger and went along, dismissing the custom as a distasteful but acceptable cost of defending my country. However, I was soon forced to realize that I'd been kidding myself. It was attendance at a contractor retreat in Boulder only a year ago that resulted in this letter and my fall from grace. Jonathan Boren from Aesir Corp was there—*"

Hunsecker interrupts again. "Continue now with a summation of Esther's grandiose allegations, and don't hold back . . . and please address Mr. Garden-of-Eden directly."

Boyden faces Manny and continues, glancing periodically at his notes. "Well, Mr. Eden, according to Dr. Brody, President Reagan's Star Wars program is a total sham, and the whole concept of space lasers shooting down missiles, nothing but science fiction. Dr. Brody claims—what she terms the *paranoid Star Wars culture*—resembles more a pop-cult religion than a crack organization of professionals. The core is composed of those brass, congressmen, and science types who realize what a multi-billion dollar fraud the whole endeavor is, but who connive to gain from its perpetuation. She further adds, quote, *motivations for the weapons culture in Washington can be boiled down to three human qualities*."

"And what pray tell are they?" Hunsecker asks, smiling.

"Cowardice, avarice, and self-deceit."

"Rescue me!" Hunsecker appears shocked, beyond the reach of absolute indignation. "The minds who proposed and conceived President Reagan's Star Wars program have brilliant track records—Doctor Anil and Doctor Eom have served the nation since Los Alamos. Doctor Mandlebrod is no less than father of the Sergeant York air defense system. How could human beings with such brains and reputations be party to such gross deception? Does the preeminent Esther offer up an explanation for this ludicrous inconsistency?"

Boyden clears his throat and looks again at his notes. "She refers to Mandlebrod as an *authoritarian science god no one dares dispute*. She claims that Mandlebrod and his cadre of hangers-on, she he puts it, *gladly sacrifice their responsibility to scientific truth in order to maintain their six-figure salaries and elite status in the Pentagon*, and so forth."

"I know there's more to this than professional jealously," Hunsecker says.

Babs and Varsana snicker in the background.

"She then goes into allegations of waste and mismanagement."

"Naturally, the whining turns up a notch. Almost time for a reality check. Go on, son."

"Dr. Brody claims she can implicate other weapons contractors in what she terms *monstrous and methodical fraud schemes* adding up to a tidy budget deficit of at least two hundred and forty billion."

Hunsecker appears incredulous. "And in what massive hole does angel Esther claim all of these billions are miraculously buried?"

"She's not specific on that."

"I'm flabbergasted!" Hunsecker's eyes are now big as ostrich eggs and his head is vibrating. Also, more laughs and nods from around the table. Manny tries to smile. Hunsecker continues. "To whom did she spill? Please refresh me."

"An Assistant Secretary of the Army—in the matter of testing fraud," Boyden says. "She claims that after the meeting she was relieved of her duties and threatened with dismissal for insubordination."

"And what does the Army say?"

"According to our Army contact, Colonel Jeeter Walmsley, the alleged retaliation is a result of her own vindictiveness—something related to a past beef she had against her supervisor."

"*EXAC-T-LYYYY!*" Hunsecker sings to Boyden, his voice deep, as if seeking an opera-like effect. "And we can find NO MERIT on this basis alone! The law is on our side, and nobody can fault us for that, not even that Democrat Congresswoman Schroeder." Hunsecker smiles and glances once more at Manny to make certain he's riveted. "Besides, there are umpteen more reasons why this woman doesn't deserve our protection or ear, not to mention the fact that she is traitorous!"

Becky is surprised by Hunsecker's intensity and theatrics. He's usually not this excitable. And *traitorous*? Maybe he's posturing for Eden's benefit. Whatever. She simply wants the misery to come to and end, and by the way:

Where the hell is Laney?

"The Department confirmed what we suspected," says Boyden. Dr. Brody went off firing like a loose cannon and tried to inflict as many casualties as possible."

"Therefore," Hunsecker says, turning to Manny Eden, *"no reasonable grounds* exist to make us believe a retaliation has taken place. She cannot possibly qualify for whistleblower status. You see?" The Hunsecker pauses, eyeing Manny suspiciously. "What are you thinking, Mr. Garden-of-Eden? . . . Are you impressed with this woman?"

"I know . . . I—," Manny says.

"Look, I can cork this genie right now," Hunsecker says, toning himself down a bit. "I happen to know that Dr. Thomas Blythe, Esther's supervisor at SDI, had already officially reprimanded her for bad conduct prior to her alleged disclosure to the Assistant Secretary. So the Department *would have* taken action against her regardless. Get it? Nowww, there goes the nexus, *WHOOSH, ZOOOOOM!*" His hands lift and cut the air like flying-wing bombers. "And, did you know that our angel Esther is an alcoholic? . . . No? She was seen abusing alcohol on more than one occasion."

"I didn't—"

"We don't have to play God, Mr. Garden-of-Eden." Hunsecker gives a little clap, and as he speaks, looks back and forth between Manny and Boyden. "Besides, her disclosure to Gates was NOT a protected activity."

"What is a *protected activity* exactly?" asks Manny. "I'm pretty sure I know, but it's confusing and—"

Hunsecker gawks at Manny. "What she *said* . . . it's that simple."

"She said . . ."

"Didn't you read your training manual? Haven't you been trained?" Hunsecker asks before smiling strangely at Boyden who reacts with a look of surprise, then over to Becky whose face remains rigid.

"I did, sir, but—"

"Her *speech*."

"She gave a speech?"

"No, no, *no*, the words, the particular *words* she used . . . Knock, knock, Mr. Garden-of-Eden. Anybody in THERE?"

"Ah."

"There is no protection for speech if it reveals common knowledge," Hunsecker says.

"It must be uncommon then?"

"Yes. The speech, in order to qualify for protection, must be *uncommon speech* . . .* " Hunsecker says and leans back in his chair, fingers fiddling absently with his tie.

Manny stares at it. What he first imagined to be a chaos of fish swimming above a black field of tie were actually mimicries of the ghosts in Picasso's *Guernica*, swirling free and frantic as bleeding white cows above Hunsecker's belly.

"But let's pretend, Mr. Garden-of-Eden, for the sake of your expanding consciousness in these matters, that precious Esther had not already thrown dirt on her grave, that the test of reasonable grounds had not been violated, and that her behavior was pristine and her dissent not yet ruled unprotected . . . and remember, Mr. Garden-of-Eden, you're no longer in high school civics class."

"Yes, sir, but—" Manny decides he has to ask a question. The idea of phony death rays is more than he can bear. "Might not Brody's disclosure itself have an effect on her whistleblower status . . . I mean, in this hypothetical example of ours?" He attempts to look unafraid and sincere.

Hunsecker appears astonished once again. "We must have a consensus on this, Mr. Garden-of-Eden . . . if OWC has no right to reverse the action taken against the employee in question, it certainly has no right to investigate the Pentagon!" A spasm of serious head nodding breaks out around the table. Only Becky remains still. "Besides, my greatest concern here is for the human beings involved, the managers being branded as reprisers . . . we need weighty, preponderant evidence or we must give *them* the benefit of the doubt, not the so-called whistleblower."

Boyden raises a finger in the air to tickle Hunsecker's attention. Hunsecker sees him, nods, and Boyden says, "It does point out for Mr. Eden's benefit, sir, that for every potential Joe or Jane Blow we often have two major issues to dispense with—the alleged retaliation because of the alleged disclosure, and the substance of the disclosure, or speech, itself."

"That's it, son. Enlighten away!" Hunsecker says, smiling again.

"To judge the substance of the disclosure, Mr. Eden, we must answer the *threshold question*. This question tests whether or not Dr. Brody's so-called dissenting speech I hold here in my hand achieves the threshold of *legitimate public concern*." Boyden pauses and fixes on Manny for a count of two, then asks, "Do you believe it does?"

Manny hesitates, sensing a no-win, also realizing that the meeting is becoming more tedious and disorienting by the moment. After a deep breath and a short pause, he says, "It seems like it, yes, I mean, billions of dollars—"

"But the concept, as such, is not ours. The Supreme Court brought it into being in 1983 for a case known as Connick versus Myers."

"This is vital to your education, Mr. Garden-of-Eden," Hunsecker says, watching Manny closely.

And not only is Hunsecker boring into him, so is everyone else, even Worm, the entire staff scrutinizing his face, his hands and eyes. As Becky examines him, she recalls the last investigator who lost his job following the first review meeting—all employees new to federal service on ninety days probation. Did Eden even know?

Boyden continues. "However difficult it may be, like the Supreme Court in the Connick versus Myers, we must be certain her motive was pure, that her desire for justice was pure and selfless."

"It must be *pure*, Mr. Garden-of-Eden," Hunsecker says, bulging his eyes to mock Manny's confusion, left hand wagging his tie like a tongue.

"Pure, if the dissenter's speech is to be protected, and taken seriously enough to cross the threshold," says Boyden. "Dr. Brody's speech fails to meet the threshold because she spoke not as a concerned citizen but as an employee bent on revenge. This is obvious . . . duck test."

"Always temper judgment with the *duck test*, Mr. Garden-of-Eden," Hunsecker says. "If it walks, talks, swims like a duck, that's exactly what it is."

"She fought with her boss," Boyden says, "and her behavior was witnessed. Obviously, she was out for revenge when she went over his head the very next day."

"And if none of this were true?" Boyden says. "We still have the Pickering Disruption Test. Did Dr. Brody disrupt her office with her speech?"

"*Pickering, Pickering, Pickering,*" Babs musically resonates.

"In a way," muses Hunsecker, "employing Pickering or Connick to validate the Department's actions against her is a waste of time. I mean, if the alleged disclosure is blatantly false, nothing but slanderous nonsense which the Department proves it is, then the retaliation is simply smart punishment."

"Good point, sir," Boyden says.

"Obviously, lies are not protected speech," says Hunsecker.

"And what if Dr. Brody won't accept the verdict?" Manny asks.

"Then throw her to the public interest piranha! Wish her the worst! We are not genies or fairy godmothers who grant personal wishes," Hunsecker says, "But now, what of your case, Mr. Garden-of-Eden . . . the Keat Linderhart problem? You should now be able to evaluate it easily, given your knowledge at this point."

"I should, but—"

"What's wrong?"

"I'm not sure, about some things, sir."

"Do you have the constitution of Marilyn Monroe?"

"Sir?"

"Has the virgin Linderhart been violated?"

"You know her?" Manny says, looking surprised.

"I know the case backwards and forwards. She committed hari-kari."

"She was punished for what she revealed on the Hill about—"

"We must have a consensus today, Mr. Garden-of-Eden, but you're determined to hero worship and waste our time." Hunsecker's face now teeters between reproach and disgust. "You've now been here long enough to disappoint me."

"But her speech . . . If not—"

"Mr. Garden-of-Eden, do you expect me to pass judgment, urge prosecution of the Commission based on her alleged observations, or your assumptions? Who are you to assume such a thing?"

"Who do I have to be, sir?"

"Someone *much* bigger than me."

No comment from Manny.

"Now listen, and you better listen carefully." Hunsecker calms to a look of bemused patriarch. "If her speech is *not protected*, the actions taken against her are therefore *not prohibited*."

"I understand."

Hunsecker pauses, scanning Manny for signs of doubt, his fingers tapping on the table. "Course, she may have been loaded with too many duties to begin with. Small commissions frequently do that to employees."

"Then what can we use as the tie breaker, sir?" Manny asks.

Hunsecker grins. "I'm not God, Mr. Garden-of-Eden. How would I know?"

Before Manny can even think of an answer, a shocking event occurs. A woman's voice, shouting down from above and beyond, suddenly explodes in the air like a stack of dropped plates:

"WHY DON'T YOU USE THE DUCK TEST?"

Hunsecker freezes.

He is surprised by the voice, yet not surprised.

Only it doesn't matter. The anti-Pickering Turk is at the gate. A female pariah-from-hell has dared to the verge. Her shout, bellowing as if from the black well of God's throat, has gripped Hunsecker and everyone else by the short hairs. All except for Becky, who finds it almost impossible not to laugh out loud.

Within seconds, the staff jerks around to gawk at the doorway, to fix on the source of the voice. But not Manny Eden. He fixates on a condition far more poignant. His precious Keat has been struck dumb, looking more like a chemotherapy victim than a whistleblower imago demanding worship. Into the flat of the conference table she sinks, waning to a crescent smear of humiliation, the faux wood table lapping without humor at her lips and eyes until she is lost to Manny.

Meanwhile, recovering from the initial shock, Hunsecker's entire physical being has undergone a divine transmogrification. Before an audience that cries out for a thumbs-up-or-down decision, the Hunsecker sprouts a spine of stegosauroid plates. With nails of black flint, he ignites a jet of sulfurous yellow vapor that gushes from his nostrils, his face wild and powerdrunk as the flame licks up and vanishes with a resounding crack.

Having reasserted himself, the boss relaxes, confident in display. He sinks back in his chair to tweak his tie again, the Guernica wraiths fanning out like a flock of macabre kites above his plateau.

He knows he has only to wait.

Silence follows.

Trying to recover, Manny Eden observes Varsana, using her as a weather vane. She has turned to face the door behind her. Her cartoon rage has resurfaced and focused once more, not on a spot above Boyden's forehead, but rather at a point somewhere to Manny's left and behind. As Varsana swivels back around in her chair, the point moves through space, her eyes following it, reeling it in with tugs and long heaves as if it were a boiling catch of shark. Then just as Varsana blinks, the fighting catch breaks air. At the end of the line, Manny's eyes intake the vibrant image of Laney Dracos bursting up to the surface.

Upon arrival, she pulls out the one empty chair at the end of the conference table opposite Hunsecker, and very cool and businesslike, positions herself and sits down. As the repercussions die away, she smiles, room-sized and slice-of-Milky-Way white, only not at the staff, but at a funny and adorable waif who resides somewhere faraway in her imaginary dimension. Following that, she yawns, flicking away a soft tear with her finger. It is apparent to all that she has arrived from the Avalonish shores of Congress, and having dined with Hill kings and hobnobbed with Fourth Estate wizards, she cannot help but dilate with ego, her breath exhausted with tales.

Nevertheless, a roomful of eyes roll nervously skyward. Just as Munchkinland natives cower before a powerful and skyfallen Dorothy, so do lesser beings of OWC squirm before the aura of a potent Mzz Dracos. Perhaps an incantational utterance or a wand wave is called for, a plummeting-down of Jayhawker shack, a godlike command to animation only possible in the White Oz.

As Laney's attention returns to the here-and-now, she glances curiously around the table. Manny waits for her other-planetary heat vision to rest on him. He tries to steel himself beforehand, only it's no use. He can't challenge her. Her eyes prove too overwhelming, too loose-cannon, too full of Senate, *Best of American Poetry*, and loud auditoriums of smoking rock.

With the exception of Becky, who places hands over her face to hide her mirth, the human tone in the room begins to find courage, waxing gradually to a state of supreme indignation. After all, wasn't Laney Dracos sitting at the head of the table also, looking down on them as if *she* were really in command?

Hunsecker though, beaming like a sportscaster who just beat the spread, beneficently sets all petty acrimony aside, and seeks, as befits a godlike boss, a higher plane from which to judge. "You were saying, *Mzz Dracos?*" he asks.

"The duck test, Basil," she says with a calm voice, assuming a relaxed posture in her chair. "You know, if it waddles, quacks, sheds, shits, etcetera?"

"Then it's . . . *a duck*."

"Precisely."

"And since you were eavesdropping in the hall for some time, what is your opinion on Keat Linderhart's protected activity status?"

"You don't know?"

"I want to expand your consciousness in these matters, Elaine."

"You won't like it, Basil."

"Why not?"

"The Constitution. I use the First Amendment as a basis."

"This is a matter of serious *concern*, Elaine," says Hunsecker, seeking the perfect tone of indictment.

"I'm simply distracted with *concern*, Basil."

"But you interfere with the ability of this office to function. And you do so in such a melodramatic and often comical way."

"Then why don't you and I do a little vaudeville routine for the staff? At least we can be entertaining."

Not allowing himself to be provoked, Hunsecker just smiles again and says, "OWC's *very own* little malcontent, our own little disruptive. If you're not wary Mzz Dracos, I'll throw you to the dogs."

Laney Dracos seizes on the opening. She whips her head around as if frenziedly searching for signs of a hungry wolf pack. "What dogs?" she asks, feigning terror. "The *Bimbo Dogs*?"

As Babs and Varsana rake her down to the bone, Hunsecker can't take his glare off her. At the same time, inside Manny Eden, a great head comes to a boil. It jolts and shudders the table, lifting it up as one big slab and slamming it against the far wall. Manny smells an odor of crackling, hears a pop of strained fuse. Something frantic gnaws at his palm. It feels like Keat. And Worm, not party to this fantasy, deliberately pokes at his socket till his fake eye spits out. It skitters across the conference table, staring briefly at Hunsecker before disappearing over the lip.

No comment by anyone is possible, and Becky is the only one who laughs, and loudly, before she can catch herself.

Her final mistake.

CHAPTER 11

Like Warm Rubber Massacre—Washington, Inc. — Nursing Gertrude — Laney vs. Emperatriz — Laney vs. The Gipper — Laney vs. The First Nancy

FOLLOWING THE CASE REVIEW CONFRONTATION with Hunsecker, Laney Dracos returned to her office to collect a few files. She had no idea the fate that awaited Becky, and if she'd known, she would have stayed at Becky's side to comfort her.

Nevertheless, during that time, and over the weekend, unusual things happened to Laney. Not least of these was a face-to-face meeting with President Ronald Reagan and The First Nancy.

On Sunday morning she recalled the events, and using an Amstraad word processor, typed them into her personal journal (along with her latest poetry drafts and fragments):

(Note to self: when completed, submit below to *Prairie Schooner*, *Paris Review*, and *Quarterly West*)

The Washingtonian

The head of (it) self-esteems
from every window
in the ship-of-State
Department—dumbing down
from the ports of that
penny-loafer alcazar
breeding Olympian hubris
with a Versailles-like disdain—

inflating and dreaming
no new Camelot round,
but only condos in Burke,
townhomes in Glen Echo,
perpetual esteem in equity.

Between attacks of carpal tunnel
and carpool palaver,
the Washingtonian roves
like a mammoth president
surrounded at all times
by a human flock
deathly afraid of anonymity.

. . . .   (*need something here*)

With up so floating memo-pads down
the Washingtonian dravels
(dream plus travel) in frantic droves
out to the Atlantic coast,
to Bethany, Chincoteague,
Nagshead, to hot sand,
peeling feet and cracker-board
houses vaguely reminiscent
of a godscape in Cape Cod—
the faces and breakers
a pure Kennedy . . .

Oct. 25–27, 1984

Gertrude Stein finally died in me by 9:00 A.M. this Sunday morning, like a vampire steaming to atoms in sunlight—but it didn't matter because she'd already done her job, I.E. clawed my brains into equal parts fear and loathing. Thank you, Hunter S.T. However, prior to matters of the 666 prez and his demon seed wife, I MUST exorcise the events of Friday afternoon:

Hunsecker's review meeting plopped like a turd, as usual, and of course I was late—some last minute admin at Ormsby's office. Anyway, I lurked outside the conference room, preferring to pass on the customary deluge of excrement. Lots of guilt for leaving my dearest Becky to wallow alone, sure, though it failed to matter because my will-to-avoid collapsed shortly after I heard the Hunsecker spewing out with his morality moronics. So I had to buck up, ride down once more like that Fort-Apache-bubblebutt John Wayne—and, yes, I took the stand and scared the shit out of everyone.

So am I FUCKING GIRLY? No! But do I LOVE getting attention? Yes!

I'll do anything for it. People I don't even know have accused me of having an attention addiction, a problem every bit as serious as gambling, sex, or heroin . . . Anyway, the real question is, why do I let that prick-faced Hunsecker irritate me to the point of dreaming him buried alive? Because he's a low life scuz? A white trash conservative with delusions of intelligence? An ass boy for the White House? All of the above? Whatever. I have to mull this out sooner or later. I don't want the 'me' I will become to look back on all this one day and fail to remember the best in passion—and above all I must stay passionate, for God help me, I believe in Heaven and I fear I'm an ignorant bitch—certainly, a selfish one at least.

Depression

The body
flat
ecoskeletal

words, too few

She was absorbed
in the
erosion of others

mesomphalos

of
herself

Have NOT yet heard a report from Becky on the subject of the 'Garden of Eden' fellow, the new Hunsecker hire from Pigsknuckle; but I know the case review meeting really shook him up—I saw the what-in-God's-name look on his face after Beast Boy shredded Keat Linderhart—and that's a good sign, sure, only I have to test him myself. Also, I'm certain that Pigsknuckle is smitten with moi. Why? Because he can't stop eye-licking all my best parts.

Will I stop him?

(Note to self: clean up the below and submit to a literary journal as "creative" nonfiction, Capote-type stuff, or some kind of hybrid expressionist thing.)

All The Gipper I Can Baffle

Following Hunsecker's case beheading, a soft and sneaky conservative came sniffing around my office, looking for a date, and I'll tell you now, what happened next was PURE POETRY.

I'm listening to WHFS on my little radio, lip-synching "Stop Your Sobbing" by The Pretenders. Wish I could sing like Chrissie—damn! And stroking my air guitar when this half-moon of face spouts to the horizon of my partition: his northern pole red as hair and his eyes of Reagan-blue vacuum. So *fucking weird*. It's none other than Boyden McCarthy, top OWC puppetcrat. As I stare at this goofy fragment of him, his entire head slides obscenely to the left, skating the top of the partition. For a moment he wobbles on the edge of gravity, then releases, and like a ball of Jimmy-Carter mercury in the poll thermometer, drops resistless to the floor.

Following that, he performs one of his make-Laney-think-he's-reckless routines. His body flaps like warm rubber massacre at my feet, as if being riddled with bullets—and he really believes this slapstick shit impresses me—but I've known for a long time that such stunts are a ploy to deflect suspicion. He's working for General Madison and Beast Boy, and each time he'd asked me out I'd concocted enough excuses to keep him off balance, to barely dismiss to our mutual satisfaction anything he might accidentally see or hear.

Only this time, the little prick surprises me.

At the moment of his entry my body is splashed like a rocking black limb against the afternoon wall. My lips flaring sinuous, pouting, malign. My hand stroking the Les Paul guitar neck, the fingers of my other hand like spider legs on speed., testing and thumping the steel strings. I imagine his report to Hunsecker: *Yeah, she was mouthing obscenities and jumping around her office like a frog on fire. She's losing it, Mr. Hunsecker! I'll testify!*

"ARE YOU A MATURE OFFICE PROFESSIONAL?" Boyden booms from the floor, looking up at me.

I just glare at him like I want to slice his nads off (he's so pathetic).

To impress me further, the little puppetcrat leaps to his feet and pushes out his arms, hands palm up, bobbing them up and down as if weighing the total value of my redeemable personality.

"Bureaucracy under Reagan is more dangerous than I ever believed possible, Boyden," I say, attempting to piss him off. "We do nothing; we help *no one*."

"Conservatives cannot afford empathy, you whining liberal fool!"

An image, a trauma, a rebirth—Boyden needs *all* of the above.

Because I'm already growing bored, I decide to screw with him, trump him in the game of brains, but before I can open my mouth, he announces:

"Elaine, your presence is *demanded*," and as he speaks, his face grins big and shiny as a campaign security badge. "There will be a *political power party* this weekend, one of the biggest of the year, and all the new conservative elites will be in attendance."

"Oh, you mean the First Nancy's psychics from El Segundo?"

"Oh, Elaine!"

"Aren't they busy predicting questions for Ronny at future press conferences?"

"Now, come Elaine, the time for sour grapes is *over*."

"But why me, Boyden?" I ask. "Haven't you noticed by now what a *liberal* disruptive I am?"

"Elaine, if you don't play the Washington game, it's not because you're smarter, or more ethical, it's because . . . well, maybe you're a little *dull*."

"Dull as an orange, Boyden."

"But you've got *potential*, Elaine."

"You're not answering my question, Boyden."

"What question, Elaine?"

"Why risk it with moi?"

"Because I cannot afford even the suggestion of homosexuality." He turns to sit on my desk, "And besides, you're the best looking woman I know. A real starlet."

Boyden attempts to act macho by out staring me. His challenged eyelids flutter like the wings of a trapped bird, and I imagine the robot from the *Lost in Space* television show appearing and shouting at him:

"DANGER! DANGER, YOU WUSSY LITTLE PECKER!"

"Look Boyden," I say, my voice seizing the opportunity to reek of pure boredom, "why should I follow *you* anywhere? You only want to *pump me* for info, and besides, what do I need from you? I'm already a savant of human nature, a moral desideratum, and the Protector Goddess of Whistleblowers."

"But that manure won't matter, Elaine . . . not where I'll be taking you."

Shoved down a few steps by the look of solemn reverence and honest terror evident on his face, I ask,

"When is this ominous event?"

"Saturday night . . . however, there are conditions."

"*No conditions*." My speech must be free!

"But certain forces will be present Elaine, things beyond your ken, wheels within wheels you may never understand."

The trembling puppetcrat introduces me in tones of fearsome gravity to a reality that he himself, even as a student of Ronald Reaganism, barely comprehends: a subterranean network of *corporate-ocracy* that overrules and undermines American democracy—a world not of Washington, D.C., but of Washington, INC.—and never mind the sense of adolescent dreams violated. I can't prevent the shouting inside my head:

Time to **GROW UP!**

Time to **GO WITH THE FLOW!**

Time to **GET WITH THE PROGRAM, ELAINE!**

"Do you *see* now, Elaine? Do *you*?" he asks.

For the sake of theatrics, a reality fist to my stomach expels my wind, and as I wilt into the chair behind me, my movements are at once retarded by implication and denial. Kaleidoscopic plates of high school civics spin before my eyes. Whole conventions of coda-soaked, slogan-raised, Republican youths in tacky blue blazers scream, *Four more years*! Then, as if Boyden's initial revelations aren't horrible enough, the prick unloads still further on me. His tongue smokes with armies of spin-doctors doing battle in the media, souls on sale for boardroom seats and talk-show appearances, form-over-substance minds hollowed to make room for corporate subsidy implants. At a gathering schemed to POLITICAL OMPHALOS (PO) by Boyden's aunt, Emperatriz Soors—heiress in reputation to the supramonde of Capitol Hill, Gwen Cafritz—all things will be made clear, astounding, and possible.

"Naturally, you'll do nothing to make me a bigger man than I already am," says the hireling, his breath regaining a more relaxed rhythm. But neither will I emasculate his self-esteem if I imitate a bureaucrat bimbo of limited ambition and unlimited naivety. And, since the palace of Emperatriz will most likely eructate with Capitol Hill godheads, all of them predatory, poll-prompted and freed of all responsibility—and attended in *Dieu avec nous* fashion by their courts of sycophants—I'd better avert my gaze when politic, wear a black evening gown showing mucho leg and cleavage, and not blubber out with any Bonzo Reagan or Californians-screwing-in-lightbulb jokes, or otherwise say or do anything that might raise an ulcer or even an eyebrow.

How can I turn him down?

"Boyden," I say, my voice soft and sad, "would I really undo years of brown-nosing and hurt your standing in blue Olympus?"

"Would you, Elaine?"

"We both want what's best of for all Americans, *don't we*?" Of course, I know we don't, and he winces a bit when I ask that, only ignores his better judgment because he's on an intelligence gathering mission for the dysfunction duo of Madison and Hunsecker and is afraid to screw up. Also, he'd like nothing better than to bang me and brag to the cretins at Heritage Foundation. They know me for crashing one of their Reagan ass-lick parties and laugh-spraying a mouthful of champagne into Chairman Danford's face after he'd told me of his Jeffersonian love for the common man.

Regardless, I realize instinctively that puppetcrat Boyden believes the sheer gravity of the POLITICAL POWER PARTY will terrorize me into reverence, choke my voice with humble pie.

However, by the weekend, I've invented my own *vox populi* strategy. And I'm determined to use it.

—|—

After spizzing away in Boyden's BMW on Saturday night, a new depression front rolls in . . . and I'm not sure why. Recently, I've found things getting darker near nightfall—the sun setting in my head also—and it's starting to make me panic. I try to yawn my way out of it, get some more oxygen to the cells; and even puppet boy remarks on the wild star burning a hole in my eye. He doesn't know the half of it. It's like black searchlight beams are pouring through my vision and dissolving things, the way hot sunlight steams the vampire Gertrude into mirage.

"What's wrong, Elaine?" Boyden asks.

"It's Gertrude, back for a quick nip."

"Huh?"

"Never mind, Boyden, I'll be fine." I don't feel like explaining, and besides, he would only use it later as fodder. My therapist, Doctor Cary Lake, told me to name my depression after someone I admire, to realize it as a whole *other being*, and so, I've named it Gertrude Stein, an author whose work both amazes and bores the shit out of me . . . okay, so as my dark little head drifts in search of ground, asshole Boyden cranks The Grass Roots on the car stereo till the stars begin to quiver: *I'd wait a millions years, walk a million miles, cry a million tears* . . . "T-38 Mashuto system!" he bellows, grinning with pride and stoking the raw wattage. I guess he figures the heavy bass tones will get me hot. Shit! I reach over and slide the bubblegum down a few notches. It's giving me a headache bigger than Mt. Shasta.

"So, uh, Laney, your band Mental Douche sound like this?" he says.

"No, more tin and acid, Slickee Boys style, and a little surf's up, like the Raybeats," I tell him, as if he really knows what I mean.

Off the subject then, because the puppet prick can't wait to impress me, Boyden reveals that Emperatriz, *The Ultimate Nexus*, is really his "adopted aunt," his step-father's older sister. Every holiday you can think of he has sent her expensive cards, then following two years of this she begins inviting him to these fancy political soirees. "I'm working my way in," he says. "She's actually doing me a big favor, Elaine, but I have to stay low key."

"How *low* do you get, Boyden?"

"That's real funny . . . but I've got some advice for you, Ms. *Tammy Pon*."

"What's that?"

"Come to grips with the reality of power."

"My version or yours?"

"You'll be rubbing shoulders with key Republicans and corporate lobbyists tonight, even White House staff—"

"A cross section of the whole regime then?"

"Those who matter, anyway. So approach with caution. Be smart and don't take sides."

"Absolutely not, Boyden, I believe in the separation of powers."

"Sure, and in the American Watch too? That one of your *powers*?"

"What?"

"C'mon, Elaine. I know all about it. You're in the group right?"

"Why ask, smart guy? You know all about it."

"Hey, Laney, I'm not playing with you, just looking for honesty."

I decide to tell the transparent little bastard a story that will make him wet his pants. I figure it will amuse me and perhaps even derail Gertrude. "Sure, Boyden, I've heard of them . . . they tried to recruit me, years ago."

Boyden's eyes triple in size, the BMW swerving. "These Watch guys are big, Boyden, *reallll big*. They're like a government within a government."

Boyden gasps, but stares at my legs anyway as I cross them.

I tell him next that a representative from the American Watch appeared at my bedroom window one Friday night wearing a tri-corner hat and a black mask. I had expected him to say, "S*tand and deliver,*" but he only taped a note to the glass and vanished. I was real scared, and the note, signed by someone named Rochambeau, told me not to fear; he would phone me at noon the following day. So, he did, and filled me in on the American Watch and their vow to make government really work for the nation by exposing and culling out corrupt managers he referred to as human viruses.

After I've said this, Boyden can hardly drive. He's so shaken and stirred. "*Shit, are you kidding?*" he asks, sneaking more looks at my legs and up to my cleavage, as if the instruments of my man-killing sex might calm his anxiety.

"No, I'm not kidding," I say.

I then describe *the secret sign*. Rochambeau instructed me to go to the Department of the Interior at an appointed time the following day and walk down Corridor B, 1st floor—this to demonstrate the reach of the American Watch. He told me that I would see people, government employees, passing me in the corridor, and they would all raise their pinky to their Adam's apple and leave it there as I walked past—kind of like a cartoon salute; and sure enough, that's just what happened: dozens of employees leaving a staff meeting in Corridor B and all of them levitating pinky to Adams apple. I was so stupefied by the vision of it.

"But that's just Interior," Boyden says, "not the whole government."

"Yes, very true. I was also instructed to take a brown envelope from a hotdog vendor on E Street and open it to receive further instructions. After my walk through the DOI, I was directed to several agencies over the course of three days, namely, Department of Commerce, State,

Labor, and lastly, THE PENTAGON, and each place I went at a certain time, people would walk past me, all of them touching their Adam's apple. I kept doing it, going along because it was all so strange and I wanted to know the truth. "

"You have to report this to the FBI, or the White House, or something," Boyden says, beginning to sound a bit frantic. "So did you *join* or what?"

"No, I didn't."

I tell him that I'd chosen to go my own way, to work the system through Congress, with Ormsby, but I sympathize and promise to keep silent.

"Well, uh, Elaine, you just broke your silence," Boyden says and smirks. "You told *me*."

"It doesn't matter, genius, because no one will ever believe you."

He gives me a frozen look for a second, then says, "Those Watch bastards are like termites. Maybe they're Scientologists or something? Subversive *bastards*. How dare they interfere with the management of government!"

Common sense, ethics, a grasp of reality—Boyden desperately needs all of the above.

—|—

Fifteen minutes of nose-bleeding volume later, and still nursing Gertrude despite my chuckles at Boyden's panic attack, we squeal off Chain Bridge Road and up a tongue of black drive. Dozens of limos which convey the "reality of power" are parked nose-to-rear so deep we have to stop and reverse all the way back to the entrance gate.

As we scrape up the Soors drive on foot, I move blindly ahead of Boyden, groping for a pale mote of window buzzing through the trees. An urge to submerge in a reality-of-power bath had possessed me, while the whole scene makes me feel like one of my favorite actresses, Susan Sarandon, in *Rocky Horror Picture Show*, the part where she and Brad are lost and seeking refuge till the Frankenfurter mansion appears in the distance—and so, as you might guess, I sing to myself:

In the velvet darkness,
of the blackest night,
burning bright,
there's a guiding starrr . . .

"Elaine? What are you singing? Mental Douche stuff?"

Boyden's voice sounds confused and weak, his steps quickening. I don't answer his stupid question. He clumsily kicks my heel as he draws up beside me in the dark.

"You need more coaching," he says.

"You need more conscience," I retort.

His face is a disembodied smudge without mouth. "Whatever you do, Elaine, don't get disagreeable on any particular issue, not like you do at the office . . . I don't want anyone to overhear it."

"Why Boyden? Can't the reality-of-power *cope?*"

"It's not your place."

"You wouldn't talk that way if I had bigger tits," I say, both palms hefting imaginary laps to my collar.

"And, if you happen to meet any, well, politicians, Heritage Foundation officers, or even Emperatriz's husband, please call them sir."

"As in *Sir Soors?*"

"No, as in *yes.*"

"Why?"

"Because they are, let's face it, better than us. . . rare, brilliant and honorable human beings."

Talk about gold bars plopping out of asses! Was this *the perfect brown-noser attitude* or what? Just as I'm beginning to itch for salvation, the North wind plummets like an angry slap, bursting the limbs above our heads into a snow of leaf flake and wood sliver. Boyden gasps and points. All my attempts at sarcasm are negated. I look up to see a scary vision of turrets, towers, and cathedral-sized windows—in other words:

THE SOORS CASTLE DEVOURING THE EASTERN SKY.

—|—

Twenty yards or so from the portal, six suits stop us. They appear on our flank like gargoyles blending out from the darkness. Secret Service types, obviously. I try not to act nervous. Boyden shows them the invite and we flash our IDs. I don't yet realize what manner of unbridled power the Soors castle really holds.

Before letting us pass, the suits once us over like we're Stalinists, and one of them is wearing some alien-looking infrared sensor thing over his eyes. I try not to snicker. Seconds later, at the grand entranceway to carnivorous Soors space, I poise myself, singing Susan again in a low voice:

There's a light,
in the darkness,
of everybody's...
liii-iiii-iiii-iiife...

Boyden swipes at his waxy red hair—one last massage to assure the forehead wave—and clutching a brass mouth of Hellenic lion, knocks three times. In response to the echo, a butler-type person, massive and frosty as Kaiser Wilhelm, heaves open the biggest fucking wooden door I've ever seen in my life and greets us with a silent *harrumph*. Gliding forward with Boyden into the Soors antechamber, I am made *parvenu* by the wine-wood light, by the opulence and circumstance, and as Kaiser Wilhelm plucks the overcoat from my back, a woman's shout erupts from on high.

"WELCOME TO CAMELOT!"

Hind legs crouch and pump. A dark, beetle-like violence swoops down on me from a Lucitania-sized staircase, her right arm high and curved as a pale horn. But what really floors me is the dress, and Dearest Me of Years to Come, I WILL NEVER FORGET THIS THING!!! Hear my words: it howls banshee-like through space, a meteor of 60s Aquarian chic. A Scocenci original, or some such.

This person is a Republican?

Twin cowls of black lace splay drastically out from the sides of the upper trunk like a pair of beetle wings, shading the arms yet baring the bony patrician shoulders. The beetle wings themselves, appliquéd with a salting of pearls, rise like an opera house roof above the rest of the dress, shadowing a black-and-white sail of satin flowing in yin-yang sinuosity to the floor.

It makes me want to laugh and scream at the same time.

"*Emperatriz!*" Boyden responds with sincere elation, his face and arms opening wide. The Emperatriz person, not surprisingly, dilutes the *frisson*. She recalls her celestial status and instinctively opts for a delicate, more stand-offish embrace—and one careful to leave the Scocenci monstrosity unruffled.

Kaiser Wilhelm and I have no choice. We must stand aside and observe a ritual ladder-dance, one in which the OWC puppetcrat assumes his rung. Once obligatory compliments and cute insider jabs are exchanged, he fixes me with a jittery stare.

My time has come.

I go cold, my throat gulping, my eyes bulging.

"Aunt Emperatriz," he says, pointing a limp finger in my direction, his body already slouching with apology, "this is . . . Laney Dracos, a *friend* from work. She's a graduate of Princeton, and, uh . . . a poet."

The Ultimate Nexus of Soors turns to approach me, and I realize I could never have truly prepared myself for her onslaught. While heavy with Gertrude, I'm forced to go face-to-face with a Washington-honed mélange of moth-like flesh and dominance, her features ballooning into focus one layer at a time, the throbbing vision of her assaulting me in successive stages. I feel like she's sucking me in, head to toe, and I also know without question that she hates me on first sight.

"*Soooo*, you work with my Boyden," she says, closing in till she smells like a cross between baked escargot and Chanel #5.

"Yes," I say, tepid but uneasy, the adrenaline rushing in me and burning off pounds of Gertrude.

"I hope you *enjoy it?*" Her voice sifts out dishonest and husky with cocktail *corporate-ocracy*, and she can't stop glancing at my boobs. "It is imperative we find warm poets who will *assume* such positions."

For some reason I can't explain, the image of that old cartoon rooster, Fog Horn Leg Horn, comes to mind, and I blurt out:

"*And ma'am, I say, ma'am, ahzzzz proud to be warm.*"

Boyden, in lieu of laughter, emits a stuttering bark. Emperatriz just stares at me, as if stupefied, and I stare back. Her eyes, pale and sea-chunky, perplex me, while her pupils, tiny breather holes bored into the scrunched ice of glaucoma, unnerve me. Her face I divide into two vertical hemispheres: the left half pensive yet sagging, as if with Bells Palsy, the right side perked yet fiercely blank. Nature and a crueler culture had conspired successfully. Her hair is a ski slope of platinum ash, and her lips outlandish, swollen with a silicone vogue—a painful red in contrast to her mothflesh pallor.

"You are so . . . *unique*, Ms. Soors," I say to her.

At the sound of "unique" her face stops. It just stops. Her body motion stiffens and halts as if frozen by a camera flash.

Boyden, noting the damage, quickly complements Auntie Emperatriz on the "power and sweep" of her presence.

The flattery injection restores movement, and she turns to Boyden and says, "Accompany me to my salon, dear Boyden. I have *much* to show you."

"You've never been more delightful," Boyden says.

Testing her wholeness, her interest in me already waned to a minor itch, she tilts her head and dares a *recherché* parody of Claudette Colbert: "*Mes péchés sont mon caractère.*" Then she adds, "And Boyden, tonight President Reagan is with us!"

WHOAAAA!

My ears are burning. The Bonzo baiter himself? The concept of it scared me. And what of Queen-zilla Nancy? What of Nancy's astrologer from El Segundo? What about that oil-sheik-loving Bush? Holy shit! My mind lurches between possibility and nightmare, my anxiety interrupted though by Boyden—his self-control frequency finally scrambled down to a static mash—and I have to laugh. He's shaking like a little weenie, only I must admit, I'm shaking a bit myself.

A short, bad, untitled poem to mark the occasion:

Searching for breath
in a rare stratosphere
the puppetcrat hands
iridesce at the knuckle,
purple-to-white in supplication,
whereupon Auntie Nexus—

following a single bosom gesture
more than coquettish—
offers her own hand,
and together, she and her
prick ship of blue drift
beneath a face-painted arch,
vanishing like shades
of Krypton into a smoking
cavern of black Xanadu.

And of course, I can't help but follow. To my doom?

—|—

We pass out of the immense foyer and into what I can only describe as the GRAND SALON CAVERN. Peering around, I see darkness for a few moments, my eyes straining to adjust. At last, I pick out shapes, several with legs. I hear the phrase "by the grace of God" uttered in the distance, and I imagine these shadows drifting within the murk to be Bible Belt Republicans, all reduced to shades, condemned forever to roam the *salon d'art* Hades of the Soors, searching for the assistant secretary job they'll never receive.
  When will they understand that mainstream Republicans hate their guts?
  Right after I ask myself this question, the voice of Emperatriz echoes ahead of me in the dark:
  "I've fashioned this chamber to absorb all possible tension."
  She addresses her anxious young prick as they stroll a few feet ahead of me, the matriarch of the Soors empire savoring the parrot tongue of art speak while extending her insect hand, palm up, as if tempting a patter of rain.
  "Through exposure to incongruous juxtapositions and deliberate enigma, my guests are forced to reassess reality, and themselves."
  Apparently, Emperatriz Soors has reassessed herself as a resident of the Bizarro World. Her voice nevertheless serves as a lifeline to guide me forward into the bowels of her abstract cosmos. Should I be grateful? No, I just get nervous again. The ceiling is invisible and this

whole place is deep and dark and sprouting with art, all of it glowing like strange plant life on an evil alien planet ... am I a fucking coward or just a hick imbecile?

I look down to see my face mirrored dimly on the floor.
Gertrude taps
at my spinal cord
with her nails,
and as a lunar slice
of cloud on water,
I gleam.

Black-velvet couches drift past me, collide like bergs and move on, their flanks and seats littered with the baggage of guest Republicans and their faux-fur pillows. A vaporous ice shaves out from beneath the black shades of lamps, end tables of ebony drinking the cold; and even as my mouth opens and my presumptions erode, I watch ghostly white hands grasp and lift nodules of dark stone fruit from atop ponds of twilight glass—the seedpods spilled esthetically, fragrant and malicious. I figure one of the Soors servants must have somehow scented the stones before the party because they smell just like Bonbons.

Meanwhile, Emperatriz, oozing her narcissistic poop, announces to Boyden, "*I consider this space to be at once unfettering and ineluctable.*"

Fortunately, luminaries of the *beau monde* species attract my attention, enable me to ignore the prattle of the Soors madam. I look on in amazement as the females chat and swing about in tastefully-contained explosions, their white-haired mates heavy with nod as the salon vault that goads their vanity drifts to gaping, black pools of void resurfacing between the champagne and whiskey sours.

"*My guests have no choice but to relax in the midst of so much provocation.*"

Relax? Sure, now the doom part.

The weird art works in the Emperatriz salon begin to provoke Gertrude even further. She's ready to gouge my eyes out for daring to compromise her sanity. I want to run shrieking, only I can't stop staring. My brain rocks with heel-faced robots of chrome velocity posing like frozen mimes and with biomorphs thrusting from the wall like petrified cow udders—and there's more! From within dark gaps of salon wall-unit the *oeuvre* of human and lesser phyla prod my dear author into further rage: tire-crushed cobras of bronze, Kali thugs of earth-goddess clay, blackamoor heads drenched in milk-marble—while beyond the phyla, impaled and frozen in space like severed chunks of moon: the GRECO-ROMAN BODY PARTS (butts, trunks, weenies, heads, etc).

In the midst of this splendor, I catch a glimpse of Emperatriz tightly clutching Boyden's biceps, pinching the puppetcrat, and I can't help wonder if she would rather be tweaking my nipples. *Yecch*! Too awful to imagine. And as if that isn't bad enough, I have even more to deal with once Emperatriz says to Boyden:

"*I am defined by this room.*"

Afloat like a shard of torso, I too am defined. But as *what*?

The head of Emperatriz bobs in the space before me like a bulb of silver crayon, while she, and the currents, the irradiant strangeness and glamour in the air, the cratered domes of Ionian skull, the inhumanity of the frozen robots—all in synergy prove overwhelming. My mind fumbles with the impact and I panic as I plunge inside myself to try to lop off Gertrude's head before she can get too cozy.

Still following Boyden and his insect hostess, I turn a corner and glimpse a fire in the distance. Though at the moment I find it inexplicable, the reality of it sobers me somewhat. I know I must grope for sarcasm, reduce the unfamiliar, keep my head balanced and buy time—but my effort fails, for a phenomenon never seen, except in newsbite distance, overwhelms my vision, growing less human in form with every step, blocking the fire and negating all reason.

"*It's him*," Boyden whispers to himself.

"I *know*," I whisper back.

(unfinished—"In Memory of Dictators")

Pampered from cradle to pedestal,
we rifle like wind through barrel,
and we are dry. Our faces strain to mimic
those of the great lords of iron and radiation.

Our display of jackboots,
Praetorian appointment memos,
and Presence Chambers were enough
to force even Gogol to piss himself . . .

. . . .

our mouths water to moats, our eyes
sticky as gravity and dead on revolution.
What once was, will always be again.
However, we regret we cannot pause,

only give advice:

Seek not.
Be your own jury.
Name a comet after yourself.

—|—

As the blinding torch of Apollo, the iron-haired Gipper rises into view before me. He melds with flames in the Soors salon fireplace directly behind him, his hands and face steaming off a Disney-rose, a nimbus of Hollywood *hallelujah* like a throb on his edges while his core of dark suit softens him, transfigures him to a vision of thunderhead curing sun over the Pacific.

Deftly, his handlers have blended him Nietzchean and St. Nickesque into a blazing tableau of I-AM-THE-LEADER. My panic is tamed a bit by a rush of astonishment and even Gertrude relaxes her claws. It's then I notice two art-deco lips of iron mounted high and cyclopean at either elbow of The Gipper, flanking the fireplace, and as frosting, only inches above his hair crown—inset between the pinnacle of the fireplace and the ceiling—a gigantic mirror gleaming with Greco-Roman ass.

All so fucking bizarre!

Emperatriz's wings flutter moth-like as she sweeps to a halt before him. She appears as if ready to ascend and swoon at the same time.

Cautious onlookers give way before her, create a large circle of space. In ceremonious fashion she introduces the jaw-dropped Boyden who reverentially shakes *the hand.* Reagan's other hand holds what appears to be a White Russian.

The president beams cute as a penitent little boy at the hostess. As an aside, I too am indulged. "And, uh, Mr. President," Emperatriz says, "this is my nephew's friend, *Ms. Loney Slackos.*"

I want to smack Emperatriz, but instead, I step up and shake with Reagan. He gives me the once over, eye-kissing my cleavage and grinning wolfishly because he likes what he sees. "Elaine Dracos, Mr. President," I say, "I work over at—"

The president dislodges from me. He gazes up. I see a dim reflection of limp Roman penis in his eyes. He gravels to my right a few feet and I turn towards him, not wishing to let go. I accidentally glimpse Boyden staring at me, his face terrified. I wink at him and Emperatriz oozes up. Before she can blabber out some brown-nosing inanity, I glide to the president's side, my entire body trembling. "I caught that recent article on you, Mr. President," I say, "a few Sundays ago in the magazine section of the *Washington Post* . . . *Mr. President?*" The Gipper's face goes blank. He refuses to look at me. "It was so clever the way you triumphed that infernal TelerPrompTer, sir."

"*Ohhhh?*" Emperatriz says, lips and wings trembling. "How did the president fare, *Ms. Slackos?*"

I turn to face Ms. Nexus, stare right into her icy glaucoma. Our eyes lock and struggle for domination. After a few moments of stand off, I say, "It's like this Emperatriz . . . the president was practicing a speech in which he accused the Democrats of making America into a desert of opportunity, but when the TelePrompTer repeatedly flashed the word desert, the president kept reading it as *dessert, dessert, dessert* . . . Cunningly though, one of his staffers solved the problem by drawing a tiny palm tree over the word to cue him."

"Clever, clever! Thank you, *Ms. Smackoff.*"

A vise grip closes on the back of my arm. For the first time I hear music. A jazz bass riff, soft piano tinkle, and an occasional spout of sax. But no vacuum is possible in the space that defines The Gipper. No sooner do I retreat a bit than other voices drone forth like an attack of cicada. I turn to meet Boyden, and behind me, a melodious Emperatriz coos the adjective "*pedigreed*."

The next voice I hear is Boyden's:

"Are you *goddamned crazy* or what?" he fiercely whispers, eyes teary and reflecting an art-deco lip.

"*America,* idol worship will be the death of thee," I say.

"What *the hell* do you mean?"

"Never mind. If you snag me a vodka gimlet over *there*," I point to one of the Soors' penguin waiters levitating a drink tray, "I swear I'll act more, uh, human. *Okay?*"

"Okay, but death by . . ." he threatens, releasing my arm and jabbing a finger at my face as he backs off, dissipating into a dark envelope of Soors *couture*.

Moments later, and despite Gertrude grinning fangs at the edge of consciousness, I snatch two vodka gimlets from a passing Oneida tray. One of them I gulp down in seconds, discarding the empty glass. The second one I nurse with smaller sips . . . so I'll get drunk, very drunk.

Real stupid?

Sure, but I had my *vox populi* plans. Don't you know? So I hum some J. P. Sousa, stirring marching band music with lots of horns, and say to myself, *Fuck that stage hogging bitch Gertrude!*

I gulp more gimlet, bolster courage with a team of Sousa trombones, RUM-TA-DAH DAH, and slip deftly into the royal circle of Reagan, my face and boobs imperious enough to force others to step aside. I do a quick reality check and observe the prez gesturing oddly. He's pumping his right arm, hand fisted, as if attempting to ram it up an invisible rectum. "Last Wednesday, I finally got my favorite saddle back," the president says, "Now I can lay off the fooze ball at Camp David."

The crowd reacts with lots of mild, ass-licking laughter. Reagan climaxes his revelation with a silly Irish jig. Loud, ass-licking laughter interrupts. As it fades, The Gipper's torso rotates. The grinding turn is accomplished in such a manner that, once completed, an art-deco piano several feet to his rear appears to jut from his shoulders like a huge black fin.

Following that, I begin to hallucinate, or so I suspect. One of the wall mirrors, hissing as it detaches itself like an orbiting solar-panel, aligns in space at such a slant above the Reagan hair crown that a mound of Roman ass—dangling pale and puffy on the other side of the room—again rises to form a guardian backside, a slash of Jove hovering premonitory at the peak of his cranium.

And I swear, I AM NOT MAKING THIS UP!

Once more, Reagan's image handlers have ingeniously tableaued him. Disguised as blackamoors or twinkling robots, they must be circulating the Soors salon, murmuring warily and paranoiac into hidden microphones, scripting and modeling and choreographing The Gipper's every twitch and squirt while micro-speakers drone damage prevention tactics into the whorl of his ear:

"*Move to the right, Mr. President,
now inch forward . . . more . . .
more . . . nowwww . . .
appear THOUGHTFUL . . . CONCERNED . . . ADAMANT!*"

Perhaps the entire salon itself was one all-consuming throb of spin-gestalt timed and tuned and rigged to accommodate itself to the demands of Reagan dodgeball.

But the moment of truth had arrived. I couldn't take it anymore.

"The Speaker of the House should be *flogged!*" I say.

"*WHAT'S THAT?*"

With a speed amazing for his size and age, the Reagan godhead jerks into damage control mode—the stratospherically black and raging eyes firing squad. It's all I can do to remain upright as his *reality-of-power* persona hammers down on me.

Within seconds though, he softens, *yes, yes . . .* Maybe it's all been a mistake? He appears to calm, entranced by my looks. "You know, Ms. Smackoff, you remind me of an actress I admire. Ava Gardner."

That one surprises me.

I spot Nancy hovering in the background, a flash of face like an ax. It chills me, for as potent and cunning as I am, facing off with her would be a little like Winnie The Poo vs. Monster Zero. Ronnie boy then chuckles, his Irish eyes smiling. "Well, hah, to answer your commentary, that old Speaker just needs to stop adding stuff to the Constitution, that's all."

Huh? What *stuff* had Tip O'Neil added?

Never mind.

I smile, sip my gimlet, and ask him, "What do you think, Mr. President, of the Beacon Hill news poll taken last Thursday?" I'm innocent, now sincerely craving his opinion. "The one that demonstrated that 76% of respondents believe America is imploding."

"We're exploding?"

"America, sir, *imploding*."

"Which poll is that?"

"The poll in which America vented its hostility at politicians."

"Who? The poll *what?*" His lips tighten.

"You know," I say, "the usual betrayal and lie stuff, rampant buck passing, kickbacks and fraud, reckless inflation of toilet seat prices."

"Trivial issues, Ms. Smackoff?"

"By the thousands, Mr. President. All counts dropped."

His face goes blank again. I almost feel pity for the amiable dunce and I imagine the whiny drone of handlers frenziedly buzzing in his ear, helping him to recover and either respond or retaliate, but after several long moments, he appears to reconcile with himself.

His blankness dissolves.

In keeping with his presidential image, he beams at me, pours it on, smug as Jehovah in recline on the seventh day:

"Ms. Smackoff, you don't need to be a rocket scientist to understand the situation." His tone is confident. "There's just not enough political courage in this town."

Hmmm? Well, whatever.

"What we need to repeal the forces of corrosion in America are win-win, not win-lose situations." This utterance from Reagan's mouth diffuses out into nearby space like a purplish, alien light. "Just give me a level playing field—that's all I ask."

My God! The speechwriters must be howling!

Before I can exercise my First Amendment rights and reply to Ronnie, Emperatriz surfaces onto my eye like a furious white comet.

"Time to become a *cognoscente*, Mr. President," she says, smiling with her droopy, plastic, barracuda face. "Degas and Pissaro have arranged themselves in your honor. I'd like you to see them before your—how shall I say—*debut?*"

"You do know the right cues, Madame Soors," Reagan says with a little chuckle, the relief apparent in his voice. "Ms. Smackoff almost had me!"

"The *bête noire* show is canceled, Mr. President," Emperatriz says.

The *what?* My urge to rip the lips off Emperatriz is replaced by a fingernail of Gertrude drawing blood on my forehead. The gimlets are pissing her off. She's waited long enough, and now, she's going to flay me alive.

I know I must distract myself.

As the newly dubbed *cognoscente* depart, my eyes strain for Boyden. He's lost in the Hades murk. I am abandoned, nothing but a lonely *bête noire*. I turn to watch Ronald Reagan grow thumb-sized, and just as Emperatriz glances over her knobby shoulder to stare at me with a look of undying hatred, the air above me explodes with a burst of light.

The hum of conversation in the grand salon sputters.

The music stops.

Gongs begin to boom in the distance. A few inches above my head, a smoky column of search beam bores through the darkness. My child-like fingers reach up to touch it, only just as they draw near, the hoarse luminescence streaks away. Seconds later, on the far corner wall near the art-deco grand, the light jerks, halts, and careens off again like a run-amok sun. Then, as if in response to the impatient crowd, the shaft returns and snaps to attention, bathing a scarecrow-ish clown squatting like a frog on the floor beside the piano.

"Greetings from THE LIBERAL DIMENSION!" the clown shouts and leaps to his feet. He flings his arms wide and drops his head to mimic crucifixion, and like one giant blob, the entire room quivers with laughter.

Following a curtsy, the clown lowers his arms, turns to his right, and walks bow-legged. Behind him, three more figures appear, shuffling into the light. One of them, a young woman, her long dark hair in pig tails, wears a plaid dress and looks like a cross between a Catholic school girl and a whorish escort model. Her eyes are gobbed with heavy black mascara and her lips red as a stoplight. Behind her limps a body sheathed in squares of wrinkled tin foil, skin sprayed with silver no-tox, a foil dunce hat on his head, his metal mouth repeatedly squeaking the word *"liberal."* Behind him, a third figure wearing a mangy lion costume, his frightened face smeared evenly with black soot, and he's holding his tail in front of his mouth like a microphone and chanting:

"Deficits, deregulation, and deunionization, oh, my!"

The audience laughs and hoots. I am stiff. My mouth hangs dumbly open. Gertrude gasps and wiggles like a psychotic child in embryo. Her mutant teeth gnaw at my uterus.

The bizarre foursome stroll about ten feet, from right to left, the spotlight following them. The clown in the lead, who I presume to be a stand-in for the Oz scarecrow, bow-legs forward with a moronic look on his face, then abruptly stops, the other three colliding nose-to-head behind him in a lame slapstick routine. The jostled clown raises his arm and points, his face astonished.

"LOOK EVERYONE, IT'S THE PRESIDENT OF OZ!" he shouts.

Upon hearing this exclamation, the light widens and the fabulous Ronald Reagan appears stage left. Everyone applauds with vigor. Reagan, looking serious, holds a small piece of white paper. He stares down at it, mumbles a line to himself, glances up at the four Oz parodies and shouts:

"I AM THE GREAT AND POWERFUL PRESIDENT OF OZ! What do you want of me, you liberal nut jobs? Have you just awakened from your poppy nap?"

Raucous laughter from the crowd. Someone nearby rasps out with: *"Nancy wrote the script."* Following that, the whore Catholic Dorothy steps forward, the other three parodies quivering behind her like vibrators turned to maximum liberal orgasm. "Your highness," she says in a shrill voice with a thick Brooklyn accent, "we came here to ask four things of you."

Reagan reads "the script" again, looks up and says, "You little hypocrites. Your leader John Kennedy told you to ask what *you can do* for your country. So why, oh why do you bother YOUR PRESIDENT?"

"Mr. President, uh, sir uh—" Dorothy says.

"Well, out with it, pedestrian!"

"Mr. President, sir, it's like this. I *need* an agriculture subsidy before I can find my way home to Kansas, and the Scarecrow's brain wants you to *not appoint* any more moral conservatives to the courts, and the Tin Whiner Man wants you *to fix* the budget deficit so he can buy fuel oil for his impoverished constituents, and the Cowardly Liberal Lion wants you to *promise* to stop fighting little wars so *he* won't get killed."

The audience guffaws as one. Reagan swivels and winks at them, glances back at the paper and says, "Alright, you whining liberal boobs, I will consider your requests, but first, you must bring me the gavel of the Democrat Speaker of The House. Bring me THE GAVEL OF TIP O'NEIL!" Reagan bellows.

The four Oz types act faint and collapse to the floor in a heap, there to vibrate and moan. Naturally, the blue blob of crowd yells and applauds madly. Reagan smiles and bows again and again, his hand waving in the air as Soors servants, looking like Jeeves cyborgs, appear and pull the shivering Oz parodies across the floor by the legs and into the shadows.

Following Reagan's departure, stage left, a portly black woman in a white evening gown smoothes into the light, and to the accompaniment of piano, begins to croon "Stormy Weather."

"Nancy Reagan's favorite!" someone says behind me.

Attempting to process the import of what I'd just witnessed, I polish off my gimlet and go in search of a big ice-water, knowing I have to chill Gertrude before she cooks me to a char. The waiter, a young guy with blond hair, shows lots of teeth and stumbles over my cleavage. I yell, "ICE-WATER" at him. I don't think he hears me. I try to yell louder. My voice quavers. Gertrude has gripped the pole of my spine with both hands and begun pulling herself up to my brain pan.

The spotlight dims to a purplish haze and the music plays on. I wander, yawning and feeling woozy. I catch a glimpse of Vice President George Bush, and his son, George Jr., talking to some CEO and Saudi Royal Family types. Junior looks like a smug baboon. I remember reading he was a cheerleader in prep school and I imagine him ramming a greased bullhorn up his own ass.

He sees me staring at him and winks.

I suppress the urge to vomit.

Soon enough, and predictably, one of the CEOs detaches from the Bush crowd. He circles around and brushes against me. He appears altogether vitreous and arrogant, his face reminding me of a Soors chrome robot. Out the corner of my eye I see him checking out my boobs and legs. He smells like the inside of a new limousine. Finally, he stiffens, and says:

"Your name, my dear lady?"

"Melanctha Von Ubercunt," I say.

He flinches. "Garner Grimstead," he says, extending paw.

"You know Emperatriz?" I ask, ignoring the paw.

"Of course. *The Ultimate Nexus*." He smiles and lowers the paw.

"I need one badly," I say with a phony pout.

"Well, then, Melanctha, you should take pains to ingratiate yourself. She'll be an ambassador one day—if a Democrat from New England ever takes the White House."

"Huh? I thought this was a Republican soiree, Garner."

"Yes, yes, but Emperatriz is practical. There are quite a few Democrats here tonight. All kinds of folks. This is a political power party, after all, eh?"

"Really? How do you know *so much*, Garner?"

"I'm on Senator Richardson's staff, flew in with him this evening."

And I thought this guy was a CEO! Richardson's one of the most influential Democrat senators on Capitol Hill. His agenda is common knowledge. I'd read an interesting feature on him in *Newsweek* only a few months ago.

"Emperatriz is one his biggest supporters," says Garner. "He gives her a voice, whenever she desires."

"That's scary."

"*Pardon?*"

"Nothing, a joke . . . So the more incredibly wealthy people Senator Richardson gives a voice too, the better the chance of him sticking around to continue *voice giving?* I mean, he needs the money, right?"

"To protect and serve the nation, you first have to protect and serve yourself, Melanctha."

I belch a little gimlet in his face. Garner frowns and glances at my boobs again just to make sure he's not wasting his time. "But Garner, seven fundraisers in one day?" Richardson sits on the board of directors of at least a dozen or so Fortune 500 corporations. No conflicts of interest, I'm sure. "The man sounds superhuman."

"He *is*, Melanctha."

"Unbelievable he can still find the time to write all those laws."

"Which ones?"

"Eh?"

"Which laws were you referring to just now?"

"Didn't he have a hand in . . . the last clean air bill?"

"That was *my* bill."

"*Huh?*"

"I cut my teeth on that one."

"*Huh?*"

"Senator Richardson checks off, sure, gets a briefing. He trusts me, you know, but it's not a blind trust thing. Some stuff is trivial. I work with lobbyists as necessary to straighten things out."

Of course, I already know. Garner's referring to "fax laws." Corporate bribe artists actually write these laws and fax them directly into the Hill staff offices. The language then goes right to the floor for a vote, often without any change whatsoever. On the Hill they call it democracy at work—some of the Dems no better than the big Elephants when it comes to shit like this.

Who will do right by us? Who?

"Then Garner, you're really the lawmaker here," I say as if impressed.

"*Noooo*, just a staffer, Melanctha. The Senator is the lawmaker."

"Of course, but you remind me of those artists who paint something and someone else signs it."

"No one has a feel for law greater than the Senator. His grasp of an issue is instantaneous."

"Where do we find guys like this, Garner?" I'm getting more impressed by the moment.

"The party picked the Senator out of a crowd many years ago."

"Oh?"

"As the CEO of TuroChem, he projected an image of internal strength, and they took notice. They knew he'd be a leader, not just another blame-game bull in the china shop."

"Well, Garner, that all sounds like *bull*shit to me."

Then, just as I knew it would, a big stone hits the puddle of Garner's face. "You don't get it, Melanctha," he snarls in a petulant way. Having wasted enough time, he moves to puncture my facade with the single most important and potentially devastating question ever ejaculated from the lips of a Washington wannabe:

"Tell me, Melanctha. What do *you* do?"

Politics

We are obsequious
cowards
true

but you have failed
us
Ozymandias

as well as all
those nawabs
of
the U.S.
pangalactic

policosmos.

—|—

While counting the peach-fuzzy hairs on Garner's chin, I explain the futility and stupidity of OWC, and my activist role therein. Soon repelled (as I knew he would be), he slides the revelation down to a rung beneath him and kicks it away like road kill.

It appears I'm just too negative or trivial for Garner.

No six figure salary.

Aren't my boobs big enough?

I check my cleavage to make sure... Only what difference does it make?

I need to set priorities.

I need ice-water.

The little Garner phony exits, and without a goodbye, taking his snarl and limo odor with him. I have no choice but to cull through the smoking blob of corporate-ocracy for that same cute blond waiter. In a minute, I find him. I get right in his face and ask him to fetch me some water, pronto. He rushes off to the kitchen and returns in a hurry, anxious to please.

Within moments, my fingernails are drumming a frantic jazz on my glass. I stare at what remains of Garner as he glides though the purple waves of Soors salon—and WITHIN THESE PURPLE WAVES, MY OBLIVION TAKES FORM. It's either the gimlets, or the lack of humor in getting rejected by that Garner prick, or who knows, but Gertrude has now hoisted herself on high and thrust her claws, deadly and deep into the core of my being.

I put my glass down, dizzy, everything going black.

Halved and discarded, panicky again, I zigzag my body through a cloud of cruel faces in search of the nearest lavatory. I must escape the mutterings of the Soors political tribe, if only for a few minutes.

I'm weak, I know it, and I hide it whenever possible.

Minutes later, I do some yoga-like breathing, attempting to suffocate an anxiety attack brought on by a Godzilla Gertrude the size of Baltimore and twice as ugly. After a bit, I stand up, shaking from nose to toe, and quit the stall. I decide to make an appointment with my therapist come Monday—though it won't do much good because the dark runs in my family. I don't believe in that couch bullshit anyway. Luckily, a bronze sculpture by Noy—plopped like a huge black turd atop a pedestal in the center of the lavatory—provides me with just the *life metaphor* I need. I have to laugh.

Might the Emperatriz have a sense of humor after all?

Relieved, I stroll towards the bathroom exit, passed by various evening gowns until I come face to face with the other half of the Reagan duo.

She pops into being like an apparition, only inches from my face. The sight of her paralyzes me as if she were Medusa herself, and even though I'm staring down at her, at least three inches taller, she rules from on high. Her type A, Hollywood-cruel eyes scratch my own eyes like fingernails, and when she speaks, her voice is painful, a razor-on-glass—just as I'd imagined it would be.

"I hear my husband *thinks* you look like a movie actress," she says. "Ava Gardner? Well, his eyesight isn't too good in this light. I apologize for the *sexual harassment?*" She allows herself a demonic grin, pushes through me into the bathroom, then turns and adds, "And you don't look a thing like her, dear. I'm sorry. More like Jane Russell . . . on a *bad hair day.*"

Yipes!

How to process this? Should I be honored by the fact she found me significant enough to attack? I just know I must exit before she has a chance to start in again and force me to forever remember myself as a sadder version of Jane Russell.

"Thank you, Miss First Nancy," I say.

She turns from the mirror and shoots me a look of practiced disgust. All *very Hollywood*. I'm trying to return a friendly smile, really, and as the door shuts behind me, I hear her spit, "*White trash slut!*"

Okay, so next I'm bumping aimless again in the half-light of the Soors museum, trying to shake off Nancy and Gertrude at the same time, searching for any reflective surfaces that might resemble Jane Russell on a bad hair day—trays, iron lips, shiny Roman weenies—also yawning intensely and snatching glops of pate and ice-water. And I'm anxious too because I sense REPERCUSSIONS.

I don't have long to wait.

By accident, I spot them over in a desolate corner of the salon, behind one of the chrome robots. Boyden looks slumped and horrified as he listens to a histrionic *Ultimate Nexus*. Feverishly she pounds the air with her fists, her beetle-crack wings all a-flutter, her bouffant lips throbbing to burst. I *almost* feel sorry for the blue prick. Anyway, throat puckered and hands damp, I back off in search of another ride home.

Only I don't make it.

Boyden descends on me in a fuming rage. He's tight lipped and swelling to purple as he hustles me out to the antechamber to retrieve our coats.

Upon entry, Kaiser Wilhelm scowls.

It must be a conspiracy.

I'm more than ready to leave anyway and figure I can dismiss anything the puppet prick can dump on me. Once outside though, in a fall of night and cold sleet, he safely erupts in my face.

"WHO WAS THE BIG MOUTHED BITCH?"

Despite the fury in his voice, his face remains tiny and bobbing in the darkness like a blur of cigarette. He slaps a hand to his forehead while bending forward at the waist. In the night, his body resembles a flaccid Reagan dick. "The President *can't relax*, even at a damn party!" he shouts at the ground.

I use a tone of voice I hope will placate. "He avoids all responsibility, Boyden." Only it's no use. An unseen object collides with my throat. It is soft but firm as a hand, and I'm snapped off balance. Awkwardly, I backpedal till I slam full force into a side of car metal and I am blinded, my eyes wet in the darkness, my window thrown open and filled with his insanely shrieking voice. "You pissed HIM off! *You pissed Emperatriz off!* You PISSED *MEEEEE* OFF!"

Then the pressure releases and he backs away.

I yell, "*Asshole! Fucking woman-beating asshole!*"

Now Boyden's scared. He grips his head and begins to press. "Why did you have to act like such a freak?" he asks from between pinched lips.

"What do you mean?"

"That bit about the news poll?"

He releases and his face snaps back.

"So he's mad over a fucking poll?"

"Oh, no, *he's* not mad."

"You just said he was. So who's mad?"

"His people! *His people* are mad! They don't want jerks like you talking to him about stuff like that. Get it?" Wild palms slap to his face, his voice cliffing up to hysteria. "It's not up to you! It's not—you *fucking* ...who are *YOU?*"

Boyden teeters on nervous exhaustion, ready to bawl. He mutters obscenities and stuffs imaginary razorblades up my rectum before turning away to reel towards his car like a drunken frat rat.

A minute later, and way down the drive, I hear a slam of door. Another few seconds, and a roar of engine, revving to spite, a squeal of tires followed by a gradual shift to distance, and silence.

Not giving a shit about anything, I hitchhiked home—a stupid thing to do, sure. I had a secret hope that some lunatic would pick me up and kill me. But no such luck. Some old fellow from Harpers Ferry drove me all the way. His name was Mr. Loveless. I'm not kidding. He acted like a perfect gentleman too, told me stories about his wife, Gail Loveless, who died of liver cancer years before, and how he still told her about his day, every night, as he lay in bed beside a framed photo of her when she was young and beautiful, the mountains of the Blue Ridge rising behind her, a tiny white cloud beside her head.

I began to bawl like a stupid baby before he dropped me off, and he apologized profusely for bringing me to such a state. I told him it wasn't his fault, told him how fucked up I was, and then he held me like a father as I cried the rage of Gertrude onto his shoulder.

Later, I felt so shitty for doing that to a man who had nothing, only air to talk to, only night to wait for.

I'd acted like a totally selfish bitch.

So typical of me.

CHAPTER 12

Ladies Night At Scandals — A Mongo Moon Goddess — Laney vs. Manny Eden — Sneaky Shit Theories — Personalities Are Such Fragile Creations

COME MONDAY, A HUGE CARTOON of Richard Nixon's face exploded by Xerox from Boyden's "My Favorite Photo," appears tacked up on Manny's inner partition wall. Taped to the edge of the Nixon lips is a white tail that emptied like a river into a word-stuffed cloud floating above the Nixon head. The words slashed in black reading:

> LIFE IS UNFAIR,
> SO MAY ST. MACHIAVELLI
> INSPIRE US ALL.

Manny's immediate impulse to trash the Nixon face is interrupted though; he stops himself in mid thrust, saying:
No. Today I will practice free will.
Self-restraint for its own sake is proof enough.
After a few sips of bad coffee, comes Keat Linderhart. He'd been putting her off all weekend. Of course, the routine OWC closeout would follow, the bureaucratic eat-shit-and-die form letter, but he can't bring himself to do it—and not because the concept of the action is difficult (Hunsecker and Boyden having provided ample excuse). Rather, it is the fantasized bond that prevents him: their love making, together with his memory of sharing on the Mozartplatz; and also because, despite his armory of new self-deceptions, she still throbs, backstabbed and moon-like in the nearby vicinity of space—though becoming more hideous and sloppy by the hour. He hopes she'll show at OWC that very day, cawing for attention and inflated to a god-sized Moloch, a scream

of grade-b zombie—the kind who gleefully devours shrieking babies before demanding with an air of horrendous bitchiness that he do his duty and exonerate her absolutely.

Only that would be too easy.

As Hunsecker said, she wasn't a whistleblower by definition. A pity, Manny thinks, I can't argue with the way the law is written. Nevertheless, he admits to himself that he'd like to cradle her once more, while she yet toasts with her cup of philosophy in the Bavarian wind, while she yet remains precociously moral, brave, and dying like a barbeque coal in the lonely Washington night. Then later, at leisure, he'd retrench and reconsider, perhaps even say to himself:

FUCK YOU KEAT LINDERHART FOR EXPECTING WAY TOO MUCH OF ME AND FOR DOSING OUT BLAME BY THE WHINING SHOVEL LOAD!

* * *

MANNY PLANS A THREE-HOUR SUNBURN lunch in Farragut Park. In advance, he tells Deejah he is going to a doctor's appointment. She doesn't flinch, just gives him the usual psycho face. What else? But before he can flee OWC, Becky Bergstein appears in his cubicle looking maligned and paranoid.

As foreshadow, she had stomped back and forth from one side of his office entrance to another, casting suspicious glances at him. But once inside she glances uneasily around with big wet eyes. She gasps and scowls at the apparition of the huge Richard Nixon gloating forth from Manny's wall, but keeps all comment to herself.

To Manny's surprise, he notes as she recovers from the shock of Nixon how drastically her face has thinned, as if a being of sadistic intention had punctured her and sucked her to collapse. With shaking hand, she picks up a yellow sticky pad on Manny's desk, produces a pen and writes:

THE TIME HAS COME
7:00 PM AT SCANDALS
CORNER OF 19TH AND M STREETS

She shows him the note for a count of five, crumples it, and leaves.

* * *

MANNY'S TREK BEGINS AT 5:10 PM. He takes several turns on side streets and lingers on corners to make sure he isn't being followed.

At 5:55 PM he enters the bar and orders a Rob Roy.

The place is breathing room only. It's LADIES NIGHT, and several white tons of hung-and-restless male are slouching needfully against their surrogate wooden mother: the bar rail in Scandals. Within the eye-stinging haze of blue neon that tearfully smudges the length of the club, the males flounder and slip. Already they've snorted at least an hour's worth of Wicked Ale, rail booze, and kamikaze shooter, and are now distending themselves into marauder soft machines, their ambitions clinging like ejaculation to a ceiling of perfect passion. Spitefully horny though, and simian with drunkenness, they choose their targets, cataloguing and rating choice cuts of female anatomy plucked from within the roil of bodies groaning slow and bladder-aching beyond the perimeter of the bar:

Glandula! . . . Yo! Yeah, you! . . . A ten, nine, eight for the MAJOR LEAGUE GAZABOS! . . . Mooooooooo!

Female bureaucrat youth unlucky enough to be nearby are skittish and dreaming of escape. "Only The Lonely" by Roy Orbison plays on the stereo, followed by "She's Come Undone" by the Guess Who.

Unlike the other groggers, though, Manny Eden is unable to focus on sex. Instead, he thrums like a tuning fork after a hard strike on White House marble. Understandably, he is anxious about the intention of the American Watch.

By 7:05 PM, he has downed two Rob Roys. With a third drink in hand, and feeling more dizzy and defiant by the moment, he plows through the warm, happy hour mass like an ice-cutter with a bad attitude, searching the floor and beneath the tables for the fizzling remains of Becky Bergstein.

By 7:15 PM, he still hasn't found her, so he perches himself at the bar as close to the door as possible in hopes he might catch her on the way in.

By 7:35 PM, she still hasn't appeared. Giving up and feeling relieved, he asks two skittish women to dance, but despite his novel *come-on*—a promise of two-for-one equity and a diversified stock portfolio in any future they might share together—while doing a damn good Groucho Marx (*Okay then, I'll leave in a huff. Make that a minute and a huff...*) he gets rejected both times. Only his ability to view the entire situation as surreal restrains the evolution of his shame, otherwise he knows he'd join the swelling and woozy ranks of the bureaucrats and photocopy salesmen, the punk accountants, and the other stiff-pricked groggers succumbing to bitterness and avenging their humiliation from a safe distance.

"Yeah, *goddamn malajusted fucks!*" this old guy in a three-piece blue suit sitting on the stool to Manny's right suddenly blurts out.

His demeanor reminds Manny of a homeless drunk who has just recalled in the midst of all this nasal-searing splendor, and with a shot of jealous bile, that he too once stalked Scandals like a magnificent prick ship in search of harbor. Only now, devolved into a balding, buck-passing mutation from Capitol Hill, he is fated like a bug for the windshield of life.

The moment Manny looks at him, his liquor-scalded face peels back like a temperamental Chihuahua. "The goddamn Washington Monument. The proof is there. All *the fucking proof* you need!"

"Proof of what?" Manny asks.

"That it's a fucking Catholic shaft!"

"How do you figure?"

"The Christian Technology Council knows all about it. The Hebes built the damn thing for the Catholics. The Council proved it mathematically."

He introduces himself to Manny as Mr. Chester Van Fleet, and proceeds to inform Manny just how "well hung and ubiquitous" the Christian Technologists are, and how, once a new breakthrough in "remote brain scanning technology" (*encephtech* he calls it) is achieved by devoted Christian researchers, we'll all be able to identify and surgically cauterize from normal society—by means of readily recognizable quirks in the brain's alpha wave—all "evil and vigorous Jews and Catholics," and not even by hiding behind lead walls or in rowdy mobs can the conspirators hope to shield themselves. Then, once these cabal lovers are corralled and blended with eternity, America will have an end to crime and war and economic instability, and even access to new immortality medicines they've been hiding from us and hording for themselves.

Manny hears "She Blinded Me With Science" booming loudly in the background.

As Chester rants to crescendo, detailing the "secret Pope-bitch defiles" of Nancy Reagan and the manner in which she "hypnotizes her Irish husband into swinishly obeying the Cardinals," Manny detects a new wave of commotion in the bar. It swells and consumes the entire place like a sudden blare of *Gong Show* orchestra. Though it's only the sound of luckless groggers acting out a new fantasy, he notes how rapidly they're approaching a state of crash dive, *oooohing* and *ahhhhhing* and slurping themselves into a frenzy. And he believes the object of their scrutiny to be in the immediate vicinity and bearing down on his position for their voices, bombinating and spearing up to mating wave frequency, are overcoming him, tugging him to their side, roaring louder and louder for want of coitus and dignity:

"Oh, Madonna! *Goddess of the Mongo Moon!* . . . *Hellooooooooo Nurse!*"

Manny turns his head, unable to check his curiosity, and as he does, the air above the dance floor morphs into a big smokey eye, and into the gap created by the eye, soundless as an eclipsing pupil, drifts the mysterious Mongo Moon Goddess the bar hounds had been baying at.

But wait . . .

Manny's brain spasms and opens his hand to drop the Roy, the glass hitting the floor at his feet. Unable to process so much startling information at once, he stares dumbly at this Mongo Moon Goddess who looks exactly like his own Keat Linderhart, the one he'd seen that night in the bathroom mirror. And this updated version, drifting through Scandals, certainly appears tall and irrepressible and cosmic enough to give him pause. She is sheathed in a dark, pin-stripe suit, her white blouse draped with a crimson-squiggle-on-blue scarf, her anemone-fingered hands caressing a martini sans olive, her hair a black-nebula halo, and her preciously arrogant, *Paramount Studio face* resembling in a disturbing way that of his OWC nemesis, Laney Dracos.

Manny stares in dumbfounded rapture as the Dracos-Keat-imago glides past him, her body at least a full two inches above the floor—and not even bothering to glance at him as she sails so brazenly by, but instead commanding the attendant and magnificent genies at her command to halt her just beyond.

Still refusing to acknowledge Manny, she turns her head at a right angle in order that her blue-socked eyes might engulf and reduce to a trivial instance the specter of Chester the Technologist. He's oblivious to her hot and shriveling stare, putting a final dab on a psycho-hate rant about "that pontificating pile of manure Pope Paul."

Before Chester can find a suitable rant substitute for the Pope, the Dracos-like phenomenon hacks him off in mid sentence, shouting at him loudly enough to be heard over a gust of "Reelin' In The Years" exploding like Steely Dan from the club's speakers:

"AND DON'T FORGET SOUPY SALES OR CARDINAL RICHELIEU!"

Chester blubbers in amazement, caught unawares, reeling with the implications. "*Richelieu?* I thought he was dead."

"Immortality medicines, my friend," she says. "All the top Catholics and Jews since the twelfth century are still alive."

Chester cannot speak.

"And there's *more*," she adds with a conspiratorial wink.

"Are you a Technologist?" Chester asks, recovering enough to become suspicious.

"No. But I'm not a fool either," she says.

"But who is Soupy?" he asks, his eyes widening again.

"Soupy Sales. Don't you know? He's an old stand-up comedian, now the Jew-in-charge of comic distraction. All late-night talk show hosts work for *him*," she says and sips at her drink, finally turning to stare at Manny with a look of mock reproach. "Where's Becky?" she asks.

"Don't know." He struggles to recover and show bravado. "I figured maybe you turned her into a Bimbo Dog."

Laney glares at him for a moment, but quickly softens. "Be careful, Garden-of-Eden," she says, "or I'll turn *you* into dog food." She smiles and says, "Now you must come with me, sir. We have business."

She attempts to entice Manny with a beckoning forefinger. When that fails, she simply yanks him off the stool by his arm and grabs his hand. Resistless and mystified, Manny plays along, sliding down the bar as Laney pulls him towards the rear of the establishment, the manic froth of Chester fading to distance.

They turn a corner and down a few steps to the dance floor. Moments later, Manny finds himself lost in a strobe-lit fog of cigarette smoke. Even worse, his love-hate partner, Laney Dracos, is unexpectedly cut off from him, erased from sight by a wedge of the bladder-bursting mob headed for the rest room.

He stands on the Scandals dance floor, feeling stupid. He glances around for Laney, his hand already lonely. The music jolts into "Rock Lobster." The B-52 lead singer grates out with *It wasn't a rock* just as Manny is jostled once more and shoved ten seconds later into a haze of heads and arms.

Rocccckkkk, the singer says.

Manny continues to glance around, aimless till Laney reappears in the distance.

Rocccckkkk.

She's no bigger than his thumbnail.

Rock lobster! Downnnn, downnnnn . . .

From where she sits, Laney sees him standing there staring at her. She can't figure him. Is he in lust or just stupid? She waits impatiently at a small table along the wall, towards the rear of Scandals, and across from a half dozen or so man-sugar dreamers—the twentysomething kind, as Laney's favorite author, Erica Jong, might say, *who yearn for a big prick spouting sperm, a six figure Hill salary, and an oh-so-petite five bedroom in Annapolis complete with a maid on weekends.*

They aren't her type, of course.

There goes a narwhal! Oooo wah! Oooo wah!

Manny approaches Laney. Drawing closer, he watches his antagonist beaming, fluttering hands and swapping pleasantries with the man-sugar dreamers—as if she were the most affable of Capitol Hill hostesses.

Must be drunk, he says to himself.

He stands above her within moments, threatening like an embodiment of machoman god—and he can't help himself. "A few drinks and no more superbitch?" he asks.

She breaks off the gaiety and looks up, staring at him as if he were a curious freak. "It's just ice-water, sir. I'm faking it."

"Okaaaay . . . and what else are you faking, Laney?"

"You must be gay," she says.

"*What?*"

"Even hateful men act sweet just long enough to sleaze my pants off."

"Okay, so I'll sweeten up." Manny dips a finger in his drink, lifts it out, pretends to brush his teeth with it, then gives Laney a big phony smile. "How's that?"

"Look, just please sit down," Laney says, beginning to look bored. "You won't get revenge on me by acting like a jerk, not in front of all these people."

Manny pauses. He stares down into her eyes, feels the soul suck. "Becky told you to meet her?" he asks, his face waxing stoic as he pulls out a chair.

"Yes, but her failure to show bothers me." Laney sips as she watches Manny take a seat.

"Why?"

"The Beast summoned her to the Presence Chamber early this morning."

"The what?"

"*Presence Chamber* . . . it's from *The Overcoat*. A short story by Gogol. You ever read Gogol?"

"No, but I saw Becky around four. She appeared traumatized."

At once, the serenely cocky face of Laney Dracos pinches to worry. "I've been out, most of the day . . . up on the Hill," she says, failing to mask a new edge to her voice. "Becky's feud with Hunsecker goes back awhile. Even Madison has reason to hate her."

"Okay, so why am I here?" Manny asks, struggling to sound indifferent.

"Becky and I want to recruit you."

"Recruit me to—? "

"Be a partisan. A resistance fighter in the American Watch underground," Laney says matter-of-factly.

"Really?" Manny tries to act surprised. "And why should I cooperate?"

"Why shouldn't you?"

"Maybe because you piss me off?"

"A man who holds grudges will fit in nicely at OWC."

"I'm not a grudge holder . . . or a fool."

"Bravo! You're one of the smart guys then," she says, toasting him.

"But why me?" he asks, staring at her intently.

"Because we've realized your potential, and besides, we're holding our annual membership drive," Laney says and winks.

"How do you know I won't betray you?"

Laney slides back into her chair. She sips at her drink and carefully watches Manny's face. "Relax," she says, "before I give you an answer, I have lots of theories I need to discuss."

"What's that got—"

"I compose them on my back steps at night. Moon-inspired theories, sir."

"Uh—"

"And what kind, you ask? Oh, let's see, like the *Theory of Sneaky Shit Ascendance*, also known as the *Grand Unified Sneaky Shit Theory*, also known as the *Shit Rises to the Top Theory*, corollary to the *New-Boss-Same-as-Old-Boss Theory* . . . got it?"

"Sure, I hear what you're saying, but—"

"But nothing . . . You mean to tell me that in your broad travels from Kenosha to D.C. you haven't figured out that sneaky shits rule the universe?"

"No."

"*Social Darwinism* . . . think about it."

"I'm thinking."

"All you need is one sociopathic shithead on top. Give this thing the ruthlessness and hunger of a snake, and if certain employee scales don't match, it sheds and sheds till only the favorite scales remain. Get it now? Simple . . . Yes?"

"I get it."

"Now you *are* a remarkable genius," she says and toasts him again. "And that's just one reason why you won't fit in at OWC."

"But I'm from Kenosha. I've been counting on fitting in, Laney."

"But you *won't*," she says, her eyes challenging him.

"Then sucking up to Hunsecker was for nothing?"

"Never mind that. I happen to know you're not an asshole, or an ass kisser." She watches him closely, feels certain she can reel him in. *The poor stupefied boy. He's struggling just to stay solid!*

"Remember all those gagging little yummies pouring out of Hunsecker's mouth, like protected activity, Pickering, motive, and *nexus*, and blah blah? That's all OWC policy crap based on years of intentionally misinterpreting the law. Madison and the Beast use law to *gut* the law . . . it's just part of the agenda."

"And what's *your* agenda, Laney?"

She places her hand gently on his arm, focuses her eyes on his, and says, "You fight for something that matters and it gets you labeled, lied about, scoffed at, yes?" Manny nods. "It's all so cornball, only you can't help it, and neither can I. We're like the whistleblowers . . . mutants, freaks of nature."

"Okay, that makes sense," says Manny, his voice soothing to neutral. "But I have no intention of rebelling against OWC. I know Keat—"

"You know *nothing*," Laney says. Her voice lowers and her face darkens. Her hand squeezes his arm as her body moves closer, till her mouth is only inches from his face. "*Listen to me, Mr. Eden. At least twice a month, the glorious Counsel Madison makes special little excursions over to the agencies. Once there, he lunches with some of his buddies in the White House blue-blood club, then patiently instructs all their managers on how best to humiliate and fire whistleblowers without running afoul of the law. He refers to these education courses as the OWC Outreach Program. He's even had a few hundred brochures printed out.*"

She releases his arm and sits back.

No answer from Manny. Laney grows irritated. "What *is* your outrage factor, sir?"

No answer.

"And I'll bet you haven't even met the Deputy Counsel from hell, Luna Goodpal."

"Huh?"

"That's her name. Her uncle's a corporate high-roller from Orange County, California. She copies whistleblower letters and evidence sent to OWC then wags her cyberpunk butt over to the agency to deliver them. Course, this is after snake brains Madison has tipped them off in advance."

"It's all hard to accept," Manny says, trying to remain skeptical.

"Not at all," Laney says. "Just place it in context. Madison is a failed nominee for Secretary of Treasury, a fuck-the-pedestrians Mayflower conservative who doesn't give a shit about democracy much less the true mission of OWC. He's just the first line of defense in keeping Reagan and his corporate family from suffering loose cannon wounds . . . outraged yet?"

"I'm trying."

"Dry as Arizona!" she shouts at a passing waiter, then back to Manny: "And he's not alone. Everyone joins in—congressmen, Cabinet members, the White House, OMB officials, lobbyists—"

"Is this a conspiracy theory, Mzz Dracos?" Manny asks sarcastically.

"Of course it's a conspiracy!" Laney barks at him as if he were impossibly stupid. "But not *always* one of smoke-filled rooms. It's a human nature recipe. Mix the right ingredients and you get the same result, every time."

"Now, I really don't get it."

"Oh, yes, you do. You're not *that* stupid."

"I am *that* stupid."

"No, you're just holding back to annoy me. You'll probably impale me with your horn then go tattling to the Beast . . . but go ahead. I'm not afraid."

"Because Senator Ormsby will protect you?" Manny blurts.

Just the mention of his name tips Laney off balance for a moment. Her eyes widen. The end result surprises him. Any hint of ego evaporates, her face softening noticeably.

"Did Becky tell you, or someone else?" she asks.

"Becky."

"The Senator was a friend of my father. They were both state legislators at one time in California. My father shot himself about ten years ago . . . Oh, don't be put off by it. Anyway, when the Senator's in a good mood I'm his honorary daughter. I trust him as far as I can, but the poor old nibs has just come under fire in the press."

"For what?"

"His biggest donor was collared for defrauding a bank in Sacramento."

"So he's a crook too, huh?"

Laney ignores the remark. "Look," she says, "there's a file of evidence at my home, a few inches thick. It's stuff the American Watch has stolen from OWC and the Beast's office over the past few years. I call it *The Golden Rules*."

"What's in it?" he asks as Laney stares through him, knowing she wants him to ask.

"Sure you can handle it, ace?"

"Gimme a break."

"How about the FEC giving the nod to voting fraud?"

"Uh—"

"Customs agents acting as henchmen for Mexican narco lords?"

"Yeah, *right*."

"FDA officials taking bribes from drug companies, HUD taking bribes from city politicians, Justice Department ignoring evidence of massive fraud at the Pentagon, HHS suppressing proof of corporate hospitals stealing billions from Medicare, and on and on and on . . ."

"Okay, okay."

"You with me?"

"I think so."

"Think harder. Gold makes the rules. We're no better than the Marcos government in the Philippines, even worse, and to top it off, these bribe artists are kicking back sacks of soft money to both parties."

"Trivial stuff," Manny says, shrugging his shoulders.

"Look, ace, the American government is the largest criminal enterprise in the history of the human race . . . is that too radical for you? Just add up the facts. Watch the magic make the Treasury vanish. And it doesn't matter whether you're a Dem or a Republican, k? That shit makes no difference. Ideology has *nada* to do with the politics of power." No answer from Manny, while Laney, desiring a more powerful reaction, decides to switch tact. "Oh, and by the way, word in the office has it that you're *fucking* Keat Linderhart."

Manny feels slapped. He begins to crackle and burn off the screen like an old newsreel. "THAT'S . . . THAT'S SO MUCH—"

"Relax, relax. A Bimbo Dog started it."

"Which one?"

"It doesn't matter. As a member of the American Watch you'll become a grateful part of our grandiose and humane scheme. You'll be able to live with yourself . . . are you listening?"

"Uh . . . yeah, sure," Manny says, still trying to recover.

Laney's voice grows stern. "We're gonna blow the trumpets and bring the walls down on those White House bastards." She leans forward and places her hand on Manny's arm again, gripping it more firmly. She knows she must bring maximum presence to bear. Manny Eden has too much potential to remain outside her control, and besides, he already knows *too much*. "So what will it be, Mr. Eden?" she asks.

"Uhh—"

"*Uhhhhhhh?*"

Manny looks down, away from Laney's eyes, and says, "I can't think, not just now. I need time."

"*Look* at me," Laney says.

He obeys.

"Didn't Jefferson himself believe in the potential of any government to go bad?"

"You just don't understand where I came from. You don't understand the pit of Kenosha."

"Hell with Kenosha! Inaction is worse."

"Yeah, well—"

"Wait too long and you'll go down on all fours."

"I won't damage my career, Elaine."

"What career? Your *fuck-the-nation* career?"

No answer.

"I'm asking you to not be a hypocrite. Is that so bad?" For a few moments, Laney's face looks pitiful.

Manny gets woozy. He realizes he's being manipulated by a master, but what can he do about it?

"Personalities are fragile creations, Mr. Eden. OWC will force you to become an asshole if you don't *act now*."

"Laney, I will never betray you," Manny says. "I don't like all this sneaky Watch stuff. I'm all for things being out in the open. Still, I will never betray you. I *swear it*." He molds a nonsickening yet beatific love expression on his face—and as if that isn't dumb enough, he tries to hold her hand.

Big mistake.

Laney notes Manny succumbing to a form of mental dissolution. Not only does it visibly retard him, but plants a scenario in her mind she hadn't prepared for. Confused and stressed, she submits to a bout of Gertrude. She avoids his stare.

"My happy pills are wearing off, Mr. Garden-of-Eden," she says. "And Gertrude is showing her claws. We'll have to finish this conversation later."

Manny releases her hand. "No, Elaine, I'm sorry."

She doesn't reply, only scoots her chair out and stands, looking as if ready to either bawl or beg for mercy. He can only gawk up at her in an uncomfortable and stupid way.

Seeing his unease, she gives him a little smile, then takes a step and fills his eyes with a blouse of white cotton. Her bosom presses against him. She clasps his head in both her hands and kisses his forehead.

A rapid evolution follows.

Laney Dracos turns from him and vanishes among the skittish dreamers of Scandals.

Manny watches her go.

"I'll Stop The World and Melt With You" plays in the background.

Manny discovers he is paralyzed.

CHAPTER 13

Deputy From Luna Hell — Cosmic Epiphanies — Death of a Thousand Bites

IN ACHIEVING HIS VERY FIRST PHILOSOPHICAL DRUNK an hour after Laney Dracos left Scandals, Manny mulled over the question of *Big-Bang-God-Soul-Life-Love-Choice-Freedom-Justice-Utopia-Reality* within a state of liquor-numbed nihilism—one which peremptorily inhaled all cosmic dilemma before flicking away the leftover imponderables like so many hotboxed cigarettes. As a result, he had reached a perfect solution before passing out in the subway train at midnight:

Fuck it all.

Too much booze, too little sleep. That's why every sound in the office now drives a cold nail into his brain. As his senses wade into static, he stares out a sliver of office window, attempting to comprehend the meaning of "day." Nearby bouts of OWC shop talk assault him, exaggerated and frenzied out of all proportion. He watches a small bar of sun fall near his toes, sips his coffee and imagines a race of beings devoid of flesh and bureaucracy, beings of pure light like tiny suns roving the galaxies, beyond Biblical prophesy and humanist dreams, beyond anything conceivable. Then he realizes, with a jolt of adrenaline born of fear, that an evolution of humanity to a state of ultimate light and intellect will result only in mass extinction.

Let's start over.

The intellect in question (*Photonsapien*), satiated with all-knowledge, minus needs and emotions, will inevitably attain a condition of perfect ennui. In other words, it will BORE ITSELF TO DEATH. How can it not?

We're doomed regardless.

He imagines countless numbers of little lights blinking out somewhere beyond Andromeda, the memories of all humanity lost.

He recalls that sci-fi book of E-Man's, the one about the strange human being with the power to create utopia.

OUT OF THE SILENT PLANET?

No, not that one.

Anyway—in lieu of pure ennui—he knows he can do a better job than the sci-fi character. To prove it to himself, he imagines scalding the earth free of poverty, disease, war, crime, government, office parks and strip malls. He replaces all tacky business zones with lakes, hills, and trees, and the asshole capital of the world, Washington, D.C., with *Ideas* alone—no more marble shacks for puppetcrats and politicians to hide in.

Who can understand his disappointment?

Laney Dracos?

He takes another sip of coffee with shaking hand, and within moments, a transmogrifying radiation begins to leak from his conscious mind. Events, places far away, even solitary objects, gain in momentum. A circle of voices claps like distant audience about 8:30 A.M. They shout in chorus, "WHERE IS THE NEXUS?" before groaning away to soft thumps, like a sound of bad plumbing.

Manny understands, and with a sense of epiphany, that he is rarely the same from one moment to the next, having existed not as one, but countless selves. He is *The Becoming Self, The Vacillating Self, The Almost Republican Hypocritical Self, The Instrument of Pickering Disruption Self.* He lives at the center of humankind's most unfathomable creations, *Time* and *Space*, left with no choice but to wish for a little hair of the dog—perhaps a Bloody Mary or a Watermelon Shooter.

Whatever it takes to cure this hangover.

That morning, he'd noticed Becky Bergstein's cell sprayed clean. Her old desk devoid of all sundry papers, moisture rings and ash fingers, even King Ludwig's jewel dethroned from the partition heights.

What could she have done?

Mulling at the periphery of possibility jams the dirt of Ed's Plant Emporium under his fingernails, and as a result, his arms lift and spread, bend back as far as he can bend them, his face turning up to the ceiling till he begins to lift, ever so slightly. He wants to rise, higher and higher, to the Chesapeake moon, the rainbow world where the American sword goddesses hold sway—a magical place, like Valhalla or Olympus.

They will understand him. They will set things right.

Before he can meet with them though, THE BOGIE comes into being.

It bawls out with a sexless voice from a deep hole on the other side of the building:

"THAT IS NOT PROTECTED!"

Following this pronouncement, a crush of shrieky and garbled ejaculations. Next, all objects of OWC begin to thaw and converge towards a common point on an invisible horizon. As they respond to these blows of psychic heat, the office objects bow and equivocate with mirage-like effect into things more compromised. Wooden desks sharpen to dull nose. Glass paperweights blister and pop. Desk calculators knead off keys to wax smooth as stream stone. Richard Nixon effigies shatter mid-air into puzzle bits before spitting through the lobby like pan-fried mercury—the totality of phenomena arguing for a speck of black hole, an asthmatic cosmic nostril winking into existence somewhere to the northeast of Manny, in the direction of Counsel Madison's office.

Can he remain a bystander while the universe collapses?

He pretends to aim for the copy machine, waving a piece of hastily scrawled paper through the lobby, but his reconnoiter is checked by two men who approach from his right. Both in standard dark suit. One lugging a briefcase of black leather.

Predators or prey?

The one with the briefcase is a fat and nervous Washingtonian in his upper thirties, eyes of doom poking out from a once-chummy face. His companion, several inches taller and nearing sixty, appears severely obligated to notions of ethics and self-esteem. He remains a Virginia culture holdout, a Colonel Blue Blood from the Blue Ridge: face of cliff, hair of pewter waxed stiff on the rims and thinning at the crest, mustache of walrus branching to handlebar below sad-and-grave-with-duty eyes—the classic look of a fearful yet morally conscious hybrid.

They pass Manny Eden in silence, penetrate the lobby, and make straight for a rendezvous in the Presence Chamber of Hunsecker. The little fat man, most likely the Colonel's attorney, whispers last second warnings in his client's ear before they both vanish from sight.

Meanwhile, still on the verge, Manny leans to his left, drawn like matter to obey. Glancing in the direction of attraction, he sees her coming from way down the hall.

I cannot deny this strange truth.

Her bludgeoning face and the oncoming repercussions of "no nonsense" mental deformity he recognizes from a collage of imaginary snapshots he'd put together since just last night. Though stupefied, he tries to use his eyes, compromised as he is by an onset of career-death anxiety. He cannot stare directly at the Luna Goodpal chimera, like he would a non-supervisory OWC employee. All he can do is back off as she erupts from the horizon of cosmic nostril, but even from a distance of several feet he is singed by the hot penumbra of her edges—the radiation evacuating from her to resolve the air into licking tongues—and Manny knows it's his fear, and the fear in others, that's to blame.

Ignoring him, Luna pumps through the surrounding space, and as reality on her rim buckles, the force of this distortion persuades all things animate and inanimate to defer to her deliberate moodiness and sense of self-importance, to bow like wind-sucked weeds as she passes.

My imagination scares me.

Jolted into fight-or-flight animation, Manny chooses the latter and somehow retains an appearance of dignity. He backpedals into the Investigatory Division, searches for human support, finds none, and retires to the coffee room, hoping to avoid more spin-off from her wake.

But escape is impossible. Luna roars through the coffee room.

Manny fumbles with a napkin and a spoon, wiping off scuzz between glances while she makes an arc that will terminate inevitably within the bowels of Presence Chamber; and in his head, she'll make that fateful arc again and again, because she's just too alien invasion, too Third Millennium, too radical killer-chic to comprehend all at once—though certain parts will always return to him and glow: her black, ego-heavy eyes; the bristles of cactus-red hair; a rangy and spa-muscled torso twisting like a turret atop a pair of black-silk legs tapering down to spikes. Her body odor like that of a hot and sweaty boy dipped in cheap perfume. And her face? Youthful though whale-ish.

An Orange County punk with scars of rainbow glitz on the lids, a dab of violet on the cheeks, lips the color of hair, and nostrils dilating (as did Hunsecker's on special occasions) with the rarefied air of *Deus Vault*.

Before she vanishes through the doorway, Manny's eyes jerk with the image of Luna. He glimpses long and glowing trails like dissipating streams of firework—the kind he sees whenever twitching his eyes while focused on a blinding light, the source slashing images of claw mark on his retina.

God, it's painful!

Once the door to Hunsecker's office slams shut, he can't stop himself. He eases his way past the brink of narthex and soon discovers, much to his surprise, that the air in this space darkens and brims with sorrowful moans. He sees acolyte Deejah Thoris slumped over her desk, her face pushed nose flat on the desktop, tears gushing down her cheeks and guttering onto a memo pad. The portrait of Ms. Plato-Prophet is inexplicably turned, face to the wall.

Manny attempts a show of lukewarm sympathy, but two voices from the Presence Chamber nibble at his attention: judicial arcanities of the Triumphant Beast, his tone subdued with *gravitas*, blending with a deep, rustic voice he assumes to be that of Colonel Blue Blood.

Harsh questions and stumbling answers follow, and just as Manny strains to winnow something comprehensible from the dialogue, a noise increases in volume within the Chamber. It suffocates the words with a membranous tonnage from which nothing intelligible can emerge.

Game over.

Manny moves closer to the door out of necessity, hoping history is being made. As he leans to within inches he is startled by an outburst of humble and shipwrecked voice—perhaps the Colonel's? He'll never know. On the brink of revelation, an event of volatile nature takes place. Particles are released during the whistleblower fission process. A light of toxic purple sprays out through the door crack like air shrieking into vacuum. Manny is buffeted by the rage of it, his skin chaffed raw.

What in hell?

The Colonel, encumbered by the weight of near hysteria, shouts:

"MOUTHFULS ARE BEING TORN FROM THE REPUBLIC!"

A second voice, Luna's, screams in retaliation:
"TRIVIAL, UNSUBSTANTIATED, AND NOT PROTECTED!"
A pause, the Colonel:
"WILL YOU ACCEPT WHAT I AM TELLLING YOU?"
Luna's voice again, pitched to a state of maniacal frustration:
"NOT PROTECTED! NOT PROTECTED!"

Following an interminable series of shrieking exchanges, accusations and denials, a final gasp is heard. The purple nimbus within the Chamber pales to the water of daylight.

Outraged, Manny Eden chases himself out the door, through the coffee room, and into the lavatory as soon as the first metallic click indicates the portal is about to swing open. He counts the pale blue and white tiles on the wall till the first footsteps are heard. When they are loud enough he exits and launches himself straight into the face of the little fat man.

Manny notes how frazzled he appears. His flesh is wet and his tie and face bleached. His lip quivers with pout, his suit scuffed to a floor mat.

"Were you his attorney?" Manny asks.

"Y-yes," he replies, weaving unsteadily on tiny feet.

"Where is your client now?"

"Here," he answers in a sad and guilty way. He raises the black leather briefcase and cradles it. With a shaking right hand he releases the snaps and slowly lifts the top.

Manny looks inside and sees the honorable Virginian. He is about eight inches long and disfigured beyond recognition. He has become only a narrow and flimsy thread of human being, a body and spirit gnawed to triviality by the most incorrigible incisors he has ever faced.

"The Death of a Thousand Bites," the attorney says.

Manny nods. He understands.

Now I know what I must do.

CHAPTER 14

Un Peu du Chose

Hello?
Is this Keat Linderhart?
Yes. Who is this?
You don't know me.
Do I want to?
No.
Why are you whispering?
A disguise is necessary. I'm afraid.
What do you want of me?
I work at the Counsel office.
Oh.
So, how goes it with you . . . over there?
Approaching the verge.
I know of your suffering.
You?
Yes.
But do you understand it?
We share a bond. I know that sounds silly.
It sounds absurd.
I've fallen in love with your morals, with your need for a cause.
I am not a crusader.
You should be honored with a statue at least.
It was only a simple decision.
But you made it with courage.
I need an army of you.
I'll do all I can.
Why are you calling me then?

I'm calling to warn you.
Is this Mr. Eden?
This is not Mr. Eden.
The secretary at OWC said a Mr. Eden was investigating my case.
Mr. Eden doesn't care . . . and there is no investigation.
What do you mean?
Nothing will be done.
Ah! The Counsel is . . . at least—
They are no different.
Hard to believe.
Not when you're here.
It's hopeless then. I am undone.
Yes.
What did I do to Commissioner Neri in his office?
What?
Tell me.
You took snapshots—
How do you know that if you're not Mr. Eden?
Everyone knows. It's common knowledge, here.
Not confidential?
No.
The OWC address, what is it?
It's, uh . . . on Vermont. I don't remember the exact address.
I'm coming down there, now.
No, don't.
I'm on the way.
It will hurt both of us.
Whoever you are, Neri put you up to this. He is a liar, like you!
No, please. Your experience has made you cynical.
A lack of it has made you ignorant.
Don't be paranoid. Get an attorney, that's all. You must—
The closer we are pushed to the verge, the more false we become.
An attorney . . . please, Keat!
I'm going to the Counsel . . . I've already talked with Ms. Goodpal.
What?
And I'm bringing a whole drawer of proof.

It will be used to destroy you.
Now you threaten me?
No, wait—
Marauder! Oh, marauder!

CHAPTER 15

Un Coup d'Eclat

I've called you in my office today, Manny . . . for a *special* reason.
What's that, Babs?
I want you to guess.
I don't think so.
Why?
I'm at a loss.
Someone told me you already know.
I don't.
You must be faking it . . . you *must* be.
Faking what?
You really *don't*?
What?
You don't know?
No.
I'll give you a hint.
Okay, but please hurry. I'm busy.
I've suddenly become *very important* in your life.
Uhhhh—
I'm your new boss, Manny.
(no answer)
B.O.S.S.
(no answer)
Manny? Why aren't you answering?
(no answer)
Mannnnny . . . Don't be an *evaderrrrr*.
I don't understand the joke, Babs.
I'm the new Deputy Director of the Investigation Division, Manny.

Didn't know we needed one.
Surprised?
Sure . . . more than surprised. I'm stunned.
The job came open, and I applied.
I didn't see a job announcement. Did they post—
Anyway, Mr. Hunsecker has asked me to brief you.
About what?
You'll be going through me from now on.
For *everything?*
Yes, everything . . . he still has his open door policy, like always. You can still communicate something private, or personal, or privileged . . . but please let me know *first*, just so I can tell him you're coming.
Of course.
But now, you and I have things to discuss.
Things?
Just a few questions, Manny, maybe a few observations. Consider our session today a kind of progress review . . . we'll expand our knowledge bases.
Ditto, Babs.
Well, there's something I have to get off my chest first, Manny.
Okay, Babs.
I just want to make sure you show me the same respect you do Mr. Hunsecker.
Count on it.
Thank you, Manny. That means a lot coming from *you*.
You're welcome, Babs . . . I think.
Now, Manny, I'm ready for my first question.
Shoot, Babs.
Manny . . . how do you like working at OWC?
Well, um, I've gotten a full dose.
I didn't *hear you*.
I'm full of it, Babs. I'm pregnant with knowledge.
That's silly.
A few months worth.
Are you trying to be *flip?*
No, honest. I'm just not ready to see you as a supervisor.

Well, you better get ready, Manny.
I will.
This is optimum organization.
I don't get it.
In this way, Mr. Hunsecker frees himself up to do more important things . . . Do you have any questions that might clear this situation up for you?
What happened to Becky Bergstein?
What has *that* got to do with anything?
I'm just curious.
She was fired.
What?
Frosting on a disruptive cake that's been a rising a long time.
She—
Shot herself in the foot. Over and over.
She—
Might learn to finally accept responsibility as a result of all this. She was the one Varsana heard ripping a big hole in one of the partitions. Destruction of government property is a dismissible offense . . . my next question, Manny: how's *your* attitude these days?
I don't know . . . what is it?
Don't get defensive.
I'm at a loss, Babs.
You don't seem to understand what OWC is trying to prevent, Manny.
But I do.
Then why the bumming face? Everyone notices it. A personal *trauma?*
What? . . . no, no trauma. That's ridiculous.
Don't get defensive.
No *trauma*, Babs.
Are you a victim of stress?
Worry . . . maybe.
But worry *causes* stress, Manny. I know some worry-stopping mental techniques you can try. When you feel yourself start to worry, yell *stop!* The mind can't concentrate on two big things at once. That *stop!*

just pushes everything else out, like a bully pushing a skinny little kid out of line.

I've *always* wanted to be a bully.

Also, wear a rubber band around your wrist. If you feel worry coming on, just snap yourself. It conditions your subconscious mind in a few days. You'll get productive again.

I'll *snap myself* into productivity.

But the bigger question still remains, Manny. Why worry? And the answer is don't, just *don't*.

And—

Stress will take care of itself. You'll be able to fall madly in love with your job again.

Doesn't it depend on expectations, Babs?

Then expect productivity, Manny. Start your day by dishing yourself out to positive people. Talk about *good* things. Have *high* expectations. But tell me, Manny . . .

Yes?

Do you really feel good about yourself?

I feel like a burn victim.

Um, okay . . . in any case, I do want to share something with you that others in this office have noticed, and that I think will help you. It has something to do with *gamesmanship*. Are you familiar with the concept?

Not *that one*.

Well, I'd like to sum it up for you.

Okay.

You come into a new office. You find out how the game is played, and you play it. If you refuse to play, it's not because you're more ethical, or smarter, it's simply because, maybe you're a little dull.

I am.

That's what it appears, Manny . . . but I don't believe it. However, I've had funny reports.

If they're funny, why worry about it?

But you've been spinning around in your office, mumbling comedy routines? Doing imitations of cartoon characters reciting the First Amendment?

It's a relaxer, Babs.

It's also *bad* for morale, Manny.
So—
Some people in the office feel it mocks the Counsel.
I'll pretend something else. *Okay*, Babs?
Are you trying to be *flip*, Manny?
No, just relieved.
Do you want me to make a report on this dialogue to Mr. Hunsecker?
We're *friends*, Babs.
But do you *respect* me, Manny?
Oh, absolutely, 120 percent, Babs.
I want your respect, Manny.
You have it, Babs.
Thank you . . . now one last question and we can call it a day.
Shoot.
Why did you call the Sentencing Commission?
Uh . . . what?
Someone on the USSC staff called Counsel Madison and told him.
It wasn't me.
He said that someone from *this office* called a certain Keat Linderhart and inappropriately discussed her case. You do have that case?
I didn't call her.
The Commission is in an uproar. Linderhart went ballistic.
Did the caller say he was me?
Yes.
Well, it wasn't me, Babs.
Alright. I'll bet she made it up. They do things like that.
Or maybe someone tried to scare her?
Whatever, she's on the way. The Commissioner's office let us know.
When?
We're not sure of land fall. Tomorrow perhaps. But if you hear anything, let me know immediately. She's a *real* basket case.
Aren't they all?
Just be professional. No more bumming or comedy stuff, okey dokey?
Okey dokey.
And you can come in and talk with me anytime you want, about anything—case files, regulations, personal gripes, whatever. *Okayyyyy?*

Okay.
Is there anything else you want to say? Any stumps I didn't blow?
Ha, that's funny.
Okay, Manny. Thanks for coming.
Thank you, Babs.
Oh, Manny?
Yes?
If you don't stand for something, you'll fall for anything.

CHAPTER 16

Manny Advises Dictator — Manny Chokes Snake — Manny Becomes President — The Origin of Morals and Idols

PRETEND YOU ARE A SUPERHERO from Marvel Comics, like Doc Strange, or the Human Torch, or perhaps an omnipotent alien like the kind Michael Renny played in *The Day the Earth Stood Still*— all flash-bang righteousness and a voice of summer thunder echoing off the planets and announcing before a pants-wetting president and both Houses of Congress:
THE BULLSHIT ENDS HERE!
Only you can't keep it up.
The dream requires too much elaboration—too many areas of legal gray and too many changes of clothing. So what's next? You simply tire, yes, and you remain more confused than ever.
Once more, you are Manny Eden. Too bad, eh? But no time to grieve. You must find a way to cope. Your revived anxiety over Keat Linderhart has forced you to throw on your scarf and trench coat and slip out of OWC. No one has seen you go, and no one really cares. But that doesn't matter. You need to locate a place where you can easily suspend all animation for a few hours, and Lafayette Park on Pennsylvania Avenue, across from the White House, is the logical choice. Luckily, the sun is out, and the morning blue and intense, only a thin veil of sky left to protect you from the endless and deadly vacuum of space—perfect conditions.
You find a bench and sit down, and without hesitation, observe the park's lost-cause-homeless as they posture and defend their spaces. Like you, the sun, and the Earth, they hurtle unnoticed towards the Andromeda galaxy. And though you eventually grow comfortable with

cosmic visions and Godot-like waiting, you remain open to the possibility of speed.

Finally, after pondering the issue of Kenosha vs. Keat Linderhart for at least half an hour, and reaching no solution, you begin to rise and rev. Just then, an unforeseen thing happens: a new dictator pomps his way up Pennsylvania Avenue and distracts you from the brink of velocity.

You watch in a state of stupor, grateful for the distraction. You count coup as his cobra of black limos perform the ritual u-turn in front of the White House, and you recognize him soon enough: crossed scimitars on black flag, his profile in the morning paper, a sense of unholy and lonesome *gravitas*. The Dictator is returning to the sacred grounds of his embassy, no doubt to be wombed by his staff into an idol of Wagnerian proportion. Overawed, you decide to wave, only you're not sure where. A black gasoline fortress, one of many, effectively cocoons him.

You recall a story about this boss-zilla in yesterday's Style section of the *Washington Post*. He'd come to this American utopia from somewhere between New Guinea and Malaysia, come seeking the White Oz of the Enlightenment in order to beg his portion of freedom's war chest. After all, Communists are everywhere, and many dollars are needed to snuff them out.

Just ask The Gipper.

While you look on, you dream the convoy coming to a halt along the curb. From one of the center cars a dark window hums down. A hand of ivory-red skin and long black fingernails thrusts forth, beckoning you to come closer.

In a daze, you walk over to the limo. A giant, turbaned chauffeur, looking like an *Arabian Nights* genie, appears and opens the door for you. It swings wide. A puff of purple smoke drafts out, smelling strongly of heroin and garlic. You hold your breath and slide into a room of gold-colored leather. The Dictator greets you. He introduces himself to you as Mr. Ultima O'Toole. He says his father was Irish, and his mother a Sikh, but you don't believe him. Why? Because he looks like a Martian. His skin is red and his eyes are three times bigger than any eyes you've ever seen, dark and glistening as scarab beetles and mirroring the spires of the old Corcoran. The Dictator is dressed in white pajamas with gold trim, and his fingers are heavy with rubies big as thumbs. His vampire-insect face reminds you in a disturbing way of President Reagan's budget chief, Dave Stockman, and his voice of sacred monument begs your understanding.

At his head nod, the convoy jolts forward and begins to circle the White House. He offers you a scotch from the limo bar, and a few gold coins stamped with his face. He says he wants an opinion from the American "man of the street" and proceeds to tell you of his plight.

Always in the crosshairs when strolling the grounds of his own country, the Dictator holds court on a golden Cris Craft yacht that plows the length of a black river known as *The Worm's Soul*. From his captain's chair the great godhead clumsily navigates its boils and bends, his rum-woozy eyes unfocused on the anorexic slab of nation that stretches on to either side of him, asleep in the heat of his bones. Those fortunate few of his Young Dawn Party, including his murderous Sun Guard, refer to him either as *The Primal Cosmic Toad* or *The Irrepressible Wonder*, depending on the season. Shit-listed mountain tribes and intellectuals know him as *The Genocidal Djin*—and they defy him continuously. Rumors chase him like starving dogs. UPI and Amnesty International won't stop lying about him. Through their eyes, you see his secret police. Proudly they pose beside their torture tables cluttered with an assortment of Gestapo dental drills, bone crackers, testicle needles, thumb screws, and meat hooks.

Moments later, you stand on the park-like grounds of a Taj Mahal palace as Mr. O'Toole—decked out like a rhinestoned Elvis—personally impales an "unfaithful" wife on the phallic limb of a solid gold tree. He tells you it's an olive tree, a present from the Italian ambassador.

You don't believe him.

Following the impaling, the two of you retire to his in-home stadium to watch a gladiatorial game wherein naked "political rebels" are forced to duel to the death with whips and axes. As you vomit and cough at the sight of the carnage, cobra-tattooed concubines, wearing three-foot-high pyramids of jaguar skull on their heads, slip into view from behind a red curtain. With handfuls of bee honey, they attend to his nibs and stroke his meat to bursting. After climax, and a trip to the palace bar for a round of parasol martinis, you lean over to the Dictator and tell him, "As President Reagan always says, Mr. O'Toole, *Do as little bad as possible, and as much good as you can.*"

The Dictator looks pleased. You've relieved him from having to deny rumors or invent moral justifications. He drops a few more gold coins in your hand and you decide to leave him with a last bit of very good advice:

"All you need do, sir, is to play by the Washington rules. Contract with a damn good lobbying firm, use a corporate front to give a million or so in soft money donations to both major parties, and don't forget to secure a team of bulldog attorneys to threaten any snoops or critics with lawsuit. All else will take care of itself."

The Dictator thanks you profusely. He calls you an "exceptional American" then signals the convoy to pull over in front of Lafayette Park.

You get out of the car and the dark window hums down. You shake his ruby-heavy hand one last time and wave good-bye. The convoy pulls away and snakes off to 17th street. As you watch it vanish, you wonder if anyone will ever realize your sensible contribution to world peace.

* * *

ONCE THE DICTATOR TURNS THE CORNER, the earth warms, and the bizarre theater of Lafayette Park comes to life. The lost-cause-homeless who have besieged the White House for the past century resume their watch from behind pasteboard shields of mass accusation. From Jackson Square to Lafayette himself, the howls of doom and conspiracy echo once more. Collaged photos of destruction, hundreds on a score of boards, line Pennsylvania Avenue and char the air with aborted nuke babies and Nagasaki death-shadows. In contrast, a few mushrooms north of the Von Stevben statue, a migrant flock of hippies groom and stretch and boil their veggie pastas. Dozens of tourist clones from Japan reel off shots of the megacephalic trombone preacher, and on the grassy lawn to the east, Suzie "Alarm Siren" McCullough and her crew from Channel 8 orchestrate a White House tableau just as a fifth grade class from Pigsknuckle, U.S., all monument-choked and agog, winds like a hobbit train between the tulip patches. Meanwhile, nearby, the schizo ex-lover of Frank Sinatra, itchy and irritable with cigarette burns, shrieks obscenities at an English tourist for gawking at the mold scab on last week's cheeseburger.

Elsewhere, in a quieter pocket of Lafayette, a half dozen or so alcoholics snooze themselves into vindication. It is rebirth they seek, their tongues babbling with a softer childhood. The bronze statue shadowing them you recognize as one of your new heroes: the renown Rochambeau, heroic spine of *in utero* America.

He strikes a pose, and in doing so, appears to inspire great deeds. You are most impressed. His overcoat is frocked and stiff as a warped plank, tyrant-hacking saber poised in scabbard, bits of iron gobbet sunken in the ground beneath jackboots (and you know that if not for this French admiral planning the defeat of General Cornwallis at Yorktown, all about you might not exist). Arm outstretched, he points to the horizon, and though you cannot see clearly from your vantage point, you recall that upon the lip of ledge beneath him, a ferocity of American goddess lunges forward, a wind-slapped flag gripped in one hand, a boulder-heavy broadsword of restorative wrath in the other. At her feet, a companion eagle lacerates the face of dictatorship into shreds of freedom's light; and together with her eagle, this honorable sword goddess assists the Rochambeau deity in guarding the entrance to Lafayette Park.

You ponder all this.

Feeling a bit envious, you decide that at the end of your sentence in Washington, you too will commission a bronze colossus, one hammered to your likeness and bolted to a dais, eyes blasted. Perhaps you will even supplant Rochambeau—striking the proper pose, of course. One of your hands will outstretch, fatherly, the other tightly clenching a writhing viper that symbolizes Washington corruption. You'll be flanked by an American goddess on your right, sword and bosom held high, and one eagle *a rebours* on your left, talons outstretched to lacerate the tyrant, the enormous black wing hovering as a protective roof above your head. Like Rochambeau, you too will encourage deeds and promote visions.

But a bigger question remains. Will you impress the tourists?

By eleven a.m., a new rain of them from Montana and Belgium, Hong Kong and Ethiopia, forms beneath the trees and sacred hero-gods of Lafayette Park. You note how they all ignore, and thus insult the savior Rochambeau. Their dismissal of him salts the wound, for already he is both afflicted and dissolved by the legendary walls of perfect White beyond, by the shadows of politician within, and the ponderous, livid, crust-busting power only a tourist can imagine.

You watch the disintegration of Rochambeau begin at the boots and inhale its way up to the head. Like muddy water suctioned from a glass, he empties until only a trace of scalp remains afloat a few inches above the earth, vague as a momentary frown. Then, from across the length and breadth of Lafayette Park, a domino effect occurs. The statues of all American heroes are snuffed. Their corks are pulled to allow their substance to stream loose over the ground like the smoke of extinguished torches. Next, the ancient clouds of oak disperse, the gobbets of Rochambeau iron, the Old World, Nipponese, and Big Sky tourists, the Sinatra-666 paranoids who rim the Grand Concourse of the Republic with their gimcrack spleen—all blotted out, smeared to anonymity, fading before a creation of otherworldly pallor known as

THE WHITE HOUSE.

An attention sponge, rightfully enough, and only now, in the presence of awe, do you comprehend the significance of it. Facing Lafayette Park from across Pennsylvania Avenue, the House projects aspects of both genesis and doomsday, and all species of Washingtonian, without exception, are made to fearfully nudge themselves forward in imagination, spasmodic as Stanley Kubrick movie apes coerced into prodding the eerie, singing surface.

You must admit though, you also harbor this ambition.

Naturally, the core of you still desires to be a Joan-of-Arc/Mother Theresa smoothed over to digestibility with a frosting of Jefferson and JFK. Only now, the posturing side of you, lacking in self-esteem, sprouts unavoidably to an alien sunflower of president, a teratogenesis of American political galaxy. Your face bristles and gleams, and whether stumping, lunching, golfing, pontificating, or pissing, you remain caboosed at all times by your train of choreographers, buff teams, staff aides, attorneys, make-up artists, and spin doctors.

Yes! YOU WANT TO BE PRESIDENT.

Nothing less will do.

And at this moment of truth, you deny the depth of your delusion. Like a child overcompensating for inferiority, you remake yourself into the image America demands. You emblazon yourself beyond the dreams of a lesser Khan or Tsar. You become puppet to a gaggle of word masseuses who idol worship you, who are too naive to assume even the potential of corruption, who believe in the myth and flawlessness of you, who even see in something as innocuous and lifeless as your gourmet leather shoes a symbol of personality deserving nothing less than a loving cuddle and a warm tongue between the toes.

By dawn's early light these word elves of yours will concoct—between sips of cappucino and Merlot—enough speech jargon to carry you skyward on great gusts of *changebuzz, renewalbuzz, new nationbuzz,* enough to aid you in laboring at your country's wreck.

YOU HAVE THE POWER!

As you muse on your newfound presidential prerogatives, three tourists approach you. They've just finished snapping a few rolls of the White House, but ridiculed Rochambeau with a snide giggle. *A pox on them!* Two are obviously twins: pale complexions of Rust Belt, old horn-rim sunshades, chartreuse shorts, and See-Rock-City t-shirts. The third one, though, puzzles you: a boyish child, sex uncertain, mouth of steel braces.

Unknown to these hapless mortals, the aura of PRESIDENT has emboldened you in ways you never believed possible. You feel cocky, bold, powerdrunk with notions of Hail-To-The-Chief. So you wait, stoking yourself till they close within only a few feet. At the right moment, they pass, and you shout at them:

"*Yo, touristas! I AM THE PRESIDENT!*"

At first, they hesitate with reflex, naturally full of gape until able to recover and scamper away, ululating like frightened quail. And no sooner do they achieve a safe distance than the boyish one pivots, in your vision just long enough for you to decipher certain shapes of mouth that form within you a devastating:

Get fucked, asswipe!

Well, you had it coming (and so does everyone else). But what has all this idiocy and mind drivel got to do with the eternal drudge of stars, the demise of Washington, the fleeting fizzle of us?

You are unable to ask for advice, for the majority of Washingtonian Janes and Johns remain fixed and silent as bedrock—no venting of rage, no vomiting of Quality Management Circulars, no vaporous leak of anxiety over the absurdity of their careers. At some point, you realize you've been duped, but unlike them you cannot live with a simple hope of equity and dreams of a mosquito retirement in Florida. In other words:

YOU WILL NEVER BE MANAGEMENT MATERIAL.

The only solution, therefore, is a heroic one. A reckless one. Or at least, one that people will remember.

Of course, this decision of yours pisses off Rochambeau. You've insulted him. "What a ridiculous boob!" he roars out. He lowers his arm to point at the gobbets of iron at his feet, and then he points directly at your groin.

You look down and nod, understanding what he means, grateful also for the male bonding moment.

CHAPTER 17

On Revolution Time — Ceremony of The Watch — Utopia By 2000 — Laney Becomes A Sword Goddess — Manny Becomes "Mr. God"

BY NOON, THE AIR BEFORE MANNY PUCKERS with a shriek of murder-scene flute, and from behind this curtain of pucker wavering in Lafayette Park space, who should step forth but Laney Dracos herself. Following Rochambeau's decree, he'd summoned his model heroine to this shooting location by means of three pay-phone calls to OWC.

As she approaches to overwhelm the background, she appears tainted. More cynical, perhaps?

He isn't sure. Nevertheless, she scares him a little. He even worries that the White House might upstage her, that she might suffer the same dissolution as Rochambeau and the other hero-gods.

Only Laney isn't in the mood for stupid mind games.

She marches right up to him as he sits cross-legged in the grass. She glares down at him, already feeling as if her time is being wasted. Her eyes look red and narrow because she hasn't slept well in days.

He wants so badly for her to smother him, dampen him with her lips, and fill him once more with her theories of evil beneath the rainbow moon.

To Laney though, Manny resembles a gawking lemur: eyes like burnt sausage patties set in a *I'm-so-pitifully-in-love* face. She doesn't know whether to laugh or run, so she just clears her throat and says:

"Okay, ace, so you got me here. Something about *catastrophe*?"

"Yes, oh wise and strong goddess."

Laney looks perplexed. "You a few cans short, Mr. Eden?"

"I greatly appreciate the time you've taken from your busy schedule to stop and give ear to this humble creep show."

"What do you mean?"

"I've only seen you for seconds at a time since Scandals."

"I'm allergic to OWC . . . so what's the five alarm for?"

He motions for her to sit beside him in the grass. She delicately lowers herself and before she can look bored or irritated, he explains the Keat Linderhart debacle, his desperate phone call, and the vanes shifting to storm. Laney, poised and tense, distracts him, his monologue ricocheting inside her like loose cannon shot.

"You look like a goddess on rage," he says.

"Three cups of coffee and a coke tense me to the point of violence."

"Okay but I want to join the Watch. I'm on revolution time, now."

"Thought you weren't into *sneaky* stuff."

"I've changed my mind."

"Too bad."

"Why? The coup been put on hold?"

"No. The Watch is formulating a new plan now, a big one. Really big."

Manny smiles like an idiot. "Look, I need you to do me a favor," he says.

"Favor?"

"You've heard that Keat Linderhart is coming to OWC?"

"Yep. You pissed her off with that phone call, right?"

Manny hesitates, then says, "I had no choice. I wanted to stop her."

"Okay, so what do you expect me to do?"

"Call her. Warn her off . . . can you do it?"

"Why should I?"

"Because it's the right thing to do, and that's what *you do*."

"It won't slow her down."

"Why not?"

"I know her type. She'll become even more ferocious."

Seeing the concern on Manny's face, Laney raises both hands and claps the air in front of his nose, and says, "I'll consider it, Gipper boy . . . but *only* after you buy me lunch."

In response, Manny produces his lemur-love-gawk again. Laney just smiles as if he'd told a joke. She kisses her fingers and places them on Manny's forehead. She actually feels sorry for him. How can the fool possibly know what a selfish, attention-sucking bitch she really is?

Now parched and high on blood pressure, Mr. Garden-of-Eden ushers his own personal wrath goddess to the Excelsior on G street. The place is expensive, D.C. vogue, skimpy on portions, and hopefully far enough way to avoid any OWC apostles who might be lurking.

They choose a sidewalk table, shadowed from Indian summer noon by a large blue umbrella. They order drinks and settle in. Laney begins by speaking nonchalantly of the many Washington Frankensteins she'd love to torch, and shortly after the food arrives, she remarks to Manny, "I don't know how to tell you this, Mr. Eden, but my pickle is perfect."

"Huh?"

"How is your Monte Cristo and Rob Roy?" she asks.

"Fine."

"You think we're safe? I'm *scared*," she says with a little-girl voice and winks at him.

Manny chuckles. "Why should the Bimbo Dogs wander this far?"

"You never know. Basil herds Babs and Pardo out on days like this, and sometimes Boyden . . . but it's Babs he wants in the back seat. The rest are a cover."

Manny watches Laney as she returns to her club sandwich. He stares at her mouth, her jaw, and fingers. All the little parts working. *What a miracle of life!* he says to himself. *You wondrous, eating, digesting creature, you.* Like that sandwich, Manny is both dissolved and absorbed by her nature.

After a long enough pause, he mentions Keat Linderhart again.

Laney says, "Okay, *okay*. I'll phone, then let you know what happens."

"Just be careful," says Manny. "We can't blow this."

"I already know what is sensible, and what is not, Mr. Garden-of-Eden, thank you," Laney says, scowling softly.

"Sorry."

"You follow my orders, boy. I outrank you."

They eat in silence for a few moments. Laney feels a bit guilty for going harsh on him. She begins tapping a teaspoon against the side of her water glass. Her bomb is ready to drop, or so she believes.

"Becky was fired," she blurts out.

"I already know," he says.

"How?"

Manny sees the confusion on Laney's face. In a strange way, it pleases him. "My new boss, Babs Easton told me . . . surprised?"

"No."

"Why?"

"Hunsecker's been grooming his bitch for a year."

Laney plucks a crescent of bread crust from her plate and demurely nibbles. She observes the cafe patrons and passers-by, her eyes flitting from one species of Washington bureaucrat to the next. To her, they are all stereotypes: the eager gopher boys, the grade-climbing blowjobbers, the overcompensating-for-inferiority managers, the bad ass Ms. Jacksons, and so forth.

Washington offers her few surprises.

"You seem too slack about Becky's firing," Manny says, a slight hurt in his voice.

"My crying is over."

"But you did cry for her?"

"Yes. I *cried* for her. Days of mourning . . . *okay?*"

"What will she do?"

"Probably go back to Portland. She hated Washington anyway."

"She worshiped you."

"We were part of the original pack from the Carter days. We couldn't get rich, so we had no choice but to attempt good deeds."

"Have you done any yet?"

"A few, but not enough to make me happy . . . so where have you been all morning, Mr. Eden?"

"Call me, Manny."

"Okay, Manny."

"In Lafayette Park, hanging out, pretending I'm president, and also advising a dictator from Mambia."

"*Mambia?*"

"An imaginary country. I will depose the dictator and put you in charge."

"I don't want to be in charge of anything. I have zero supervisory ambitions . . . and I know you worship that goofy ass Reagan, but now you want to be him?"

"No, just president. I have to become president before the CIA can put you in charge of Mambia."

"Right . . . by the way, how did you get so *horny* for Ronny?"

"I grew into it."

"Reagan's an affable dunce at best, a political sociopath at worst, " says Laney.

This irritates Manny.

"Why don't you plan a Gipper bash and invite the whole DNC?"

Laney frowns. "Whose toadies flushed the law down the OWC toilet?"

"Okay, but Reagan can't eyeball each and every—"

"Shit paddies grow mushrooms, Manny."

"He can't—"

"Oh, and I just saw your precious Gipper at a party in Virginia. Too bad you weren't there to watch the happy doofus perform."

Laney tells him all about it and watches him freeze in near disbelief. He almost reminds her of Boyden, but she pushes that comparison out of her mind. Boyden is a wimpshit. He has no conscience, no compassion, and even less sense—a perfect Reagan Republican. Manny is different though, original, just somewhat deluded.

"Look," he says, his voice low and recovering, "Forget Reagan, I'm on your side, no matter what."

"I suppose . . . if not, you'd just lie, repudiate him for my benefit."

"Thanks."

"Okay, so now you're in the American Watch."

"Just like *that?*"

"You want an induction ceremony?"

"Uh—"

"Okay, fine. Hold out your fists."

Manny obeys. Wasting no time, Laney hums "Thus Spake Zarathustra," the theme from "2001:A Space Odyssey," while slowly dripping water from her glass onto Manny's knuckles and simultaneously dubbing them with her butter knife. "*Mr. Manny Eden, by the power invested in me by the Most High Wizard of the American Watch, you now possess the rank of knight templar of the first order. Protect the weak, serve justice, be true to your nation, and ordo vigilante.*"

"What's that mean?"
"Be forever vigilant . . . or something like that."
"That's kinda cool and funny, but—"
"Right. And now we are *two*."
"What?"
"We're all that's left. There used to be seven of us at OWC, like Seven Against Thebes, or *Seven Samurai*. Ever seen that movie?"
"I thought—"
"Wrong. They're all gone. Fired or quit."
"Shit."
"Becky left me to watch alone. And now I have *you*."
"Yes . . . you do."
"And what about Rochambeau, you ask?"
"I was getting around to that."
"We *are* Rochambeau."
"Huh?"
"You and me."
"So there is no single—"
"He represents all of us, Manny. He points the way, just like in Lafayette Park."
"But who wrote the letters to me?"

Laney smiles. "*Je suis Rochambeau*," she says with her best French accent. She once again kisses her fingertips and places them on his forehead. "*Arise now, Sir Eden. Go forth and battle evil, and do not return till victory is ours.*"

Manny grabs his butter knife and salutes Laney. He lowers it again and grins, a speck of butter on his left eyebrow.

* * *

AFTER LUNCH, WITH PLANS TO MAKE, the two of them wander back down to the walks of Lafayette Park, but Laney grows irritable in the sun, and her face, in Manny's eyes, appears to weaken. She feels herself being emptied, the heat on her skin reminding her of youth, and youth recalling an attitude straining to remain *positive*.

Once they meet the edge of tree shadow, she relaxes somewhat. "Lunch was fair," she says to Manny, turning her face up to the windy branches above her. "You really didn't have to."

"My eyes needed kissing," he says.

She levels her head and stares at him suspiciously. "How so?"

"They want you in them all the time. I've lost all control."

Laney takes his confession lightheartedly—the ultimate rejection. As they stroll she raises her left hand even with his chin and wags it back and forth, *whish-whish* slapping him—a symbolic punishment, as well as a means of defusing the tension. Though difficult, Manny manages a phony laugh. He quickly steers the conversation to the subject of *Utopia By The Year 2000*.

Laney remains skeptical.

"No matter how much new blood you inject, the gold and germs of this city will foul it sooner or later."

"Then you're back where you started," Manny says.

"Precisely. We must tear everything down, build an *anti-city* . . . Politicians and bureaucrats—all extinct."

"But if that happens, how will we martyr ourselves?" Manny says, prodding for a reaction.

"I'm *not* a martyr, sir."

"Then we do good because it makes us feel superior?"

"You say *we*, but you mean *me*. And you've got it wrong again."

"Then why?"

"Why am I a do-gooder? . . . I've thought about that for a long time, and the answer is outrage, mixed with equal parts philosophy and hate. I don't know . . . maybe it's genes. My father was a crusader and it killed him."

Manny decides to lighten things a bit. He wants to make Laney laugh. "But in my utopia, you won't need all that."

"Unlikely."

"The whole point is to transcend the bounds of current civilization, create a race of super beings."

Laney laughs. "What else, *Mr. God?*"

"Everyone gets a wish, but they have to run it past me first."

"And you reign as Emperor Eden in the Garden of Eden?"

"No. There's no government. I've been thinking about this, even though I want to be president. I just have to stop being selfish."

"Will the Capitol or White House be the first to go?"

"Both at once," he says. "We'll reduce 'em to postcards."

Laney laughs again and Manny smiles, happy to have impressed her.

Their lunch hour climaxes at a phone booth on the corner of Pennsylvania and 17th—Rochambeau, his eagle, and the American sword goddess scrutinizing Laney's poise and resolve from a distance.

Manny digs his boyish toes into the earth, but like Rochambeau, Laney raises her hand and points to the horizon—a sign for him to get scarce. She doesn't want him breathing down her neck when she attempts to make contact with Keat Linderhart. She has a plan and it must remain secret.

"What about the coup?" he says, slowly backing himself into a train of idle bureaucrats crossing 17th. He'd do anything, even feign a devil-may-care recklessness to impress her.

"Patience," she says. "Democracy yet survives."

* * *

WITHIN HOURS, MANNY EDEN BECAME THE DREAM Laney Dracos had exposed, a ghostly identity like a smoke-and-mirror portal through which she passed. By fall of evening, a new and destructive self was born in him, and one hidden from everyone but her. Laney was promoted to the pedestal of AMERICAN SWORD GODDESS, and she assumed within Manny the Oz-like qualities of courage and morality, genius and compassion. She was Keat Linderhart, the warrior queen Zenobia, and the most intelligent human on earth, Marilyn vos Savant, all put together—the composite lodged in a housing of angelic creation. Whereas he, on the other hand, had shaved himself down to *Mr. God*.

The circumstance was complex.

It was displayed to a weary Laney Dracos during the following week with a series of notes placed in her drawers, an urgent phone message to her from a dummy government contractor in Patuxent called Ordo Vigilante Inc., and one hastily scrawled note of explanation from *Mr. God* himself, cryptic to everyone but her:

```
Dear Sword Goddess,

Next step: no more senators, congressmen, or
staff. They've written to ask you for mercy
because they know you are special to me. Per-
haps they can find a useful role in our new
utopia? Maybe as shrub trimmers? Call me and
let's talk about it.

I keep leaving you stupid notes. I can't help
it. We are two, but I want to be one.

Your Servant, Mr. God
```

The above was all necessary. For on the way back to OWC, the afternoon Manny left her moral in the eyes of Rochambeau, he found himself able to split like a chromosome: one half of him carrying on mundane, the other half veering off, reckless as a caricature of teen love seeking a time and place more suffering. In short, his doppelganger, *Mr. God,* decided to boldly reveal himself to the woman who had stung him.

By means of two more notes, *Mr. God* (not Manny Eden) told Laney of his meager gentry ambitions and of her likeness to "sun" as envisioned by the poet Roethke. To *Mr. God*'s surprise, he was also further drawn to her by traces of what he believed to be deeper traits of sensitivity and vulnerability, and thus, able in only a few hours to plot his own love perfection.

And this imago he created was precisely what he needed to defile.

Laney Dracos refused to respond to his *Mr. God* notes, and this circumstance only nagged him to insomnia, left him cowardly and doomsaying, even distracted from the whistleblower business at hand. How relieved he would be to discover a flaw in the woman (perhaps perfection itself?) the prognosis of meltdown lifted thereby.

Meanwhile, he had to tough it out.

So whenever she passed him in the hall at OWC, it was not Manny Eden she ignored, only that humbled ape, *Mr. God*, who had so recently confessed and wet himself. However, it was none other than the real Manny Eden who Laney brusquely shoved aside by Friday morning, and without apology.

It occurred to him, despite the buffer ego of *Mr. God*, that she carried out her incommunicado thing a little too far. He wanted to know what the hell was going on with Keat Linderhart. While the distant shouts of Hunsecker lacerated the OWC air, Mzz Dracos clobbered him in the hall with an insouciant hip, hot coffee slopping onto his hand as a result. He yelped and flogged the air like a clubbed seal as her silent progress continued upon an air cushion of genie sigh.

As usual!

Later, a baffled and hurt Manny cared for his burning paw in the lavatory. He winced at the gush of cold water hitting his sore flesh. The pain made him believe he had found the elusive flaw.

Perhaps he would use it as a window on deliverance.

CHAPTER 18

Silence of The Wimp — A Rodent Snack — Glyphs Pressed to Mutter — Luna Attacks — The Impossibility of Morality

A WOMAN'S PLAINTIVE YOWL shatters the OWC calm. The cry erupts inevitably from the depths of Presence Chamber, and as a result, Manny Eden's rejection pain and self-derision cease to matter. Torture devices rule the day. Shivering victims present thumbs for screwing, iron maidens forced to wait, anal pears fed to upraised asses.

The Garden-of-Eden hesitates, scans for snickering eyes, and backpedals a few feet, willing to suppress the knowledge of pain until two figures arise from the lobby to block his retreat: chlorine-eye Babs facing Worm with the speckled-trout-hands.

Worm has cornered her deep in her own territory. He appears desperate. A few minutes have whittled out all rancor, peeled him down to a hide more transparent and pensive. Susceptible to even the mildest of winds, he appears not brash with Babs, but rather supplicatory, hands lifted and shuddering to the farthest tip as if pleading a cause to a merciless idol.

"You must want to *know things*," he says to her.

"I know enough," Babs says. She looks frayed but in control, gripping her dress, her knuckles iridescing with waves of strain.

"I want to see you as a mental giantess on a throne," he says.

"So that's why you ride me, Mr. Quigley?"

"An erogenic yet brilliant oracle . . . ho, Eden!"

Worm's hand flops in the air, wags and sinks again.

"Yes, sir!" Manny pretends he's happy and oblivious.

"This woman believes me to be a romantic fool," Worms says to Manny.

"I said no such thing," Babs states vehemently. "You have no right to spread it around. No right!"

"Calm, calm little goddess," says Worm.

"I'm on the brink of something here. You're trying to ruin me!"

"Ruin, how?" asks Manny.

"He is casting dispersions," Babs says, pointing at Worm.

"I never." Worm appears hurt, lip fallen.

Manny opts to change the subject. Turning to Worm, he says, "Mr. Hunsecker has selected your oracle here to be his deputy."

"Whoaaa!" Worm pops like a slice of hot bread from a toaster.

Manny nods.

Babs' hands relax and smooth down her dress. She smiles in an overdone and embarrassing way, flushed as she is with triumph for the first time since her long ago marriage to Sven.

Worm recovers. "What a surprise," he says, remaining blithe as possible. "I didn't know there was an opening."

"Openings appear when necessary," Babs says to him.

Manny Eden stares into her chlorine eyes, and lifting her arms as if to fly, she props herself against the side of a blue, wavy pool. Her skin drinks in waffle-golden quaffs of light. Her egret-nimble legs float up to pump a froth of water into Manny's face.

"But Eden here—" Worm clutches her by the arm and shakes it to recapture her attention. "Eden knows of wars, limb heaps, and Walt Whitman. I only want the same for you."

"History won't pay the mortgage or make me a better deputy," she says.

"History will . . . " Worm begins to fumble and quake. He's losing, and he knows it. Just then, another yowl, like a flash of heat, singes the faces and walls of OWC.

"What's happening in the Presence Chamber?" Manny asks Babs.

"The *what?*"

"Uh, Mr. Hunsecker's office?"

"Just a minute . . . just a minute!"

Babs freezes, squinting and intent as Superman having ingested Lana Lang's strangled cry for help ten thousand miles away. "I think Mr. Hunsecker needs me." She turns and struts off to snuff the flames with a dose of atomic breath, but returns in less than half a minute, shattered as if by Kryptonite.

"He wants to see *you*," she says to Manny, her eyes gurgling.

"Me? Why?"

"I'm not sure. Someone's in there demanding concessions and complaining about trivial issues."

"Who?"

"She waited for hours . . . hurry, Manny, *please!*"

* * *

YOUR FIRST OFFICIAL SUMMONS to stand amazed and dutiful within the sacred space of Presence. Perhaps you should stuff your shoes with broken glass, or bolster yourself with a passage from the Torah or King James, for the Chamber is a gateway to sacred *boss space*, one requiring atonement, and raging from time to time with mythological beast-kings and their barkings, fiery judicial quotes and exculpatory "isms", and various swoon-like noises following either the delivery of a victory speech, a mercy weeping, or the cluckings of duck test refused— as well as any *truth collars* taking the form of memos as needed.

So you slink forward, steeling yourself, and as you do, a dark wavefront washes over you. It rips at you with a hundred black Shiva hands, for just beyond the verge of Chamber, courage, fair play, and reason are snuffed, become heroic pretensions reduced to flags fallen in the struggle. Regardless, you persist, attracted as you are by the suckhole of command, and perhaps, even by a need for a self-destruction you can not yet admit.

Within moments, you achieve the verge of Chamber. You edge yourself inside, and once there, begin to mutate. Paralysis is assumed within a pocket of crayon-purple twilight. Hunsecker has pulled wide the curtains behind his desk in order that he might paste the morning like a cliff of light across the room. To your surprise though, a translucent purple film masks the window and serves to channel the light, allowing only one peculiar and nerve-scraping wave to filter through. Thus is

Hunsecker's head effectively dabbed with craters of toxic hue—and with the prey effectively stunned by this technique, you know the Beast can probe for weakness and smite all the more easily.

"Thank you, thank you for coming, uhhh—"

He cannot recall your name, though he sounds genuinely grateful. You are perplexed, and as Hunsecker stands behind the obstacle of his desk, he motions for you to step forward.

A woman's voice interrupts: "Who is *this?*"

Pivoting to your left, you see her sitting on the edge of a chair. The sight of her scares the living shit out you. She is poised and bulbous and blinking at you like an owl that has just spied a rodent snack. Obviously, the source of recent bitterness. She's closing on sixty, plain black-and-white check dress, shoes soft and unheeled, hair of Presence phosphorescence cropped short and unflattering above her neck. She adjusts a pair of comic yellow glasses up on her nose, and in a pseudo-profound manner, pulls in her brows and squints as if to penetrate your disguise.

Hunsecker glances suspiciously from her to you. Meanwhile, she says nothing, allows him to stew. Moments later, shrugging her shoulders—but in such a way as to indicate her resignation at being disappointed—the owl woman rises to her feet, shifting to one hand a large black briefcase which had, until just that moment, rested on her lap. She walks right up to you, gets in your face, and says:

"Are *you* Mr. Eden?"

"I am," you answer.

"Well, you can't *scare me off,*" she says.

You don't answer. The head of Hunsecker gouges like a black thumb into the corner of your eye. Your feet are anchored, tapped into a subterranean chill that constricts its way up from your stomach and into your throat.

"Don't you know..." she pauses, takes a deep breath, and shrieks at you: "IT'S ME, KEAT LINDERHART! I GUESS, MR. EDEN, YOU THOUGHT YOU COULD SCARE ME OFF!"

After pounding that in she shoves past you, four inches below nose level, moving to rest her briefcase in a delicate way atop a credenza pushed flush against the wall and opposite Hunsecker's desk. She unsnaps and flips open the lid, withdraws a handful of papers, and traces a wide circle around your silently screaming form and back to Hunsecker, the stack risen on high, and purple, as if it were a sacred offering of inestimable value, and Hunsecker's desk, an altar awaiting sacrifice.

"Have you spoken with this woman before today?" Hunsecker asks you.

"No. The case was a dead end . . . the meeting—"

"Here is the proof!" the owl woman spits out, leaning over the desk. The papers beetle only inches away from the crater-dabbed visage of the Beast who pretends his eyes cannot part with the vital image of you even for a moment. "HERE IS THE PROOF, MR. HUNSECKER!"

The last shout slaps him to attention.

He recovers quickly.

"Proof of . . . your *improbity*?" he asks.

As her hand dips towards the surface, losing to gravity, Hunsecker snatches the stack from it. He sits down with it on his lap, flips through in a perfunctory manner for a few seconds, and then, tactless as possible, and with plenty of contemptuous wrist action in full view of Keat's terrified eyes, slops the whole pile onto his desk with a loud bang.

In response, she slumps and says, "I've been treated *horribly*, Mr. Hunsecker, oh *horribly!*"

"Try taking deep breaths," he says.

"They want to destroy me, Mr. Hunsecker! Won't you accept MY PROOF?"

He won't answer. Instead, he swivels about in his chair, grips and tugs the sail of purple film, nudging it up a few inches—just enough to allow a blinding plate of sun to jet forth and cut the room in half. You are severed at the waist as the air around the Triumphant Beasthead swirls with a soup of hot and glistening fusoria, a golden souvenir snow of dust rendering his face even more blackly damning and Jehovah-absolute than ever.

"Cowards and liars, all of them!" Keat Linderhart bursts out, flicking her hands like an overheated child.

"You are bordering on insanity, Ms. Linderhart," Hunsecker says calmly.

"TRULY EVILLLLLLL!"

In the midst of theatrics, you feel the need to distract yourself. You juggle the choices until you become a gull above the Chesapeake shore.

All hollows and wind, falling towards a spit of sand, tapping out words on the paper of eye while the cowardly and frittering Yankee Doodle "self" is peeled away to reveal a tube of stale macaroni . . .

But you cannot so easily separate yourself from obligation. You too are downtrodden with whistleblower trivia and with the values it demands of you. Therefore, following a peel down of conscience, helplessness moaning along behind, you arrive at images you find strangely consoling: a smudge of cosmos beneath your fingernail, a glowing slash of America with sword, the city of Washington broken and tumbled beneath eons of ocean.

Shine, perishing Democracy!

"Please, HELP MEEEE!" Keat's voice sounds like a wet finger skating on china.

"I don't understand, Ms. Linderhart," Hunsecker says.

"The people at the Commissions are afraid that honesty will destroy them."

"But for some curious reason, *you* are afraid of nothing."

"I was between. Only now, I have passed to the other side. It was almost enough to make me evil."

"A moment of truth, Ms. Linderhart?"

"The choice was incredibly hard, much harder than you think."

"Why couldn't you just do your job and keep your mouth shut? Such a condition as you've described at the Commission is inevitable. No one, certainly no one political in Washington, would change that."

"I take my job SERIOUSLY, Mr. Hunsecker. I'm a professional—"

"Professionals don't go off whining. They take their problems in stride."

"*ET TU*, MR. HUNSECKER?"

Keat clasps her hands into a stiff ball of prayer knuckle, and begins to bow, back and forth, geisha-like, become a living haiku of purple mantis. Hunsecker though, full of rising action toward climax, only expels himself at her, one long whoosh of exasperation from his mouth shoving through the cosmic dust swirl like an avenging fist. And of course, he begins to inveigh with *The Lean*, his shadow not only bloating, but rising up to a black conehead that spears out to impale the far wall.

"Corporations have a right to exert influence, Ms. Linderhart," he pronounces with a gavel-thumping tone. "After all, we do live in a democracy, and they are the ones who will suffer from the laws."

"Criminals deciding their own punishment?"

"*Criminals?* You are arrogant Ms. Linderhart, like your superiors said. You set yourself up as a godlike authority."

"I support the law, and the Commission."

"You only sap their morale."

"This is . . . OUTRAGEOUS!"

"Did you stop to think how you placed your fellow workers in jeopardy?"

"MY PROOF, WILL YOU ACCEPT MY PROOF OR NOT?"

"Cork your cannon lips, Ms. Linderhart."

"YOU EVIL MANNN!"

"Get some therapy. It's important to both of us."

Following this advice, Hunsecker swivels in his chair again and with one hand snaps the sheet of purple film up to the ceiling. In response, and with a sound of pipe striking bone, the light comes brawling in, the hurled lava of morning scalding you to a feeble vampire.

Though shocked and groping, Keat is soon galvanized. She snatches her limp stack from Hunsecker's desk and scuttles like a toy owl over to her briefcase. She hurls the papers back in, slams the lid, and snaps shut the locks. She grabs the briefcase, piston-struts defiantly into the Triumphant Beast's tower of cold shadow, and screeches at him:

"I DEMAND A HEARING FROM LUNA GOODPAL!"

Hunsecker's face slides like mud. "Not possible," he responds, baffled and strobing.

"LUNA GOODPAL!"

"What do you really WANT, Ms. Linderhart?"

"LUNA GOODPAL!"

"WHAT YOU REALLY WANT IS TO STAB THE PRESIDENT OF THE UNITED STATES IN THE BACK! ISN'T THAT IT, MZZ DEMOCRAT?" Hunsecker bellows loud enough to be heard outside the building.

"EVILLLLLLL!"

Vibrating to tremor, Keat Linderhart is poised to flee. Her mind stutters between hope and futility, her body pregnant with self-righteous immolation. Hunsecker, sensing the kill, stands up from his chair. He instinctively lurches forward to begin the chase, leaps as though over a puddle and straight into the sharp corner of his desk.

"GODFUCKIT!" he shouts, wounding himself in the thigh.

At this point, Keat disappears, and everything accelerates.

You go into motion. You bump from wall to wall, unable to resist being born along in the wake, sucked into vacuum created by a monstrous entity roaring ahead like a comet unleashed from a Washington hell more sanctimonious than any human being outside D.C. can possibly imagine. And before you realize it, you are in danger, coughed like debris into the lobby.

First, you notice the black jaws of Keat Linderhart's briefcase reopened and gaping from atop a chair on your right. Following that, a wild swing to the left focuses you on the hysterical Keat screeching:

"BRING ME LUNA GOODPAL!"

Her body lamb-shivers with the predatory image of the Hunsecker who faces her, attempting to appear *Deus vault*ish, but only succeeding in looking like a befuddled purple ham.

Then suddenly, just off the shore of their infernal dialogue, the complication of Laney Dracos becomes fact. She enters the room alone and stands to face Hunsecker.

Your adrenaline races.

Her eyes are bristling and sharp, her image straddling the earth of carpet, remorseless and profound as an American sword goddess set to battle The Hun. And yet, something isn't right . . . *what is it?*

You sense a scary hesitation.

You fight down a compromising panic.

Meanwhile, on the other side of the room, Worm Quigley, having briefly appeared, dissipates into background, the upper half of him swimming like mad towards the rear shadows, his lower trunk stuck in the ground and humming like a shaft.

"I WILL HAVE A CONCENSUS!" Hunsecker shouts. You watch him wobble, one hand shooing away the threat of Mzz Dracos, flapping in the direction of Worm's retreat. "Move on. Move on," he orders her. "There are no absolutes here."

"Not so," Laney says, her voice cold and strong. "Keat Linderhart has a need for our assistance, and you are denying it."

"You're *such* a virgin," he says, then to Keat: "You do know how to squeal, both of you. What a performance!" He claps his hands, follows up with a small mock bow. "Where is the audience?"

"WHERE IS LUNA?" Keat yells.

"Shut up!" Hunsecker is quickly reaching his limits.

"SHE WILL OPPOSE THOSE WHO WOULD DESTROY ME!"

"What theater! Bravo!"

"Which of your sacred canons did Ms. Linderhart violate?" Laney asks.

"Among others? *Never* go over your boss," he snaps.

"But her conscience won. Too bad!" Laney snaps back.

"*Authority* depends on the ability to *enforce*, Mzz Dracos."

"How convenient for the evil trolls you call friends."

"Evil? That's so much liberal bull, and besides, someone else made these decisions. I'm only trusting them," he says.

"So like a good bureaucrat, you refuse responsibility."

"I AM NOT A FRAUD!" Keat yells.

"Right. You're a hireling for the Democrats!" Hunsecker proclaims.

"She only tells the truth," Laney says.

"Sorry, Mzz Dracos. I don't practice self-deception like you do."

"COWARDS AND LIARS, ALL OF THEM!" Keat shouts.

"We translate law into *reality*," Hunsecker says, slapping hand to palm.

"The reality is—"

"NO FREEDOM OF SPEECH!"

Keat begins to sniffle and moan.

Hunsecker points at her while staring at Laney. "And she was outside the scope of her job."

"That's your law, not mine," Laney says, her anger flushing her red.

"She divulged to a congressman, not to a person designated to receive such information. Therefore, her activity is *not protected*. That's the law!"

"THAT'S THE LAW? I AM UNDONE!"

"Also, she *was not* the first to mention the corruption," Hunsecker adds.

"But she was the first to be slapped." Laney says.

"THEY ARE RELENTLESS!"

"She made statements which contradicted agency positions in official press releases. That's insubordination and *not protected*."

"WHERE IS THE NEXUS?"

"I have memos in my possession, Mzz Dracos, evidence she'd been making derogatory remarks about her superiors before the hearing. Therefore her motive is the result of grudge, her action without merit, and her activity *not protected*. Ask any court!"

"LUNAAAA?"

"SHUT UP!"

"You have a White House personality, Hunsecker," Laney says.

"And you have a Democrat agenda, Mzz Dracos."

"My agenda should be obvious, you suck-up fascist prick."

"Egregious insubordination! Egregious!"

"I WILL NOT RECANT!"

Hunsecker then grins, not triumphant or serene as you might think apropos, but in a manic and screw-loose way, because he's noticed, as you have, how the walls and ceiling in the lobby have begun to convulse. From all across their planes, tiny wormlets of viscid latex, followed by loosened and drifting plates of drywall, converge at one point. Like imploding pond ripples, they fuse to form a moon of bone latex, the entire phenomenon about six feet off the floor and whorling snailpace over the far wall and towards the open doorway like a Channel-7 lapse photo of a Caribbean hurricane. Simultaneously, a cold moan of wind shivers the entire building. Keat Linderhart shrieks:

"SHE COMES!"

Seconds later, Luna Goodpal appears.

As if in answer to Keat's summons, she lunges through the doorway. Streamers of hot scintillation lash out from her edges as she circles. She jabs like a knife-dancer, in and out of space, violently snapping her head and lips at each spectator in turn.

That is, until she sees Laney Dracos.

You can't get a clear look at your beloved goddess because Luna snaps and rankles in the space between, but you will never forget Laney's face surfacing near the contorting rim of Luna, nearly eclipsed and pulled out so far to funhouse mirror-taffy. You will also remember stepping back in awe to watch the battle of the antipodean super beings: *First Amendment Valkyrie* versus *Punk-Ass Republican Circe*.

The two women tense themselves, lock eyes and clench fists, and as they circle one another, Luna repeatedly screams, NOT PROTECTED! from between lips the color of hair while Laney shouts back mightily in kind: NO CENSORSHIP!

After a minute of standoff, the Luna sniffs a fear and switches tact. She draws for Laney a picture of Senator Ormsby shattered like a hull of old political ribs, one scuttled and dying slow somewhere on the shore of the Ozarks, Mzz Dracos' jugular exposed at last to the death bite. Unable to deny this, Laney begins to retreat, losing to spasms that distort and weaken her face.

You recall hours later that you wanted to call out to Laney, to comfort her and bolster her, only you were too shocked by the event to even speak. Is that what you wanted?

Following Laney's exit, Luna Goodpal stomps an imaginary crushed form beneath her heels. She then vacates the office-gray waste, satisfied as she is by the WIN-WIN situation. She rips off a page of scenery as memento and hauls it behind her like a tail. You watch her go, and turn to look around the room.

You are alone.

* * *

SHAKING LIKE A WIMP AND SEEKING someone to corroborate your outrage, you open and close the boxes of office cell that remain in OWC, all of them wrecked and discarded like smoking scraps of shell casing.

You discover no survivors in the post holocaust ruin, only Worm.

He sits motionless in a chair behind his desk. His face is fitted with a paper mask, a life-sized photocopy of the Union Head looking jaw-gouged and tongue-slapped—not even holes cut in the eyes so he can see.

"Why are you wearing that mask?" you ask, anxious and heaving in place.

"*I made it last year for a Halloween paty,*" Worm says, his voice muffled by the mask. "*I wear it when I want people to leave me alone.*"

"Did you hear what just happened?"

"*Didn't hear a goddamned thing.*"

"Keat Linderhart! Can you believe it?"

"*Begone, you crusader prick!*"

"Laney . . . I don't understand."

"*Assign the enforcement of morals to someone else,*" Worm says. "*I've neither the stamina, the time, or the clout.*"

"How about a conscience?"

"*No.*"

"Why?"

"*I'll tell you. This agency is weak in its relation to other powers, everyone scared of making the wrong move. Forces out there combining, Eden, and its siege time, liberal passivity and conservative feudalism growling at the gate.*"

"What?"

"*But be careful. Matter has its own agenda. Only a master intelligence could affect such a cosmic sabotage. The evidence abounds if you open up, examine the distances involved. You must tap into the animistic root of rhythm, the brainwave of the earth, of rocks, ocean, insects, fossils, everything.*"

"That sounds like so much *bullshit.*"

"*Well, yeah, you got a point.*"

CHAPTER 19

Hunsecker Fears an Act of Congress — Hunsecker Enlists The Help of Manny

The following day, mid-afternoon:
Over here . . . Mr. Garden-of-Eden! Here!
Huh?
Inside my office . . . this way. Quickly!
Okay.
I apologize for nabbing you out of the hall like this.
No problem, Mr. Hunsecker.
It's just that matters have gone ballistic overnight.
You look tormented, sir.
That doesn't begin to describe it. I feel as though an attempt on my life has been made . . . but this is *hush, hush,* off the record.
My lips—
Have you sent the Linderhart closeout letter yet?
Not yet.
Good, good. *Don't* send it. We need damage control . . . I'm grateful you're not efficient.
Eh?
The press is involved now. But they'll probably backpage it. OWC is *always* backpage.
I thought it was no page.
Have you been defending Elaine Dracos?
What?
Mzz Vendetta. Have you been *defending* her?
I've defended no one.
Least of all *me?*
I don't get it.

Are you trying to be *flip*? No? ... Do you smoke? I need a cigarette ... I just heard you were defending her.

She's a permanent topic of conversation, but—

The press is involved now.

What?

Vendetta is the culprit. Everyone *knows* the Queen of Shakedown.

Everyone, sir?

Have you sent the Linderhart closeout letter yet?

No.

Counsel Madison hasn't changed his mind about this case, but technically it's still open. A reporter from the *Post* asked him for a comment on the incident yesterday, then everything went ballistic.

What happened?

She's pulled these stunts before. Everyone's in a constant state of tension. Counsel Madison is infuriated. He doesn't blame me. The Queen set this whole thing up and we all fell in ... you too ... you might be a TV star, Mr. Garden-of-Eden, or at least a star on Capitol Hill cause *you were in it too*. That's right. You kept your mouth shut, but you're in it, you're inside, no doubt, accessory to the fact.

The fact of?

A shakedown! Are you *stupid*? What could be plainer? There'll be a hearing on the Hill, an investigatory hearing. A staffer from the Senate Governmental Affairs Committee called just one hour after the reporter.

Who—

What a sense of timing! Counsel Madison will be at the hearing in two days. He hates those Democrat vipers. But that was the plan. She's pulled these stunts before. You remember that big black briefcase, the one Linderhart was lugging around?

Uh, huh.

Okay, it had a video-cam tucked inside—a real secret-agent job, inside job, and you and I are featured. The Queen of Shakedown set the whole thing up ... Did you know she's a zealot? That's right. A zealot. And do you know why?

No.

She's unhappy, full of rage. She's near breakdown. Her mother was a tyrant who beat her regularly. That's right. And now she's transferring her rage onto us. You see?

That's really odd—

No, not at all. It's *drama*, Mr. Garden-of-Eden, drama. She's the *queen of drama*. She's got a personality disorder. She's compensating for her lousy childhood. You see?

Yes.

I know these things. I understand psychology. Do you? Do you read Freud?

No.

But I watched myself. I protected myself. No one can blame me for *anything* I said yesterday, right?

I suppose . . .

No comments? I don't mean to smile, but you look quite distraught, Mr. Garden-of-Eden. Are you a Manipulator or just an Evader?

I going to relax.

What happened to your English? . . . Anyway, the case is still open. Remember, you're my man on this.

I'm more than a man, I'm Mr. G—

We've been dragged up on the Hill four or five times for damage control, only this time . . . Congress might get fed up and blow our budget stump. The White House might demand sacrifices due to bad publicity, but I'm not worried. Neither is Counsel Madison.

OWC could shut down?

No! Ridiculous! Just firedrills, firedrills. Don't believe it. Nothing will shut down. I'll keep you informed. *Dolores capitis non fero. Eos do.*

Eos do. Check.

Stay low and I'll let you know how to follow up.

Stay low. Check.

I have confidence in you, Mr. Garden-of-Eden.

Yes, I've always believed that.

These people don't understand the president's program.

Check.

So wise, so young, do never live long.

CHAPTER 20

Like a Morose General Patton — Magical Thinkings Beyond Good and Evil — Ashley Madison Befuddles The Democrats and "Rolls With The Punches"

NO DIFFERENT THAN MOST, Ashley Madison sounded like distant ocean, timeless and empty as a conch. If you held the OWC Counsel snug to your ear and listened hard, you imagined the dissolving swell of oblivion. You forecast a demise of the human species. You groped frantically for "self." But on certain days, when Ashley was exorcised of oblivion by a fear or anxiety—resembling less a carnivorous plant-in-wait than a paranoid mammal measuring out the cave of its refuge—the sound of ocean would be demoted to background, overcome by the staccato of interior monologue necessary to evasion. And on days such as these, Ashley would take his cue from that lovable old tyrant Winston Churchill. Just as Sir Winston had reinvigorated himself with marathon steam baths before each new fray, so too would Ashley rejuvenate his own being by exposing himself to the cruelty of the nearby Potomac shore.

Now on this particular day in early November, Ashley was half with sun and blowing cold as his future. Somberly, he slipped out of OWC before noon to stroll the distance down 18th Street, his large, power-politic body passing beyond the granite-mesa bastions of bureaucracy and crossing Constitution Avenue to land upon the parklike expanse of the Mall. Upon skirting the obstacle of duck pond, he stepped onto the nearby lawn, and feeling Churchill-like—but looking more like a morose General Patton dreaming Napoleon's retreat from Russia—plodded up a shallow ridge and down the lee side. He soon arrived at a solitary wooden bench facing the river.

As the wind tore the lid off the Chesapeake and skipped it like a cold slamming rock up the Potomac, Ashley forced himself into a state of self-examination. Not able to collapse into dementia, or seek the maternal warmth of sympathy, he believed himself doomed. ROLL WITH THE PUNCHES was his motto, his philosophy, and its implications the litmus test of his personality. Being a Mayflower conservative, a true "blue blood," he never found it necessary to reason why others suffered vicissitude or whether notions of personal misfortune or tragedy were in any way relevant. Those who failed to ROLL were utterly dismissed. Life was, after all, full of blows, and you had to expect them, whether telegraphed days ahead by the spleen of an enemy or arriving out of the darkness like a hurtling freight—as had this most recent and frightening one.

Two days were woefully insufficient to rehearse Ashley for the whining liberal barrage soon to assault him on Capitol Hill. An oversight hearing, sponsored by a few Democrat senators of the Governmental Affairs Committee, had been called suddenly, to rehash once more the minutiae of his Counsel activities—and motivated no doubt, as before, by the loose cannon lips of a malcontent Democrat mole planted in his own OWC by the name of Elaine Dracos. And as the Hill cyclops tensed its thumb, Ashley's resolve and sense of duty were compromised by the threat of public humiliation. He knew the White House would only endure so much before a resignation for appearances sake became necessary. Therefore, seeking to ROLL ASAP beside the Potomac, Ashley rehearsed his answers to the GA Committee. He knew he must get it straight, cover all his bases, and he yearned for realism.

He concentrated hard till he felt the limelight of press and senatorial scrutiny stoked to a furnace on his skin, felt himself prickly and chilled to the palm, fingers desperately pinching his legs as the interrogation pounded him fast and hard:

Counsel Madison, is it the policy of OWC to intentionally misinterpret the law in order to create a false basis for avoiding it?

His tongue was stuck; like the Sons of the Pioneers, he needed a drink of cool, clear water. "Of course not, senator," he would say.

Then will you please respond to statements made recently to the Washington Post by Congresswoman Gottlieb of Pennsylvania, namely, "How disappointing to see the agency Congress created to help remedy the ills of Washington succumb to the same disease it was designed to treat. We have a tragedy in the making each time a conscientious individual seeks justice from an agency poised not to serve as fair counsel, but only as his or her executioner—the law itself being the weapon of choice."

Ashley Madison could only reply: "I will respond, senator, by noting that the honorable Congresswoman is just a politician at the end of the day. If she sees an opportunity to embarrass the Administration . . . well, she has a reputation."

Counsel Madison, your stated policy since taking office is to weed out the truth by administering polygraph tests to whistleblowers who seek your help, yet you have never insisted or required managers so accused to submit to the same tests. Why is that?

"If I had reason to question their integrity, senator, I would have insisted."

Counsel Madison, did you actually teach a course to managers on how to fire whistleblowers without being caught by OWC, advising them how to construct the charges so as not to give the appearance of violating the First Amendment?

"The briefing was open to everyone, senator, all part of our OWC Outreach Program, and it was designed to inform the people out there just how OWC works. A lot of stories were going around up until this time, a lot of ignorance."

Counsel Madison, how do you respond to Senator Ormsby's comment, that stricter judicial review would discourage OWC from capriciously violating the law?

"I must say, I am offended by that remark, senator. OWC under my direction is instructed to meticulously apply all legal precedents in the decision-making process. If anything, we follow the law too closely."

ROLLING, ROLLING, ROLLING!

Ashley was used to it. He'd rolled plenty (way too much!) since throwing in his hat with the Reagan team. This past year, the White House had not only passed him up for a Secretary of Treasury nomination, but Commerce as well. After a few feelers of low-key indignation were cast by him into a West Wing pond stocked post-election with Golden State piranha, he was promptly saddled with the "honor" of OWC.

Nothing less than a punishment, a tragi-comic damnation to obscurity!

No doubt. Those white-stocking bitches!

He knew he should have shut his fat mouth and hoped for an Assistant Secretary slot at worst, perhaps at DOD or State. How could he help but now imagine himself suffocated in a suit of Lancelot white, his Republican sensibilities violated? Even the White House trust placed in him regarding "loose cannon control" and "protecting party business interests" failed to placate his rage. What offense had he committed to deserve such a trivial agency of *l'enfant terrible* bureaucrats? More importantly, why hadn't his fellows at the Heritage Foundation used their connections to help him rectify things?

Fair weather friends and morons. Cowards too, all of them!

No answer was ever forthcoming.

A devastated Ashley retreated to his baronial estate in Great Falls, Virginia, there to lower Old Glory to half mast. He secluded himself for days, attempting a hyperconsumption cure by chomping down chocolate truffles, macadamia nuts, and steaming handfuls of cuttlefish nonstop while gulping Hennessy cognac and watching taped reruns of his favorite *Firing Line* episodes—but all that wasn't enough. Eventually, even the sight of William Buckley began to nauseate him, and therefore, with trifling effort, and more cognac, he soon slumped to his own version of *Ecce Homo*: razorslashed and bleeding upon his white patrician columns, his mouth snorting words of despair, "*Eloi Eloi, lama sabachthani!*" beside his favorite black stallion, Bucephalus, till a flashlight thrust in his face by Olivia (his soon-to-be-estranged wife) awakened him in the horse stall at two o'clock in the morning.

Such episodes, however, were *positive* inasmuch as they pragmatized Ashley, for following two weeks of hangovers and eruptions of high octane flatus in the presence of business associates (prior to OWC, Ashley had been CEO of Aesir Corp, a DOD weapons contractor), he found himself frantically searching day and night for the means with which to dampen the effects of a petty White House.

In short, ROLL TIME!

The idea of a cooling-off vacation occurred to him, but upon recalling his last experience, Ashley horrified himself.

Following any hiatus from the office, four days to a week or more, his head still boggled with Beijing or Rome, his mind yet raw with the nails of a million other lives scratching in the earth beneath his soles, he found himself strangely unable to respond in a normal fashion to his work environment—once even experiencing the onset of an eating disorder and depression near manic in intensity.

Ashley consulted his Jungian analyst, and decided, poised on the verge of career-death angst, that rather than seek outward he would turn inward, *roll with the punches* to unplumbed depths, focus exclusively on refitting the drifting puzzle states of his wounded psyche. He moped into his personal library, intent on distracting himself till he could invent a plan. Impulsively, he skimmed through a stack of history books on the subject of America's birth, as well as one novel, *Last of the Mohicans*, and then, with a bottle of Hennessy, a box of truffles, and the ammo of imagination, began to dream a history more suited to his own globe-spanning passions.

Would his Jungian analyst approve?

Probably not, and it mattered not a jot, for as a court favorite of King James I in 1623, he would be issued a royal patent to colonize America. Boldly he would sail up the *silver-flefhed waters of the Patawomecke* like Captain John Smith, seeking the most defensible knoll from which to anchor the new Palatinate of Lord Madison.

In his gloss-stroked beaver hat, Erol Flynn pirate shirt, and golden cod piece etched with a virile swan of flapping Zeus, Lord Madison would claim his empire. *Show them British steel!* he would cry, and as often as necessary, for empowered by the sweeping proprietary rights granted him by the royal charter of King James, he might *Make War* (without the boring necessity of having to conduct press conferences with sniping Jews from the *Washington Post*), or *Peace* (if a good night's sleep required it), *Coyn Money* in his own image, *Enact Laws*, or even pluck virgin nubility like a true feudal master. For purposes of leisure, he might wander the tide waters of America, and from there, encased in an envelope of pure light, he would stride, the divine hum of his godhead drowning out the *crye and noyse of the savages*.

Ashley realized instinctively that if he set cowardice at defiance, it would be a simple matter for him to gather dumbstruck worshipers by the tens of thousands, to accrete the flotsam of empire. *And why not?* Imagine the entire Powhattan Confederacy bowing to him, the White Manitou of the East! From the Rappahanock he would stir the Monacans, from Albemarle Sound the Weapemeocs, the Chowanocs and Nottoways further west, the Cuscarawaocs nestled between the Chesapeake and Delaware bays, and the Piscataways simmering restless beyond the Patuxet. From the gangling tribes of the Nacotchtanke he would winnow out his Janissaries, forge a bodyguard of chthonic red goliaths whose bodies would be berry-slashed and writhing with skeleton chalk.

With his gore-hungry army assembled, he might strike west for fabled realms of golden sand, or else turn north to do battle with the Iroquoian Empires—and just as Prince Madoc of Wales left his trace in the tongue of the Carolina wilderness, so too would Manitou Madison leave his own mark, and in fire-told legends and ritual as far west as the Ohio.

This was not to say, however, that a man of Ashley's superior abilities—not to mention Nietzchean values—would be denied a role in a virile democratic scheme.

Damn all Democrats to hell!

Though gagging on the notion of suffrage, and infused with his own *fuhrerprinzip* morality, no one could dissuade Ashley from bathing in the heat of those forces branding *the will and flefh* of the new Republic.

By 1765, Lord Madison would declare his presence!

He would take up residence in one of the finest colonial mansions in Alexandria and dub it ... *Halcyon House*. With Captain Meriwether Lewis he would stand, celebrating with 27 reeling toasts the Captain's momentous plough up the Missouri. Mornings Lord Madison would reserve for snipe and golden eagle hunting in the tidal swamps, evenings for Old World balls and public dinners, Saturdays for accompanying the illustrious John Tayloe and his pedigree trotters out to the

Jockey Club races. He would inspect the thousand-times-a-thousand stone swipes and punctures wrought by the masters Franzoni and Giovanni Andrei in the Captiol's interior; and of course, his own *Great Head* of *gravitas* would be slashed and rubbed into immortality by the crayons of St. Memin, or made over into deathless watercolor by Boudon.

Alas though, all would not remain roses and savor of sweet meat.

Like his Britannic Majesty's minister, Sir John Merry, Lord Madison had found it necessary to placate (and far too often) the brazen, tobacco-chewing blackguards of the new Republic. He could not help but share the observation of Sir John who, in his London dispatch of 1807, defined democracy as "the dregs having got to the top."

Of course, this observation did not apply to Lord Madison, and this decision of his was not motivated by vanity or self-conceit. No. He simply and rightfully placed himself. True, he'd been overlooked for Secretary of Treasury and Commerce, snubbed by the Reagan wunderkinds, but unlike them, he possessed a *true pedigree*.

And what was that?

Without resort to Bacon-like empiricism, and scorning the biology of proof, Lord Madison declared his heritage as matter-of-fact. If forced to defend his honor, say, against an attack by the wily likes of a Democrat such as Congresswoman Schroder, he might forcefully dredge up the horn-and-hoof march of Darwinism, as well as the value of Rand-like genius in order to defend his position till the whining Democrat enemy either conceded or withdrew in disorder—and though he might nibble in symbolic fashion from cheese coalesced from cows of Republican teat and drawn through the snow all the way from Massachusetts to be offered as a gift to President Jefferson, he would fume furious, and with a sense of degradation, whenever he recalled this same plebeunctuous fool escorting that outrage of the century, Dolley Madison, to the seat of honor at an official state dinner—then further estranged upon hearing President Jefferson (that hambone!) so brazenly pronounce the ceremony of official functions to be tainted by the "corrupting vanity of the European court," and thenceforward, to proceed "pele-mele from the onset."

Such events, as Lord Madison was well aware, only further obliged the low born to crowd out the more pedigreed citizen, to hold rollicking, liquor-frothed dialogues with President Jefferson, and to boor him (he so richly deserved it) with their ills and petty triumphs whenever caprice suited.

And President Madison? No different. Even worse! The imbecile allowed his body to be shoved about in the common tide that sloughed itself upon the White House lawn whenever his wife Dolley produced one of her infamous *levees*.

Lord Madison, on the other hand, scorned that feeling of vertigo the low-born imposed like a decree of will, rendering him so utterly sod-nailed that it required weeks of enforced solitude in the Blue Ridge and at least a dozen golden eagle trophies before self-esteem could be restored.

Nevertheless, the grandiose, feather-tower of Dolley, always cut a swath through the throng—her comet tail of troupe stumbling on behind—the drunken mob of the *levee* parting before this female Moses, and in mimicry of the due respect accorded the European pantheon.

And did not this "instinct for deference" prove Lord Madison's point? *As natural as the food chain!*

Deference or no, Dolley Madison was only to be loathed for her vulgar habit of receiving the sons and daughters of sod farmers and file clerks with the same cordiality as she received the European *corps diplomatique*. Naturally, her habits enraged Lord Madison (thank God things had come full circle in the Reagan 80s!) because Dolley, by means of her careless mouth and foolish gestures, devalued him and all his peerage. How had even Dolley failed to realize the concept of Rightful Domain? She inferred by her behavior that we have obligations towards the offspring of clerks when in fact we only have obligations towards our peerage.

Lord Madison realized all too well that a "democracy" of Jefferson and Dolley, that such a chaos of interfusion and lack of values, could bear but one type of offspring, and his name:

MEDIOCRITUS.

My God! What I would give for the rebirth of Plato!

He recalled Charlton Heston's famous final cry in *Planet of The Apes*, and he relieved the stress by shouting to himself:

"DAMN THEM ALL TO HELL!"

When engaged at the GA Committee hearing two days hence, leaning down upon that cold wooden table, mouth before a microphone, the Democrat sons and daughters of Mediocritus would certainly inquire of him:

Lord Madison, do you perceive OWC to be a positive force for good?

Trying not to laugh, Lord Madison would somberly reply, "senator, I perceive OWC to be in the vanguard of those who fervently desire a better America."

Would you say, Lord Madison, that a retaliation policy exists within the government, the effect of which is to not only silence dissent, but to promote corruption?

"If retaliation ever comes, senator, I would think it responsive, spontaneous rather than conspiratorial as such. In any case, OWC would not support it."

Would you not say there is a tacit policy on the part of managers?

"How could such a thing exist? It sounds like a contradiction. I have never seen it. The managers I know are all dedicated to serving their country."

Under law, Lord Madison, OWC is in effect duty bound to become an institutional whistleblower if it discovers an agency of the American government pursuing policies of gross waste or criminal activity. During your tenure, or to your knowledge, has this circumstance ever come about?

"OWC is ardent in the performance of its duties, its employees loyal, and if evidence ever came across my desk that another organ of the United States were pursuing such a malevolent course then I would not hesitate to take action . . . however, senator, this has never been the case."

As the eternal foe of democracy continues his fantasy of thrashing the senators, a vagabond schizo of the city, sexless and sheathed in a crust of urine-yellow ice, babysteps several yards away and parallel to the edge of the Potomac shore. Lord Madison sees him, and in response to his summons, a chorus of screeching tin slithers loose from the lips of a Nacotchtanke band as they burst from behind the cover of oak, scrambling to close a ring of face about the shuffler.

The vagabond takes no notice. His tiny tot feet wade through a slosh of brain until spear points are thrust forward. Death follows at once, and the Democrat interrogation continues:

Lord Madison, has the OWC ever violated the First Amendment that guarantees the freedom of speech, or through neglect ever allowed it to be violated?

"The aim of OWC, senator, is to discover that speech most deserving of protection. We are tireless in the pursuit."

Lord Madison, two employees of the Energy Department, Mary Wagner and Isa Kaplan, have signed affidavits stating that you met with the Secretary of Energy to provide advice on how to fire whistleblowers whose cases were pending before OWC.

"I do not, at this time, recall such a meeting, senator."

Do you recall a remark you made to a Mr. Arthur Daniero, a division chief at the Energy Department, to the effect that whistleblowers deserve what they get because if they weren't so stupid they would see the firing squad lining up ahead of time?

"I never made such a remark, sir."

Lord Madison, what comment do you have concerning your letter to Jonathan Neider, Whitehouse Counsel, specifically to the passage that states, "I've never met a true whistleblower in all my life. These so called righteous paraders are more akin to bag people and nutzoid cases, and more concerned with pettiness and revenge than with righting wrongs."

"There was a movement underway at OWC at that time to separate the wheat from the chaff, senator, to strain out those responsible clients from the irresponsible, the effect of which was to make our operation more efficient and more answerable to the public."

Lord Madison, is it true that out of over a hundred cases of criminal misconduct perpetrated by over a dozen government agencies since 1980, that OWC has never ordered a single investigation to be conducted, and that out of nearly two hundred cases of reported retaliation against employees for whistleblowing, OWC has never ordered the agency involved to cease and desist, not even in a single case?

"I can't speak for my predecessors or their staff, senator, but our Uncle Sam is not one percent as corrupt as you believe him to be. The majority of issues involved here are really, taken as a whole, quite trivial.

They have little or no impact on the vital issues facing this country. I can assure you."

The Nacotchtankes were howling, dismembering, and fiercely chirruping. Dolley Madison, weeping and repentant, was finally buried in the earth up to her neck. Lord Madison felt the coldness of the day revitalize him, and at last, he stood and began his long trek back to OWC, his body throwing shadow beyond the Mall, his thoughts focusing like sun through a magnifying glass onto the face of Elaine Dracos.

THAT PERFIDIOUS, DISRUPTIVE, DEMOCRAT BITCH!

Lord Madison, one final question. Is it true, that to all intents and purposes, OWC has been transformed into a White House spin team that in reality exists only to shield the Administration—on the one hand by suppressing evidence of corruption, and on the other, by seeking to impugn the motive of the client?

Lord Madison would not sleep until he buried Mzz Dracos up to the neck, and right alongside that CLERK-COURTING WHORE, Dolley Madison.

CHAPTER 21

The Powers of Rodin — Pecking Order — Year of The Rhinoceros — The Glue of Common Loathing — Something As Basic As Heat

AT THE CLOSE OF EVENING, PATHOS from the day's industry at OWC, having pinched Manny's nervous system like a trauma, shoved him before a bathroom mirror and forced him to go face-to-face with himself. The confrontation continued for several minutes until he grudgingly accepted a role as superhero in his own psychocinema production. The current shooting location: Hunsecker's office.

The most recent take portrayed Captain Garden-of-Eden defending the fair Tammy Pon while salvaging what little of his honor remained by making use of both fury and physics to suspend the Triumphant Beast in mid-air above his own desk, prepped like a funeral slab to receive him. The death blow fallen, the camera eye zoomed onto the godhead of darkness looking like a bloody melon on the vine. Another close-up revealing the final breath and slump to lifelessness.

In the second act of the film, Captain Garden-of-Eden suspended his Hamlet-like rage in order to search America for his rock-singer love, she having vanished on a leave of extended illness following that disheartening manifestation of the surreal Luna. It was vital upon finding his heroine that he restore her confidence, rejuvenate her by any means necessary, for she was braver and stronger than he, and he knew America's faithful would perish without her.

Meanwhile, as the self-absorbed Tammy wandered the Washington burbs, aloof and unavailable for conflict, wounds and outrage deluged the mail room of OWC. The despised whistleblowers were left hanging by their thumbs, their fingers plugging a thousand dykes from St. Croix to Anchorage, their conscience tested in a war of nips and bites spread thin by time, apathy, and a Gulag psychology. They resisted the corporate mob of Washington Inc., fought their snarling bosses in the halls and on the elevators, living each day in a conspiracy of fear. They cured their ignorance with the burden of knowledge, and as one, said to themselves:

> *We are the conscience of*
> *a smug and stupid people.*

* * *

FULLY AWARE OF THE URGENCY, and the time bombs set and ticking, Manny wastes no time finagling Laney's address from a suspicious Deejah. At 8:30 A.M. the next morning he borrows E-Man's old '77 Datsun and drives out to Laney's place in Falls Church, VA.

The day is blue and mild. He pulls up to the curb, feeling calmed by the appearance of her home: a vintage, sun-yellow Cape Cod with maroon shutters, a row of azalea bushes flush against the house, and an open-air porch with two pine rocking chairs. The car parked in her driveway (and Manny gasps when he sees it) is a fire-engine red, '65 MGB roadster—and in *mint* condition.

Manny gets out and walks up the drive. He places his hand on the hood of the MGB. It is cold. He rings both the front and kitchen doorbells, even fogs a few windows. No Laney appears. He finally gives up and inserts a note in the front screen door that he will return later that evening.

At 4:45 PM, he arrives once again in E-Man's car, slowing to a prowl. Her MGB has vanished and his note on the front door has been replaced by a bright yellow slip of paper. The new note, scrawled in Laney's shaky hand and nearly indecipherable, instructs him to meet her at noon the following day in the park across from the Corcoran Museum on 17th Street.

She will be the one "disguised as a tree."

Near the appointed time, Manny Eden halts a block down Vermont Avenue and pretends to linger. He wants to make sure no one is following him. He eases like a gawking tourist through Lafayette Park, walks in two circles, and seeks Rochambeau's horizon, south to the Corcoran.

Minutes later, he finds her.

She is *sang-froid* and cross-legged beneath a 19th century poplar tree, staring up to the sky through black sunglasses, the poplar limbs playing over her face like a dozen dark fingers. Despite this distraction—and her looking like lumberjack tomboy in red plaid shirt and blue jeans—Manny notes her new weakness.

"I'm on double-secret probation," she announces as he walks up to her, saying so without looking at him or even moving a muscle. "Suspended from OWC, two weeks without pay." She tries to stand. The muscles in her face slide to earth, resistless due to lack of sleep. She yaws west as Manny pulls her up by the hand. He sees how bad she needs corrective action.

"You've been followed," she says, glancing around uneasily. "Bimbo Dogs are on the periphery."

"Bimbo Dogs? Where?"

"*Don't be a fool.*" She slips around the poplar trunk and flattens herself against it as if hiding from long distance lip readers.

Manny watches and feels the sudden urge to weep. Laney trembles against the tree. Manny advises her to wade into the depths of the Corcoran art gallery. No one can shadow them in there—her footsteps, even their breath, loud as lightning cracks in those vast and somber rooms.

"I *need* art, Mr. Garden-of-Eden" she says, nodding. "It will help straighten me out, give me perspective. Yes, but it's too dangerous here. I know a much better place, further away, a safer place."

Obeying her tersely whispered instructions, Manny waits a full minute before following her body west to 18th Street. He takes the first left onto E St., then down a block and a half to the granite maw entrance of the GSA agency. She knows of a government shuttle that departs from there every half-hour for the GSA district building several miles away, not far from *L'Enfant Plaza* and the Mall.

She fails to explain the significance of that, and Manny doesn't ask.

At the appointed rendezvous, they step into the shuttle van, both flicking identification at the driver. They take a seat in the back, and Manny whispers:

"What have you been doing the past couple of days?"

"Testing my will to live," she whispers back.

"How?"

"Soap operas and vodka."

A couple of suits in corporate blue board the shuttle. Laney fails to notice. She stares out the window and away from Manny. He clumsily places his hand on top of hers, his hand feeling not like his own—more like a cold fish, like Worm's hand.

"Hunsecker broke the news," she says, "a *letter charging insubordination in the presence of witnesses.*"

She lays her head back on the seat and closes her eyes, motionless till the van turns off Constitution Avenue. As they approach the brown and crumbling acreage of the Mall, Manny inquires about their final destination.

Laney answers with a face devoid of life.

"*The Balzac Park.*"

Manny still doesn't understand. Before he can form a question though, Laney gazes at him and says:

"*And by the way, Manny, I need something to hate.*"

"As usual, I don't get it," he replies.

"*Focus, Manny. Focus. For starters, I don't know whether to hate the whole human race or just Ronald Reagan.*"

Before he can respond, one of the suits turns in his seat and glares at Laney. He is bald and jowled, his eyes far right Republican—the kind that shoot deer after church on Sundays. Laney sticks out her tongue at him.

Manny glares back till the suit reverses himself.

* * *

SCOOPED FROM THE MALL, the Balzac Park is an open-air sculpture museum just north of the Hirschorn. It sinks into the earth, looking like an enormous pit, the sides squared off with sheets of black granite.

After a long and silent walk from the shuttle drop-off, Manny and Laney descend the marble staircase into the depths of the museum. Laney strides purposefully over the dead grass towards a statue by Rodin known as *The Burghers of Calais*. Manny is right behind. To him, the statue appears like a cluster of monkish giants—big feet and extra facial misery for effect. In imitation of Laney, he takes a seat on the dais beneath *The Burghers* and glances around at the variety of humanlike images scratching up from the grassy floor. Included among these, another prominent Rodin, *Balzac*. a black spike of author at least fifteen feet tall and driven deep enough to become the sullen crux—his literary highness orbited on all sides by sculptured plumps of fertility goddess, several sluggish biomorphs that look like muscles or clam feet, an *ecce homo* icon of phalloid tusk, plus two womanoids of tin chasing one another in a circle, their black moons of ass dripping off behind.

Laney refers to this bizarre exhibition as the Balzac Park because of Rodin's *Balzac*. Why else? Her favorite spot though, on a granite shelf beneath *The Burghers of Calai*s. Looking up, her eyes trace their too-awkward and wretched faces, and she recalls how they have always justified her penchant for martyrdom, her redemption from futility at any cost. The sneer of *Balzac* only piques her pride, levitates her above the equivocating mass, but *The Burghers*, as counterweight, depress and provoke her to purpose in the most melancholy way she can imagine.

"Senator Ormsby is dying," Laney says.

She lowers her head to stare at Manny. He turns to look at her sunglasses reflecting the black moons of tin, and despite this distraction, it all makes sense: Luna Goodpal's threats and Hunsecker's triumphantly delivered letter of insubordination. Ormsby had been crippled by a heart murmur only last week—a ripple of shock on the Hill and restrained laughter from the White House before he promoted himself to an attack and a fall like a scream. Now he grope-talks like a baby recovering *gahhhhh oooo-gahhheee* in his cabin somewhere in the Ozarks, sending greetings from the warhorse pasture (with his wife's hand because his won't work) and warmest regards to *My Elaine*.

"Madison will stalk me now," she says, her voice emotionless.

"He has nothing better to do?" Manny asks.

"Nothing better than to prolong his revenge."

The Burghers halo her head like an aura of black teeth. Her sunglasses are now ponds of Manny's face, and in her eyes, a tusk of *ecce homo* rises above his ear, dark as Rodin's bronze. She removes the glasses and stares at him, her blue-socked eyes gone Burgherlike. On the lip of the dais she sits, hunched forward, one fingernail nervously edging the wave of her mouth. "OWC knows I tried to engineer that hearing on the Hill," she says.

"I know too, but—"

"Of course, Hunsecker must have mentioned it . . . Senator Ormsby scared the face off that weasel."

"So what happened to the hearing?"

"Sorry, no hearing," she says, nonchalant.

"Hunsecker told me—"

"He was wrong. Lord Madison and his minions are safe."

"Why?"

Laney turns from him and stares straight ahead. "Retaliation is a fine art in Washington. Did you know?"

"What? You talking about Hunsecker?"

"Madison is far more dangerous. I'm too exposed now."

"Can't Ormsby write letters with his wife's hand?"

"He might ask one of his colleagues to jolt Madison with a phone call, sure, but it would be a one-time shot, not a Damocles sword like Ormsby. Madison knows that. He'd be cordial, bide his time and seek me out later, everyone else wearing me down with trivia in the mean time."

"So it's over?"

"No, sir, it's not." She turned to look at him. "You want it to be *over*?"

"Course I don't."

"Then what?"

"I want you to be safe."

"No worries. I'll make Mzz Dracos invulnerable again."

"At OWC?"

"I still have press contacts, Hill contacts."

"Why not just look for another job?"

"Doing what?"

"Uh—whatever. Lobby for a non-profit, or something."

"Not that easy, Gipper boy."

"Well, you just dropped a few contacts."

"The employers of Washington will smile wide enough, sure, maybe even do me a favor or two, then turn skittish if I push for a job because I have a rep around town as a disruptive personality. Even the non-profits want good bureaucrats."

"But you're still Sigma Chi sweetheart on the Hill, right?"

"Oh, sure. *Fucking* BS. So many donkey and elephant emperors minus clothes and up to their weenies in shit."

Manny laughs.

Laney deadpans him. "Just knowing Papa Ormsby was around kept them off my back. But they all want pecking order, zero squawking about right and wrong, especially in the presence of certain senators who shit gold bars . . . these people are *groupthinking* on a completely different plane. You just don't get it."

Manny stares at her and Laney stares back. She laughs to herself as she watches him zone like an adolescent boob between adoration and arousal. A slight smile forms on her lips and she asks him:

"Are you in lust with me, Gipper boy?"

He smiles back and says, "Your morality tips me over the edge."

"Oh, bullshit. I'm growing more evil by the day."

"Talk about bullshit."

"I'm begging the asteroid to hit."

"Which one?"

"The one that will bring back the dinosaurs."

Manny forces a laugh. "Better a tyrannosaurus than a politician, eh?"

Laney deadpans him again.

"That's funny," he says, "but seriously, you don't have the personality for evil."

"Evil *is* a personality. I came to this conclusion only a few days ago."

"Yeah, well, there's really no such thing as *evil*, Elaine."

Laney responds with her stop-being-a-moron stare. "Haven't you even accepted my sneaky-shits-rule-the-universe theory yet?"

"Not yet."

She ceremoniously clears her throat. "Well then, my dear *ignorant* bastard, will you believe me if I tell you that science has proven a series of flashes and electric shocks will condition worms into creatures afraid of light? Do you know that experiment?"

Manny nods.

"So you see, like worms, we have knee-jerk reactions, only conditioned by the city of Washington. This place works on us long enough, produces enough disgust and fear, and it changes us into things, like rhinos for instance. It's that simple."

"*Rhinos* . . ."

"Stupid, dangerous things. They're here, on the loose . . . all around us."

"Um—"

"And right now the herd belongs to Ronny."

"There you go again."

"How can you deny it? This is his fucking year, and the old man is ridin' high."

"You're not a rhino, Elaine."

"But I'm talking about something much stronger, something as basic as heat." Laney bores her eyes into Manny, her hands lifting as if to slap him.

Manny marvels at the sight. Is she part Italian? Whatever.

"Haven't you heard the expression, 'He brings out *the worst* in me?' Well, how long before the worst *sticks*?"

"But you drive a mint condition MGB."

"Huh? How did you know?"

"I left a note at your house, remember?"

"Oh, yeah, right. Lucky I didn't mistake you for a prowler."

"And if you had?"

"I might have cut you in two with my Smith and Wesson 9mm."

"What? You have a *gun*?"

"Durn right, partner." She winks at him, and her face saddens. "By the way, have I told you I can be driven to murder?"

"No."

"How, you ask? Just enough hate, or maybe the end of everything that makes life worthwhile." Tears begin to form in Laney's eyes as she stares at him. "I could do much worse, like grab a hammer and drive a nail into Hunsecker . . . will you hold him down for me?"

"You need a vacation, Elaine."

"I loathe him inside me."

"*Inside* you?"

"I can't stop going to bed with the little prick. He's like a doll who stares over my shoulder at everything I do, commenting on it, sneering, insulting. He pops up out of nowhere like a black light bulb and I have to answer to him, argue like a maniac."

"That's pretty bizarre. Maybe you should talk—"

"*Fuck you.*"

"Come again?"

"You remind me of Hunsecker. You pop out of nowhere and pester me."

"Come again?"

"See how *evil* I am?" Laney asks and wipes her eyes with her fingers.

Manny decides to quickly change the subject. He can't bear to see her cry. "Sure, sure, and what about the coup?"

"The coup is past and it failed. The black tower still stands."

Needing no more urging, and with a calm voice, Laney carefully explains the disaster. She makes him recall his imitation of flotsam and the scene of surreal confrontation while towed helpless by the Triumphant Beast's wake as he chased the pathetic Keat Linderhart.

"Remember the screams of free speech? All pre-arranged," says Laney.

Before Keat Linderhart could launch her do-or-die siege she'd met Mzz Dracos over coffee, the time and place chosen beneath the gaze of Rochambeau. They decided that Ms. Linderhart would breach the OWC gate with inhuman patience, gall and mouth, towing the CIA-like briefcase owned by Elaine, the videocam tucked secretly inside (purchased a year previous for just such an occasion), hopefully capturing for an uneasy and fixated audience of Senate staff notables the spectacle of an evil OWC rampaging over the rights of an innocent.

But the outcome?

A dark screen of toxic mud, hoarse female ejaculations magnified to hysteria, a dim trail of Keat's hair followed by an explosion of white light and gigantic torsos drifting up to eclipse it; and the second scene even worse—the ill-placed briefcase angle shaving off the compromising vision, more shrieking, and Laney's humiliating retreat, step by step into hibernation.

"The tape unusable?" Manny asks.

"A fucking disaster. I had to shut things down soon as I saw it."

"What about the *Washington Post*?"

"The same, and besides, they've finally gone over to the White House. The word just came down from my contact there."

"What do you mean?"

"The First Nancy has been doing garden parties with Katharine Graham, owner of the *Post*. Management is so intimidated they're scared to run any copy that might be seen as critical of The Gipper."

"Yeah, right. So now all production has ground to a halt?"

"I have to wait, make myself invulnerable again, like I said."

"But only if Madison, Luna, and Hunsecker cease to exist."

"It's possible I can make them *cease*."

"You kidding?"

"I have a smoking gun, if I want it. Deejah is helping."

"Gimme a break."

"No, really. She hates Hunsecker worse than any of us. There's nothing like the glue of common loathing. Also, she worships me."

"You mean like I do?"

"Not sure. Anyway, she says Hunsecker has been real antsy over intercepting correspondence from Veterans Administration, demanding she open all mail and check thoroughly for evidence of a certain Dr. Bo Hammer who's a surgeon at a VA hospital in San Jose. Hunsecker breathed down her neck, but she smuggled out a copy of Hammer's letter. It seems a story popped out in the San Jose press, something about a score or so unexplained deaths. VA believes Hammer leaked it . . . course, they maintain he's a shakedown artist attempting to cover for his own mistakes, but they want him bad and figured he might be ignorant enough to contact OWC."

"Anything else?"

"He sent evidence, including a videotape of nurses abusing and starving infirmed patients. It's explosive. And it trails right to the Counsel's office. Deejah overheard Madison telling Hunsecker that he'll be *watching this one closely*."

"The Gipper be praised!" says Manny with a voice like Ireland.

"Fuck that Gipper bullshit! Madison's sniffing around cause the VA secretary is close pals with Reagan. They ride their little horseys together."

"As well they should."

"Yeah, right. Anyway, in theory, if I can get a copy of the tape, and maybe even land Hammer himself a spot on *Sixty Minutes* is a sure thing. I know a news director over there."

"JOE BLOW!" Manny shouts, jumping to his feet, overcome with elation for Laney's sake. "The walls will come a tumblin'!"

Laney looks up at him with her best cruelty-mixed-with-apathy face. His burst of enthusiasm annoys her, even threatens her. She informs him that Hammer has been calling OWC every day, leaving messages no one would ever return, frantically complaining either about the slow death of the patients or his own various tortures.

"Use any means, and help the doctor. You must!" Manny can't check his excitability.

"Why is it my responsibility, Gipper Boy?" Laney asks. "I'm not the one killing patients. I'm not the one persecuting him."

"You know what to do," he says.

"You're not answering my questions."

"You *know* what to do."

"You're so insistent with *my* life."

"You have a contact at *Sixty Minutes*. You can put a stop to it."

Laney throws her hands up and stands to face him. "Ohhhh, you sure? . . . Look, a reality check. The war between OWC and Elaine Dracos has gained no real ground. She's had managers fired and press stories run. I've even forced Counsels to the Hill to deny their crimes, but the bureaucrats only go into hibernation and reappear later, deadly and useless as ever. So what the fuck's the point?"

"You're just making excuses."

"I'm telling the truth, Manny."

"You have a responsibility, Elaine."

"I have *nothing*, Manny."

"You have knowledge of the facts, Elaine."

"So does Congress and the president, Manny."

"But you're better than them, Elaine."

"I AM!" She pops her eyes to dinner plate size, white heat curdling into an expression of mock horror. "WHAT ARE YOU DOING TO ME?" she shrieks at him.

"Alright, alright . . . fuck it all then," he says.

She steams his face with a cold cloud of breath.

"ARE YOU MY FUCKING CONSCIENCE NOW?"

Her skin glows cold and raw.

"ARE YOU MY FUCKING CONSCIENCE, MR. EDEN?"

She shudders involuntarily with cold, looks as if she might buckle.

"Want a bullet?" she asks.

As Manny Eden turns and departs, Laney frames herself against the medieval nightmare of *The Burghers*, icelets running like half-frozen tears in her hair.

"You see, Mr. Garden-of-Eden? I'm talking about something greater, something AS BASIC AS HEAT!"

Manny remembers her dwindling to a panicky soak somewhere behind him.

"Mr. Conscience! I haven't played myself out," she yells. "I'll come out on top! Trust me!"

He is almost to the granite staircase, Balzac sneering on his right.

"Hunsecker is in me now! DON'T LEAVE MEEEEE!"

Halfway up the stairs, Manny notices a crowd of heads above him. They are all hunkered beneath umbrellas and poking with one gaping face over the wall and down into the pit of Balzac Park—crackers disgorged from the Arkansas Moose Lodge bus: mothers and daughters, uncles and pops and little shaveheaded skeeters gawking at the phalloids, braying at the monstrous fertility flanks. But just as he closes in on their faces he sees how jolted they are by an animal-like cry shrieking up from below. Laney Dracos, it seems, has finally confronted *The Burghers* with the sobbing truth.

The Arkansas clans stutter for a moment, appearing uncertain before scampering away, their faces blinking out like dull sunsets, wits of grits assuming a new murder brought to climax in Washington, the murder capitol of the USA.

Panicked at the sound of the cry, Manny forgives her everything. He turns, and as he runs back down the steps, he bellows over and over:

"I'LL HOLD HIM DOWN FOR YOU!"

December 5, 1984

Dear Counsel Madison,

I will get straight to the point. I'm writing to inform you of a new brand of murder, and those who are about to die salute me as Dr. Bo Hammer. They reside at St. Anselm's Hospital for the American Soldier in San Jose, California.

I cannot scrub my account down to a sterile chronology, though the events are causally linked and I attempt to be as objective as possible (see Attachment I) in my observations. Regardless, you may inquire as to my motives for writing. Besides attempting to right a serious wrong, I need to relieve my own guilt at not having reacted sooner. I wish to share my outrage at what has transpired, and in doing so, reveal to the world those conditions which allow a tiny group of individuals to engage in legal murder.

Under normal circumstances it would not be simple matter to dichotomize such a complex circumstance into one of two boxes—the first labeled good, the second, evil—but at St. Anselm's the boundaries glow, marked off with a violence hard to understand unless you have experienced it. On one hand we have a few good doctors, and on the other, a disastrous policy enacted by a hostile staff. The latter are judged by their behavior in the conspiracy—one of willingness as regards the circumstance, and retaliation as regards their response towards anyone who questions their actions.

Pardon me for this tangent. How much easier it is for us to condemn a dangerous policy than to single out and condemn those responsible; but is the difficulty dependent on lack of facts or lack of nerve?

Nevertheless, St. Anselm's is run by Dr. H.L. Xavier. Don't f**k with Dr. X. is the first thing one hears from the lips of a colleague here. If he stares at you cold, they say, you're a safe zero in his eyes, but if he begins to smile, you'd better get out the want ads. However, I found Dr. X to be a meticulous man, as was evidenced by the hospital's commitment to hygiene. Such a man, I reasoned, would not tolerate incompetence or sloppy procedure. My tenure at St. Anselm's thus began uneventfully, Dr. X's efficiency providing the type of working conditions I considered optimal.

As I've already noted, the events are fleshed out in objective detail in my attachments. I'll sum up though by saying that certain doctors here, and one in particular, cut on everything from eyes to hearts, and without any qualification to do so. The worst slasher is hampered by a tremor, proof enough of a nervous system suffering repeated alcohol dosage. When I confronted him with his impairment he denied it and became indignant. His most recent patient, a Mr. Marv Colson, died from a botched appendectomy only yesterday.

There are other major issues too that involve at least a dozen medical staff: fraudulent credentials, terminal incompetence, and severely negligent nursing. My colleagues have distanced themselves from me on all these matters.

Ms. Margaret McElvy, the Director of Nurses and longtime friend of Dr. X, informed me privately in her office one day that I was a vindictive, interfering sneak, and that the real reason I'd been whining about all the duties the nurses allegedly had failed to perform was because I hated at least two of them for ignoring my sexual advances. What I really wanted was to trip one of them up with trivial complaints in order to get my revenge.

I had reported several nurses to Dr. Villamayor, a senior administrator at the hospital. I reported them for neglecting patient medication, for haphazard monitoring of critically ill patients and for allowing the more infirm to stew in puddles of their own feces for excessive lengths of time—one patient, a Mr. F. Garner, for a period of five days. A few patients informed me that the nurses were getting revenge because Garner had complained about not receiving his medication on schedule. I also noted they were watching soap operas in Nurse McElvy's office when they should have been on duty.

Because of my efforts, Dr. Villamayor became furious with me. He asked me why it suddenly mattered so much to me and then stated that administration had enough problems to focus on and I should be more sympathetic with them and do less griping about peripheral matters which were none of my concern anyway.

That same day, I worked my way up to the top. I carefully and rationally explained it all from start to finish to Dr. Xavier. I told him also that I didn't think it served our profession or our conscience to let the men in our charge die of nurses and slashers considering they had miraculously outlived all the fire and shell an enemy could throw at them for three wars in a row. He stared at me cold throughout my talk as though he'd heard nothing, then proceeded to find me at fault. According to him, I was a troublemaker, a misfit malcontent, and a suspected sexual harasser. He didn't hold out much hope, but he would wait and see if my attitude changed.

My long letter of complaint to VA headquarters in Washington only resulted in punishment. I'm now doing bedpan duty on the graveyard shift, and everyone is giving St. Anselm's a clean bill of health. Someone threw gasoline on my car last night and lit it on fire. I know it was McElvy's brother. Also, Dr. Xavier appears on the edge of mirth whenever he sees me.

I sincerely hope, Counsel Madison, that you will help me on behalf of the naked and the dying here at St. Anselm.
Please. Help us.

Sincerely,

Dr. Bo Hammer
Assistant Surgeon

Attachments

CHAPTER 22

The Needful One — Laney's Death Dream — The Stone in Laney's Head

STARE INTO THE MIRROR. Look into your own eyes. See nothing there. Pinch your nose. Slap your face hard enough to make you wince. So what? What are you really? You don't know, so give up. You are simply Elaine Dracos.

Too damn bad.

After the strange episode of Balzac Park, things get even stranger. You're on hiatus, suspended from OWC for one more week, and Manny Eden won't stop pestering you about Dr. Hammer. You tell him to back off, give you space—but you're just delaying because you really have no intention of helping that poor bastard Hammer. It was a mistake to imagine it, even to tell Manny. It's just not safe, and you've called Deejah Thoris and told her to cease and desist any dealings with Hammer. Only now, how to prevent Manny from realizing your hypocrisy? Also, how to prevent him from noticing how often you float and frown upon contact with earth?

Are you falling in love with Gipper Boy?

It appears his Chevalier-like tiptoe into your delicate heart valves has succeeded in pricking to life a trait you consider dangerous: an annoying state of "almost love." Uncertain on how best to absorb your confusion, Manny convinced you of his potential as a crying shoulder (the least I can do, he says), and anchored himself to contain your various onsets. Does he deserve you? No! Regardless, you nickname him *Daddy Boy*, and in return, he dubs you, *The Needful One*.

Each night, during the week of hiatus, his phone rings at three A.M., and when he answers you say something like, *Daddy Boy, I woke up in a closet tonight*, or, *Daddy Boy, I woke up gasping for breath high above the earth tonight*, or, *Daddy Boy, I woke up on the Massacre Coast tonight*, and so on till he becomes exhausted from insomnia and threatens you with nullifying all relations. Whereupon you immediately rage over to his place to strike him about the head area with a blunt dose of your personal trauma regarding age, death, love, utopia, politics, the horror of your job, etc. till he gives in, and cushions you, and strokes your cheek like a Daddy Boy.

He jokes with you, and you invite it.

He cajoles you into believing you are simply passing through one of life's "panic zones," a kind of haunted house wherein the jackets of old hopes and illusions snag unexpectedly on the door knobs of new realities. No matter, he knows you must avoid a descent into madness in order to restore yourself.

Of course, you do not believe this, not at all.

* * *

DOCTOR HAMMER WON'T RELINQUISH HIS GRIP. Deejah Thoris calls you at home and tells you Hammer is now dangling from San Jose with straining fingertips. Deejah kicked out once, twice, and an apology as he fell away, a sudden *Wait! Please!* before the connection dissolved over three thousand miles of copper and glass. However, you can't be bothered with the details, for in the days which follow, Needful One, you dream recklessly of Instant Rub lotto wins, your ascension into Heaven, and swimming pool limousines.

As a Nemesis-in-embryo you drowse in Manny's arms, sheathing his fingertips, mutely apologizing for your earlier violence, and offering apology too for your bouts of life terror. You drive him from his place to your dollhouse Cape Cod in Falls Church, your face wet with tears as you lead him, sophomoric and awkward as a drunken boy through the gravel of your drive. And his illusions at this time, naturally, come fast and furious.

See the girl with the Alps in her hair, you say, and there you are, his Needful One, eclipsing a moon mountain shoreline at dusk. You point and laugh at this poster photo taunting you from your bedroom wall:

an aroused and godlike sea-maquette of seraphic resolve, poised to ascend from the shore of La Punta Spartivento, Italy, 1982 . . . My *immortal, partisan pose*, you say, dosing your voice with fatalist sarcasm. But Manny Eden only pales and turns away. Is he jealous of your history? Who knows? Maybe the word "partisan" reminded him of that doomed whistleblower from San Jose.

To cheer him up, you tell him by-the-way you can do a great imitation of Lulu in the old 60s movie, *To Sir, With Love*, and to demo, you sing the theme song with your sexiest voice.

Afterwards, the Daddy Boy is so horny he squirms for over an hour.

* * *

WITHIN THE WOMB OF YOUR CAPE COD, watercolored with lighthouses and eyeless masks, you open up to him even more. Night after night you pulse with tales of absent-but-fondly-hated Mother, ghostly U-Boat towers near Kitty Hawk, the ponies of Asateague, and the Outer Banks with Father till seventeen. Your lips are moist and pulpy as heart, warm with love as you release to him whatever child-self returns to comfort you. Only a larger question remains. How might you atone for your schizophrenic meandering, seek forgiveness too? Completely unnecessary, for your very change of nature had frightened him.

It was your first attempt at a suspense thriller kind of love: his wok-steamed prod, your vaginal time vault whose time had not yet come. *Dear Daddy Boy, I think the panic zone is to blame*, you say, exasperated. *Even steam won't help me, now*. But this explanation of yours does not satisfy him. He is afraid to hug the cliff of your expectations, his next step a death plunge.

Soon enough, though, you begin to weep like the soppy and selfish bitch you are—for yourself, for him, and even for Hammer. In vain he tries to console you with a tableaux of sanguine future, and one bereft of the American life sicknesses you both know so well. But you will hear none of it. Needing to encourage only more self-pity, you imagine horizons dark with rage, red-penny moon tides of misery, ecosystems of anguish old as Africa's Rift Valley and pointlessly nourishing the stones of a corrosive earth.

He explains you are part of it too though. Even the lament of all Masada, Constantinople, and Europe's lost nobility steams from your lungs, trickles out of you even as you speak. You only smile and reply softly:

What would you expect, Mr. Sun King? I am ninety percent tear.

* * *

DRINK YOUR COFFEE WITH SHAKING HAND the next day and complain to him of feeling swallowed. He immediately knows what the problem is. You're aching for new climes. A real vacation. In lieu of that, he opens a *National Geographic*, and soon you are full of Roman baths and the New Guinea coast. Above the sea, young gods of Portugal play and drift like balls of heat. Old gods of the Tamil and Trobiander walk the cliff rocks on bare knuckles of moon.

How to conjure further for you? *How will he distract you?*

Playing the Daddy Boy again, he tells you to relax, to imagine the grandeurs we can never compare to, the wastes we can never cross, the delusions we can never create. Ignoring him though, you casually speak of a new utopia, a "House of Life" you have erected in your sleep, and one devoid of government, religion, and fools. You also describe to him the strange dream you had last night. Once again you drifted in a cloud of stars above the earth, and a squall of black eyes appeared in the space around your body, drinking you in parts like tiny vacuums.

You believe this dream portends your death.

That reminds me, he says, Did I tell you that scientists have just discovered the universe to be fractured and drifting apart? *No?* Well, I read about it in the *Washington Post* yesterday. You see, big lumps of it, like the Hydra-Centaurus Galactic Supercluster, have been freed from the domination of Bang, summoned off like warming bergs, become plasma factions persuaded to revolt by a black hole tyrant somewhere beyond the rim of the universe and so distant that no one can see it. While you, Needful One, hurtle towards this enormous sucking thing at thousands of miles a second and all you can do is dream and sketch utopias. The great anarchist Bakunin, and even Marilyn Vos Savant, would be proud of your audacity.

Now, what about Dr. Hammer?

* * *

EVIL-LOOKING AT DADDY BOY, if he dares hint at Hammer, you and he tour the local geography, attempting a poetic, lunch-and-alcohol antidote. Come the morning and off you go to a Bukowski-laced picnic in liebraumilch sun; undoglike days of fried chicken, pina colada thermos, and Anne Sexton at Accotink; chicory coffee, smoked bluefish, and Hart Crane at Occoquan; *Tetelestai,* Pinsky, and Blue Moon Ale at Mason Neck. But poetic revelation and calories fail to console, and Manny assumes solutions more inebriating, more vast and final are in order.

At his suggestion, you strap two bicycles to the rack of your MGB and cruise, soon adjusting your eyes to bask in the fog of the Blue Ridge. On the drive up to the mountains that day, you tell Manny stories of old Virginia, the Shenandoah Valley, and the bike paths there which steam free of ice by noon; and you tell him that if he wakes up early and goes deep into the valley to stand and face the Mennonite Church of Murphreesville, says a prayer to their hero Jacob Wisler, then turns to his right and walks about thirty yards, picking his way over the shallow bed of Lubber Run and up the grassy bank, he will come upon the ruin of a 1936 Packard chassis. At this point, he will stumble backwards like an Oz-struck scarecrow, narcotized as he is by the morning boil of life in the onsweeping valley before him, the turn of earth on this particular day creating a swarm of sun flakes on the grass and cool-moist meadow hair.

Later, the two of you coast the Shenandoah on bikes, and the remnants of past encroachments become visible.

My God, Manny says to you, *the ancient farms are here.*

Farm homes, old farm songs.

With water and lonely atom for companion they lean, slacken and decay in the hollows and sapped out glebes now grazing field. You both pick the children out, the dresses of yellow and peach, Sunday biscuits, the autumn geometries of old crop machines. Farmer Joe and Mary slip their hands around your waist and you *do-si-do* very so-so in that barn behind Miller's place. And it all returns to bury you: the edge and beauty of the day weighting you down, cold as sunlight on iron rust, making sorrowful the many fields of swallowed plow, the yards of graying silo tin.

Does it matter to you, Needful One?

Oh, yes, for as you inhale the place like a toxic vapor, examining all the pallor and fragility, you mellow to a pensive drone. You darken and appear weakened by tales of loss only you can imagine. Whereas, Daddy Boy can only think once again of cheering you. You begin to weep and weep some more, and he wants to make your water his. You leave that foolish and bumbling Daddy Boy wondering what to do. You clap-clap over wooden bridges fording cobbly streams, and coast through pasture lands all fog-puffed and filled with grazing horse. He tries to make you laugh by badly imitating Hunsecker presiding over a review meeting—only his effort falls flat.

You skirt the bank of the Shenandoah River, and calmly swerve your bike from the path. He calls out to you several times. You pretend not to hear as you clatter alone towards an old spine of fishing pier, your private Gertrude goading you on.

Loudly, you sing your own gospel music version of "Rock Me on the Water", your face frail and blank as you coast off the pier, your bicycle back-end cartwheeling up and dumping you head first into the dark water.

* * *

SHRIEKING *GODFUCKINGDAMMIT Princess Needful* while driving you home, he sees the burbs coming at him soft and slippery as boiled papaya under his feet and you—wearing his jacket and the heat drumming dull in the car and about ten cups of Quickie Mart styrofoam littering the floor—either vomiting hot and brown into your empty purse or else scooping out a droll "Rock Me on the Water" from your waspish throat hollow, or else waving your hands like a maestro of your own silent film comedy while making just the kind of eccentric demands and proclamations you might expect to hear uttered by any goddess of self-imposed immortality who is convinced the human race should repent its ways and worship her as a myth.

* * *

NAKED AS LIGHT AT DUSK, Needful One, and your Electric Melon shooters made of vodka and cran-orange have not only cured you but cajoled you into searching your drawers for candles. You locate five in a box, insert them into holders, place them on the mantle and fire them all. Another few Electric Melon shooters and you begin cavorting and dipping in ritual circles like a deranged Beelzebub, becoming more ridiculous and violent by the moment. Your forefinger shadows rise and crowd the wall, substitute for horns. And as you move away from the light, arousing to grotesque proportion your chthonic blades of loin, you shout with a possessed voice a spew of words that neither of you understand:
   Antecessor! Antecessor! Come and carry us to Blockula!

* * *

IT'S SUNDAY MORNING AND YOU'RE SMILING, barefoot and full of legs in short terrycloth robe, shoveling up a side of bacon on the gas stove and ignorant of his blissful face responding to you from the dining room. What about Dr. Hammer, he asks you. You say nothing. Instead, you recklessly flop the bacon slab over in the pan, and as you do, he hears a loud spat of grease. You recoil at it, scratch your forearm, and slap the side of your face as if swatting a mosquito. Turning the bacon again, you slap yourself once more, only hard as a paddle-on-butt, hard enough that a piece of stone spits from your head and skitters across the tile floor of the kitchen, coming to rest with a hollow sound.

Later, a curious Daddy Boy finds it and says nothing to you, not at first. Like a dug god from a relic mound, it reclines on its haunches, cracked and squat and howling of mouth. It leaves behind a trail of sacrificial human even in miniature. Manny won't tell you that the face of it eerily reminds him of Hunsecker. If he understood the significance of it, he would demand you keep striking your head till you shed every stone.

* * *

HOW MUCH TIME DO YOU HAVE? Well, only seconds are left, uncaptured . . . towards midnight and you and your *âme damnée* are cuddled at your place watching television, a perfume commercial of slo-mo erotica: lots of lean arrogant bods and windy silk fluttering against a background of monochrome Wyoming. Daddy Boy, you say, Do you see that magnificent woman on a motorcycle sculpture, the moon in her hair, prairie and cliff at her breast, snow in your eyes?

He cannot answer.

Being a romantic is killing me, you say. Meaning is extinct. I have only this niggling piece of gray life pie. What of trips to Singapore and the *Cote d'Azur*, junkets to Rio and the power of corruption over senators?

Since he cannot control what he cannot give, Daddy Boy relates to you his own fantasy of total earth transfiguration, a subtle rusting of sapien creation in order to begin anew. He has dreamed his own utopia, a perfect one, after having read a book about failed American utopias (he is trying to impress you). He discusses strange things too, like the evolution of a "Transhuman Consciousness" or "Over Mind" to replace the individual. Instead, oh Needful One, you would cut corners, choose the form of a gang-busting God, a mere wave of hand that makes everything perfect in seconds. Frustrated and changing the subject, he purposely recalls a certain Bimbo Dog with chlorine eyes and pretends her frolic in his sexual shallows.

And how do you react?

You only snort in disgust before laughing and swimming towards your Daddy boy, become a face of teeth and bubbles and eyes of tombless summer blue. You have noticed his isolation, seen the fruit of agony in the sea and taken pity. Lowering your dark hair beneath the swell of television light, you nibble at his thighs and stomach, tickle as a minnow up to his neck, higher and higher till your face fires hot in the sunglassed blue and your lips flutter like sea-quail along his cheek. He embraces you then and carries you to the shallower bath of bed, overcome with your perfect woman-ness. He kisses you and pushes till you say *More* with the suddenness of it, *Go deeper, Manny Eden*. And soon, you take him into your mouth, creating enough motion with your tongue to make him surge and call you *Dearest love*.

Later, as you both lean to the current, your eyes caked with saltspray, your bodies collapse where the sea as a drowning man weakens, and the sand sprays in fossil fans from your fingertips.

CHAPTER 23

Ashley Gets Even — They Won't Survive Dr. X — Laney Goes Rhino

DESPITE MANNY EDEN'S PLANS TO DISSOLVE Washington and create a new utopia of bureaucrat-slapping supergods, the business of OWC must be attended to, the cruelty of government career endured. Mortgage and landlords leave no other choice. Therefore, on the Monday following the two week suspension, Manny and Laney take the subway into D.C. and soon find themselves entering a cold lobby of glass and stone decorated with pots of paper tulips. The space itself, though claustrophobic, oozes a lesser twilight in comparison to the OWC Hitchcock floor above.

Manny escorts his Vendetta over the iron-on tiles, his hand clasping her arm to steady her. He notices among the lingering bureaucrats, a large, dark-suited man standing directly in their path, solemn in pose before the elevator and looking like a morose General Patton. A few feet later, the general spots them. Immediately dismissing Manny, he excites himself just enough to glare at Laney, a grain of preeminence tainting his anger blue.

How can Laney not notice?

In response to this browbeating, she trembles ever so slightly, enough to alarm Manny. She flip-flops as if in last stage chrysalis, facing humiliation anew, and only seconds later, after a slight attitude adjustment, emerges and makes herself available. She wriggles free of Manny's lifeless hand and proceeds to reveal her new self to all present. The charm grill of her teeth, white as noon frost, inflates and consumes her face.

"Counsel Madison, *hello*," she says, her tone disturbingly sexual.

A group of OWC legal suits linger nearby. They watch in paralyzed silence, noting that the catalyst of Laney's new self now wears a barking face attached by a bridge of white collar to a torso the size of a warehouse. "What have you to gloat about?" he asks as she boldly invades his space without taking the hint.

"Absolutely nothing. I have no reason to," Laney says, happy as fresh mint.

"Then why hover so close?"

"Because a power sheathes you," she states without a hint of flattery, "a defiance that makes others uneasy."

"Nonsense. I'm a diplomat."

"You're a leader, Counsel Madison."

"Transparent flattery, Elaine . . . why are you laughing?"

"I recall Senator Ormsby remarking on that same quality."

"What?"

"*Politics*." She winks at Ashley.

He winces. "The Senator actually sympathized with your position here. He realized that no one in the Administration could credibly support a whistleblower without running the risk of career suicide . . . no one blames you."

The elevator door opens. Ashley shifts his bulk sideways to allow Laney to enter before him. She thanks him in coquettish fashion before sweeping grandly ahead on like Dolley Madison herself, opening the smile grill so wide it makes Manny quiver.

Once they're all inside the elevator, smudged in brass, stiff and dark, Ashley introduces a "gentleman gun" who up until that moment had been lurking at his rear. "Ms. Dracos, meet Jay Van Weberhoff," he says, "an aide to Senator Monroe of Indiana."

Van Weberhoff, a Clark Kentish hireling of Yale-pale fur, shakes Laney's hand overlong during the introduction, squeezing it in milking fashion just once before release. "Jay is down from Mars, I mean . . . the Capitol Dome, to inspect our operation here," Ashley says, sounding convivial. "You see, Elaine, I'm a *very* popular fellow these days."

Van Weberhoff chuckles and nudges the glasses up on his nose, while Ashley orders his cinderblock head of General Patton to adjust itself until nose to nose with Laney's face. And as their eyes lock, he asks her with a boyish voice:

"Now, uh, Mzzz Dracos, one more time, I want to get this straight. You mean to say that Senator Ormsby . . . *admired* me?"

Laney smiles nervously and says, "Yes."

"You mean the Senator might even *console* me, if he got the chance?"

"I'm not sure—"

"You mean that *ignorant, fossil cracker* actually felt sorry for me?" Van Weberhoff spits air in lieu of guffaw. The Counsel coldly appraises Laney's dumbfounded face and continues the interrogation. "You mean that *anti-Christian, tree-hugging, union-loving, invalid liberal prick* actually saw fit to forgive me?"

"Well—"

"Then his stroke was sent by God!" Ashley shouts.

Van Weberhoff chortles out loud this time, and like a carnival horse, stomps his foot on the floor of the elevator—a skillful display of the Washingtonian art of brown-nosing while overcompensating for inferiority at the same time.

Laney, restraining herself with little or no effort, ignores Weberhoff and says calmly to Ashley (who continues to bear down on her like a well-oiled engine of doom), "The Senator is doing well out in—"

"Didn't that prick Ormsby have his brains yanked out through his nose, Elaine? Isn't that what they do to mummies before they bury 'em?"

"That's rather—"

"Wait, I'm sorry. He was your *mentor*, yes?"

"Well, yes, Ashley, but they had to dig deep." She smiles at him as if to share in the joke.

"For *what?*"

"Why . . . for *the brains*, of course!"

"OH, HO! That's funny!" booms Ashley, thumping the air with an explosion of laughter. "I've always thought of Ormsby as a mummified old prick!"

"You have no idea what an old prick he really was," Laney says and laughs along with him.

Next, a melodramatic pause on the part of Ashley Madison. Executing a silent and solemn look of gravitas, he inquires with a voice gone soft and innocent, "But do *you* blame me, Elaine?"

"For what, Ashley?"

"Attempting to do my utmost for President Reagan?"

"Ashley, you're no different from the best of them."

Manny doesn't know whether to scream or vomit. Laney now sounds and looks like one of those television housewives who has just been rejuvenated by the promise of a new and miraculous toilet bowl cleanser.

"Like The Gipper, you do as little bad as you have to, and as much good as you can," she says.

"I appreciate that comment, Elaine, as well as your newfound optimism."

The elevator door opens onto the OWC Hitchcock floor. The reflexive surge to escape begins. When Ashley isn't looking, Manny squeezes Laney's arm from behind, pulling back slightly and attempting to rein her in. She yanks loose from his grip and calls out to Ashley:

"Oh, Ashley! Lunch today?"

"Certainly," he retorts, checking his momentum just enough to complete a half-turn and add, "but leave the *choir boy* at home."

"Of course!" she says, standing rigid and following Ashley with her eyes as his bulk eclipses the door to OWC. Van Weberhoff, in tow, turns back once, just long enough to slime Laney's body with his eyes.

Laney smiles at him, real wide. Plus she gives him a little wave.

For Manny, this is the end of reality as he knows it.

* * *

EXPERIENCING THE PRESENT AS ONE UNNAMEABLE ROAR, the "choir boy" hesitates before burning himself again. Imitating great playwrights, authors, and non-existential philosophers, he attempts to expand a vision of the past he has known, claim it as one paradisiacal and ceaseless present without chance of falter, that is until Elaine Dracos turns to him and states with a voice sucked dry as a Nevada test range:

"I told you I'd make myself invulnerable again . . . proud of me?"
"WHO ARE YOU?" Manny asks.
"*Shut-up*," she says, her face turning angry.
"I thought you were invulnerable."
"I'm in the business of survival, sir. Please get to the point."
"Oh, *Ashley*! Could you have brown-nosed any deeper?"
"Asshole."
"And speaking of assholes, what was that shit about Ormsby?"
"Madison loathes Ormsby, equals lots of schmooze points. Get it?"
"That's obvious."
"And he has every right to."
"He, *uhhhhh*—"
"Don't make something of the Senator he's not. Ormsby is a criminal no different than the others."
"That sounds a little too vicious."
"How would *you* know? You've probably never seen the man, much less spoken to him."
"But I don't care about that, not now."
"What then?"
"Whether you will blow the Hammer whistle or not."
"You mean, will Elaine Dracos needlessly impale herself for your benefit *or not*?"
"They survived Normandy, but they won't survive Dr. X."
"And what about my *own* death? Will it be REVOLUTIONARY?"
"So this is going to be a repeat of the Ziska case?"
Laney gasps. "Who told you about *him*?"
"The Bimbo Dogs."
"That case is none of your *fucking* business."
"You sold him out."
"I didn't make him become a whistleblower."
"You unmade him."
"I wasn't responsible. He knew about the snipers."
"But—"
"And no one else would corroborate his allegations."
"So now Hammer fries too?"
"He has to take responsibility for himself."

"I thought *he did*."
"It's not really convenient, or even smart. Not *now*. Don't you see?"
"I don't."
"You mean you *won't*."
"So what happens after lunch with Madison? Drinks at the Willard?"
"That's none of your concern."
"Why? You going to fuck him?"
"If I have to."

CHAPTER 24

Manny Loses It — Dropping The "Utopia Stone" — Up From The Slime-House-of-Saud Office Park — Hebrews, Hittites, Greeks, and So Forth

5:06 P.M. LONG AFTER LANEY'S MUTATION in the face of Counsel Madison, the Garden-of-Eden arrives at the Rosslyn metro station in Virginia to catch his bus, the 1Z. As he waits outside in the cold dusk of his whimsy, nine buses full of reality-phobes come slushing in from all over the target area, ablating the curbs in transit and coughing out hostages. Shivering on the metro jetty, Manny transcends reality and enters the realm of total transfiguration.

Only how to concentrate?

Mzz Dracos' mental sclerosis has rooted him to an alien tableau: a darkening western sky slashed with a scimitar of moon, a mote in God's eye gone fractured, hot, and listing between two office buildings rearing high in the Rosslyn twilight. While he watches, a black power cable sagging across the street rises up to meet the moon, edges the cusp, then eclipses a blemish or two. Moments later, a bit of gleaming lunar rind appears beneath the underside of the cable, unsheathing atom by atom.

Experiencing his first "Earth turn," Manny realizes that no realization could be more humbling or empowering. It's one thing to learn of "turn" in a science book, quite another to come to an intimate knowledge by perception, struck with a notion of numberless days produced by rotating bulk—a poor excuse for *Time*. But no sooner does the weight of *Time* evaporate than a bout of *terraphobia* overcomes him. It stays with him until the Earth relaxes and becomes his possession. He can kick it, hug it, stroke it, enter it, even become contemptuous of it. In comparison to Earth, he is scaled to salmonella, or less, but still able to plunge his fist down through sheaths of rock fat and earthmuscle to grip the hot magnetic heart.

Never has anyone else been capable of such a feat.

In seconds, Manny Eden sees the asteroid coming.

He evolves to a concept of Earth-as-prison.

He predicts nothing less than utter extinction, and as he does, a 24P bus mashes the ice before him into slowly thickening water. It grinds past to make for the ghettos of south Arlington, its husk loaded with the ferociously poor and late-of-dictator. It snuffs the new moon from his eyes and blunders on.

Manny gazes through his own winter breath clouding the box-like buses passing by, the crowds of dull *sheeple* walking up from the depths of metro station, and he knows that a phase-by-phase renovation into utopia is inevitable.

One way or another, he'd been planning it for weeks.

In response then to Manny's new loathing of all things, a godlike urge-to-surface rumbles into orbit beneath his feet. Groans of plate and hot core coagulations bore into his foremost consciousness, cajole him to create a leviathan obsessed with release, shrugging awake like a planet fetus within the womb below. From the Antietam cornfield to Selby Bay Marina, from the Germantown hollows to the wild acreage of Locust Shade Park, from Annapolis to the Glen Echo Hills, true utopia is now possible, and all because of him.

Thank you for making paradise a child of rage, Manny Eden.

* * *

5:14 P.M. AFTER BOARDING THE 1Z to Arlington, Manny "Mr. God" Eden thinks it all over very carefully. He realizes the evolution of his utopia (*The Most High Noosphere, New Erehwon, The Transhuman Consciousness, Manny Town*, or whatever) must be conceived on the move—the flux of transfiguration energies gleaming and bold with supervision. Also, unlike the other ill-conceived "utopias" of America's past (Woman-in-the-Wilderness, the Fourierist Phalanxes, Icaria, Zoar,

Orderville, the Bohemia Manor), this particular Eden of his god-philosopher vision will not undergo entropy or founder due to the influence of mammon, squabbling malcontents, or autocrat saviors who have achieved a state of self-delusion and distance. All potential glitches will be worked out in advance. The sheer size of his utopian pregnancy will smother any whiners who might seek to remain unhappy for the sake of unhappiness and the need for attention.

NOTHING will be allowed to upset the scheme.

Mr. God finds a seat on the bus and looks out the window, sees snow flakes beginning to fall. But this has no effect on him. Instead, as if sitting on a throne of magical toilet, he shouts to himself:

"I AM THE CREATOR OF THE FIRST AND BIGGEST PLOP!"

Several passengers turn to stare at him.

Fix 'em in the crosshairs, Manny Eden. Bombs away!

* * *

5:22 P.M. MR. GOD DECIDES THE COMING OF UTOPIA will be a time of radical change bubbling out in two major phases which, though distinct in impact, will occur simultaneously: **TOTAL HUMAN ECESIS** (the translation of sapiens to a utopian state) and **BZNESS-GOV-ZONE DISSOLUTION** (a total meltdown of all extant power structures)—a consequence of that finger-gag nausea experienced by all truly sensitive beings whenever overexposed by life and the *Washington Post* to the elite cretins of the D.C. metro area: IRS officials, tobacco lobbyists, incompetent bureaucrats, panhandling congressmen, used car dealers, sleazy land developers, equivocating bureaucrats, divorce attorneys, White House psychics, speedtrapping cops, fast food grungers, dangerously stupid bureaucrats, and so forth and so on.

There's no business like show business, Manny Eden!

* * *

5:23 P.M. MR. GOD PLOPS.
   The ripples begin.
   The wave shock expands.
   Much to his irritation though, the other passengers in the bus are oblivious. They sit blandly in their seats, watching the snowfall get heavier. To alarm them, and at his insistence, the snow sucks into the bus, in from the blizzard darkness and racing swarm-like through the windows. One terrified Indian mother down from the Andes, her eyes sunken and black, shrieks and tightly wraps her infant in a sweater. She flicks snow from the tiny lashes while she rocks and whimpers a paternoster. The bus driver, a craggy Sikh in his fifties, allows his fear-cooled hands to slip from the steering wheel, his mind going into a nerve skid. Of the four other passengers besides Manny, three leap screeching from the bus at such time it veers off the highway—one of them, a pudgy yes-mammal, accomplishing the feat with such force that he is dumped bawling and newborn onto the slush of a lawn the bus has crossed without leaving a mark.
   Just before the crash into a utility shed (an accident of no more or less importance than the fall of snow) the Sikh driver turns to rubber. Upon impact he jolts forward, his turban flying off his head. He clips the corrugated tin roof like a spongy nerf before skipping like a flat stone over the icy ground, gravity finally slowing him just enough to fill his eyes with a black sky of snowing stars. And neither he, nor any of the other former passengers realize it, but the mysterious man who remained dark and calm is now three feet above the ground and floating cool and furious as an all-powerful Nemesis towards the Potomac, his newfound telekinesis stalking the White Oz monuments and offices, his thoughts gouging out craters and rippling suburban landscape as far as the mind can see. Not a single construction of humanity exists that is not threatened.
   Don't forget to leave the libraries and museums, Manny Eden.

*　*　*

6:39 P.M. SUBURBAN YOKELS ARRIVING HOME from D.C. sample the first wave of Mr. God's utopia as a heavy slap to the organs—especially the stomach. Seconds later, it phases to a screw, tight and deep in the forehead, aftershocks of wave inducing rage and grand mal seizures in some, incurable vertigo in others. Upon completion though, and after only minutes, utopia flushes itself out to the eyes. It bubbles up from the pons and old mammalian brain baggage, up from the primordial mind chowder with unbalancing visions of flight, teeth, and snake.

Mr. God, above all others, knows that true epiphany requires perspective.

Less conscious things, leaftips and fintertips too, feel the nudge of utopia and begin to respond. Within their envelopes of soggy cell, their fluids and creature-feet quiver and warm as if microwaved, or jostled by an eruption of sun, the first comber of utopia fibrillating all local flora from mold to oak, all fauna from doe to dust mite, even thrumming down to the tiniest crack in the coldest floorboard, down to the invisible insect dust.

At the same time, Laney Dracos, weakened as she is by the pulse, and hallucinatory glimpses of up-from-the-slime evolution flailing in her eyes, slips from the edge of her bed to the floor. Attempting to stand, she is forced to her knees by the vision of an aroused Ashley Madison with a prick hard-on the size of the USS Liberty. She cries out. He looms above her like a black moon eclipsing all light. His three-piece suit is replaced by martini boxers and a trunk of gray-haired flesh, his General Patton face smelling of stale truffle and looking like old wax.

Damn your need for revenge, Manny Eden!

*　*　*

7:42 P.M. ONE BOTTLE OF MOOSEHEAD BEER and Mr. God reclines in his bed at home, focuses more clearly, extends his vision. In other words, he gives all the victims time to breathe.

Later, his roommate, the E-Man, rumbles in looking like blisters over-easy. He slams the kitchen cabinets, searching for a box of mac-and-cheese. Someone has eaten the very last one. E-Man asks to borrow five bucks for a steak-and-onions at Mt. Gyro. Mr. God coughs up, but it reminds him of what a dump Mt. Gyro is, and of the asshole dump owner, Daddy Papadopolis.

Poor old Daddy P, he says to himself. *How to tell him his Macedonian lamb spits are doomed?*

At Manny's insistence upon killing the Moosehead, the Mt. Gyro franchise in Annandale begins to perspire and rearrange itself. Whole colonies of bacteria sizzle and spit from the formica like beads of steam-pregnant water. Ovens and fryers oxidize back to the days of the Beer Hall Putsch. Spitted flanks of lamb hatch flame-crested bowerbirds that launch themselves like Aztec demons into the dining room, there to dive and crap on shrieking customers. Attic-vase Greeks come to life and prance about on the wallpaper, squaring off into phalanxes and hurling Ionic obscenities at one another before brawling onto the ceiling, shreds of limb and head zigzagging the air like confetti.

Daddy's number one kitchen man, Chef Bobo, blames the Turks and blows his nose over the souvlaki. But the owner of Mt. Gyro, Daddy Papadopolis, swears vengeance and loads his Walther PPK.

Nevertheless, a Pyrrhic victory in the dining room appearing certain, the tomato paste resolves to sweat, the customers resolve to leave, the milk congeals to grass, and the usually surly waiters siphon into crocodilian smiles. As compensation for his loss, the pitiable Daddy P sprouts an oily lawn of hair and sheds fifty-eight pounds. Utopian pizza will be delivered *I-Dream-of-Jeanie*—i.e., magically. Mr. God is not without mercy—and besides, he can't imagine a utopia devoid of pizza.

Will utopia also include a weight loss clinic, Manny Eden?

* * *

8:10 P.M. ONE MORE MOOSEHEAD AND THE ELECTRIC corridors of Bzness-Gov-Zone begin to ebb like heat towards dissolution. Frantic executives, bosses and bureaucrats, blame the snowing stars, the French, the Chinese, Pol Pot, Galactus, Gorbachev, an invasion of libertarian wizards from Middle Earth, everything and everyone but themselves.

Regardless, a state of total anomie is apparent.

Mr. God lies in bed and whistles *Moonlight Sonata*. Bobbing chunks of light are seen to mass at a distant point in the east, and like enormous air raid columns, swerve and bore through the atmosphere over the entire target area as if advertising the grand opening of a new shopping mall. They waft against a cloud bank in the west, and their glow illumines human-like shapes moving like vast and dark gods above the distant Massanutten Mountains.

What might these apparitions be?

Gargantuan Toad Dieties of Mambia? Senatorial behemoths of the suburbs?

No one knows.

Meanwhile, Lucinia Lombardo and her cousin Baal Hinsley of Falls Church (neighbors of Mzz Dracos) have climbed high as possible atop the shingle roof of their home. In the explosive darkness, their bodies wobble with the import of mythogenic visions to the west, below Venus, and to the north, below the star Polaris. Lucinia, a shrill-mouthed Anabaptist, screeches, "*Millennium! Millennium!*" while eighteen-year old Baal, looking like insanity, jabs her finger down at Mzz Dracos (as she looks dizzily up from her front yard) and shrieks at her:

"*Your Antecessor comes! The way to Blockula opens!*"

Laney Dracos though, stumbling about in her housecoat and still perspiring the portent of an aroused Ashley Madison in martini boxers, takes a more radical view. It is her opinion (she keeps to herself) that the shadows of gods roaming the horizon symbolize not only the western Lamb and Satan, but all the Elder Gods of the Hebrews, Hittites, Greeks, Babylonians and so forth—ancient super beings awakened from hibernation and now preparing to depart for more gullible

worlds, humiliated beyond endurance by the more powerful and televised idols of the Reagan White House.
Is The Gipper really that influential, Manny Eden?

* * *

8:36 P.M. HOUSE-OF-SAUD OFFICE PARK, Bowie, Maryland.
The night shift abandons its post.

White shirts pour thick as spilled borax onto the black-turf hexagons which separate the glass buildings. Rude feet trip over the basalt mini-fountains and step on exposed necks. Brains erased of career and sex think only of escape—the whole scene reminding Mr. God of a rampaging herd of Toho movie extras goaded into stampede by a rubbersuit Godzilla.

A few hystericals beseech Allah and bleed themselves with razors. Other pitifuls simply bawl or start fist fights for distraction. Most of them desperately seek the familiar blue and siren of police. Alas though, these middle class victims of stick-and-carrot can do nothing but snap as row after row of House-of-Saud office glass tightens at the waist and explodes to sand with a bomb rolling crack heard as far away as New Jersey. By morning, the office park will appear like a field of gutted hives the size of up-ended ocean liners, only a half-life of Zone remaining behind, hugging the earth like fog and crackling with sparks.

Conscious of eruption from all quarters, Mr. God sheds the final grace necessary to Zone demise—the entire pastiche of petty ambition and power structure shaved to a stubble and pre-heated to utopia by his beneficent animosity.

Farewell, and fuck thee off! Mr. God shouts.
Farewell, ye McNeighborhoods, McPeople, and McJobs!
Farewell ye sharper-image strips!
Farewell ye billboards of bimbo pushing cigarettes big as nukes!
Farewell ye corporate, subsidy-sucking remora!

And of Mobil-Texronoco gas, nothing will remind but a few clusters of socketwrench sculpture encircled by wreaths of black rubber flowers.

Congrats, Manny Eden. You've ended our dependence on oil and car mechanics!

* * *

9:02 P.M. DESPITE HIS WISDOM, MR. GOD KNOWS the whole of humanity will knee-jerk with condemnation of him—and soon, for the loess of utopia, mounting in the atmosphere like a volcanic trail of Mt. St. Helen, will shiver the Earth one degree more and bolster the antitrades, at the same time disrupting the magnetic field—thus pausing migrations, puckering the oceans into pole, and summoning the queer climates, phenomenal droughts, and tepid surface tides of *El Nino*.

Regardless, it is all for the good. He can't be stopped.

What will remain then of America's corporate products?

Answer: only one small pond of neon potholing the landscape. Liquescent and unbearably pure, it will goad whoever happens to see it into a bad taste of nicotinic bimbo, orange-sherbet sports jacket, Ayn Rand flatus, and the combustible, black crockery effect of urban Buffalo.

Who needs capitalism in utopia anyway, Manny Eden? Or communism for that matter?

* * *

10:08 P.M. THE STARS NOW NESTLE one inch deep. Some believe them to be the tears of angels. After a third bottle of beer, the cloud screens of Virginia go null. Manny might squeeze off another wave of utopia, but he'll wait till morning, crisp out the details under the shower.

As his own filth will dissolve and dribble into the drain, so will the monuments of Washington melt and sluice into the Potomac, away to the Atlantic before washing to sandcastle on the beaches of Europe. Like water-soaked witches, all contrasts to Washington's impotency will thus deflate, relieved as they are of inspiration. Rather than gawk stupidly at idoliths and obelisk (reduced by Mr. God to postcard), a new race of utopian beings will meet the original idols themselves—the voice of American democracy made corporeal.

Many heroes and political philosophers of various eras and stages—attended often by the likes of Dolley Madison, Diderot, and Voltaire—will wander like minstrels about the new land, inhaling the scented corona of utopia into their blood before exhaling their gratitude over the smoking hills, lakes, and river banks now bereft of all greed and government. Though made only of circuits and harvested flesh, they will be solemn with compassion one day, fire-eating with righteous *isms* on the next, and easily engaged by the casual command:

"Tell us now of America's best and brightest democracy."

Dolley, Diderot, and Voltaire meanwhile, having viewed the carnage of the American ruling class from a distance, will be shocked into utter confusion and forced to search for scapegoats.

Voltaire will blame the Pope.

Diderot will blame Catherine II.

Dolley will blame the British over the cursings of Chef Bobo who won't stop blaming the Turks.

But what about the new residents, Manny Eden? What of the future superbeing, Homo Utopius?

* * *

TUESDAY, 7:01 A.M. BLACK SHOED, MOUTH WASHED, and full of cheese omelet, Mr. God is on his way to OWC and feeling a strange equanimity. He'll conjure Rosslyn, the White Oz, the termite nations of bureaucracy one more time, and as a bonus, do lots of nasty things to people he doesn't like.

For example, he will:
- Lower Hunsecker by the ankles, thrashing and screaming into a pit of jobless whistleblowers.
- Handcuff Luna Goodpal to a sincere evangelical.
- Tell Babs how fat she looks and how powerless she truly is.
- Force Boyden to work for the Peace Corps.
- Perform JFK imitations till Varsana shrieks in pain (and continue doing even more of them).
- Exhort the cosmos to more ridiculous forms in the eyes of Mzz Dracos so she'll note with horror the catastrophic consequence of her evil temporizing.
- Videotape the vigorous paddling of Madison's big fat ass and send trailers of it to the White House advertising a midnight premiere at the Key Theater in Georgetown.

And so forth.

Only Mr. God cannot suffer notions of Laney as a traitor to her species, not for long, so in true Mr. God fashion, he simply alters her. In less than a moment he cloaks her in god flesh, makes her sunset purple, gold, and all colors of glower, and he launches her into the marble hallways of Washington, there to swirl like an awakening sword goddess of WW I, like America herself anxious to battle The Hun. Her true and righteous nature she will reveal to the multiplex predators of Washington: the bribe-peddling lobbyists and democracy-for-hire "consultants" of K Steet, the fact confabulators of all desperate Democrats and Big Lie Republicans, the managerial Morlocks and the career yes-mammals at the agencies, plus the many other status quo preservationists and special interest barnacles who perpetually corrode the hull of good ship *Democracy*.

By 8:00 A.M., his Supreme Vendetta will bubble up with pouting lips and blue-socked eyes. Her *J'accuse* energy will recombine the words on their memos into an eerie image of her face. Her pointing finger will erupt from the skin of their wall or desk to dispel the self-delusion and rationale necessary to evade responsibility, while those blinded by the crackling aura of her presence will collapse to the floor, weakened as they are by fits of weeping gratitude—for they'll realize this flashing storm front of spirit to be not only their salvation, but a benign force even more powerful than Captain America, Ms. Marvel, Ronald Reagan, JFK, Queen Zenobia, Simon Bolivar, Dolley Madison, and the entire Justice League of America put together.

Thus will Laney Dracos serve as model for the evolution of humankind into Homo Utopius.

We can't praise you enough, Manny Eden. You are a true visionary.

CHAPTER 25

Throbbings of Worm — A Desperate Catfight — The Cops Bust Laney — A Note About "Self"

12:30 P.M. ONLY ONE BIMBO DOG ANIMATE. Not even Worm sign yet. It might be a blazing morning outside or a dark tornadic afternoon, everything blended in OWC to post-utopia static.

The Investigation Division had recomposed itself since the appearance of Luna Goodpal, snapped back to form like good bureaucrat rubber. Meanwhile, members of the House of Saud royal family, having already landed at BWI and taken limousines out to the office park, come together and form a row of human sheets. They fall to their knees as one and pray to Allah for revenge.

Will he hear them?

From behind his Eracto desk tank, Manny Eden plunges down once more to grip the heart of Earth. What remains of Washington now bakes mellow with a soft blanket of Northern Lights, and Laney Dracos, taking a break from her Nemesis duties, stretches her body across the top of his desk to become a sun-winnowed mouth, an American goddess of light and lip muscle and Aurora Borealis mane, her left hand invisible due to his distraction. He leans forward to gently kiss her and a ringing phone enters his fantasy like a tweak of panic.

Manny picks up the receiver and hears:

Do you know how much I hate you, conscience?

The imago Laney deflates out of sight, her Olympian lines and sinful Ava-Gardner-gaze replaced by a voice that sounds soft and weak.

Laney?

You're killing me.

Please—

Want a nail?

No.
I had a dream last night of being raped by Madison.
You're kidding, right?
Who would kid about a thing like that?
Where are you? I want to see you.
Childe Harold on Connecticut . . . our smoking gun met me here.
I don't get it, as usual.

After Deejah hung up on him last week, he bought tickets and flew in from San Jose two nights ago, figured he had nothing to lose. He called me at work yesterday afternoon.

Hammer?
We met at the Prometheus statue, Hains Point Park. He slept at my place. . . . and I didn't have sex with him, if that's what you're thinking.
I'm not.
It doesn't matter. This whole thing is a big mistake.
Then why are you doing it?
My motives are purely selfish. Remember I told you Hunsecker was inside me? Well now he's been replaced by you.
Huh?
I want your pointing finger out of my head.
That's funny . . . listen, just relax. Afterwards we'll go to Florida, start a worm farm, whatever.
No worm farms. We're finished.
Why?
Um, let's see . . . how about no more paycheck?
We'll make do.
How? By renting a tree house in Lafayette Park?
No, I mean—
Never mind, it's all set up.

She tells him The American Watch (*ha, ha*) has finally found the whistleblower needy and noble enough to crush "the White House groupthink project." The extreme visibility of martyrdom will bring sufficient public and congressional rage to bear. Laney would televise Hammer into mythos courtesy of *Sixty Minutes*. The producer is excited and standing by. *Oh, yes!* Also, Hammer has the official OWC rejection letter, a second copy of the nurse killer tape, and as bonus, a cassette of Dr. X in denial over the abuses.

Elaine, are you crying?

Listen, I would never have gone to bed with Madison. I just said that to hurt you. Did you believe it?

Yes.

I'm sorry. It was so cruel and stupid. Please forgive me. Please.

Forget it. I want to help you.

It's time. Deejah is here with me now and she's freaking out.

What?

She gave her notice at OWC last week. She's moving to Oregon, but she's too agitated by something, as if a psychotic break is on the way. I brought her along as a witness . . . another mistake.

Why didn't you ask me—

I didn't want harm to come to you.

And now you need a saner witness?

Yes, and hurry, my man of Kenosha. We have windmills to conquer.

* * *

YOUR FEET CRUNCH into the mulch-blackened aisle of Ed's Plant Emporium, your chin not soft but hard as stone. Your indignation borders on wrath. Your entire being is pumped with notions of justice. Though no glory is possible, your voice will be heard, and given your state of mind, nothing can stop you now, not even the vision of a snickering Syd Drummond waiting for you in Kenosha.

Regardless, your spirit and dash are abruptly impaired by nothing more harmful than simple courtesy. Halfway to the hall, an entire head and torso drifts forward to block your path. It floats limply between your body and Laney's salvation. A cold trout of hand flops to within an inch of your chest. You choose to ignore it.

"You see Hunsecker?" Worm says.

"Where'd *you* come from?" you ask.

"You see Hunsecker?" Worms says again, "He had the funniest damn expression on his face just twenty minutes ago."

"A look funnier than usual?"

"I'd say one of triumph. Worm has never seen the like."

"I don't have time for this shit," you say, and as you restart your momentum, Worm moves again to block you.

You violently shove him aside.

He sputters out *"Fuck you."*

Less than a minute later you're free and half-running up 18th Street. It takes you nearly ten minutes to cover the long blocks between OWC and Childe Harold at Dupont Circle. Panting and sweaty, you brake for knots of mulling suits, Big Sky tourists, and bewildered Star Eyes. You curse at them under your breath.

It makes no difference.

You approach the rendezvous point from a block away and notice a crowd, still small at thumbnail-size distance. They're mobbing in the front of Childe Harold, heads slanted earthward. They appear to be observing something taking place on the ground. A few are waving their hands in the air. You hear distant shouts.

You suddenly feel panicky.

At a distance of half a block, between the trunks of legs, you see a churning blur of color, as though someone had unfurled a large flag on the ground and it now flapped uncontrollably in the wind.

You run faster.

You arrive on the scene just as the crowd bubble bursts.

Onlookers, five or six of them, backpedal with quick but tiny steps, as if someone had aimed a lawnmower at their feet and pushed. From out of the gap rolls the cause of their repulsion: a two-headed, four-legged thing fused together like one freakish human body.

In response to this chimera, the crowd shouts back.

For a moment, you glimpse the Hunsecker. He's staggering in the background, reeling in confusion, drops of blood splattered on his face. The wild and thin Deejah appears next, coming up from behind him to hover above the thrashing shape and make sorcerous symbols in the air with her hands while screaming half-intelligible incantations.

To your surprise, the chimera responds.

As if conjured into being, the faces of the thing flash into view, freeze just long enough for you to recognize one of them as Laney Dracos and the other as Luna Goodpal.

Near paralysis, you force yourself to try to stop the violence. Before the faces can blur out of sight though, you stall, brought up short by the virtue and impact of Laney's ferocity. At this point in the conflict both women look considerably frazzled. Their lips are bloody, fistfuls of hair screeched out onto the pavement—though Laney appears to be gaining an edge. She presses a vigorous assault against her antagonist, hammering down blows despite her own wounds and exhaustion while Luna, fighting mechanically for her life, looks groggy and beaten; and no sooner does Laney struggle atop Luna, pinning her school-boy style, than a D.C. police siren whoops to a groan in the background.

The crowd quivers and mutters.

You fear for Laney's safety and you move to pull her up just as a huge black-female cop bursts through the wall of bystanders like a violent bulldozer and unhesitatingly locks her nightstick around Laney's neck. The cop twists it cruelly and jerks the woman you love into the air, choking her in the process. Laney frantically grips at the nightstick with both hands, her eyes bulging.

You shout as if demented: "YOU'RE KILLING HER, YOU BITCH!"

You lunge forward, thrashing your arms, until a white-male cop, big and wide as a porta-john crapper, roars in and drives the butt end of his own nightstick into your chest, knocking you backwards onto the pavement.

In horrible pain and feeling like broken ribs, you immediately struggle to sit upright, fighting for air as the waves of agony leave you breathless.

You try to focus.

The crowd goes blurry.

Not a single hand is lowered to help you, and the first thing to resolve in your eyes is Luna Goodpal, her body still prone on the sidewalk, her face weepy and scratched and pointed up to the clouds. Her tears have flushed so much red eye-shadow down her cheeks that it looks as if she's been crying blood.

You glance around for Laney. She is nowhere to be seen.

A rescue ambulance pulls up behind you with a single blurt of siren and disgorges two paramedics toting a stretcher. You hold your chest and push up to stand, noting the object of their attention not to be the tearful and bleeding Luna, but rather a heavy-set, middle-aged man who looks a lot like General Patton. He lies fallen to earth some yards away to your right, slumped against an iron sign pole, his head dipped into a gluey pond of half-dried blood that bonds him to the pavement.

The parameds, undaunted, scrape him up like an overdone sausage and slap him square in the stretcher, clamp an oxygen mask over his mouth, and haul him into the ambulance. They drive off with a series of low and exaggerated siren whoops. You hear a male bystander squawk to a friend that "the bitchin' catfight" started in the dining room. Before you can inquire, a befuddled Deejah, smelling like spilled Cabernet and looking like brains-on-acid, stumbles over and informs you between mental rifts that the bloody side of beef just towed away belonged to none other than Counsel Madison himself.

Her information registers in you and it makes no difference. Your mission now is to locate and buttress your peerless Vendetta.

"Where is Laney?" you ask Deejah.

She points north, up the street, and begins to mumble to herself.

You edge through the bodies and search till you find Laney a block away and handcuffed in the backseat of a cop car. She looks roughed up, her hair in her face. Otherwise childlike, trance-eyed, and wedged between two of D.C.'s finest and most monstrous.

You don't hesitate.

You immediately poke your head inside the cruiser, your face alarmed with concern. Laney refuses to look at you though, as if she is embarrassed, or severely depressed, or both. All you can say is "*Laney*" before the cops shout at you to "GET MOTHERFUCKING SCARCE!"

You had heard tales of abusive and hostile D.C. cops, but thought them exaggerated, until now.

* * *

AS SOON AS POSSIBLE, YOU TAKE a cab to the precinct where Laney is incarcerated, only the cops have slapped her in a holding cell and won't allow visitors. Bail set at $50,000. The charge: assault with a deadly weapon.

Nothing you can do, at least not yet.

After a sleepless night, you stay home the following day, repeatedly calling Deejah at OWC as well as the sergeant on duty at the precinct. By eleven in the morning you fall asleep on the couch in the living room, observed fearfully for a full three minutes by Molly Moon who believes you have gone insane and might spring up any moment to strangle her.

By noon, Deejah calls you, and using a muffled voice, tells you Laney has just phoned her. Dr. Hammer posted bail for her before catching a plane to meet his fate back in San Jose. He felt guilty over everything that had happened. Regardless, Laney is out and on her way home to Falls Church—and by the way, Hunsecker is fuming like a madman around the office, demanding to know the whereabouts of that "Garden-of-Eden snake."

An hour or so later, after taking an afternoon bus and walking several blocks, you arrive at Laney's house. You note with a sobering dread the crazy way her MGB has recently left the street, run over the walk, and gouged a muddy gully through the azalea bushes in front of her house.

Dazed with fear, you ring the buzzer again and again before slamming your body hard into her front door, bruising the wood for an answer. You then clamber over the still-warm hood of her car and kick with both feet through a bedroom storm window. You wriggle inside the house, cutting your arms and clothes on the broken glass, and after a frantic search, you find Laney unraveling in the living room.

She reclines on a leather ottoman, her office clothes mauled and still clinging to her body. Her head is tilted back. Her mouth closed. Her eyes only slightly open. Sleepy and disturbingly peaceful—one of them puffed into a dark shiner.

You cry out with a strange, animal-like sound.

You feel for her pulse and breath.

You collapse onto all fours with another cry before lurching up to fumble the phone off the wall.

You pushtone for a 911 ambulance, gobble out the address with an alien voice, and quickly return to her.

Laney, God, oh fucking fucking God!

You see bottles of valium and percocet on the coffee table.

You can't make her vomit.

You cup her head and lift her off the chair onto the floor.

You breathe yourself into her, inflate her and deflate her, punch her chest like you've seen on television.

You feel her evaporate—a rare and clean vapor between your fingers and wet kisses, going slow as heat.

You see the envelope she left for you atop an end table.

You continue to try and revive her till the parameds show up.

After the parameds have failed and carried her away, you weep till you are utterly exhausted. Hours later, you read the letter with blurry eyes:

```
Dear Manny,

I went looking for you after they let me out of
the police station. You weren't home. I wanted
to see you, thank you for all that has hap-
pened. Anyway, I believe in Heaven, but I'm
afraid I'm a dumb bitch. As a precaution, I
wanted to leave you something of myself, trans-
late myself onto this paper for you to keep—
only the words won't come. I cannot capture my
"essence" because I don't know what it is. I
thought about it, in that pit of D.C. jail last
night, and the difference between whatever is
commonplace and whatever is special, that de-
fines ME and no one else, is impossible to
know. I'm just a fool stuck between a past I've
lost and a future I can never have. So please
accept my apologies for being unable to ex-
plain my "self". I only know that I have to
move on. You are the American Watch now, the
only one left! Keep it burning, my good friend.
Help the doctor if you can. I know you love me
and I'm sorry for that too. I've been selfish.
I should have possessed more courage. I should
```

have tried harder. Maybe next time I'll listen to you and pack for Florida. Anyway, goodbye Manny. Don't be mad at me.

Yours Forever In The After,

Laney

CHAPTER 26

Madison's Version of Events — Manny Goes Mannequin — A Moral Obligation — "They Just Wanted to Kill Her" — What Really Happened at Childe Harold

FOLLOWING HIS TRAUMA, Ashley Madison returned to OWC to explain in dour but patient fashion (to those fireproof few who dared inquire) the mystery of the purple railroad-track that puckered his forehead from nose bridge to scalp. In meticulous, though artful fashion, he engineered the image of a "malicious and guilt-ridden" Dracos gone rabid with malice aforethought and splintering a bottle of Heinz on his cranium—the bottle not simply hurled like shrapnel but launched through space with her own blunt-object essence adjoined to the payload, the weapon streaking to the target like a missile whose human booster refused to detach—and this sorry performance enacted only because of the one critical though justifiable mistake Ashley had made prior to the assault, namely, his successful challenging of "her delusory sense of reality."

Like the rest of OWC, he had deduced, based on available evidence, that Bo Hammer was simply a bad doctor and a sexual harasser, and one who employed every tact possible in an effort to save his job—and everybody at the table, including she, *knew it!*

Of course, Mzz Dracos could no longer live with the lies and guilt. It finally caught up with her—not to mention with that SOB Senator Ormsby.

How pointless and self-destructive!

"That hypocrite liberal bitch," Ashley said to Hunsecker in the elevator lobby just prior to the weekly OWC director meeting. "What *more* can I do for my country?"

The Counsel grinned directly into the face of Hunsecker, and the Beast, grateful as a true brown-noser, grinned back at him.

As Ashley turned from Hunsecker to push the elevator button, on his way to buy a hot chocolate from the snack shop, he heard Hunsecker say behind him:

"What do *you* want?"

Curiosity aroused, Ashley swiveled his head sideways. He stared through the dim light to see the choir boy named Eden, a rather gaunt and pale fellow, standing about five yards away, just outside the door to OWC. He was glaring darkly, his mouth open, his stance mannequin-like—left hand raised slightly, right hand crossing his chest as if contemplating the pledge of allegiance

"You modeling a bad attitude, mister?" Ashley shouted.

The choir boy didn't answer. Ashley shrugged.

The elevator door pinged and opened. The Counsel stepped inside and pivoted to face the lobby, laughing to himself as the door closed, having just caught sight of Hunsecker glaring back at Eden with his infamous "Triumphant Beast face."

* * *

ASHLEY'S HEARTFELT WORDS TO HUNSECKER had occurred a few minutes after 10:00 A.M. At this time, all OWC division directors, already huddled in the main conference room, reduced themselves to passive posture, coffee and notepad at hand. Such a cadre of Reaganized conservatives and head-nodding brutes appointed over the past several months of Ashley's tenure as Counsel certainly did not dread these weekly meetings. They viewed them instead as an opportunity to demonstrate their loyalty to the three major principles of Ashley's enlightened regime, namely:

1. Reinterpretation of liberal public law with conservative regulation;
2. Careful investigation of speech potentially deserving protection;
3. Application of policy and ethics necessary to protect both the White House and the Republican Party.

* * *

DEEJAH'S FACE AND MIND HAD PUCKERED from that moment earlier in the day when Manny related to her the dialogue in the elevator lobby between Hunsecker and Madison. Laney simmered on their foul breath. Her death grinned out from the black stove of Madison's mouth. Her life dipped casually into the obscene puddle of Hunsecker's brain.

What vendetta could ask for more?

At this point, for Manny Eden, the sobering ratio of life-to-time weighed heavily against the two bosses while the act of murder became a moral and Hamlet-like obligation. Besides, would it not serve the greater good to burn such viruses from the body politic, to rescue scores of human lives and even America herself from the certainty of further injustice, degradation, and harm?

"Laney lost her temper, but wanted good," Deejah said. "You only want revenge, Manny Eden."

"No, Deejah," he replied stoically, "*I have transcended revenge.*"

Deejah's hamster-pink face burrowed deep inside her parka. Watching Manny, she became afraid. He looked feral, savage, capable of any monstrosity.

It was near 5 P.M. A long black escalator lowered the two of them into the hypogeal twilight of the McPherson metro-station. On the fringe of the landing terrace, Manny Eden stood idol-like as a glazed Deejah dug with quaking hands through every pocket in her parka in search of a rail pass. She was nervous because she knew Manny Eden was determined to learn what had really happened at Childe Harold.

She finally found the pass in her pants pocket. She bit it with her teeth to straighten out the kinks and proceeded through the pass gate only to pause halfway through, violently jerking her head to one side. Her gaze fixed on a *psychic burr* (a hint of Harmusal, imperceptible to ordinary humans).

Fortunately for all present, her brain anomaly evaporated within seconds, withdrawing its claim in order to resume its spelunking through the pre-psychotic caves of her unconscious.

"But all I want is *good*," Manny said as they descended the final black escalator to the loading platform. They stepped off the vanishing lip of stair and walked about twenty paces through a random sample of Star Eyes, Morlocks, and yes-mammals. Deejah behaved as if she'd heard nothing he said, her eyes gaping wide. "A double celebration is in order!" she bubbled out to Manny.

"Excuse me?"

"Hammer was followed right from Dulles airport."

"Wait. *What*?"

"VA in San Jose told the White House all about it. They had Hammer followed. Laney didn't stand a chance."

"Okay, so my—"

"She fluttered like an angel when she saw Counsel Madison. You could see the blood gush into her face ... I felt a neck between her teeth."

"Madison and—"

"The hate ran through her body, flushed itself up the roots."

"You're talking about what happened at Childe Harold, right?"

"A double celebration is in order!" exclaimed Deejah once more.

Manny could not grasp the nature of her impulse. Her eyes wafted over the alveolar roof of the subway esophagus and narrowed in focus suspiciously, on double alert for any phenomenon snapping off from the *Transepochal Trunk* to join the current life stream.

After a few moments, she phased back to "reality," Manny staring anxiously at her. She told him that the Beast, Madison, Luna, and scaled beings she'd never seen before burst in on Laney. They rattled their swords. "The Prophetess Danilo has one too," Deejah said. "A big sword. King Arthur gave it to her. *Excalibur*. I would have gladly loaned it to my lady dragon."

"Sure, sure, but what happened in—"

"*Excalibur*," she said wistfully.

"Deejah?"

Though his tone bordered on reproachful, Deejah only grazed lucidity. Her face went fish-gobbling blank for few seconds. She appeared as if ready to sneeze. A few Morlocks stared sidelong at her, one male grinning derisively. Her eyes returned to Manny Eden. "We were all crammed in a large booth," she said. "Laney asked Counsel Madison so polite to stay. Oooooo . . . a producer from *Sixty Minutes* in New York was on his way, and he might want Counsel Madison in the interview also."

"And then?"

"Counsel Madison said, *I won't be hung by a bunch of fucking Jews.*"

"And?"

"Luna screamed at Counsel Madison, *Get it! Get it!*, and Laney threw her glass of wine in Luna's face."

"Madison tried to grab Hammer's evidence?"

"He tried to get the tape, but Laney was losing. They wanted her to die, right in front of them. That's why they all came, took time out from their schedules. And a bald fatty from Congress was there too. His name was Chain E., or Changey, or Chicanery, or something like that. He was standing there, outside the booth, watching us like a buzzard, talking sideways out of his mouth."

"She—"

"I . . . I—"

"What?"

Deejah's eyes crawled over him, rested in a frightening way on his zipper before moving up again to his face, shivering nervously as if teetered over an abyss. Manny simply grew more impatient, up to his eyes in hate.

Even small doses of utopia had now become impossible.

"Counsel Madison surprised everybody. He just reached out and grabbed the folder with Hammer's stuff. Laney tried to stop him. Hunsecker kept shouting at Hammer, *You only want to destroy the president!* He was like a monster. Laney accidentally scratched Counsel Madison's hand while they both yanked at the folder, and Counsel Madison punched Laney in the face—"

"*What? He hit Laney?*"

"Yes, really hard, in the eye, and Laney was crying and she swung and hit Madison with the ketchup bottle. Luna then stood up and slapped her hard as she could."

Manny forcibly shut down his temper, tears forming in his eyes. He asked Deejah coldly, "*What was Hammer doing?*"

"He tried to save his stuff while Hunsecker kept screaming in his ear. But Counsel Madison was acting on orders from the White House. I heard Hunsecker talking about it. I know it. They all wanted to kill Laney. They all wanted to be part of that . . . that's why they came."

* * *

A TORNADIC HOWL QUAKES THE AIR in the subway.

A storm comes. Lava meets the sea.

The commuter train arrives.

The sliding door opens and Deejah swishes through, breaking the ice of bodies. She stops to lean against a pole of chrome. Manny wedges himself in, grips the pole as the air around him is cut off, Deejah's hamster-pink face only inches away.

Washingtonian body odor wades in like a thick and reeking gum. Manny hears a muffled pummeling of earphone bass. Directly before him, a wall poster of several erogenous youths, faultlessly yuppie and all laughing and waving cigarettes that by some miracle have been made smokeless—the realization of this deception depressing him further.

Years later, during his incarceration at St. Elizabeth's, Manny would write in his journal:

```
The train jolted and I was shoved into Deejah.
I apologized. I was too dazed to control even
my own balance. Instead of bawling further, or
continuing to dwell on suicide and murder, I
listlessly followed Deejah off the train to
Dupont Circle, and we talked. She informed me
she had an IQ of 187. She reminded me of the
mad chess master Bobby Fisher who saw con-
spiratorial cabals wherever he looked. She told
me she'd gone to college at Georgetown, her
undergrad in history, but quit after one year,
as she put it, "mercifully plucked from academia
by the hand of Ms. Plato-Prophet and released
```

to toil as apprentice priestess in the service of Harmusal." Her Prophetess later dispatched her back to Washington as a Seed. And at the thought of her divine mission, her eyes focused on me clear and hard. "Go now," she said, "and dwell no more on vengeance. At the dawning of Harmusal, all will be settled." I said, "Whatever," and shuffled away to ponder the mystery of her belief, not only in such a phony god, but in the possibility of true justice.

CHAPTER 27

The Sublime Perception State — Seven Screams — Death of a Counsel — As Far From God As Angels Can Fly — Deejah's Final Peace

THE FOLLOWING DAY, DEEJAH CAUGHT the subway train back to OWC. On the journey there she detected a feeler from the cosmic godbrain worming its way into her mind stream. It corrupted her erotic fantasy of making love to The Prophetess on the Oregon coast. Her own hand snapped with sucker-like fangs onto her right breast, and as a result, Deejah could only whimper and claw at herself, her emotosexual needs bitten off at the head. She knew this was a warning to her to cease all obscene and superfluous thought and resume the *Sublime Perception State*. The feeler had slapped her to attention and she was properly chastised.

DO NOT THINK AND BE.

How could she have forgotten?

Upon exiting the subway train and walking up to street level, she performed the ritual incantations taught her by Danilo, all necessary to enter the *Sublime Perception State*.

Once there, she did her duty. She mentally recorded the haunch of a ground sloth protruding from beneath a trash dumpster, two protodogs yipping at homeless prey in Farragut Park, and one mini-rhino snorting and pawing the pavement on the corner of 17th and G streets—prelude to charging the dwarf Zinjanthropus who'd been teasing it with a stick from several yards away.

Returning to the office, and feeling relieved, she ate a breakfast snack of bagel and juice at her desk. She began to log the OWC mail. At a particular moment between the ages of Earth, as she reclined in her chair—tinkering half-consciously with logging a fraud-and-retaliation trail of tears that began on Capitol Hill and ended in three or more congressional districts—her mind unraveled further to a glowing ball of body, a meteor of woman congealed to a thousand parts loathing and equal parts compassion. Deejah watched her Lady Dragon score a fiery trail in the Washington night, her brilliant ego enflaming whole tracts of marble forest, gouging craters in the trembling Mall, igniting dormant lava beds beneath the White Oz crust. Her final theomachy between Good and Evil having ended conclusively, the victorious Lady Dragon held aloft her exhausted arms so that Deejah might enfold her and thereby renew her strength—and this fantasy continued until Deejah became distracted by a noise.

The source of distraction occurred on the floor above her head.

Sounds indicated the hanging of a picture frame. Scrapings and scrapings vibrated into her feet. She imagined the positioning of the frame just so and parallel with the lines of room. Following that, the six dull knocks of hammer necessary to hang it. One final knock and Deejah heard a driving nail of scream. Then another, and another, the same intent and death-ringing scream repeating itself seven times. Very horror-movie-like, and with a hint of drama and echo, as if the throat that unleashed it bellowed down a stairwell.

Deejah slid from her seat, chilled and instinctively groping for a cup of coffee that wasn't there. She was temporarily blinded by the airy howl. Moments after sight returned, she behaved ambivalent, even contemptuous (after all, she did possess the rank of Deputy Hierophant).

Ambling into the stick furniture lobby of the Investigation Division, she halted and looked around. She saw Boyden. He was poised to inspire, only a foot away from Babs Easton who stood facing him. Neither bureaucrat spoke or breathed, their faces solid, their eyes fixed on divergent angles. They envisioned a creature vaguely like themselves, a crying animal thing somewhat discomforting, and yet, for some reason, unable to inspire pity.

Before life returned to all present, an apparition arrived to upset the tableau. It impacted harshly with the image of Deejah's self. It shoved her body and entire civilization aside on its way to assume a pose at center stage: the face thin and pot-holed, the eyes like blue beetles on caffeine, a tacky purple tie focusing rather than diffusing an image of hideous rage. The apparition eclipsed the entire room. It shouted: THAT MONSTER EDEN! HE SHOT THE COUNSEL!

* * *

THE BLURRY HAIL OF LIMBS NEXT, the gray and greasy stairs of EXIT running up to her face, and Boyden, Babs, Varsana, Worm, and dozens of other bureaucrats she'd only noted the presence of in times past, but did not comprehend, all rumbling into an unprecedented future no different than a frantic herd driven to one motive by distant thunder.

The mob slammed aside the ponderous fire-exit door and boiled like carbonation up to the twelfth floor. Outpacing them by pure force, Deejah was one of the first to confront a wall of suits: OWC bureaucrats bunched tight as a hive in the secretarial anteroom, straining and squirming in the doorway to Counsel Madison's office as if caught in a panicky act of escaping a fire.

Before Deejah could react, a new shriek of discovery curled out from the Counsel's office and broke like hurled glass against the back wall. Deejah glimpsed Ms. Mason, Counsel Madison's secretary, standing wobbly for an instant apart from the crowd before withering to her knees, her face faded to bone.

Ignoring her, a curious Deejah attempted to join the human fence, force a gap just big enough to allow her skinny body to slip through. Only it was no use. She heard sirens, dim and fading somewhere outside, and saw Laney Dracos standing beside her, smiling at her peacefully, her face haloed by a dawn-pink light. Deejah said to her:

"*My Lady Dragon, now that you are as far from God as angels can fly, sing for me your sounds of purest good. Drown out the noise of all evil beings.*"

Soon enough, the voices of walkie-talkie police muffled all the bureaucrats, prelude to a swarm of blue uniforms bottlenecking the hallway before squeezing like unleashed wrath into the anteroom. They barked savagely and blew whistles and formed a flying wedge to violently pierce the boil of office mites clogging the doorway to Counsel Madison's office. A consumed Deejah followed in their wake, and once inside, the sight of Counsel Madison's corpse loosened her bladder.

The pee ran hot down her leg.

Then she saw her friend, Mr. Garden-of-Eden, flying past her. He was lofted above the earth by a gaggle of blue demons. His arms were severely pinned back by cuffs, his eyes bold and frozen, his face cut and puffy as if he'd been beaten by the mob.

Once he disappeared, a fresh round of shouting burst out.

Deejah stared again at the fallen Counsel. The bulk of his remains were dressed conservatively: pinstripes soaking in a thick gulp of blood, the inert meat inside as if dropped from a great height to land against the broad wall of his oaken desk—and strangely enough, in the exact same puppet-dumb slouch recently assumed against the pole outside Childe Harold, as if he'd connived to gain maximum sympathy by acting out the old crime scene, reposing here where all might witness the sad consequence of one conservative martyr having indulged a liberal malcontent for far too long—the only difference between that incident and this one being the condition of his head which now resembled the apparition of Union soldier tacked on Worm's partition: the lower horseshoe of jaw shot completely away.

Whatever remained was sprinkled like gooey hailstone all over the carpet.

"HE DROVE THROUGH HERE, waving a gun like Arnold, uhhhh, *what'shisname, God!*" Ms. Mason, now recovered, shouted with a squeaky but convincing voice at a Moby Dickish bureaucrat as Deejah edged her way back into the buzzing mull. "MURDEROUSLY INSANE!"

Deejah struggled for bearings, every new word spoken by Ms. Mason jamming her nervous system into a robotic lurch and misfire.

"Like the one who smashed his car through the front of the AECOR office building in Bethesda and went hunting for bosses!" A paranoid mind, Ms. Mason said, her hands chopping the air, "no different than that she-beast Dracos who for no reason tried to kill Counsel Madison with a ketchup bottle!"

* * *

COUNSEL MADISON'S BODY BAG looked like a brown cocoon. It shadowed the carpet where the sunlight flowed in. The cops departed after dusting for prints, taking photos, and marking off the crime scene with tape.

The remaining crowd dispersed to put their own spin on events, and the press arrived to do a pinball routine. Hunsecker himself burst in, panting like a beast and demanding more explanation of anyone who would listen.

He desired his own future relieved of loose ends.

Deejah though, pinched herself into silence. Feelers thrust out from the cosmic god brain reminded her that duty came first.

The end could come at any time.

And such certainty filled her with relief, for her dream of a new and secure life for all would soon be realized.

Never had she felt saner, or more at peace with herself.

CHAPTER 28

The CEO — Varsana Claims Grope — Keat Linderhart's Car Accident — The Dong Hobbit — Uncle Pharaoh's Flea Tent — A New Life

A post-Madison evolution of OWC employees and others:

DEEJAH THORIS
Immediately following Counsel Madison's death, Deejah quit OWC and moved to Oregon to live with Danilo. She became Vice Priestess of Transition, her job to coordinate the settlement of new Harmusal acolytes. Her duties included, but were not limited to, processing all financial forms necessary to relieve new members of their assets, as well as all forms necessary for liquidation of said assets prior to deposit in the church treasury. In 1989, Deejah questioned Danilo's failure to reimburse members who wished to retire from the Harmusal community, and after a heated conflict with Antipater (the dwarf deputy of Danilo) over his theft of a member's wallet, her body was found at the base of a cliff on the Oregon coast just north of Humboldt State Park. Danilo's Vice Priestess of Public Relations, Madame Electra, told police that Deejah was severely depressed, and that she refused medication and counseling. No one was ever charged and the matter was dropped.

BOYDEN MCCARTHY
Left OWC one year after the death of Counsel Madison for a management analyst job at the Pentagon, remaining in relative obscurity until Donald Rumsfeld became Defense Secretary many years later

during the administration of George Bush, Jr. Working with Rumsfeld's people, Boyden played a large role in squashing all internal opposition to Rumsfeld's policies in Iraq. He became so loathed in Pentagon circles for his ruthlessness and spontaneous suck-up ability that upon being appointed directly to Rumsfeld's inner circle as Deputy Assistant Secretary of Contractor Relations, the Mummy-faced bureaucrat was nicknamed CEO (short for Cocksucking Electric Orifice). However, in 2003, and much to his surprise, CEO was abruptly terminated from the Pentagon on a trumped up charge of insubordination because he'd made the mistake of pissing off a four-star Army general who, unknown to him, had just returned to Rumsfeld's favor. The ex-CEO currently lives with his mother in Madison, New Jersey, and is unemployed.

KEAT LINDERHART
Quit the government six months after the fiasco at OWC. She worked odd jobs and lived in Maryland for another year. In 1987, she perished in a car crash on I-495 while driving to a friend's house in Rockville. Her car swerved into the guard rail and flipped. An autopsy later showed her blood alcohol level to have been well above .08. Her last will and testament left several million dollars to various charities that focused on children's health. It turned out, oddly enough, that she never had to work at USSC in the first place. Her death left many questions unanswered.

SYD DRUMMOND
Took over the *Kenosha Morning Sentinel* in 1992. To everyone's surprise, he improved the paper, both in terms of content and profit, and turned out to be a fairly able businessman in all other matters. In 2002 he received a triple bypass operation, and in 2003, his wife Amelia divorced him because of an incurable sex addiction he'd successfully hidden from her for years. He currently lives in a one bedroom apartment just outside Kenosha and still runs the paper, preferring to telecommute and remain close to his beloved porn collection—one of the biggest in the state of Wisconsin. His chosen moniker in Internet sex-chat rooms is *The Dong Hobbit*. He is being carefully watched online by FBI agents posing as teenage girls.

BABS EASTON
Left OWC in 1996, having served as Director of Investigation for over ten years. She did a brief stint at NASA, but quit her job after only one year following a succession of poor performance appraisals. In 1998, she divorced her husband Sven and married a wealthy stock broker from Los Angeles by the name of Bradley Foster. In 2001, following the dot.com crash on NASDAQ, she divorced Brad and moved to Fresno where she became part owner of a day spa. In 2004, following a butt, lip, and boob job, Babs married one of her spa employees, Miguel Alonzo, a nineteen year old massage therapist from Oceanview.

VARSANA PARDO
Retired from government service in 2001 with full benefits and moved to Sunrise, Florida, just north of West Palm Beach. Upon settling into the Golden Pond retirement community, she quickly established herself as a force to be reckoned with. No one could beat Varsana at bridge more than two times in a row without running the risk of discovering themselves days or weeks later the subject of defamatory rumors concerning their sexual orientation and/or their financial status. As a result, several of the women in the community became terrified of her. An exodus from Golden Pond began in 2004 after Leslie Charbonneau's husband, Bing, decried Varsana's toxic mouth in the presence of many witnesses at a community dinner. He termed her a human bacteria out to destroy the healthy body of the community, and for his efforts, a police detective was dispatched to question him the following day regarding a charge of sexual assault brought against him by Varsana. She claimed that Bing had groped her the night before just as she emerged from the ladies room, and that his bacteria speech was just pay back because she had rejected him. The case was dropped following several police interviews with Golden Pond residents who all swore that Bing never left the table after Varsana went to the bathroom that night.

THE E-MAN
After an especially nasty fight with Molly Moon over the disappearance of a cheese danish, E-Man packed and drove long and hard and didn't stop till he got to Nevada. Once there, he sent a goodbye letter to Manny

at St. Elizabeth's, then worked various odd jobs in and around Las Vegas. His best job was slot counter at the Suspicious Lives Casino.

YOLANDA PEEL
Quit OWC in 1986, worked at the Government Printing Office, then at USDA for five years as a secretary before moving back to her home town of Raleigh, North Carolina. She married in 1994 and had three children with her husband, Ricardo Bond, a shoe store manager from Brooklyn. Yolanda did not regret her early retirement from Washington, and swore to herself she would never ride that rhino again.

BASIL HUNSECKER
Retired from government service in 1991 with full benefits. After dabbling unsuccessfully in the Washington real estate market, he moved to the small town of Mascot, Texas (pop. 827) in 1993, not far from his sister, Emmilene Hunsecker, and there, began his retirement in earnest. In those parts his nickname was Uncle Pharaoh, due to his rare, flesh-eating disease that eventually starved his face to a mummy-like appearance. In 1995, out of boredom, he bought a flea market on Hwy 90 and renamed it Uncle Pharaoh's Flea Tent. He sold out in less than a year—in part because his employees stole from him on a daily basis out of an intense need for revenge, but mostly because customers couldn't stand the sight of him. On a trip to Monument Valley in 1996 with his sister and her teen daughters (who screeched in horror when they met him), Basil lost his pain meds the first day out and suffered in such severe agony come nightfall at Motel 6 that he died of a pain-induced heart attack before morning. By dawn his skin was hard as a pencil. He was buried in the Mascot cemetery without a headstone. His sister could not afford one.

WORM QUIGLEY
Retired from government service in 1985 and died of a malignant brain tumor eight months later in Shreveport, Louisiana, in the presence of his son's family. In his will he left his Civil War memorabilia to the Confederate War Museum in Richmond, Virginia. Upon reception, they trashed it, but sent a Thank You letter as a matter of course.

BECKY BERGSTEIN

Did not return to Portland as expected. Two days before the death of Counsel Madison she found a job at the Government Accountability Project (GAP) in D.C.—a non-profit organization tasked with the mission of watchdogging Washington. Given her expertise with OWC, she readily produced reports and insight into its machinations. Her products were then shuttled to Congress, GAO, and the news media, and as a result of her efforts, many whistleblowers were warned away from OWC, and limited reforms were finally instituted by Congress. Following Manny's arrest and later incarceration at St. Elizabeth's, she began to visit him often. They became close friends, and she secured excellent legal counsel for him. Upon his release in November of 2004, Becky asked him to marry her. He agreed, and they now live together in Bethesda, Maryland with their Golden Retriever, Bolivar, and their two tabby cats, Kilgore and Trout.

MOMMY K

Became ill from stress following Manny's incarceration at St. E's, but recovered quickly and moved up to the Washington area to be near her son. She rented an apartment near St. E's and took the city bus to the asylum, visiting as often as she could and always bringing food, hope, and encouragement. She often worked with Becky on her son's case, and the two of them became good friends. In 1993, she was diagnosed with pancreatic cancer and died three months later. She was 62. Becky was with her till the very last day.

MANNY EDEN

Following the shooting of Counsel Madison, Manny pleaded not guilty by reason of insanity and was sent to St. Elizabeth's Mental Hospital in D.C. for evaluation. While in St. E's the White House and select senators pressured the administration of St. E's to keep Manny locked away for a good long time. However, once Manny's opposition effectively ceased to exist, and a new change of management at St. E's had taken place, he was released after only twenty years. With Becky Bergstein's help, he secured a job at the Government Accountability Project and now works there as a field investigator. The national recognition of his martyrdom never took place—i.e., he never appeared on any talk shows or *Sixty Minutes,* and that was okay with him. He was just happy to be free and attached to Becky. Unknown to her though, he occasionally visited Laney's old Cape Cod in Falls Church, and always very late at night. A family lived there, so he was careful not to alarm anyone. He would park blocks away, enter her yard via a church parking lot, then sit on her back steps and whisper her name, straining his eyes through the shadows for any sign of her. But she never did appear. He continued to whisper her name for many years, and later, just to himself, wherever he might be.

EPILOGUE

THE WHISTLEBLOWER'S LAMENT

In search of a signal peak, I stumble, stranded on the waste coast with the ostrich and hyena. Escape is required, but earth-like movements of culture call me to gravity. The first tug I feel as the gentle, managerial art of nit-picking. Innuendo follows, accusation, threat on a whim. In the daylight stalking hours I am made to appear in the digestive lairs of bosses the way kings once summoned suspected traitors or imprisoned usurpers. On Monday mornings apprentice brown-nosers prowl the halls for me, alert as predators having sniffed a wound, a bleeding in the air. Unsigned confessions next, white collar noir. MS. BITCH-SLUT SHAKEDOWN QUEEN ostracized from happy hour. My phone beeps, grows too hot to hold whenever accusations slur from my lips until I drop it, my nerves needing the convenience of hope. Other employees' wives, coaxed into harmful deeds, make a point of collision, in the park or at the post office—evidence of my humiliation left behind for the news hour that never comes.

—Unknown

(anonymous note found in
Lafayette Park, Washington, D.C., November 1984)